Advance Praise f
Ghost T

"A haunting and immersive read."

—**Eva Wong Nava**, author of *The House of Little Sisters*

"With lyrical prose that evokes the mystique of 19th-century Kyoto, this meticulously researched narrative weaves together historical authenticity with the ethereal allure of "yokai" folklore. Prepare to be captivated by a world where every shadow conceals a mystery, every whisper harbors a secret, and every choice echoes in worlds seen and unseen—a mesmerizing journey that will linger in your thoughts long after the final page is turned."

—**Jake Adelstein**, journalist and author of *Tokyo Vice* and *The Last Yakuza*

"What a spectacular phantom ride! Natalie Jacobsen's *Ghost Train* takes you on an unforgettable journey to mythic modern Japan."

—**Daisuke Miyao**, author of *Cinema Is a Cat: A Cat Lover's Introduction to Film Studies,* Professor and Hajime Mori Chair in Japanese Language and Literature, University of California, San Diego

"A work of fiction—and in some respects otherworldly—this book is solidly based on research of Japan's history and folklore, as well as the author's personal experience of living in Japan. Lush with detail, enhanced by passages of the author's personal poetry, *Ghost Train* is a wholly unique and remarkably beautiful coming of age story."

—**Shirley Miller Kamada**, author of *No Quiet Water*

"A charming tale of an enchanting time and place brought to life by a gifted young writer. Students of Japanese culture will especially like this book, filled as it is with revealing historical detail. I learned a lot."

—**Robert Whiting**, best-selling and critically-acclaimed journalist and author of Pulitzer Prize candidate *You Gotta Have Wa* and *Gamblers, Fraudsters, Dreamers, and Spies*

"Jacobsen makes impressive efforts to get the details right and respect the subtle complicated reality, [with] genuine respect for Japan … the book is peppered with poetic snippets presented in a variety of visual formats that add style and depth."

—**Sean Michael Wilson**, graphic novel writer and winner of Japanese government's International Manga Award

GHOST TRAIN

GHOST TRAIN

Natalie Anna Jacobsen

幽霊・機関車

ナタリー・アンナ・ジェイコブセン

SelectBooks, Inc.
New York

This edition is published by SelectBooks.
For information address
SelectBooks, Inc., New York, New York.

First Edition

ISBN 978-1-59079-564-4

Library of Congress Cataloging-in-Publication Data

Names: Jacobsen, Natalie Anna, author.
Title: Ghost train / Natalie Anna Jacobsen.
Description: First edition. | New York : SelectBooks, 2024. | Audience: Ages 14-plus. | Summary: In 1877 Kyoto during the Meiji Restoration Era, Maru Hosokawa, a samurai's daughter, encounters ghosts, mysteries, and a kitsune who offers her help in exchange for confronting a demon, as she navigates the challenges of a changing world.
Identifiers: LCCN 2023047049 (print) | LCCN 2023047050 (ebook) | ISBN 9781590795644 (paperback) | ISBN 9781590795651 (ebook)
Subjects: CYAC: Fantasy. | Visions--Fiction. | Mythical animals--Fiction. | Japan--Fiction. | LCGFT: Fantasy fiction. | Novels.
Classification: LCC PZ7.1.J3735 Gh 2024 (print) | LCC PZ7.1.J3735 (ebook) | DDC [Fic]--dc23
LC record available at https://lccn.loc.gov/2023047049
LC ebook record available at https://lccn.loc.gov/2023047050

Book design by Janice Benight

Manufactured in the United States of America
10 9 8 7 6 5 4 3 2 1

For those who
never felt brave enough to be defiant

For Maru

Summer stifles land,
the gloaming looms above,
and eyes await the Fall.

Mother Hosokawa

A Note for the Reader

The glossary at the end of this book lists some of the Japanese words used in the text and identifies historical events referred to in this story to enable the reader to connect more deeply with Japan's history and its folklore about the yokai. It is intended to be a brief guide. As in all cross-cultural learning, greater understanding comes from immersion in Japanese culture and interaction with Japanese people.

While some of the Japanese words have English equivalences available, the words were selected for their specific usage and nuance and were identified as integral to the Meiji Era and setting of the story in Kyoto.

Acknowledgments

This story is my love letter to Japan.

I feel I must state clearly that I am not Japanese in my ethnicity. This book is a true work of fiction, and my depictions of characters and perceptions of their voices are all fabrications of my imagination and cannot replace the voices of those who are born and die in Japan. Since high school, and continuing to the present, I have been learning from Japanese people and studying Japanese culture and history.

Around three thousand documents and excerpts from literature and academic works were referenced to enable me to capture the atmosphere and details of Japanese culture in the 19th Century. My years of living, working, and studying in Hokkaido, Tokyo, and Kyoto bolstered my firsthand experiences that brought this story to life. It was a joy to immortalize walking through the streets of Kyoto by way of Maru.

The folklore discussed in this story are real. Japan's rapid societal shifts and the expansion of Japan's infrastructure from the introduction of gas, electricity, trains, and foreign influences brought great economic growth in the first decade of the Meiji era. This also cultivated a landscape ripe with rumors. Some attempted to prove the validity of their myths by causing violence to spur rejection of the changes and inspired my interest in writing *Ghost Train*.

I had tremendous help from invaluable kind souls who made suggestions to keep the story in my novel as authentic and historically accurate as possible. It is with deep gratitude that I thank:

Alec Jordan, for sharing resources and direction. Scott Jackson, who gave me an introduction that changed my life.

Daisuke Miyao and J. Keith Vincent, who became instrumental sources of information pertaining to the late Edo and early Meiji eras, helped me to give voice to the characters displayed throughout the story. Their patience, kindness, and willingness to share their knowledge humbles me.

Sean Michael Wilson, a manga artist of samurai tales, for providing resources to learn about emotions and reactions during the Satsuma Rebellion.

"Rin" Satoshita of Mainichi Kimono, who graciously consulted with me about the terminology of wardrobe and geiko practices in Kyoto. Her historical and cultural notes gave me critical insight into life inside an ochaya.

Yumi Ninomiya, manager of the shop Talis in Tokyo, answered a multitude of questions surrounding Japanese astrology, fortune-telling, and other peculiarities rooted in the supernatural.

Mie Tanaka and Shintaro Suzuki, for sharing their family stories and superstitions in the Meiji era, and for their gentle suggestions and everlasting friendship.

Nick Edwards, Steve Moloney, and Matt Pernsteiner for assisting me with the strangest translations at the oddest hours. Cassi Brown and Candi Waller for their prayers. Lou Torchia for his grace.

Sarah Adams, for reading it first and urging me to finish it. Fellow authors Demri Redmond, Sara Sciacchitano, Akiko Terai,

B.L. Jasper, Waverly Knight, Rachel Kitch, CW Rose, Deborah Wong, and Astiya Batyr, who made me feel my story deserved to be read. There are hundreds more near-strangers who heard my pitch and have been by my side ever since; I'll never forget their kindness.

Roxy, Kaitlyn, Elizabeth, and Jess, for reading something so wildly different than usual. Zahra, Kelsey, Caz, Tina, Marta, Saz, Kat, Rainer, Lorie, Daniela, Marek, Erik, Matt, Yu, Ashley, Saki, Kenston, Manami, Erica, Akane, and Olivia for cheering me on. Mike and Daniel for telling me to write the next one. My coven for their love and magic. The teachers who helped my writing flourish. Susan McCormac for her support. Sally Suzuki, my "Japanese half;" for riding this train with me.

The people who made it legible: my editors Nancy Sugihara, Kenzi Sugihara, Tess Massey, Nicole Arch, and Kyle Panas who willingly became immersed into a far-away world in a distant past, and took it upon themselves to research the language and history to help fact-check and clarify the story. They are sculptors who polished it for publication.

Kenichi Sugihara, for shouldering the immense task of managing this publication and guiding me step by patient step. His enthusiasm helped me to remain calm and confident through the process.

Janice Benight, for the beautiful exterior and interior design.

My parents, who fostered my love of writing early in my life and offered boundless encouragement by flying with me on all of my whims. They generously and selflessly gave me the opportunities that shaped the writer I am today. This book is a reflection of and dedication to the love they give to me and my sister Emma.

Thornton "Max" Hare, my loving husband, who patiently followed my every emotional ebb with the progress of this book and provided the space, peace, and unbridled encouragement I needed to complete it. The fruition of his unwavering support is in your hands.

And finally, to Japan: Thank you for giving my heart a home I return to again and again.

Prologue

A scream ripped through the red-drenched sky, scattering the birds. Billowing smoke blotted the sun balancing above gold-capped blue mountains. A mist that had draped the forest suddenly evaporated.

The locomotive pummeled by, the trees bracing in its wake.

In the front seat sat an older man with a furrowed brow who appeared discomforted by the humidity crowding the cabin. His foot kept track of his conductor's cap lest it slip below into the machine's claws.

It was early sundown, and the engineer began to push onward at a desperate pace. Glowering, he pulled out his stopwatch in the fading light and squinted at the glass. He saw it was beaded with moisture, skewing the arms and bending the numbers.

"Bah," he scoffed and went back to maneuvering his train through the thicket. This corridor approaching Kyoto was his least favorite; it was a place whispered to have lurking shadows that portended danger.

The train was now nearing the curve where his predecessor had been found, his body severed and draped across maroon-stained rails in a malicious attack the Imperial Palace took personally. The culprit—some suspected oni—hadn't been discovered; but when he was given the job of replacing the unfortunate conductor, the frightening rumors were quelled, or perhaps drowned out by the roaring engine. Danger be damned. The monsters they feared weren't real.

The truth was that Kyoto itself, the old, stubborn capital of western Japan, was a city clinging to the last gasps of Edo Era traditions, and refused to adapt to the evolving eastern capital, Tokyo. In Kyoto he had put up with vile rumors: that his train brought disease, war, and demons and a grotesque charge—that it consumed blood for fuel.

Some believed their new emperor had betrayed his people by accepting foreign machines from strange lands and diminished them by introducing shameful notions that disgraced Meiji's vision of a united nation and integrated world by the twentieth century. Someone had believed that slaying an engineer would stop Emperor Meiji's machines altogether.

This was folly. To the old man, his sleek locomotive was beautiful and bore immense power as it traversed the land, carrying the future in its compartments far more swiftly than horses and old men with backs bent from their heavy sacks. He knew Japan would be left behind if it was not in motion with the world's turning wheels.

He adjusted his posture, ignoring a pang in his lower back. It was nothing compared to the importance of his duties. He owed this to a day he was hunched over his diluted barley tea, reading in a paper that the emperor needed fearless conductors.

The reward was his vantage point: he saw stretches of coastline dotted with black ships, sands of the west, and rising cities in the east. He huffed with pride over his role in what would someday be an esteemed history.

There were few locomotives, and only his connected the two capitals. This weekly pilgrimage ushered in a new era under Emperor Meiji, who boldly asserted old Japan no longer existed, and a better Japan would be born from his ascension.

The man's reveries transported him to a daydream of smooth white steps beneath rippling green roofs where the emperor bowed to him in gratitude for driving the train even faster than the foreigners who built it. He had donned robes fringed in gold. Crowds cheered when the emperor presented him his medals. At last, they had united Tokyo and Kyoto. He, the conductor, had done the impossible! His train alone had brought the ancient city of the West and the new Eastern Capital together.

His toothy smile wilted when a barbaric cry filled his ears. His dream vanished. He jerked his head up and saw a train racing down his tracks.

His head felt cold with dread. There was nowhere to go. The trains were face-to-face on the same silver path. The engine's stark blackness and a bright yellow eye were heading toward him. It was unmistakable.

Sweat and tears dripped from his eyelids. He had a fleeting thought that he wasn't the fearless man he claimed to be.

He dug his heels into the floor while his hands fumbled for the brake. The train was meters away. If he could pull the brakes fast enough, it might spare the machine. His sweaty hands were slippery. His throat narrowed and his ribs shook. The train was bearing down faster. It would be upon him any second.

A whistle shrieked in his ears as he clasped the brake with both hands and pressed his feet on the dashboard to use all his weight to stop the engine before it was too late.

His hat cascaded into the beast's bowels. His calloused hands burned as he gripped the brake tightly and yanked with all his might. An unearthly scream escaped from behind his teeth. He curled into a ball to wait for the crash.

But he felt nothing.

His train was slowing to a halt. Steam poured off its sides in heaves. His heartbeat pounded rhythmically with the final sputters of the locomotive.

He sat up and rubbed his eyes, his adrenaline still curdling his blood. The tracks were empty. When he stood up, his legs buckled from cramps. He grasped the door handle and cursed when the heat singed his palms. He growled and kicked the door open, spilling on the tracks below.

Behind him the train cars, rocking from the sudden stop, appeared to be intact. He glanced at the train's front and leaned on the scraper. It was too hot to touch; he recoiled and looked along the tracks, imagining blood of former engineers' running along the rails.

But there was no blood. There was no train. Only a forest of trees smelling damp, and the woodsy thick, hot air choking him.

Around the bend, the tracks were concealed by tall pine and bamboo branches, and the familiar breeze was absent. All around him was an eerie silence—even the frogs and cicadas held their breath. He instinctively held his ground, his limbs tingling and ready for the unknown.

He stumbled over the track ties, crunching the ballast as the sun's final breath grazed the earth's curves before darkness. Something was wrong. He tried not to think about the last conductor's fate.

He had heard screams. He saw a train. But this was impossible. Schedules were so tight there was never an overlap. And if it had been there, where was it now? A train couldn't disappear. The alternative explanation, that he was delusional, was equally unacceptable.

A rustle in the cedars sent a chill down his spine, even as sweat pooled under his arms. He tried to prepare himself to leave, hoping to find a way to mend his torn courage, when a glimmer of gold caught his eye.

"What is this?" He bent over a cluster of what appeared to be fur and reached in gingerly to touch it. It bristled at his touch as if it were alive. *An animal.* But unlike any he recognized.

"This can't be—!" what if the thing was under his engine, clogging the gears? He'd have to pry it off. It might have harmed his machine. What the hell would he tell Tokyo?

He scoured the edge carefully but found nothing amiss. In relief, he straightened his suit, ignoring a voice that hissed a warning: his service could turn into sacrifice, just like his predecessor.

No, he told the voice. There were no monsters. An animal had only been grazed. It had not met its demise. His machine was not mangled.

He climbed aboard with a pinch of the hair between his fingers and relit the dashboard lantern to get a closer look. He saw it was golden and firm and sparkled with an ethereal quality.

"Kitsune!" he shouted and dropped the hair. The floor was covered in scattered shards of a fox spirit; its needles seemed ready for a fight. He kicked the hair away in fear and disgust.

If a train had disappeared, and if this was fur of a kitsune, it could mean only one thing: the presence of yuurei. A shiver ran through his chest. He had to be resolute; it couldn't be a ghost.

When he was growing up, he heard tales of seeing yuurei. In those days, intimidating folklore taught children moral lessons in disguise. Later, when sipping cups of rice wine in dark bars, he had listened to engineers and conductors tell of yuurei taunting them after sundown. Stories about ghosts were not supposed to scare men who served the emperor. Yet he had seen the strange creature's steam and heard its terrifying animalistic cry—just like a train.

He frowned. This folklore was from the Edo era of yesterday. The Meiji era stood for science, machinery, and a shining tomorrow. The presence of kitsune, yokai, and yuurei were superstitions of the old world. There was a rational explanation for what happened, but he could not pursue this now. Going down that path could become a disease from which he'd never heal. He pushed aside his thoughts.

The sound of the watch *tick-tick-ticking* brought him to his senses. His deadline awaited him. Tokyo counted on him to improve the world's image of trains—he had to show their power. The emperor needed him. It was time to leave the ghosts behind.

He sat up taller, settling his bones on the hard wooden seat where he'd be least likely bothered by aches, and cranked the gears.

At last, the machine's belly grumbled and expelled a belch of steam, lurching it forward into the steeping darkness. The hums of the ancient forest returned.

The starry sky blinked above, and yellow eyes peered from the forest walls to watch as he rolled onward.

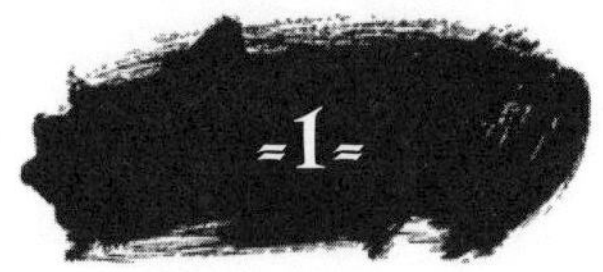

1

Fireworks exploded and a roar of cheers met the sparks curving downward.

Maru clutched a banister, steadying herself on the uneven rooftop under the rosy sky of the bursts, wishing she was flushed with excitement instead of looking pale with despair. With a thump of her foot, her superior Mitsu, a maiko, motioned for Maru to bring out the sake and mind her tasks. The sculpted scold on her painted lips served as a reminder of Maru's place. She wasn't meant to enjoy Kyoto's summer Tanabata matsuri as much as Mitsu and her company did. The geiko and maiko sat in a circle on squares of red woven blankets in an area reserved for only a few at the festival. In her previous life, she would have been alongside them instead of cowering in a corner with ghosts.

They watched Maru fill the sake cups. Her hands trembled as she poured the wine and pointed to the booms overhead with apologetic nods before retreating so they could give a toast in synchronized celebration.

Maru was meant to serve and to be seen very little, as any good, self-respecting shikomi should, even though she shouldn't have been a shikomi at all. "Cheers, ladies," proclaimed Adakichi, who was the senior geiko of the group and Maru's okaasan; her "mother" at the ochaya. The others pursed their lips to keep their personal opinions concealed out of respect for her position while she spoke. "Thanks to you two," she said, "for holding this city together better than Meiji does." She gave a special little nod to the last otoko geiko of Gion, the famed entertainment district.

"And here's to the men who will keep our cups full!" Their laughter rang out as the fireworks burst, and they clasped their hands over their mouths in delighted gasps. "Perhaps Maru is otoko?" Mitsu asked. "It would explain her sulking."

Maru ignored her, seeking respite as she viewed the falling sparks, pretending to look for something or someone. It was true that she enjoyed looking at the stoic bamboo homes along the river with balconies held up by stilts. She saw through their lamp-lit windows that they were filled with families and friends. Onlookers adorned in iki kimonos stood against velvety mountains as if they were etchings in an ukiyo-e woodblock print. People waved fans and pinched tobacco pipes as they sat on the grass slurping oysters next to tilted lanterns. They basked in a tranquility just out of her reach.

The sounds of taiko drumming and the crowd's cries carried through the streets.

"Yoi! Yoi! Yoi!" the swirling dancers chanted below her.

Maru had longed for a glimpse of the normal life she'd once enjoyed with her father and friends before she was thrust into this geiko-filled world. Below her she saw people trading coupons for charcoal-fried sweets, fishy-smelling bonito covered noodles, mochi stuffed in pickled leaves, and soft beans in buns. The wafting, curling smoke of grilled fish beckoned her.

She banished the temptation to join the crowd below, knowing Adakichi had to release her before she could leave; it was a rule she still struggled with after nearly a year of obeying her okaasan. And permission was unlikely to be granted during the season's first matsuri. All of Kyoto was there to celebrate summer and chase away the oni and yokai who rose after their winter hibernation. Maru's role was to keep the sake cups full, nod approvingly at the customers' conversations, tidy their blankets, and brush off the jokes made at her expense. It was nothing but a ruse.

While acting as a shikomi, she still had to exhibit her great respect for her father and defend her family's legacy, lest she fall short of expectations. She turned her eyes to the sky, craving to somehow fall into freedom. Although she had no blanket or sake, she had the best view of the fireworks. Waves of nostalgia hummed in her heart. As a child she had demanded that her father put her on his shoulders to watch the festival. She was carried into a sweet daydream she often had when alone.

Her reverie was interrupted by a voice of a woman saying, "He couldn't accept that I was unmarried and insisted I take his hand."

Adakichi quipped, "Did you respond that you would take his money instead?"

Maru was not allowed to participate in their gossip. Not only did her rank limit the dialogue she could partake in; she was limited because she knew little of the intricacies of dealing with men. And this was setting aside the disdain she held for nearly everyone who came as a client to their ochaya for entertainment. From the start of her employment at the ochaya, she was bored with all of the shuffling in and out. The men always wanted the same despicable things: to drink too much and pinch young women's behinds.

Added to this was the fact that because geiko and their ochaya dealt primarily with entertaining men with their singing, dancing, and conversations over tea, these were usually the only activities during their gatherings outside of work.

"At least he wasn't coming from Shimabara. Those oiran see the worst," lamented a younger maiko speaking about the prostitution district. Maru thought she had seen the girl before, but couldn't recall her name—its number of syllables would have revealed her status. Thankfully, she could distinguish maiko from geiko by their hairstyle and number of kimono layers or type of collar they wore, a talent she now possessed after serving Adakichi for nearly a year. Against her will, she had collected many skills.

"This man rambled on about how easy they have it in Edo, *sorry*, in Tokyo—bah! The Eastern capitol's name change will simply *never* stick! But sickness takes lives there; I've heard there are many lanterns snuffed out in the oiran brothels," scoffed one thin geiko with white painted shoulders and three stripes carved down the back of her neck, formal for the matsuri. Lanterns were doused when a business closed. Maru felt cold at imagining long alleys in complete darkness as inhabitants suffered inside.

"Yes, it's dreadfully isolated there. I heard the police bar their doors when they get sick to stop the spread of the infection," quipped a full-faced maiko.

Maru knew there were far worse fates than celebrating the festival on a Kyoto rooftop, and being trapped behind a barred brothel door was one. She counted her blessings. She had been placed at an ochaya in Kyoto's Gion districts that had smooth stone roads, delicate willow trees, a dainty red bridge, and an aura of quiet respectability compared to the rowdy and dingy unkempt alleys of Shimabara reeking of vomit, sweat, sake, and lust.

When sicknesses swept through the streets, often the only way to contain it was by locking the doors to the infected ochaya and brothels. It was rumored in rural villages that they were also set ablaze.

Tomosuke said, "If I didn't know any better, I'd assume this quite youthful emperor is out of touch. He's quick to dismantle centuries of well-being with flimsy laws."

"He is trying to unravel three hundred years of damage done by the shogun. There had been pitiful leadership in their bakufu, mayors who were monsters and greedy and cruel landowners," interjected Adakichi.

Maru hung her head. The bakufu, consisting of daimyos and the Tokugawa shogunate of the Edo period Adakichi spoke of, had ruled the land lawlessly before Emperor Meiji ascended. The earlier government kept farmers poor and nameless and the merchants starving while the feudal lords and samurai class were wealthy. Conflict between the shogunate, the great land rulers, and the hungry common people often ended in bloodshed and men's heads on spikes.

"It's easy for you to brush this away. Your ochaya has always been in good favor regardless of the leadership. Others have resorted to bribery to keep their lives," said a geiko as she tucked a strand of white hair beneath her black, waxy wig.

At risk of losing their own income and rice allowances, Maru knew most ochaya solely served the shogun or samurai before the emperor offered protection to all classes. She knew this because the samurai were the reason she was able to work in an ochaya in Gion at all—and spared the hardships of another destiny.

"Consider that in the last ten years we have been blessed," Adakichi said to soften her remark. "Lighted streets, warmth in winter, guarantors and even insurance for our business. Even a semblance of sound politics. We can't fault Meiji for inheriting an exploitative system. He's put many back on their feet . . ."

"But it has come with a steep price," retorted a mousey geiko.

Yes, Maru thought. A price that included her father being away while she remained stuck here. His new-world duties in his business took him farther and farther away from Kyoto. Maru felt her teeth clench.

"I'll say! It's why there are only two of us left," said one otoko geiko, Tomosuke. "Meiji is afraid of a man confident in so many colors." He chuckled, "all he wears is a kon-iro-blue."

"But ever since the shogun bowed out, we are expected to rule our own streets and defend our homes. If there were no samurai, there would be no one to protect us." When the moon-faced maiko criticized the emperor, Maru's ears perked up.

"The samurai were never much use when I was young," Mitsu chimed in. "Their time soured like vinegar." Maru dug her nails into the beam, showing no facial reaction as she bore the opinions of other maiko and geiko.

"Have you seen their new force? In black and red?"

"They are hardly men; they are merely boys compared to the warriors who—"

"Those 'Akebono samurai' aren't 'warriors.' They disgraced us by ushering in this nonsense and dragging in 'Emperor' Meiji. They should have stopped when Tokugawa assassinated their traitorous pals and their teahouse went up in flames with the bats."

"That was years ago! You speak of it like a personal betrayal that occurred yesterday."

A pang tightened her stomach. Her father had been an early advocate for Meiji. Risking their lives, allies of Meiji and the samurai met under the cloak of night in the Akebono ochaya to plot the overthrow of the ruthless shogun of the ruling Tokugawa clan. Her father had escaped that fateful, fiery night.

"Samurai can't be reformed in any way," said a shrill young geiko, sipping on sake. She was an atatori to one of the older geiko here, and acted the part with her snide, bold remarks.

An older, retired geiko said, "If that's to be believed. I heard they won't accept samurai in Meiji's army now. They have new loyalties. This emperor is obsessed with preparing us for things that will never transpire. Endless talks of threats from foreign foes."

Maru couldn't help herself. "The real foes are those quick to abandon the ones who saved you from starvation under the shogun."

Silence speared the conversation. Maru dropped her head to avoid Adakichi's glare, knowing she would catch her hand as a punishment later at the ochaya.

Finally, a soft-spoken maiko broke the quiet and the curse that Adakichi cast at Maru with her furious eyes. "Well, if I took the throne at fifteen, I wouldn't have even a wisp of an idea of where to begin. I, for one, commend him." The drum of the conversation returned to its beat.

Maru watched shapes in the matsuri's bonfire smoke grow while she smothered the fumes raging in her chest. Her life had been defined by hearing "The emperor did this, the emperor did that." In the earlier days when her mother was still alive, her father would proudly tout Meiji's ideals while her mother pointed out his policy contradictions. He used to scoff and brush this aside, and her mother would glance at Maru with an indecipherable look. Then Maru would agree with her father, leaving her mother in the garden with a poetry book. But those quiet sunny days when Meiji's ambitions were merely ideals ended long ago. Here on the rooftops, geiko came together to exchange their experiences of living out his policies, and Maru realized the discrepancies in his policies caused the polarizing opinions about his reign.

"Serve them," hissed Mitsu, to discourage any more of Maru's unsolicited outbursts that had deserved Mitsu's sneer. And Mitsu's reactions were always indicative of Adakichi's response. Their small ochaya often put Maru in these situations, pitting her against two formidable women who had taken her in as a favor to her father.

As a shikomi in the first stage of becoming a geiko, Maru was still below the apprenticeship level of a maiko. Her training to become a geiko was a discipline she diligently, although grudgingly, wanted to learn to impress her father. In his absence, he had entrusted her to the ochaya to teach her the viewpoint of the emperor's new world where women of any status have the possibility to rise in their rank. He had said, "Accept this opportunity with pride, Maru. Few in the past have had this privilege to change paths."

Adakichi reminded Maru that at first she had been disappointed to find her "inexperienced" and "ill prepared for this world" but hastened to tell her that she was not inadequate as far as her thinking. She was simply older than other maiko at her stage of training.

While most maiko began training around age ten, Maru was nearly twice that age. Being part of a samurai clan had sheltered her from needing to work. Now, with societal changes, her father wanted her to embrace this new way—and thankfully, because of her clan status, she was granted an exception to begin as shikomi. "You are fortunate. You'd much rather be this than a farmer with a worn back," her father told her. It was to the chagrin of maiko, whose families had worked all their lives for generations for their daughters to have Maru's privileges, that Maru was here on a family recommendation alone, something most would have been grateful to have. Now she might be bound to a fate that wouldn't have been hers if her father had simply returned home to his clan and taken care of her. It turned out that she didn't enjoy fending for herself outside the clan walls.

But to Maru, this was all temporary. *It would be worth a year of pain to have a lifetime of rewards,* she told herself. In one year, her father would return home again as a wealthy man, and they'd begin a new life together.

She pulled a fresh bottle from a basket and poured the sake wordlessly, without a smile, the only show of her disdain for the clients around her. Chasing down the drunken men to fill their empty cups with sake felt like using a torn net to catch fish in a storm.

She was considering revisiting the rooftop corner when Adakichi nails dug into her arm, stinging her skin but carefully concealing the wound from others. "Can you fetch us some tasty bites from below?" Her words seemed to slither.

It wasn't really a question. This was well in the realm of her duties. But she had a surge of excitement about being allowed to join the celebrations in the streets. Maru nodded obediently and descended the stairs into a pulsing, tightly-packed crowd dancing erratically, moving with the beat of taiko up and down the main road in Gion. She felt as if she picked up her feet too high, she would be carried out to sea. She usually saw herself as an anchor to buoyant joy, always drowning and unable to reach it.

Only a year, Maru reminded herself. *Father promised this.*

The red sun dipped to sleep, but light from the fireworks and lanterns bounced off banisters, and oiled-paper window coverings flooded the pathways in yellow. Open doors welcomed the parties inside. She was enticed by intoxicating smells of soy-glazed chicken.

Feet flew in harmony with the sounds of sizzles, stamps, and hollers.

Maru couldn't resist melting into it all. She crossed into a rickety alley where she maneuvered herself around pots of unruly ivy before slipping through its crevice into an open street of yatai stacked with stacks of tofu flat-cakes, charred chicken legs over embers, and spear-roasted onions.

Flailing arms thrust zucchini and boiled unagi toward her face. Though her stomach rumbled, she declined by flicking her chin. Children ran amuck in fundoshi thongs, their sandals long abandoned. She felt like the crowd was eating her alive.

When she ducked under a flag, heavy feet threatened to trample her toes that were protected only by thin tabi in her tall, wooden geta. She feared being pulverized by rowdy dancers.

She dodged ladies in large outfits with poofy skirts she hadn't seen before. She tried to get a closer look at them, but the ladies were already consumed by the crowd in a blaze of color. Boys wearing oni and other grotesque monster masks shouted as they passed.

Ah! She finally smelled the sasamochi! And pickled plums, salted cucumber, and mugwort cakes! In an open window, a family sat beneath red lanterns strung up by ropes across wooden beams. A boy was transfixed by the fireworks as his father took sips of wine and ate their supper.

Loneliness seemed to coil around her ribcage. She swallowed her feelings and listened to her heart beat with the reverberating drums.

Just one year, she told herself.

At last! Finally standing before Adakichi's favorite sasamochi vendor, she fumbled for her coin purse. The disgruntled lady shooed away prying children and shouted at a group of drunk men who bumped into Maru. She wished her father was with her to bare his teeth at them.

As she gave the woman a coin, someone pushed her, and her knees buckled. When she whipped around to exchange angry words with the person, she saw that a tearful child with stained cheeks and greasy hair was regaining her balance. Her robe was askew. She had dried blood on her knees.

"Maaaaaaaamaaaaaa!" the girl screamed. The drums drowned out her cry.

Maru bent over her. *Was she hurt*? Nobody should cry at a matsuri.

The little girl's pleading eyes were locked on Maru. Her small hands reached out. Her face appeared to be stony blue in the yellow light. Maru was entranced.

"Go on, git!" barked the sasamochi woman at two handsy boys sneaking treats. The small girl with eyes bigger than moons leapt backward in fear and was swallowed in the blur of dancers. "Vagrant rats," spat the woman. Though she was gone in a blink, Maru thought a shadow of the strange little girl remained.

Maru paid the woman and tried not to be jostled or crushed against the walls as she craned her neck looking for the girl.

"Maru, Maru!" Over the taiko she thought she heard her name but saw nobody familiar in the sea of faces painted yellow by the gas lamps. Was it the girl? Was she possibly calling for her mother?

"Maru!" Someone collided with her back, nearly sending her toppling and then pulled her away from the dancing stampede. "Oh! Kiku, it's you!" Happiness flooded her heart.

Her long-time friend hugged her shoulders and dipped to snatch Maru's basket out from the flying feet. "Ah, they aren't so bad." Kiku helped herself to a smashed sasamochi.

Maru said, "I need fresh ones! The geiko aren't drunk enough to ignore these not-so delicious seasonings garnishing them."

"Here, let's trade baskets. Madam would throw you out before you finished setting it down."

"I'm deeply indebted to you," Maru said with a small bow.

"I think you owe me for several other 'last times' I helped," Kiku responded. "You're so clumsy for someone who works in a teahouse!"

It was true. She didn't feel any more self-assured than she was at the beginning of her involuntary apprenticeship. This agonized her. She wanted to be more worthy—not just a woman of a certain status simply waiting for marriage and a domestic life. Because of her gracelessness, and untidy ways she took after her father, it became Adakichi's mission to guide her to be more patient and disciplined so that she would be ready to learn the entertainment skills maiko and geiko practiced.

But Maru thought she'd need a miracle to progress in these abilities. This was partly because she believed she wasn't meant to accomplish these arts. She had been taught that the daughters of clans didn't work.

She had begged her parents to let her stay at home to be with the clan. But her father ushered her along, saying women were meant to work outside the home and build a good reputation now that they were under the Meiji regime, rather than reading poetry all day as her mother often did. "Embrace the new ways," he'd said, or it would mean he had wasted his time at warfare. When she moped, he dug in his heels. He sent her childhood tutor away, saying he was pushing her from "trite binds of planned destiny." He then sent her to school to integrate with other Kyoto girls, where she finally settled down and made friends.

She protested again when he pulled her from her Confucian lessons ("how much more meaningful interpretation can they pull from your brain through your nostrils?") and knocked on the ochaya door so that she could find "a new path." Her journey was now different from all the women in her clan before her. Her father told her to be proud, but she was ashamed.

In contrast, Kiku had a rambunctious personality that sometimes clashed with ochaya mothers, but her external poise was professional, and she looked the part. When Maru met her in school, she knew Kiku would find success. She came from a wealthy line of musicians with an impressive repertoire of clienteles—the emperor's family included—and a stature that made her self-assured, unlike the rest of her family. Her docile parents believed Kiku was better suited to work in the entertainment districts of Hanamachi, including Gion, with the ochaya and geiko where she could freely tease the men and banter with them to her liking. Maru envied Kiku's confidence and straightforward path. Her own family's loss of wealth had made her own path crooked.

Kiku shouted over the excited crowd, "These nitwits are always clamoring. As if we won't have a matsuri every night this season." Maru decided not to add that she should be enjoying the summer celebrations with her father. Suddenly she missed the rooftop view high up from the crowds where she could enjoy the fireworks without fearing for her life—even if it meant tolerating the presence of a few who loathed seeing her breathe.

"Where is your okaasan?" she asked Kiku, struggling to keep up with her friend's nimble pace.

"Eh, hosting some party indoors. She's not keen on fireworks. The best patrons never are, and my okaasan knows it."

Maru responded, "Adakichi is up on Koroku's roof with some other geimaiko."

"Oh? No clients tonight?"

"No. But we'll get the post-matsuri crowd."

"Good luck with them. Total drunkards, mega idiots." Kiku tucked a rogue fold back into her obi belted around her waist and then grinned. "Did you make your wish yet?"

Maru had been so busy with the chores for the Tanabata matsuri that she hadn't yet paid a visit to the shrine to declare her wish for the year.

"Well, come with me! That's the whole idea. It would be such a waste if you didn't make your wish!" shouted Kiku.

A soft wail tugged at Maru's ear. She paused to listen for it again, remembering the little girl. Had she found her way? She instinctively looked at a shadowed corner of the street and was certain she'd spotted a small figure. But when she got closer, she felt only a lingering impression of an unfinished story.

"Come on!" Kiku dragged her through the alley, jolting her back to the present.

They dashed like tanuki avoiding the end of a broom, their giggles louder with each crossing. With their robes gathered and their hands clasped, they slowed down at the shrine illuminated in a canyon of lanterns bearing Shinto symbols. In the small park nearby, young men and their girlfriends were pointing at fireworks cresting the stone walls. Screeching children chased goldfish in a barrel with their nets as an older gentleman sat near, watching over them.

Beneath the red torii gate to the shrine, the girls bowed and smoothed their robes before hurrying past the stone and bamboo temizuya full of purified water to write their wishes.

Kiku went to work as taiko rumbled, pressing her nose to the paper. "All of these lanterns, and I still can't discern anything," she said, while Maru ambled on.

In the last three summers, Maru's father hadn't taken her to write a proper wish, and she was out of practice of praying for her desires. All she wanted was the impossible, anyway: to be out of the ochaya, have her father at home, her mother alive, and the emperor lead Japan to peace. But to condense these into something that made sense was a problem since she didn't have just one wish.

Kiku said, "Oh Maru, write that you want a husband like every other girl, and tie it up."

She haphazardly settled on "*I wish to have my father and my life back*," and then sped after Kiku who approached the moss-covered pond to tie her wish with the thousands knotted in the thrush. Maru struggled to wrap her note around the sasa branch, feeling embarrassed as Kiku watched her wrestle with the leaves.

"Who knew this would be so fascinating," Kiku said and laughed. "Did that drink really do you in?" Maru wasn't laughing. Everything seemed hard now that she was on her own.

But finally it was secured! Relieved, she admired some leaves with wishes carved on them by a stick, harkening back to ancient times before the emperor made paper commonplace.

"I can't even see the lovers up there, can you?" Kiku asked, scouring the sky for the two stars that were to unite that night over the matsuri dedicated to them. Before Maru could reply, Kiku pointed behind her, exclaiming:

"Oh! I see a fox! I wonder if that's good luck." Maru watched its yellow tail disappear into tall lilies; her glimpse was always a little too late, but her heart fluttered in anticipation all the same.

They prayed at the temple steps and returned to the crossroads to part ways. Maru's face fell, and Kiku noticed her sadness.

"Let's ditch these baskets. They won't miss us for a while. Come dance!" Kiku hid the baskets between two potted junipers and pulled her into the street.

Their bodies were pressed against a dozen faceless dancers, chanting:

"Yoi—yoi! Yoi—yoi!"

Maru grabbed Kiku's hand and found herself laughing openheartedly. Kiku lifted her hands over her head and sang. Maru recoiled at first. The feeling of freedom was a dangerous gift. But then she raised her own arms and chanted in between their bouts of laughter:

"Yoi—yoi! Yoi—yoi! Yoi—yoi!"

Kiku flipped a coin, snagging a bottle of the yellow stuff from a nearby vendor that all the boys drank from a box around their necks. She tipped some into her mouth before passing it to Maru.

Bleck! It was so bitter. She grimaced as it dribbled down her chin.

"What is that?" Maru shouted over the music. Kiku shrugged and drank more of the unpleasant drink.

"Yoi! Yoi!"

The dance halted as the drums rose in a crescendo, everyone raising their arms and spinning, kicking their knees up in the final steps before leaping high with a unified shout:

"YOI!"

Fireworks were rapidly fired off, illuminating the rooftops and clouding the horizon. Their light cast dancing shadows as if spirits were coming alive alongside them.

"Ahhh this is the best part, right here!" screamed Kiku, her breath reeking from her drink as they embraced. The air was thick with music, sweat, and chants. A glow emanated from the street.

Grandmas on balconies looked after grandbabies, kids sitting on shoulders shouted, and men smacked glasses while girlfriends clung to each other. Dancers spun, lantern-adorned floats teetered as the weight bared down on their calloused carriers, who sweated under bandanas. Everyone became one animal, roaring, coaxing in the fortunes of the season, celebrating love, banishing oni.

On the precipice of the song's climax, surrounded by flurried colors of yellows and purples, Maru found it easy to believe how the kami—spirits and gods alike—could be appeased by the dancing that chased away evil yokai and yuurei that grumbled at joy and lusted for the fear that was born in dark solitude. She felt a happiness here that sparked something inside even more than the fireworks reflected in her eyes. Maybe it was summer nostalgia; maybe it was everyone putting aside what the emperor had said that day.

The drumming and rapid rhythm of feet reminded Maru that she was with her best friend, surrounded by all she ever knew. Her heart's heaviness should have evaporated and left her with ease.

Then a new beat started, and Kiku dropped her hands. The feelings of invincibility subsided. They downed the last of the beverage before making their way to say goodbye.

As Maru ascended the stairs, each one was harder. Her stomach was clenched. She was hoping Kiku was right. But Adakichi's eyes were lightning striking her heart. She had dawdled, and realized the lesson for this failure would leave some marks.

She retreated to a rooftop corner to make herself invisible until summoned again. She watched geiko and maiko lean back in laughing silhouettes against the fireworks' glows.

As the taiko steadied, the crowd breathed into a slow-moving golden snake, expelling the magic. Maru munched on pickled ginger and salted cucumber over rice; a dish her mother used to make. It was the only thing sour enough to take away the knot in her belly. As she chewed slowly, she knew she should be grateful to be safe on the rooftop among prestigious company, yet she longed for something she couldn't have. While she wanted to be far away, it was here beneath the fireworks that she felt most connected to her father, her past, and a feeling of happiness that she once knew.

But the joy she yearned to keep danced behind the matsuri's haze, a veil too heavy for her to raise alone. The happiness she'd shared with Kiku would soon be a distant dream.

On a nearby rooftop people took turns gazing through a telescope toward the mountains, where Maru could see a glowing torii. She saw the gates of the shrine jutting out of the blue pines before being clouded by a stack of smoke. She watched the plume, mesmerized. The only time she saw smoke as black as this was when a kettle went unattended. But this smoke was moving across the horizon.

Echoes of fireworks dissipated, and the sounds of drums faded as she watched. *Was she the only one who saw this?* She whipped her head toward a geiko who was now rating the clientele. Maru looked back to be sure she wasn't seeing ghosts.

It was there, passing in front of the mountains. Coming toward the city.

She stood, feeling a sense of duty. She needed to say something. Her father would do the right thing.

"Shikomi?" she heard someone say. It was Mitsu, sidling up by her. "Your face is revealing your fears."

"There's something—" But Maru couldn't explain the black thing she was seeing.

"Oh!" Mitsu relaxed. "Oh, it's the train. Okaasan mentioned this. Mind your mouth."

Maru instinctively looked over her shoulder before fixating on the snarling smoke—a black lion leaping across rooftops as it stalked the edge of the city. "It's so—"

But Mitsu had already sat down. Maru was accustomed to sudden abandonment. She turned to the horizon that never betrayed her, that always whispered "there's more to come."

Dinner sloshed heavy in her belly. She had heard the train announcing its arrival at odd hours, but had never seen it. The emperor's machine had catapulted Kyoto's people into a frenzy of anticipation about their grand future. Although clients solicited Adakichi's opinion, she was certain if she never acknowledged the train, using it for travel wouldn't become a routine, and the train would soon be discarded as an "inconvenience." ("We need to go to it? When men with donkeys can come to our door? These whims of men come and go; I'll catch the next invention.") And thus, she kept Maru and Mitsu from making queries.

So when Maru finally saw the train, seeing it brought a sense of relief, but she quickly became aware of how damp her palms were. She shook off the feelings that something about it was sinister. Against the skyline of shanties, pagodas, and juniper, the darkened machine carried with it something unrecognizable, as if she were cracking open a new book. She remained still, watching its smoke thin as it reached closer until the ashes concealed her view.

The train vanished as quickly as it had arrived—just as her father had left Kyoto when winter's first snow fell and the fat flakes erased his samurai days.

"And she never looked at apricot pits the same way," Fujiwara burst out in laughter as he slammed down his drink. On his right side, Mitsu put her hand on her mouth, her eyes betraying her wish to remain modest. The rooftop perch where Maru had enjoyed watching the matsuri seemed far away, and her servitude entertaining the clients was a stark reality.

"Cheers," roared his companions, as they sloshed their wine.

Furtively checking that everyone had enjoyed his joke, Fujiwara took a triumphant swig.

"More, sir?" Maru asked, kneeling next to him.

"Ah yes, more. Yes, always more."

More laughter. *Breathe deeply, she told herself.* In the flickering candlelight she saw Mitsu's smirk as she watched Maru flounder as she ducked beneath the drunken men's flailing arms, chasing them down to keep their cups full. Adakichi was upstairs in her okiya living quarters attached to their ochaya. She was getting ready for the performance, leaving the maiko and shikomi to "ply the clients gently." It was rarely gentle.

"My dear shikomi, please me the most, and—" he said and reached out to grasp her calf but missed. "My comrades, you should see her play cards. She plays a ruthless, mean game—and always wins!"

His salacious laughter filled the room, and she felt like screaming. But she only wavered slightly, forcing her eyes to remain steady so that she would not reveal her disgust. Kiku was right. They were mega idiots.

"Say, you're searching for a new stage name, aren't you?" he inquired.

"I believe you are mistaking me for the maiko."

"You two are like sisters! You had me fooled." Mitsu huffed at the disrespect. Maru knew they had little resemblance, except perhaps in how she painted her face, which she learned from Mitsu after some pressure from Adakichi. As a shikomi she rarely painted her face, but a matsuri was a special occasion that warranted her formal look.

He told Maru, "When you, too, graduate and need a new name, you should call yourself Apricot after me." He slapped his knee, spilling his wine. His breath reeked.

She stole a look out the windows and wished she could coax a breeze to come in. But the dark tapestries hung without swaying, the odors of tobacco, incense, and the kettle's heat mingling with the callous laughter of their guests. The post-matsuri crowd was indeed the worst of all. Daytime clients who visited for tea, gossip, and music were the best. They were typically older and quiet and had refined tastes. Evening guests were usually unbridled. They enjoyed being riled by dancing and games with the geiko and maiko. Maru felt tired and longed to be dismissed so she could rest on her futon.

Finally his attention shifted. It would permit her to go to her cool tatami and relinquish the stage to Mitsu. She prayed for a diversion to let her retreat to the pantry. Perhaps Adakichi was ready to perform. Sometimes she wondered if Adakichi held back on purpose to give herself a sliver of peace that Mitsu, and especially Maru, couldn't afford.

"Apricot is a perfect name for her. She has beauty of the fruit's blush," said Fujiwara, as the other men's murmurs cooed "that's so." "And I bet her juicy softness—"

"I am keen to hear the conclusion of your thoughts, but am afraid I must interrupt you," said Adakichi, sweeping into the room like a relieving breeze.

She was saved. Maru had nearly collapsed from the tension of holding herself up. They had kept the oil lamps burning a long time. It was a costly investment to serve them at night.

Adakichi's robes swirled, reeds in a pond rippling. Her red lips were pursed, eyes sharp, an unfaltering arched gaze fixated on Fujiwara.

"It's like you have never seen me before," Adakichi said with a small smile.

Fujiwara leaned his head next to Maru. He appeared entranced and unsteady. "My pillow, Little Apricot," he said as he tugged her arm.

Maru grit her teeth, knowing the name was an acknowledgment of his endearment, that her acceptance might garner them more wages on this night or a gift the next day. Mitsu, long accustomed to the guests' jibes, had advised her to imagine her kimono was a thick skin that could absorb disdain and discomfort, since there was little else to arm herself against men like Fujiwara. Maru pulled a pillow from the cabinet and slipped it to the ground.

When Adakichi clicked her tongue toward her newly-strung shamisen, she had forgotten Maru wasn't allowed to touch the instrument because she was from a samurai clan. The taboo was an old tradition.

A thin, sinewy line divided their worlds, and Maru wanted the boundary to be respected; it was one of the few clan customs Adakichi had permitted her to retain. Maru intended to shed her samurai identity in the ochaya for protection, but remnants of her ancestral devotion lingered. While being in a samurai clan meant less and less under the new emperor, she found herself clinging to belief many regarded as archaic. But if guests knew they were being served by a samurai daughter, her clan would suffer humiliation, and they had endured enough in the nine years of Meiji's reign.

"No, I'd like the maiko to bring me the shamisen," said Adakichi in a rushed correction of her order. Maru's heartbeat quickened as Mitsu pried herself from Fujiwara's hawk-like clutches to oblige their okaasan. Maru spied the wrinkle on her nose when she placed it next to Adakichi, who kneeled on her pillow, hoisted the instrument and smiled as she sang,

The geisha of Tatsumi goes walking,
Bare white feet in black lacquered clogs.
In her haori jacket, she's the pride of Great Edo.
Ah, the Hachiman bell is ringing.

And with that, Maru felt the tension in the room melt away. Adakichi song signaling the end of the jokes and jabs that had rattled her brought her one of few pleasures she had experienced lately. She knew she would soon taste fresh air and relax on her futon. The customers' laughs would be washed away like other memories of the night.

Kokki-fukurei, her father warned her. *You will understand as I have come to.*

At last, pleasantries were exchanged, and the customers tipped back their final drinks. Mitsu presented a plum-colored pouch of a soft material Maru imagined a queen in Paris dressed in, a kind that shimmered depending on how you smoothed it.

One by one hands dropped copper in the pouch. The opinion that "the newer ochaya on the west bank are abysmal at entertainment" was shared by Fujiwara, who promised gifts. Gion and Ponto-cho ochaya of the east were the renowned; few could compare to their prestige. Mitsu thanked each patron dutifully, moving her lips as little as possible. They leaned on each other, belting out songs in slurred words, Fujiwara calling after them: "Warm up Sakura—nay, Sayako—for me." Adakichi remained bowed until all patrons except him had stepped into the night.

His prolonged presence was an occurrence they were accustomed to. He rarely succeeded in his eternal hopes of snatching a maiko to walk him to brothels in neighboring wards afterward; discipline was too strong here, where Adakichi's rule enforced the emperor's prohibition of such mingling. Before Maru had been brought to the ochaya, Adakichi had dismissed a maiko "acting more of an oiran from Shimabara," involving them in scandal and leaving her in need of a way to repair her reputation.

Maru had meant to be the answer to her problems—a favor to them, and a favor to her father. Surely a samurai daughter knew about keeping their respect and maintaining a low profile.

Her chest tightened. The intruder known as unfairness kept creeping in, but she had to suppress it.

"Fujiwara, would you like some tea?" asked Adakichi.

He nodded. Her fist clenched at his response. She didn't need more work. Blood rose to her head as she stooped to find the flint and struck it to the fresh cedar. Red sparks cascaded until smoke filled the pit. She took the kettle to the hook above where it was draped by chain over the banister. Smoke crept up her sleeves, tickling her wrists and adding warmth to the garments that enrobed her.

Flustered by the heat from the kettle, Adakichi and Maru shifted uncomfortably.

Fujiwara paced to find a new perch. He had the attention of three women and was relishing in it; a grin seemed plastered on his face. Mitsu's lips were dry from the paint, and Maru knew that her ochaya sister did not dare to lick her lips and give away that she too was exasperated. Their patience was waning.

"Why so solemn, Apricot?" he inquired to her dismay. She couldn't let him describe her in such an ugly light.

She scrambled for an excuse, remembering it was better to admit the patron was close to being right, even if it was not the truth. In this case, he'd read her thoughts correctly.

Adakichi stared her down. The women hated it when she got more attention. Maru was merely a helping hand; they were professionals. Geiko's art relied on shapeshifting into what clients wanted to hear, preserving their true lives as mysteries. They were dancers, singers, and conversationalists for hire. They were friends for an evening. Unranked Maru could shatter this illusion.

"I am nostalgic about the matsuri."

Mitsu cut in, saying, "No, she is just aloof. She was gripped by the train instead of the fireworks. You'd think differently if you'd seen her." Maru wondered why Adakichi never retaliated for Mitsu's pessimistic pettiness. A pang pinched her side from the injustice.

Fujiwara roared, catching Mitsu off-guard. "And here, I worried that shikomi was tired of me! A train! I guess ol' Meiji found a new conductor since his other one was murdered?"

Maru suppressed her nervous laughter.

"But I do know when a young lady lies. Geiko and maiko are wily, but you are not and need some polishing." He glanced at Adakichi. "I might be a man, but I'm no fool."

"Then shikomi will oblige if you are curious, but I urge you to understand her feelings are immature."

"Nonsense, I adore her like a daughter."

I'm not your daughter, Maru thought. It was quiet; the candles flickered a warning for her to hold her tongue. Maru thought she heard the creaky window in the pantry open behind them. Mitsu pouted, but Adakichi's face remained blank—it was her technique to keep from revealing her rising temperament.

"It's my father . . . I miss him," Maru admitted, tilting her head down to match her statement.

Fujiwara laughed. "An honest answer! But tell us. What takes him away from a daughter?"

"He is a businessman," interjected Adakichi. "It is how she came to us; he was a former client in debt to us." Mitsu twisted her mouth. Even she didn't know Maru's true story.

Fujiwara's face beamed, a fire in his eyes. "A client . . . Your father may even be my competition, right?" he asked with an impish grin. She wanted to wipe it off his face.

"What business is his?"

"He trades with the Portuguese—pottery and vases." At least that's what she knew from when he left her the year before and explained what was taking him to Satsuma where the boats from Portugal came with goods. He had said the other ports were weaker. They specialized in the wrong imports, and he needed to go to the southernmost port to regrow their wealth.

"Ah, Satsuma . . ." Fujiwara rocked back and forth. "And when did he embark?"

"Before last winter."

"He's been away for quite a while compared to business partners who have made the same venture. Someone is not as good at business as me. Or is a liar. Does he write to you?"

Maru shook her head.

"Huh, a businessman who undoubtedly must be successful and yet his daughter is here, alone, without receiving word of her father—" He paused to think about this. "Perhaps he got tangled with that uprising in Satsuma. Eh?"

She felt something would explode from her body. She had dodged those rumors before—the rumors that threatened to swallow her legacy: that a girl who grew up in the famed Hosokawa samurai clan's home was forced to take a job somewhere outside their walls. The story of her tradition would be broken, entangled with the southern rebellion whispers. *Was her father there?*

Despite changing her name with Adakichi's help, the rumors breached her work. The pierce of gossip still stung, and Adakichi's eyes buried into her skull. This was personal, and risked both her good reputation and Adakichi's fine reputation.

"No, he is there for trading purposes," she repeated. Her father was now a merchant, having hung up his armor years ago when the emperor ascended to his rule, ending the fractured barbaric reign of the shogun. He had been proud to help, and just as pleased to retire the past ("There is peace in an empty scroll," he'd said.) But not all samurai had willingly been stripped of their title and role, which Fujiwara now hinted at—some were unhappy rebels causing trouble.

"He went to advance our business. In fact, he's been there many times. Satsuma is his southern home," she continued, repeating his lines. It was not so controversial, she thought, as everywhere was tumultuous with so many wanting in some way to reclaim, restore, and rescue their idea of a united front after being shattered and torn by Tokugawa shogun leaders for centuries. This just happened to be the longest he'd ever been away.

Maru added, "Now that trade with other countries is open, he was eager to assist—it was an opportunity. The emperor gave us duties, right?"

He smirked. "To garner his daughter a great husband, no doubt."

She thought quickly. "So long as Madam Adakichi accepts me, I have no need for one."

"That is so. She understands me more than my mother—or a wife could." He chortled.

Mitsu stared into the crackling fire. Maru imagined she was praying to keep her composure.

"Well, trading is a dangerous business. Those Portuguese are fickle; I myself deal with Southern traders who come through Kyoto. They come here for licenses, you see—the Satsuma government isn't in agreement with Tokyo, so they need a true liaison to work with them legally." Fujiwara chuckled. "They're rough. They bargain with threats. He is either brave or stupid to linger there or will be caught up in something dangerous. I pray it is not the latter. We are stronger today, thanks to *merchants* like him."

Maru was confident he believed the rebellion rumor. But her father had never hinted to her that he was anything but a merchant now, and she wouldn't let Fujiwara tarnish his name. She would not utter the bitter term and call him a rebel samurai, when he was not.

Mitsu waved her fan fervently, concealing a sly grin that made the bats in Maru's stomach take flight. *She can't know.* Maiko like Mitsu treated insider information like candy to sell.

Embers beneath the kettle collapsed; she leapt up, and Adakichi bristled, coming back to life.

"Business is such an unpleasant topic to end the night on, as are life stories with no clear moral," said Adakichi. "How about one more tune for you. She'll make apricot tea."

Maru found an apricot left in the unhinged cedar box with a soft cloth and knife. The first few strums of Adakichi's shamisen brought the stillness Maru desired; she found comfort in the lullaby melodically plucked, building to the moment when she'd sing.

Maru rolled the fruit over. The flesh was taut, but if she pressed firmly, indents appeared.

Your heart

She sank the knife into the skin, hearing the soft pop below her hand.

Flip-flops and changes

Juices spilled over her thumbs, staining the cloth. What she wouldn't give to savor its sweetness. But this apricot felt rotten.

Like a marionette.

She slid the knife across its circumference until she could pry it open. She was being careless, letting so much juice escape. She knew Adakichi could not see her, but she knew Mitsu, ever competitive, might rat her out if she caught her being sloppy.

There's someone

She tore at the pit heartily, ripping its fibers, dropping it triumphantly.

In the shadows

She squeezed a bit into the cup, and placed thinly cut slices on a thin, bamboo-woven net.

Pulling your strings.

Adakichi's voice faded, replaced by the whistling of the kettle. Maru grasped it with a blackened towel and poured water over the slices.

"Politics do not even escape our music," Fujiwara said. "I suppose you are insinuating there is something suspicious happening—or perhaps you do not consider me genuine?"

"Certainly not. I took it for a noncommittal lover. Politics are pervasive. Change is our only constant, and we look for inspiration in nature, and our hearts."

"When Meiji ascended, the feeble had no family names. Now they do. They have an illusion that there is power in a name. Those blasted engines blacken our nights and steal our virgins for blood to run on," he sputtered. "We are all marionettes of the emperor."

Mitsu almost dropped the cup. Adakichi never flinched, but Maru felt her shaking. It was an ugly rumor, a vile story that trailed them all. Maru's legs wobbled as she served the tea.

"Apricot. It comes full circle," Fujiwara mused, glancing at Maru.

She locked eyes with him. He'd alluded to her real name—*full circle*—Adakichi had only referred to her politely as "shikomi" to clients. Did he know her? He was in their ochaya for nights on end, yet she knew nothing about him. Why had she not listened closely when she was lectured about who's who in Kyoto during her preparatory conversation lessons? Did he know her father?

Or worse, would he wander into the street announcing he had found the samurai daughter?

"What is your name, anyway? Must I always call you a fruit or 'Shikomi'?"

"It is preferred," interjected Adakichi, as Maru simultaneously answered "Maru," without thinking.

She answered quickly, relieved that maybe this was the first time he'd heard it, and she had practiced caution and worried for no reason. She was able to exhale.

"Shall we consider consulting the almanac to see if your ventures are aligned with the stars?" Adakichi made a move to open her fortune-telling book that all good geiko used. Maru saw it as a desperate attempt to distract Fujiwara. It usually worked. ("My business is blossoming thanks to her, my one real confidant!" he used to boast.)

But he ignored Adakichi. He had eyes only for Maru.

"What an unusual name, *Maru*," he mused, having a sip of his drink. "This sweetness tastes like you.

"You'd think her father had played a joke on her, wishing for a boy. Apricot suits you better." Fujiwara raised the cup and drank, fibers clinging to his teeth, tea gushing down his glistening throat. It reminded her of frogs and their bulbous throats that bloated when they sang to the night. "Name aside, I reckon you would be a demanded commodity at Shimabara."

When he left, Maru still smelled apricot permeating the room and threw open a window. She then extinguished the lantern outside to signal they were closed. Mitsu swept the tatami while Maru and Adakichi cleaned the cupware. This was when they dusted away the dirtiness of the clients, that also helped to scrub away their comments and glances that felt pressed into their skin.

"Mind the night soil, and then sleep. Finish the cleaning tomorrow," Adakichi whispered.

Maru hated selling their day's waste that was turned into night soil to the farmer for his fields. Usually, this was the maid's job.

"Okaasan, may I finish cleaning the cupware first?"

Adakichi walloped Maru on the back of her head.

"I insist, Mayuki. Tomorrow you must be fresh. Your father would want it this way. Unless you don't agree. Isn't this a game you'd like to win, too?"

"*Yes,* Okaasan," Maru said. *Mayuki.* Her "stage" name was meant to strip her identity. Adakichi was reminding her that she could toss her into the river and drown her if she wanted to.

Mitsu pretended she would not pry into her problems because she wanted to be polite to her. Or perhaps her desire to be cruel had dried up for the evening. She announced that she was going out to see a friend, waving away the tension. But Maru knew Mitsu loved clawing her way into Maru's secrets, and envied the tenuous thread that bound her to Adakichi.

Adakichi nodded absentmindedly. Maru knew she must attend to the outside chore before she was left alone with her okaasan. She lugged the bucket of night soil from under the wooden toilet flap and replaced its perfumed cedar leaves. She then slipped on her geta to meet the farmer who would soon be rolling through Gion looking for products to fertilize his rice paddies.

The cobble streets were covered with the full moon's light. Now that the fireworks and smoke were gone, she could see the sparkling stars. Maru felt relief from the headache that hampered her progress. She longed to be lifted up to the sky to fall into the black tapestry above and allow her pains to take flight. These small moments were the only time she could reclaim peace.

She tugged at her obi. There was little escape from the humidity itself or the discomfort of each labored step carrying the heavy wooden crate.

Father is a businessman, she told herself. But Fujiwara's teasing, malicious voice and his smirk lingered in her head. She was dizzy and hot from the thoughts spinning in her mind.

Maru knew Adakichi would punish her for her outspokenness and make snide remarks disguised as lectures. She would tell her to back off more, let the maiko lead, and let men win now and then. She would remind her gaining loyalty required exhibiting humility. Adakichi knew the art of saving face: when to strike and when to confide in half-secrets and half-truths.

Her neck itched. How she longed to undo her hair and robe entirely, but if someone saw her behaving improperly, it would be the end of her relationship with Hanamachi.

Thankfully, she was alone. The bamboo-gated windows and tapestries were silent. Curved branches of cherry trees kissed the stones. Lattices of wisteria filled the air with an easing fragrance. There was no summer breeze; even the cicada were quiet.

And where was the farmer? Had he already pulled his cart by? She listened for a sound of wheels and made her way toward the river to see if she could catch him.

She thought back to her last conversations with her father. He hadn't implied anything about an "uprising." He had lamented about problems with the ports, or was it the pots? What was the truth—the other countries came here for lights and their rights? Or did they come for a fight?

She dropped the crate to wipe her brow. She was plagued by voices of evil yokai in her ears, whispering new memories into existence and throwing doubt on her truths. She leaned back and drank in the air, gasping for relief from the odors of the night soil.

Her father appeared in her mind, smiling quietly and extended a hand that felt weathered and strong from years of gripping a sword but gentle enough to hold hers carefully and make her feel safe.

Maru came to her senses, shaking off the memory of her mother's words:

"Don't coddle her so."

She picked up the crate and ripped off the roots of the weeds Fujiwara planted as she turned to go through Gion and over an arched bridge. Willow trees curtained the nearby okiya that was shuttered at nighttime. Focusing on details helped to distract her from thinking about bigger strains that kept her up at night adrift in an endless sea of woes.

Where was the farmer? Adakichi would seek her soon, and she'd be in trouble all over again. She'd hide the night soil in her room; its stench was something she would mind less than Adakichi's punishment. She needed to go back, even if her feet resisted her direction.

Then, a movement caught her eye.

She was sure it from an animal. She stilled her quickened breathing, hoping the creature wouldn't notice her. Her eyes were weary, but she could distinctly see something crouched in a shadow.

Under her narrowed gaze, a golden leg emerged, stepping into the moonlight. A cat?

No. A fox! The way it stared at her made her wary.

Its paws froze. Maru heard her heart churn louder than the river rushing. She shook off her fear and stepped forward confidently, but her kimono was so restricting and her geta so loud, they betrayed her. She hoped someone was around—even Fujiwara would be welcome.

"You," said a voice from behind.

And though Maru wanted with all of her might to continue on her path, she knew she had been seen and couldn't rush away. She had to answer.

"Yes?" But she saw no one. Just gingko and building edges steeped in blue and silver.

"Where are you?" she asked, aware she was no longer polite, much less composed. *Come on*, she thought, turning this way and that.

She saw only the fox. It was pulling itself slowly forward, displaying a limp.

"You there," said the voice. It came from the same direction.

Who was calling for her? Everything rushed through her at once; it didn't make sense—it couldn't be—

"Please," cried the voice. She saw the fox's mouth moving. "Please help me."

Maru let out a shriek. She turned quickly, stumbling to get away, discarding the crate.

"Please!" she heard as the voice faded.

She dashed past the corner, zig-zagging her way through the streets to shake off the yokai, afraid it was at her heels, ready to nip. Every shadow, every flicker of light startled her as she pressed on faster. *It's a dream*, she told herself, for visions of a demon were even worse to admit. She didn't look back, running as fast as she could until she slid open the ochaya door, her geta heel catching its edge and sending her into a heap on the hard pine floor.

When Maru awakened, she saw through the cracks in her bamboo shades that the sun was high. So was the heat. She found herself sitting upright in her okiya bedroom, her heart beating wildly. Memories of the night before appeared in bursts. Her nighttime yukatabira and futon were damp and in disarray. Did her dreams make her toss and turn?

No. The fox did! She clutched her chest and felt her stomach drop. Should she tell Adakichi about the talking animal? She feared being accused of having a delusion. But desperation made her consider it. The presence of a yokai usually implied greater danger abound.

The loudness of being alone rang in her ears. Nobody, not even her father, had prepared her to face what she presumed was a demon—and her mind offered no rationale; no voice materialized to give her an answer.

She could only pray she'd never see it again.

A tingle in her head convinced her to part the mosquito netting and get prepared for the day. She yelped when she found a fresh bruise on her hip. Peering beneath her yukatabira, she pulled out her kobuse-steel tanto blade with relief. It was barely larger than her hand, shorter than the common swords her father had wielded in the past. He imparted the tanto blade to her when he left.

"Just in case," he had said.

"In case of what?"

It felt like she was holding his hand. She hadn't found a use for the blade yet, except for cutting flowers along edges of a field on afternoon walks or slicing a melon for sharing.

She was grateful it didn't need to be drawn last night.

"Your mother would use words as armor, but in this new world, this will better serve you than a dead poet's ink dried on a page."

Her eyes lingered on her stash of pages, inked heavily with her tears and words depicting a lonely, confused young woman. Writing was something her mother had inspired her to do, and though Maru wasn't half the poet she had been, writing was her only solace inside this bamboo cage. She would hole up in her room for hours, lamenting about the lyrics she'd never share, waiting to be summoned to do chores. All her life seemed to be spent in waiting.

The reminder of chores from the night before motivated her to rise for the day. She tallied what she'd need to do: the sweeping, coordinating pantry restocking with the maid, washing a smoke-pressed kimono, meeting with her hairdresser, dusting the harp, and polishing a tea set for the day's clients. She might need to fetch a new pair of geta for either Adakichi or Mitsu.

Mitsu was spared from most of the chores, having paid her dues for years when she was in residence as a shikomi before becoming a maiko. She was now nearing her graduation to geiko, biding her time as she refined the arts of conversation, personality, and dance before opening an ochaya of her own after she made her debut. Then Adakichi would need to find another maiko to help earn enough wages to keep running the ochaya.

Not many ochaya were attached to an okiya, a house owned by a geiko who gives lessons and room and board to geiko-in-training. This arrangement made their rent quite high and their list of chores long; they were expected to take greater care of the place where they worked and lived. Most okiya and ochaya had more maiko as tenants, but Adakichi's strict rules and steep rent kept many at bay. For Mitsu, living there was far more convenient and created less drama than staying in an okiya with competitive maiko, sharing futons with someone who would sell secrets to their okaasan to advance her own career. Mitsu had proven to be an admired ally of Adakichi; and though she could be short-tempered and disdainful, she never stole from Maru or hit her as Adakichi did.

Maru hoped her father would return and she'd be long gone before a worse maiko came.

Downstairs, the interior cooled overnight, thanks to the tatami mats that retained last winter's breath, expelling it in summer. She thought she heard the ochaya exhale at her arrival.

Adakichi's face was fully done up, her painted snow-white skin accented by her black eyebrows, deep eyes, and red lips. Her hair was up in a bun with elaborate ornaments. It was early; had a client booked for tea? Had she missed the hairdresser? Her hand covered her belly in fear of being admonished for being late. But Adakichi was calm. Over the year, Maru learned this meant she was on the brink of being displeased, which could take the form of a strike. And Adakichi didn't know yet that Maru hadn't managed to sell any night soil.

"I am sorry, Okaasan," said Maru, bowing so deeply her forehead touched the floor. She wanted to get ahead of the punishment.

Adakichi clicked her tongue. "You'll help with cleaning later. Mitsu was out rather late; youthful energy needs to be put somewhere more useful. But first, we must take care of errands at the market. That emperor's train made deliveries." Her lips tightened.

Maru was taken aback. The train? She had been preparing for a punishment, not an invitation to go to the market. Every flick of Adakichi's wrist made her flinch.

"Summon Mitsu. No ochaya should out-best us in the latest fashion."

"You, as well?"

Adakichi usually prevented non-clients from approaching her.

"You didn't think I put on makeup and a wig as heavy as iron because I enjoy the extra layers in this heat, did you?" And that's why patrons admired her: she balanced feminine talents with wry humor—the kind men approved of—and what Maru aspired to have.

"We will talk on the way."

There it was. At least it wouldn't be a physical retaliation. During daytime, Adakichi sharpened her tongue to dissect Maru's misdemeanors with words instead.

Gion was bustling, despite the sun bearing down. The meandering machiya, pieced together with a preciseness in its straight edges and layers of frames, protected them from the crooked city. Shopkeepers dumped water outside doors to suppress the dust as passerby carried baskets. News of the train gripped the city. Many were rushing to see what it brought; others were nearly frowning. Not everyone approved.

"Ohayou!" Patrons and neighbors put a hand in the air when they passed.

By the river the sky opened, revealing the waterfront's expanse. Paper lanterns hung off balconies and willows lined the banks where children teased fish with kite tails. Some wore cloth that clung tightly to their bodies. Their foreign style startled Maru. Had she only now opened her eyes?

"Those striped uniforms the children wear in the water—where are they from, I wonder?" mused Mitsu.

"They are rather disquieting," murmured Adakichi, before a wide smile filled her face.

Horses pulling carriages of older ladies passed by. Yatai-keepers offered sugar-coated strawberries, which they politely accepted. Adakichi frowned when Maru took a nibble—perhaps she wasn't forgiven yet for her careless indiscretions.

Her father's absence made her frantic. Prone to clumsiness and uncertain about how to carry herself and orchestrate her words, she felt she was constantly fighting to survive. Although he said he'd return to see the "greens bleed into reds," there was no telling how long he would be.

Fujiwara had verbally cut her with this remark. Maybe the uprisings in the south had interrupted her father's work. Or perhaps he had a completely new home and workplace. Far worse, he might have been killed and she'd never know.

She didn't want to remain with Adakichi. *It's all temporary,* she told herself; but as she heard the words in her mind, she felt her throat close. The thought of her father never coming back constantly stained her mind. At the very least, there had to be repercussions if Adakichi believed the rumors about her family. As someone who was trying to gain favor with the palace, Maru was a liability to her. She couldn't afford to pay Adakichi back for any business she lost because she took Maru under her wing.

She remembered when her samurai neighbors pretended they didn't recognize her after the war ended and clans disbanded, now without income after their surrendered status. Her father was able to build a new business and change his reputation. He was no longer connected with sword and bloodshed. She had to trust his decision to send her to the ochaya while he was away, saying it was "double the income" he could earn elsewhere.

Her hand quivered, she took another bite. The taste took her back to childhood reveries—picking strawberries in mountain gardens, the sensation of curling her toes around cool grass, her father chasing after her head wrap when it fell in a field, her mother calling her. Shards of light danced between the branches.

Careful to see it is not Jinmen Ju you pluck! They might bite back—trust me, her father had told her, laughing and picking her up.

"Shikomi," said Adakichi sternly. Maru snapped out of her daydream, realizing she was several paces ahead of her. She bowed to her and resumed her correct position. Adakichi pinched her side hard under the guise of adjusting her obi to confirm she was always in the wrong.

They rounded a large intersection with the tallest buildings in Kyoto, including a four-story restaurant filled with patrons hanging out windows with wine and tobacco pipes. A worker was swapping the placards of today's fish. Monks cut through the crowds in their flowing dark orange robes. Purple, red, green, and white flags strung up by gas lamps caught the sunlight, dyeing the streets in color. Young men sat on a wall sharing a beer, knees bent to prop themselves up.

"Good morning, ladies!" they called out. "Can we come by tonight? My boys are so lonely."

"You'll need your father's invitation; no first-timers, and men only!" Mitsu replied.

Adakichi was tense. Maru knew she hated being mistaken for an oiran—and Adakichi, an esteemed geiko, was not a courtesan. Even Mitsu's long darari obi should have given away her own position as a maiko.

A geiko's art centered on music and dance rather than on mastering sweet nothings whispered in the dark and other intimacies that oiran were known for.

But it was geiko who used to open brothels that held dazzling performances to create great anticipation for clients awaiting their night with an oiran. Geiko were once guardians and mothers to the young women who kept company of daimyo and shogun through the nights, whether they were bored at home or just stopping in Kyoto on their journey elsewhere. Later when Meiji changed the laws, there were years of confusion over the palace's remapping of districts to permit geiko to practice their art, but only if it was done separately from oiran's practice, which were driven underground.

Adakichi insisted that geiko and oiran had, at last, a distinct business from oiran, and she regarded it sacrilegious to conflate the two. She claimed that boys and men who have a good laugh at the expense of these women were harmful to geiko and reflected the city's negative perceptions of their art.

"Men will not treat us with dignity or respect for our art unless we uphold our own dignity of character," Adakichi said. "Maintain your control to earn their respect. They will then pay us enough for the lives we wish to have."

Mitsu was silent but nodded in agreement. She had been trained for over ten years by Adakichi and was comfortable with her authority, while even the smallest pressure to behave differently was a strain for Maru; each mistake she made was a wound that refused to heal. But Maru never wanted to become accustomed to their emotionless practices.

They crossed the bridge, the arch that became a treacherous walk in the heat of the day.

Adakichi continued, "Men who are under our skin may as well be under our sheets. And we are not oiran—so men have no place beneath either our skin or our sheets.

"But Fujiwara *would* make a fine Danna someday as a 'work' husband. As your dedicated, faithful patron, he would provide an insurance of income for life; a familiar face to entertain and rely on. Mitsu will need one. Mayuki will need one too if her time comes. He is a good businessman, and we must keep him trusting us."

I won't be here long enough to need one, Maru thought.

"He was one of the first families to align with the emperor, forging an allegiance and shunning those who stuck to the feudal ways of the shogunate like rice on an old pot. He is a master at playing different sides. A man like him craves secrets as commodity to hold others in debt. It's not our duty to take away his power from him. Remember. Men who crave power will align themselves with its helm, regardless of the head that wears it."

Had she made a mistake by revealing her name? Had she just threatened her own existence by bringing a curse on her family? A tightness in her throat under the collar of her robe made it hard to breathe.

Adakichi faced north over the river and mountains, toward the darkened outline of Sanjo Bridge, shrouded in a golden haze of parasols.

"I never tire of this view," she said. Mitsu quickly agreed.

Boats flowed down the river and disappeared beneath the bridge. One low pleasure boat with a tent was rocking from the ruckus inside; a group of rowdy men entertained by oiran cracked open fresh scallops right out of the river. They teased the girls under their robes in between turns at their card games. Soon the fishermen would venture out with their wide nets under the grey and peach skies of the misty morning sunrise.

Adakichi continued with her lesson. "Do not let your thoughts about your work stir your emotions when you are alone. Despite the difference in your levels of hierarchy, maiko and shikomi do not serve each other but their clients. Maru is your imouto, Mitsu. You protect her and cover her mistakes. Work together. Don't let men unravel you with a careless comment."

She grasped the top of the bridge post, facing the silvery carpet of river.

"This work is a culmination of my trust in you and our coalescing of art and our practices, and you two must work to carry this on and preserve it."

"You won't be having your Hiki Iwai soon, will you?" Mitsu asked with a laugh.

Adakichi took the joke in stride; she was far from retirement. "I am asking you to avoid manifesting personal resentment in veiled remarks in front of our patrons."

Mitsu gazed into the distance, her stiff lip indicated she was hearing but not listening. She had a perpetual fog hanging in her harbor that kept Maru at a distance. Maru had been trying for months to lift it and become sisters-in-arms. But night after night resulted in Mitsu thinking Maru threatened to take attention away from her, and Maru solemnly reminding her she was just passing time until her father came to her rescue.

The three of them moved on.

There was a symmetry in the city. The corners of the shops and homes stitched together with straight bamboo fences and sills that kept everything orderly. Their edges caught the sunshine. Everything seemed in place as the streets bustled with carts carrying bushels of rice, old ladies stirring barley in barrels. Music wafted, interrupted only by temple chimes. Tattoo-covered firefighters climbed ladders, dumping water on roofs. A man swept his broom shop crammed to its brim; next door, a merchant read a book on his stoop. Two men in wide-split trousers carried a former daimyo in a palanquin. A spry man carved a shakuhachi flute out of bamboo, eyeing its shape after each cut. An orange cat stared at her from a windowsill. The curtain in the window was drawn.

The itching on Maru's neck came back, and her stomach churned. The shadow of the encounter with the fox had made her jumpy, and the feeling of being watched by more than street-goers tugged at her. She tried to shoo away her fears.

Coming to the west side of Kyoto typically denoted a special occasion or a need for specific goods from another district—such as robes, books, and musical instruments. She used to accompany her father to attend events here until she went to school, and now the teahouse had become her full-time responsibility.

Maru remembered racing her father to her favorite mochi shop, both eager for the sweets. Everyone made way for them. Shoppers passing by talked to her mother, who often bore a worried smile. Maru devoured the sticky treats, the syrups dripping, while her mother was busy keeping up appearances. The past was a happier place to meander.

But now the shadows and hurried whispers seemed to tiptoe in their wake, following them over the bridges and into the wide streets filled with faces she didn't recognize. So many plain-clothed merchants pushed by. Where was the music and wind chimes? She missed Gion.

A curl of smoke filled Maru's nostrils, bringing her a familiar, rich smell.

"Meat!" she gasped. She was breathless—meat was everywhere.

A crowd was ogling, in vocalized harmony, sizzling skewers of beef a butcher with a long beard and bloody robes spun over coals. This must be the first time they were seeing meat cooked in the streets, thought Maru. It had been accessible to clans like hers, but here it was not being prepared for a special occasion. It was available for all to devour casually.

She had an urge to step in and tell them all about her own experiences with meat, but instead she gripped her hands at her sides.

The butcher rubbed his belly as he spotted them and called out, "Adakichi-san, a pleasure! Step right up." He waved his hands, boasting loudly, "Finest cut for the finest lady!"

Adakichi pinched it and sniffed. She cupped her other hand over her mouth while she bit her blackened teeth into the juiciest meat Maru had ever seen.

"Oh, my! This might be the best thing I've ever had!" she cooed.

"Ma'am, it'll soon be as common as fish."

As common as fish! Fish had only been available for samurai during the time of the shogun, but today it was considered cheap and eaten by all classes. It sounded like an insult. What would be next?

"Is this really possible?" inquired Adakichi. Maru recognized her tone used to engage a client and encourage them to carry on the conversation.

Merchants, one of the lower classes, clamored to have the opportunity to speak with a geiko. Ochaya had been reserved for shogun and daimyo. With the dissolution of the higher class under Meiji, this butcher was more of an equal, but he couldn't yet afford her talents. And he would need an invitation from one of Adakichi's current clients. Maru gave Fujiwara until the end of summer to bring a famed butcher through their doors.

"Fish, indeed. Cool, with natural salt. It will certainly be a treat for you; it's a little difficult to prepare." The butcher was reeled in.

Maru felt less entranced. She had a suffocating disdain for everyone reveling in this newfound meat business; it was old news for her. She couldn't help feeling something was being taken from her while everyone else was gaining something. Meat had been *her* thing.

Adakichi was bantering with the butcher who practically begged for her attention, the way she liked men to act.

Feeling bored, Maru turned around and saw some familiar people, including Kiku—a solace in her barren landscape. They were wearing fashionable robes, and their hair was swept up in curls adorned with ornaments—unlike her own flat, looped bun. They were trading gossip with bright rosy lips.

Maru suddenly cared little about Adakichi and the meat man. She desperately wanted what she missed—a normal routine of attending school and seeing her friends—something Adakichi and Mitsu couldn't satisfy.

"Hello, hello!" she called out to them.

Her sudden appearance tilted heads in her direction. Maru stiffened.

Kiku sidled next to her and squeezed her elbow. "No after-sickness? I could lie down for days."

Maru laughed stiffly, and the two women exchanged a look.

"Everyone is well? How are you, Ai? Tane, it's been a while—"

There was a pause, as if they'd been talking happily without her. It was rare all four got together since school, and Maru found it difficult to slip into conversation. Much of what she knew depended on her relationship with Kiku.

"Those robes are pretty," said Maru to Tane. Tane blushed. She was a gentle, modest young woman from a family of merchants who ran a noodle and teashop in southern Kyoto.

Maru then turned to Ai, the gorgeous Ai, a jewel of a girl with her perfectly snowy and slender face and small nose wearing a dress bigger than life itself. It had one of those big skirts from the matsuri!

"Ai! This is—" Maru was at a loss for something to say. Ai had been waiting for this. She twirled round and round, showing off her big curls and strange robe that was wider than her arm span and swept the air with every swish.

"It's what all girls wear in Europe. It's so romantic! I feel the most luxurious breeze," she said.

"I thought she looked like a pastry, but she isn't as edible," added Kiku. Ai hit her lightly on the arm.

"Your taste is—" began Tane, looking Maru up and down before coughing.

"Madam has the tastes of a grandma," offered Kiku for levity.

"Oh, these, yes. A little dated, but customers like them," Maru quickly said. The noise of the city was coming into focus, and she was feeling nervous. "I've missed you all; it's so different now." No one seemed to return her enthusiasm.

"So different," echoed Tane. Her voice was raspy.

"Not so different; the boys we teased are now the men we torture," Kiku said. "And it's a better time for good fortune. You missed the news. Ai's family is searching for a husband!"

Ai was always expected to be the first to marry. Maru couldn't think of anything worse.

"The interviews have begun. One of them is with the Abe family," gushed Ai.

Maru was almost knocked over. Her family always walked on gold. It was not unexpected, but a sour thought crossed her mind: everyone else got what they wanted.

"Anyone would be lucky to marry into your family," said Kiku. Though the Abe family purportedly had kami blood running through their veins, Ai's family, the Nakatomi clan, was wealthy. They owned the famous Kamigamo shrine with a lineage of prominent Shinto priests; it was there they also oversaw the famed horseracing that brought nobles from Tokyo to gamble. Many people clamored to be friends with Ai, but her parents hand-picked only a few to be her trusted friends. It was a privilege that tested everyone's composure.

"When? How soon will you know?" said Maru. "I wish we could share a drink!"

The girls looked at each other with uncomfortable glances.

Kiku broke the silence, "Her parents are arranging it all. We are sure there'll be a match."

"Yes, of course, her parents know everyone," agreed Maru. Matches were common for a family carefully selecting someone who would not detract from their distinguished family or muddy the bloodline.

"And about your father. You are not too difficult for him to make a match for you?" asked Ai.

A dark playfulness lurked in her question. Ai either knew her father was away and was reminding her of her situation or had forgotten she was vulnerable. Maru wasn't sure which was worse. If her father was with her, he would undoubtedly be facing similar dilemmas; he'd be interviewing families who were prospects but had less to offer. She batted away the nuisance of having to consider this.

"Ah, no, he is—well he is still in Satsuma. Trading, if you recall."

Tane wrinkled her nose. "Aren't traders working with the Spaniards? Aren't you nervous about the possibility that he'll be kidnapped?"

Maru couldn't help opening her mouth in surprise.

"No, surely not," she said.

"He is clearly one of the rebels. He never could let go of his samurai days," scoffed Ai. "She is saving face. She wants to be a geiko after all."

Maru sighed. They had been through this before; dirty silk that would never clean.

Tane giggled, an insidious look in her eyes. She was instantly worried when she glanced at Maru. Although Tane was shy, she never passed up an opportunity to get in Ai's good graces. When Maru's father retired his samurai ways, he also relinquished their title and status, making Ai's family more powerful than her own—and a more enviable ally.

Maru shook her head. "No. Being a geiko is not what I want."

"Oh, of course. But your father cannot afford having you at home anymore, can he?"

Maru bit her lip and tasted blood. Ai often pushed the boundaries of their assigned friendship, but she rarely had a response loaded in time to fire back in such a cunning way.

"Maru wouldn't lie," said Kiku, softening her voice. "Your father is trading beer and sake, right? It's a good business; he's supporting your clan just fine."

"Double the income!" Her memories were evaporating as she grasped to recall what he told her. She hadn't a clue what the Portuguese were known for. She'd thought it was pottery. But between Fujiwara, Adakichi's disapproval, and her friends' prompts, her memories blurred. Her father always shut the door when people came by to discuss business.

"I heard the Spanish are only good for tomatoes," Tane offered.

"What wine does a tomato make?" Kiku quipped back. "I suppose, if it works on men and turns their loins, it's as good as any to me. I prefer mine knocked out; how to achieve this is inconsequential."

Maru's face flushed. She remembered a summer ago when Kiku had seduced a rickshaw boy by the riverbank, nursing him sake and doing as they pleased until flies got caught in their hair. "It was all in silence, for boys say the dullest things when their behind is bare," Kiku had said. Once when her father was away, Maru lured a boy of her own, but she loathed every moment of the encounter. She had sought solace afterward from Kiku under twilight's giggling stars and found herself tantalized by Kiku's laughter-glistened lips, wondering how she could be more like Kiku.

But last summer was eons ago. And today any quiet innocence was gone; their world was in a new disguise. Why were her friends doubting her so? She had little patience to spare, worn from all she expended to the men she served, and now sanded further by Adakichi's hands.

Ai interjected, "She can't even lie properly, when there's no need for a samurai family like hers—"

Pale faces turned to Maru. Was the world coming to a standstill? Whispers were swelling with the dust that swirled at their feet.

"Maru," Ai continued, her brazen eyes staring at her friend.

Maru blinked, and her father's stern eyes looked back at her. *She would be found out.*

"It's Mayuki! Out here, you—!" She stopped short of cursing her.

The hum was growing louder.

"It's so criminal to disregard your own ancestry."

She blinked. Yellow eyes flashed before her own. She sprang at her, pressing her fingers on Ai's lips, startling them both. She peeled off her lips. Her palm was stained with Ai's rouge.

The humming ceased, and prying eyes looked away. The sun seemed brighter. Her throat opened to let the air fill her chest.

"Your okaasan may be looking for you," suggested Tane with a gentle firmness.

"Go, and maybe your father will bring a husband! Must be why he's taking so long!" chirped Ai.

Kiku conveyed an apology with her eyes.

"There you are," said Adakichi, coming up beside her. "Are these your acquaintances? Ah, Kiku, how is your okaasan?"

"She sends her wishes, Ma'am!" said Kiku brightly.

"I am sorry I wandered away," said Maru quietly.

Adakichi measured the girls and their robes.

"Say, how about we go to Chiki-san and see about new robes? I hear she received some from Europe," she said calmly. "Let's see if we can outrace the storm."

The train. It was now a savior.

Maru wiped away the tears that threatened to unleash her inner turmoil. Her friends had hurt her more than Adakichi's nighttime strikes. She quickly buried all desire to mention the fox she saw the night before, fully aware her trust in them may have been misplaced, after all. She was running out of people to embrace.

Why did calling this "temporary" bring such a burden of loss?

She only wanted to go home.

The three young women stared as Maru left with Adakichi. Her neck burned. She wanted to look back but was afraid of what she'd see. It was a relief when a sudden shower took away the opportunity.

4

They sheltered in a darkened shinise. The bent-over woman in thin blue robes who ran it looked older than the shop itself. The incense holders and stoneware she sold to temples were stacked high.

While Adakichi and Mitsu engaged in polite conversation with her, Maru steadied herself, remembering the company she kept. Her friends couldn't compete with her social status—even Kiku who worked for another high-ranking geiko didn't hold a candle to Maru's position.

But it did little to calm her. The rain rattled the cracked window glass and dripped through the thatched straw roof, her heart jumping at each sound.

"The samurai were responsible for installing new roofs," chortled the woman through gapped teeth. "The palace heeds no calls from an old woman." Raindrops hit Mitsu in the face. She glared at Maru, looking for a way to somehow blame her. "And I can't afford the strapping young roofers."

Thunder shook along with her laugh.

"The emperor still posts his decrees, does he not? You could write a request there for the public, couldn't you?" Adakichi asked, sipping on pale tea.

Maru shifted around in a dusty corner, the knotted wooden walls watching as she gingerly touched ornaments that looked back at her, and a childlike curiosity played with her heart. They were not yet ordained or blessed for the temple; their emptiness of soul struck her as unnerving. Here, they were simply statues.

"Yes, every morning! You should hear the clatter. I want to brandish my broom!"

Lightning lit the room. Cornered by statues, Maru moved out of eyesight, wishing she could say a prayer now for protection. But no one would hear her.

"One thing after another . . ." the old woman muttered. "Only death will end it."

The lightning startled Maru as she reached out to touch the smooth stone of a shape that could be a fox. She recoiled, afraid it was a warning.

She realized it was looking at her.

"You're hardly alone; we must keep his vision in mind," assured Adakichi.

Maru's gaze was locked on the stone in an image of a fox. "Can you see me?" she whispered, maintaining a small amount of hope. Her voice was masked by the quickening rain. Thunder echoed; the shelf shook, and the fox wobbled. She grabbed hold of it, but it knocked into its neighbor, fracturing its front leg.

"He makes his proclamations and bats take to the air!" Her okaasan's voice was shrill.

The mouth formed a shape. *Yes.* She let go of it abruptly and pressed her back against the shelves, disturbing the statues. They all turned to look at her.

"If we were in Edo times, someone would have cursed him for his inflictions."

Lightning struck, and the shadows cowered; the glint in its eyes had disappeared. The rain's beat tempered, and sunlight returned to the corners, illuminating cobwebs.

Adakichi beckoned her, and they left. Maru barely noticed when they arrived at the palace. She was so consumed by thoughts and stony faces she didn't hear Adakichi say why they had been diverted there. The courtyard soldiers wore pants that clung to their legs *(in this heat?)* and their hair was tucked in their collars. They strutted like dolls, bearing permission to bully children who were out late and escort home grumpy old patrons yelling in sake bars. She'd never become accustomed to them, preferring the familiarity of samurais' style of ruling, the arranging of negotiations and helping people in need.

If only there were other samurai still around to take her in while father was away. But they too had disappeared during recent wars, surrendered their arms—as her father had willingly done—and moved north to seek a change in lifestyle, as far as she knew.

"What a strange woman," Mitsu remarked. Adakichi remained mum.

The shouts from the woman standing on an overturned barrel brought Maru to the present. The protestor's hair was slathered by the rain and she wore an old robe. It wasn't uncommon to see a displeased citizen complain at the gate, but the wild look in her eyes and her gibberish worried Maru.

"Pale faces at sea! On shore! Night falls, demons pounce! The emperor's deals in—"

Maru longed to be back in the shop corner with the fox statue. *Why had it drawn her in?* She didn't know yet, but she felt it might have an answer.

People in iki kimono and large skirts like Ai's were gathered in front of the palace decree board, ignoring the protestor. Today there were excited whispers—a hum stronger than cicadas. Adakichi pursed her lips, craning to see what the fuss was about. She heard voices going back and forth. Maru fondly remembered her father reading the posts for her.

"Who is an e-l-e-c-t-r-i-s-i-a-n?"

"—more foreign intervention, spilling into our city—"

"Not like Chiba, wiped from the cough—"

Half a dozen prints, some from earlier days, depicted matsuri wagons pulling a train, and included long decrees. They were written with such formality that she had to concentrate to comprehend their meaning. She read one from the emperor.

By Order of the Emperor

> In continuation of fulfilling The Charter Oath, our cities will embrace the ways of allies and commence the construction of an infrastructure to strengthen Japan from within; advance and assure negotiation in equalizing treaties; provide a foundation upon which our collective Self can realize our greatest powers. Construction is to begin immediately to connect our most prominent cities as a priority; and further reach all in the coming years and ensure equity across prefectures and orders through safer, reliable communication methods that will illuminate a forward future. The installation of new technology is to deliver electricity for the benefit of all classes; permitting all to fulfill personal aspirations in alignment with their governments. This promotion of welfare of our empire further increases distance between the evils of the past and dissuade discontent, and introduces new, purposeful customs to improve knowledge of the world.

"Well, that is quite an announcement," said Adakichi. She received a response of quiet laughter. "You can never get too confident in things that go the way of the samurai." Maru bit her tongue in resentment. Usually Adakichi wordsmithed her opinions over sake with her clients, privately confiding she dreaded interpreting their response. But here, she reveled in her opportunity for a show and demonstrated her careless attitude toward Maru's family. Although Maru tried to mimic the stillness of the stony statues, she felt her lower lip quiver.

"It seems we will expect visitors to build us something grand to keep us from sakoku."

Sakoku. Maru recalled the word with a shudder—the terror of her father lamenting the dangers of the shogunate's Sakoku policy that closed Japan's borders and isolated the country from the rest of the world for hundreds of years.

"'To connect us all'—does the Tokaido road not do the job?" a young mother inquired.

"He wishes to put us in a better position to rival our adversaries—not so much a 'war,' but petty scuffles brought on by farmers when they run out of stipends," remarked a merchant.

"We should have confidence. The announcement abides by the 1868 Oath, which all citizens took with the emperor," said Adakichi.

"Ba! Progressiveness is merely a rejection of what has worked all along."

"A failed experiment," spat a gruff man. "Goals of yesteryear are today's ghosts."

"We are as close to unity as we've ever come. If we determine he upholds his values, then—"

"Which means they are out of touch and forget quickly the ways of Edo," claimed an older man in a tight bun and clean robes.

"Taka here preferred the harsh ways of shogun, bloodthirsty and selfish."

"Aside from this ele-cu-tree we must resist the urge to execute edicts without public discourse. He is restoring goodness and eradicating troublesome behavior that put us on edge."

"Everyone forgets the Tokugawa shogunate kept us at peace. They banished Western influence, and rightly so. This emperor and his imperial government already gave us their terrible locomotive, that loud thing that stinks of something rotten bleeding out—we had no choice."

Peace must have unusual definitions as of late, Maru mused, recalling her father's tales of Kyoto before she was born: assassinated leaders' heads propped up on fences in the dawn, children captured for ransom, crops burned to starve rivals. The peace of today was one he had fought for to keep the streets free of blood, the paths to school safe, and dry collars around their necks. Over two centuries ago, the Tokugawa and "Great Unifier" Toyotomi forced Emperor Go-Yozei's hand to establish a new hierarchy, rejecting the direction the emperor was taking his subjects. This included war with Korea, worldwide travel, and a visit to a place called the Vatican where citizens worshiped a different god, all of which drove the shogun to form a bakufu, close the borders and rule with terror, threatening the lives of others who adopted outside cultures as their own. Each leader was more terrible than the previous one, but each asserted he brought peace and had ended the civil wars. People like her father saw the clans become too powerful and dangerous, and fought to overthrow them and restore order under an imperial emperor.

"Yet, sir, you wear an outfit delivered by that train," said a younger lady, wearing one of those wide skirts and waving a fan. Indeed, the man wore dark pants and a funny jacket, which Maru saw as silly rather than impressive.

"Maybe if they employed samurai to do more than needlework—" the young lady suggested.

Maru thought about how many had been proud to turn to merchant life; but there were strings of insults about their choices.

"Samurai are plenty busy," retorted another woman.

"With yet another self-pity tantrum in Satsuma province," snorted a sunburned man.

"My husband's cousin found himself to be quite the hand at woodworking. They all have their passions," said the woman, eyeing the man.

"Meiji destroyed true passion. Vague flourishes of his pen change our city. It will happen. All will be taken from us! They tear down Buddha, rip the tapestries of families who swore allegiance," an old man said, wiping his face. "They subject us to the ways of foreign entities who are our enemies! Samurai protected us, and now outsiders pry us open."

"I hear ol' Saigo is still accepting pupils at his Shi-gakko academy," a dark man said. "I heard they plan to engage Meiji. That is, if they can ever afford a gun over a hoe."

Saigo! She hadn't heard that name since the war when she was a child. Father once admired him for his military organization in the face of Tokugawa's bakufu. To hear he now opposed their emperor made her chin drop.

"No, my brother returned from nasty battles missing a hand. He says it was a mess in winter. Now he is without work. You may be jesting, but there is nothing ripe there."

Maru wondered if her father looked down on the samurai who joined Saigo, breaking their oath to lay down their arms for Meiji as he had. Once a friend, now a foe.

"We let this pot boil, never knowing we are the ones cooked until we are on the plate."

There was a murmur of agreed bafflement. Maru studied Adakichi's face to see if she detected a threat or was refraining from giving her opinions. "All of our traditions had a beginning," said Adakichi calmly. "With patience we will find agreeable new ones."

A few women with tight waists and frilled fans nodded in agreement.

"BLOOD! YOKAI! MEIJI!" The protestor screamed, toppling over. Adakichi rushed to her side before a soldier stepped in. "We will handle her, ma'am."

"Well, she needs no handling. She just has a tendency for hysterics."

He put his hand out to Adakichi and then hoisted the woman to her feet and tried to hush her.

Adakichi gave a curt bow and ushered Mitsu and Maru through the palace gates. "Sometimes it is best not to interfere with men who know no better," she mumbled.

The bright courtyard under the white midday sun stung Maru's eyes as they approached the open hall. Wide red columns upheld the lofty teal roof adorned with dark wood and gold carvings. Wings of the palace and cedar guarded the main hall in the shape of a horseshoe.

Up the marble steps and inside, a high-beamed ceiling and a bright red carpet on the dark wood floor greeted them. A window on the far wall gave them relief from the stagnant air and opened to a lush garden with knobby dogwoods tipping over ponds of orange fish. The room was so grand, filled with art, she wondered how Meiji could spend time in Tokyo, away from his magnificent palace here in Kyoto.

Adakichi said a word to the guard. Leaning closer to the art, an image of something white at the base of a tree in a painting caught Maru's eye.

Maru saw a fox's yellow eyes blink in the painting and jumped.

"Someday you could perform here. It is always an honor for a geiko to be within these walls and presents your name as one of the most prevalent in the business."

"Did you see the fox move?" Maru said, pointing to the image of the fox.

"Paintings don't move, Maru," snipped Mitsu as the guard returned.

"Yuhiko, it has been a while," said Adakichi, bowing to an old man in billowing robes.

"Aki, it's too hot to see such a warm face. Ah, is that Maruya?"

Her old name. The one meant to stay hidden. He knew her family. Maru could do nothing but smile and bow, scrambling to remember his name. His face looked familiar.

"Don't tell me you forgot; your father was a longtime friend of Kira."

Kira! "This heat has made me delusional," Maru laughed nervously, glanced at Mitsu whose head was tilted. "I remember our dinners!" She wanted to conceal how elated she was to see a family friend, and how safe she suddenly felt.

"Tell me, how is he lately? I rarely see him in the market."

"He is away on business."

"And left you all alone? Who cares for your clan?"

"I am not alone when I have Okaasan," she gritted her teeth. "And there are some caretakers. We are fortunate," she added to save her father's name.

"Ah, do not be modest. I know you miss him; he always spoke how after every job he looked forward most to going home to you."

"That was long ago," she said softly.

"But what could keep him so long?"

"He is far away, trading art in Satsuma," she said, feeling braver from her recent practice.

"Ah," he paused. "We have a handsome collection of art and the most exquisitely detailed vases from afar brought to us by traders from Satsuma." His eyes narrowed. Adakichi remained still, and Maru knew she was summoning ways to hit her.

"I would be delighted to show them to you on your next visit. And I hope to see your father's collection." Mitsu was leaning in closely, her eyes hungrily devouring the details. Maru felt uncomfortable; the more Mitsu knew, the more she could hold over her head or sell to her own friends; and by daybreak, her secret would be out. She had to tread lightly.

Come to think of it, her clan did have a collection of ornate vases, which she presumed he picked up in his jobs; a thank you for vanquishing an enemy, rescuing a child, or enacting revenge on a daimyo. She suspected their collection paled in comparison to the emperor's.

"It would be a delight to Mayuki, I am sure," said Adakichi carefully, prompting Maru.

"Forgive me, is Maruya not her name? I must have become a really old man."

"She needed something more suitably feminine. We thought Mayuki added beauty." Mitsu tilted her head again.

In truth, Adakichi helped her change the kanji characters of her family name to deflect suspicion about why a samurai's daughter worked in an ochaya, although with those close to her she could still use her name shortened to "Maru." Fujiwara's similar comments made her cringe.

"I hope he returns soon to you. I cannot shake the oddity that it has been so long; we have carriages arrive so frequently from the south."

"Thanks for your concern; I am accustomed to this from the days of his former work."

"As long as those days are behind him, I am sure, too, it will be any day now."

Maru thought a shadow lingered on his face.

Adakichi broke the silence. "And I see you have found employment with the emperor!"

"Yes, many of us have found a home within the walls we were told contained our enemies," he said. "But you learn your hopes for the future might align with those you once fiercely fought."

"A fine idea!" Adakichi said. "If only more of us knew the emperor's intentions were never bearing ill will and trusted he will make the right decisions."

"Continue to pray," Kira said. "You are here to enter in the lottery? Adakichi, don't be so abashed; anything you request will be granted. You have friends here at the Gosho."

Maru thought he was rather pretentious to use the Imperial Palace's formal name. People rarely bothered using it since Emperor Meiji moved his primary residence to Tokyo.

"Ah! Is it that time of year? Did you say a lottery?"

"Yes." Kira shifted his weight, putting hands behind his back with a slight bow. "New policy of the emperor. Those who partake in the grand parade in the Gion Matsuri at the end of the season must be assured by the palace that their intentions represent his mission."

"Well then, we want to go by the book, as they say," Maru saw Adakichi's mouth become thin.

"Consider your name entered. And I think the emperor's office will oblige, after an interview. Always a joy—aside from the beastly heat."

"I did come to ask about the decree. If you were to come by for tea . . ."

Maru's eyes began to stray. She was thirsty and itchy. Kira was one of her clan's strongest allies, a powerful daimyo who owned much of the land of Kyoto before the emperor rose. After the fighting subsided, he stepped down to support the transition of power through negotiation for long nights with her father and other clans. She imagined him and her father once fought side-by-side, taking on rivals, defending against traitorous shogun making coups. It felt odd to see him eagerly working for the emperor as a baron, abandoning his rankings. Here he nestled at the bottom.

Her father had refused such a role, angrily saying they sold out for copper and artificial power. After the samurai fought for Meiji's ascension, a creation of a court rendered samurai useless. He agreed to lay down his arms in retirement on the provision of peace, but to become a man of the court was another story. He had chosen to take the "nobler route" and be of the merchant class, trading his sword for a pen. He was certain the power was with the people, as Meiji touted. It had been their motivation to overthrow the shogun, who kept classes limited and poor.

But here Kira was, without any qualms. She wished her father could be there, to see he was healthy and happy and above all, safe, and able to return home every night.

"My daughter! Please! Help!" A scream from a crumpled woman with a bent leg at the staircase broke their engagement. Guards rushed to the wailing, inconsolable woman.

Kira rocked on his feet, concern writing itself in the corners of his eyes.

"Missing . . . never strays . . . young . . ." the woman shrieked.

"Oh, that poor woman," said Adakichi with a strain, as if she were frustrated.

"Hmm." Kira's lips were tight. Maru looked between him and the woman, as an urge to help welled up. But Adakichi raised a solitary eyebrow and Maru hesitated.

"Please!" the woman banged her fists on the ground, bowing as she begged for help.

An assistant and guards dragged the screaming woman out of sight.

"Will they help her?" Maru asked.

"Hmm," said Kira again, his jaw chewing on the thought.

Maru trembled, watching the woman's feet disappear behind the corner, her cries echoing until they became muffled.

"Unfortunately, we have more business; it's quite a busy day," Adakichi said.

"Every day seems so," nodded Kira, gathering himself. "With the train, we can receive news sooner, but does it make the days longer?" He laughed. "And a telephone will be right behind, once we get those wires installed.

"Ah, the train, yes. Didn't they say the emperor found a new conductor?" asked Adakichi. "It was unfortunate, if the harrowing rumors are—"

Kira tilted his head in a way that was inquisitive.

"Rumors. The bane of the rationale. Be well and on your way, and I'll pay a visit soon. And Maya-ru-ki, if you see your father soon, which I pray you do, have him come by."

He saw them out and back to the bright palace grounds. Maru's mind wandered to the bright day her father had taken her to see Meiji ascend, and he was crowned beneath the sun.

They stepped through the busy fabric district of Nishijin, filled with rows of long factory buildings with open windows and a whir of seamstresses. A small girl in the quiet street ahead wandered aimlessly alone, her robe sliding off her shoulder. The girl looked like she'd been crying. Maru's heart leapt in empathy, the helplessness the stranger exhibited was a familiar feeling.

The girl's eyes found Maru, and her crying ceased. Her paleness was ethereal beneath the sun. Her eyes were searching and sharp.

Maru exclaimed, "Oh!" She thought, *Could this be the woman's daughter? From the palace?* "Okaasan! Please wait!"

Adakichi turned and Mitsu stopped next to her.

"I think the girl—"

"What girl?"

"The one who is—" Maru gestured that the girl was right behind her, only to realize she was gone.

"She was probably just playing," suggested Mitsu.

Maru noticed the cicadas' hum had stilled. They continued onward, but Maru kept looking over her shoulder. Uneasiness seeped under her ribs. Had the sunlight already changed, or were shadows moving?

A yellow light appeared again, bringing with it a pain behind her eyes and a tightness in her chest that made her feel faint.

"Mayuki?"

Adakichi stared at her with a look that dared her to disobey again.

Maru gasped for air. She found it difficult to walk but turned around to see if the girl was there. She shivered when she saw the street was empty.

They came upon a narrow alley sloping beneath a second-story walkway, nearly missing the entrance to the "good" fabric shops. The only clue to the store's location was a sunburned kimono hanging against a bamboo fence as if this was meant to persuade shoppers the store was an inconsequential place to visit.

But Adakichi stepped through the turquoise pine trees to a tidy, pleasant space. Chiki's shop was for women of a high class. She knew Maru's clan had ordered robes from here years ago when her mother was alive.

"What do you think of that disturbed woman?" Maru asked. "Will the emperor help her?"

Adakichi turned. "She must be an invalid, wailing like that. I'm sure her daughter ran off with a lover. They always do." She was spiteful and sharp when no one else they knew accompanied them.

If the girl was the woman's daughter, Maru didn't think she was old enough to do such a thing. And there had been the girl at the matsuri, too, if not the same one. As she tried to remember their faces, their looks and eyes blended as if they were one. Maru frowned.

Adakichi said, "Mitsu, why don't you see Kohako at Kazurasei about getting a new kanzashi or kushi? Your hair will need something shiny for the next matsuri."

Mitsu ducked behind a noren bearing Kohako's kamon. An orange-golden animal in the window licked its paw.

The fox!

Maru blinked, and saw it was only a tabby cat. The city was strange today. . . . Perhaps her eyes *had* played tricks. Her life might be in confusing, scattered pieces, but she certainly could not be seeing or hearing talking animals.

Adakichi dipped behind some bright red tapestries. The building was tall, and a high window let light spill in. A juniper bonsai rose from the wooden floor cut around it. Talismans from customers hung from branches bearing names of faraway shrines.

The walls were chock full of hanging cloths. In the loft, someone was sewing. A woman with a pointed face, free of eyebrows and wrinkles, rushed toward them with a deep bow. She led them to a low table beneath a circular window overlooking a garden, and a young woman brought teacups and chewy sweets.

"Help yourselves, but you must regale me with talk of the town."

Adakichi launched into the sights they had seen, except for mentioning the woman at the palace. "We did not yet see the train, but my! The town is busier with so many new shops!"

"The trains have brought many new styles. We are quite unbridled in our creativity these days. Have you seen those large bustles?"

"Bustles?"

"Maybe not. It's the style of a new silhouette. The top of the dress scoops, you see, instead of being a triangle, the way our robes cross over the bottom half like a parasol," she said, putting her arms out to demonstrate. "Foreign women have such a peculiar perception of their bodies. It has been illuminating. I have prints to sew them. It is quite complex, a bit like a bird cage."

"A dress or robe with a bustle sounds quite difficult to make."

"It is a challenge, but I manage," said Chiki politely.

"Nevertheless, my maiko needs some new robes. She needs to be fashionable," said Adakichi. "And we need a robe for her naming ceremony, come autumn."

Maru was ashamed she had assumed Adakichi brought her along to pick out new robes. But of course, she knew the biggest day in Mitsu's career—her official debut—was wildly more important than everyday robes of a shikomi.

"I have every pattern imaginable, and men want to follow the traditions here in Kyoto, so we share the value of our legacy. I presume you have credit from a client?"

"You can bill it to Fujiwara's name," called out Adakichi. Fujiwara, ever flaunting his wealth and eager to boast about dressing his 'favorite geiko,' kept an account open in all designer shops so that Adakichi could stop by any time for a robe to be made in his name and worn by a woman during his next visit. If his visits were frequently scheduled, Adakichi would send an order with the maid and have armloads of robes delivered. It was how many ochaya could afford such luxuries.

"Allow me to humor your shikomi for a bit. Show her around. Say, what color pleases you most?" Chiki didn't even wait for Adakichi's approval.

"Do you have plum?" Maru asked nervously. She was recalling the midnights when she and her father shared salty pickled plums as they looked at the constellations from their rice paddies.

"Dear, we have it all! You would look like a European empress in plum."

Chiki found one as rich as a summer evening, dotted with white thread, conjuring fireflies. When Maru stroked it, she felt she could spiral forward into the depths of its sky.

"How about his one?" Chiki held it up to Adakichi in triumph, prompting a half-hearted nod.

Maru was elated but felt her guilt surging.

"Thank you," she whispered.

"There is no need to thank me. It is a nice break from the old shogun wives. They have lost their power and do little except throw their money around to reduce their boredom here."

Mitsu slid open the door, bee-lining in. "Sorry I am late. Kohaku-san had so much to share."

"That's why Adakichi sent you," laughed Chiki.

"Ah, sorry to interrupt." Chiki's assistant appeared. "There seems to be a discrepancy in the books. I am having difficulty finding a credit available under Fujiwara's name."

"Hmm. It happens," said Chiki slowly. "Adakichi, are you comfortable proceeding with this?" Adakichi tilted her head, signaling a question was lingering. "He must be mingling with other company besides ours. Take off Shikomi's robes. Let's save the poor bastard a bit. Bill him for Mitsu's clothing."

Chiki nodded and patted her assistant on the arm.

Maru's heart sank. She knew not to get her hopes up. She once fashioned an idea for her father to consider: she would serve as caretaker of the house while he was away. She thought this would be a good alternative to living at an okiya, and she could prove to him her capabilities. He mulled over it for days, building her hopes. But in the end he denied her request, shattering her. "The Civil Code requires you to be twenty. Living at the okiya will enhance your future, and it will feed you." All she heard was that he saw her as a child.

Her mother had claimed, "You spoil her so! She sees the world an endless stream of gifts . . . she needs to learn."

"Not in Meiji's world. She will have it all handed to her. It's why I fight for him. He sees prosperity for us. No more millet. No more death," her father had asserted.

"She holds your hand for everything. What happens the day you can't hold her back?"

"And you don't reach out your hand to her at all—yet you claim the title of 'mother.'"

They settled on maroon for the maples of autumn and pride. The predictable selection left little satisfaction to Maru. Not that her opinion had any weight.

"Chiki, we have been an intrusion too long," said Adakichi, rising.

"You are never an intrusion. Please, take this basket of grapes and these early oranges that came in this morning."

"Grapes! A lucky treat. Are you sure?"

"They always taste better when shared."

Maru plucked a grape and lifted it to her mouth.

"Oh! Peel, peel first!" Chiyo showed her how to peel its skin and pop it into her mouth, gushing with flavor. "Look at that pucker! Some are sweet and make the sour ones worthwhile."

On that note, the three bowed and stepped into the pool of light. Maru, unable to keep her smile to herself as she stumbled after Adakichi, clutched the basket of fruit, remembering fondly that oranges were her father's favorite, and promised to be sweeter than the grapes.

"Does anyone smell, well, something dead?" asked Mitsu.

A shadow passed behind them and caught Maru's eye, but she blamed it on the heat and the sting in her heart biting back.

The next day brought the tsuyu season, which meant rainstorms daily and a ripe Earth. Maru's curiosity about the fox ebbed, and her melancholy flowed; and when the ochaya was blessed in a ceremony on the Grand Day at Yasaka Shrine, she hoped it would cleanse her by association. She had expected to attend the event, but a slip of her tongue in front of clients and a complaint to Adakichi ruined this possibility. She was told to stay home to clean with the maid, who admonished her with a frown when she replaced the night-soil box.

At least Kiku had given her a friendly wave when she passed through Gion wearing a split-peach-bun and carrying a stack of lunchboxes of cool buckwheat noodles, seaweed, and citron slices—a summer staple.

The next night had them all tense again as thunder bellowed and lightning entered the dim sitting room. But guests clanked their glasses, drowning out the rainstorm. Maru juggled cups to deliver their wine before she was asked. She was careful to step over the patrons' legs stretched out on the tatami, across the table from Fujiwara. He was as persistent as tsuyu.

He shouted with delight when he saw Mitsu wearing a robe he selected and rambled about the cost. ("Nothing mixed about it: no cotton. Just pure silk like her"). Nobody mentioned the delay in credit placed at Chiki's.

"Thank you, peach!" he chimed at Maru, who was pouring wine into his cup. (Another damn fruit.) He cursed when he didn't see her return a smile, but she later swore to Adakichi that she had "subtly done so!"

"Your shikomi is elusive about her emotions. Mitsuki wears a natural smile as jewelry to pair with her new robes, as she should. If I wanted to guess what a woman was feeling, I'd get myself a wife," whined Fujiwara.

"Indeed, when Shikomi advances to a maiko, her lips will need generous amounts of paint. She will clear Kyoto's stock of rouge," said Adakichi. "Although even paint-plumping cannot command the lips to behave properly if the face they're attached to is stubborn."

Adakichi had commented before that Maru's lips were quite thin, but now added the remark that she had "more than made up for it with her forehead," suggesting she had wit (although Adakichi noted, "I have yet to observe this myself."). These were desired traits among geiko, who needed long-term clients—a necessity often at the mercy of how clever their conversations were. She felt lucky that she didn't need to reconstruct her whole skull.

Her thin lips aside, Maru's main problem was that she lacked confidence. Mitsu could toss comments right back to people. Instead, Maru was skittish, preferring to absorb knowledge by observing things. But Adakichi cajoled her to ignore her insights, implying they were often wrong. She had years of work to do before she could gain their trust enough to even become a maiko. Which, of course, she had no desire to be.

She continued to repeat to herself, *It's all temporary.* She was just carrying stones across a river in a storm.

"It's fortunate, then, the trains will frequent the city more. We shall order a whole delivery of rouge just for Shikomi!" exclaimed Fujiwara.

Lightning outside washed them in bright light as rain pounded on the roof. When the thunder bellowed again, Mitsu exclaimed "Raijin is up to tricks tonight!"

Maru instinctively touched her belly, recalling that when she was small her mother told her to protect herself from the rain god. Summer storms were frequent and offered relief from the engulfing heat. Maru longed to wander in a garden and feel the rain and moss underfoot. Here is where the incense was hung, and she had to watch out for someone spilling wine on her new robes.

Opposite them, the guests sat comfortably, arguing about the appropriate soy and salt level needed for cooking soba noodles and how the fresh cold noodle soup towering with mushrooms and leafy vegetables was different in each prefecture. The conversation was bright and full of arm-waving.

"Please, chase away the rain with one of your songs!" called out Moto, one of the guests.

Adakichi was still upstairs, waiting to make her grand entrance. It was up to the maiko to ensure the guests were properly riled up, ripe, and had demonstrated enough patience to earn her presence. It helped to achieve a balance of respect and adrenaline.

Not that clients were likely to go anywhere in this rain.

"She is readying herself to put on a perfect performance for her favorite man," chuckled Mitsu, lightly touching Fujiwara's wrist.

"Ah, I hardly imagine she needs to practice."

"You know how it is; you are your own biggest mountain." She took a sip from his cup and gave him a little smirk.

Maru listened. She was happy not to imbibe anything. She was not allowed to reject invitations to have a drink, but Adakichi wanted them to remain sober and refined. Maru was certain younger girls were drinking under the table at other ochaya, but Adakichi was adamant about her ways. Sometimes geiko and maiko kept a towel under their necks to let sake drip from their lips to the cloth so they could fool the patrons.

"I should very much like to summit your mountain," Moto cooed. Maru wrinkled her nose.

"Aren't you allergic to upright movement? She'd have to climb—" Fujiwara said as he laughed.

"I should be proud to keep you safe from the ghosts," Moto stood, wobbling, and pretended to wave a sword. Mitsu shrieked with laughter.

"Maybe that's the sword you use when you lie," said Fujiwara.

"But what demons are out there?" she cried, ignoring him.

"Scores of them," Takeda said. He was a good-natured, hunched-over man who was lonely more than anything else. His wife had passed away a year ago. Maru pitied him but remained uncomfortable befriending him in the presence of Fujiwara, who could not resist exhibiting jealousy with comments to her that stung like wasps and lingered longer than the stinger's welt.

"*Hyakumonogatari Kaidankai*!" Fujiwara cried out.

Takeda offered to explain what he knew about the game of telling ghost stories.

"This was the name of a parlor game played by samurai to test each other's bravery long before Meiji came around. They'd gather in a darkened room at nightfall and form a circle surrounded by brightly lit candles to protect them from yuurei. Each samurai took turns telling their most frightening ghost story. When his tale was finished, he would extinguish his candle. With each candle that went out the light faded and more spiritual energy was raised as the distance between our world and the world of kami became closer. When only one candle remained, the final samurai demonstrated his bravery by blowing it out, proving his readiness by striking the yuurei hiding deep in the shadows." Takeda paused to take a deep breath in the humid, smoky air.

"Then, tell us your story and let's see how strong your sword is!" commanded Fujiwara.

"Deep beneath the very tatami upon which we sit could lie a yokai so mischievous that it can wreak havoc upon a whole family. For you see, when your house shakes, it might not be an earthquake but instead a monster," Takeda began, wagging a finger.

Maru's breath quickened. There were so many tales of hauntings during the quiet moments of the day. She hated hearing of demons crawling around, possibly surrounding them. A flickering lamp raised bumps on her arm. It felt like little feet were scampering up her spine.

"But what gives it away are the creaks in the floorboards, for what else could cause your home to groan except being pressed by a yokai?

"And how do I know? One day an old woman named Yuka called some strong men to her home because her house creaked at night. She feared it was riddled with beasts waiting to snatch her by the ankle—and pull her under!" Takeda exclaimed, grabbing Mitsu's thigh and trying to sneak his hand up her robes.

"These brave men waited for nightfall. Not long after it was dark they heard the first creak. They dismissed it, thinking it was only the wind. Then they heard a second loud creak. And a third.

"And at last the whole house SHOOK!" Takeda shouted. Maru covered her ears.

"They rushed out for fear the entire house would come down upon them. The roof, the very bones of the house, were quaking on their own.

"And how was this possible? One man was certain Yuka was right: she had yokai living under her feet. He brandished his sword and drove it right between the floorboards." Takeda stood up and mimicked the thrust of an enormous sword. "The creaking stopped. Blood oozed from the boards. The house stopped shaking. And the yanari disappeared!" He sheathed his invisible sword and sat down.

"Marvelous!" Fujiwara clapped and pinched a candle. The room darkened.

"Our house creaks at night," Mitsu whispered to Maru beneath their applause.

Takeda wiped his brow. "These stories take the wind out of an old man like me," he chortled. "But you keep me younger. Let's see, how about the tale of the Ubume—"

"Everyone knows about her: she's boring," spat Fujiwara, blowing out a second candle.

Maru shuddered. She would be grateful not to hear the recount. As a child she mistook evening winds for wails of the ghost of a mother whose infant died during childbirth. It was said she haunted the streets looking for children to snatch up. She thought about the woman at the palace who wailed indiscernibly about her lost daughter and wondered if the girl in blue torn robes had found her way.

"If that is the case, may I gauge your taste for something true?" Takeda inquired.

Fujiwara leaned in, wide-eyed. His breath was hot and bitter as he panted hungrily.

Takeda said, "It is a rather new phenomenon, its presence was first noticed in Tokyo, but warnings are making their way to Kyoto to protect our dear maidens. You see, Tokyo has had cases of kidnappings of young women."

Mitsu and Maru looked at each other.

Takeda began his tale. "This monster was born a boy. His father was training him to be a soldier to Meiji. Even at six, the boy would fight anyone. Even his teachers lost, but insisted he must be disciplined. He outsmarted everyone and spent his days drinking until his face was red." Takeda puffed his cheeks and clapped them, staining them red.

"He became so unruly, the school sent him home. He was becoming unpredictable and violent. He drank. Teachers feared for their lives but were too scared to admit it."

Maru thought this story was familiar. He belched a rank, drunk breath.

"His father came by, but the boy transformed into a demonic menace, slaughtering his father and then bounded into the woods.

"Ruckuses, fires, and growls were attributed to him. Men foolish enough to lose their wits to sake, succumbed to attacks. He fed on their flesh and grew.

"Then he moved on to Tokyo, and his tastes changed. He hungered for women with a pleasant scent that drew him into a frenzied state of lust."

Maru sighed. This was Shuten Doji, a mythical demon in a modified classic tale. The long-slain monster's head sat in Nara, guarded in a temple. Fujiwara grabbed Maru's hand. Although she flinched, she didn't back away out of obligation.

"And one by one, noble women and common girls were kidnapped and their innards ripped out, their blood drained. In the morning, neighbors would find empty shells of their skin."

As Takeda continued his tale, the rage of Raijin shook the house, and lightning slashed the sky. A candle flickered in the corner and Maru released a breath she didn't realize she was holding. She was startled by the presence of what she imagined was a chochinobake licking the flame. She avoided looking at the window, as she had done since childhood from fear of ghosts looking in during a storm.

"Each night police wandered through the drunkest alleys looking for the thirsty yokai, their legs trembling at every corner." Takeda pried open his eyelids.

"But he was too strong. He cut off soldiers' heads and grew wilder. Tokyo banned maidens from leaving their homes after sundown, so they would not risk becoming the oni's next meal."

There was another clap of thunder, and the last candle went out.

Mitsu screamed. Maru looked up, only to lock eyes with a figure peering through the window in the pouring rain. Its silhouette looked sharp and menacing. Its eyes were golden, its teeth long.

Takeda laughed and relit the candles, the wicks gasping awake. "If you listen to travelling merchants, they tell you of the horrors: the curfews, the smell of blood at dawn. A fire took out half of Tokyo last week, did they tell you that? Done by his new lanterns. They tell us the future will save us, but I fear we will all be dead at the hands of this emperor and his monsters."

The face vanished from the window. Maru quivered, shivering in the hottest season. People kept mentioning strange animals, bleeding, and the smell of flesh burning. Maru shook her head, trying to get these hideous, dismembered bodies and faceless creatures out of her mind. So many men only wanted to get attention from relating frightening tales.

Takeda wiped his eyes, reddened from coughing.

"Moto, your warrior skills will come in handy," Fujiwara said, laughing. "There are many foes."

Raijin screamed again, this time on top of the house. The rain was louder than before. It was how Maru imagined the ocean: crashing waves trying to consume the shore.

"If Moto is the only thing standing between me and an oni, I will be singing my death song," came a voice from the staircase, a wisp of jasmine flowing down to the parched room.

"We all feel like rather big mice here," Fujiwara said.

"Yes, I am here," Adakichi said. She went to her harp. "I arrived before you no longer wear your heads."

"She casts away demons better than Takeda," Moto told them.

"Ghosts are no charm of mine." She took her pillow on stage and played over the thunder, casting away fears with her songs. When the audience's consumption slowed, Adakichi matched the storm's tempo as if she controlled the clouds. Finally, The Thunder God retreated, after having idled so long listening to her tunes.

Adakichi turned from her harp to see the men lulled into semi-unconsciousness. Normally she was dissuaded to bring clients to the brink of sleep, but Adakichi did it to quell the storytelling.

"Gentlemen, how are we feeling?"

Takeda tried to answer, but this resulted in coughs. Adakichi laughed. "More vegetables!"

"I happened to pick some up from the best source, Ogawa's farm at the edge of town. His daikon is so mighty." He measured the length of a daikon with his hands.

"Don't oversell yourself there," Fujiwara remarked.

Takeda lunged at him, but a cough sent him sideways, gasping.

Adakichi swept away the commotion by reading their fortunes with her almanac. The stars in their eyes aligned with her pages of dreams of marriage and successful business. This was her passion. Her voice rose with excitement as she revealed information about their future, much of which was gleaned from what they had told her in the past. Maru wondered if Adakichi could tell her future. When they seemed satisfied, they agreed they'd heard enough and donned their straw coats to shield their silk clothing from the rain.

Fujiwara promised to send them fresh-cut flowers the next day. "Unless you'd rather have a whole rose bush! They are importing them from China; I'd gift almost anything fine to my princesses."

But they customarily declined.

Mitsu and Maru began their evening chores, opening the windows to allow the smell of petrichor and bamboo in to replace the stale air. The silent routine allowed Maru's burrowed worries and longings to surface, persistent in their cries for attention. She wrangled with her emotions by engaging in some ferocious scrubbing. With every dunk of her cloth in the water barrel, she tried to wash away the discomfort the clients had brought.

"How did the topic of demons come up?" Adakichi interrupted. "Rarely do men find entertainment in children's ghost stories."

"But what he said is curious. Is it true that maidens are disappearing in Tokyo?" asked Mitsu.

"The young woman at the palace—" said Maru, thinking of the small girl.

Candlelight reflected in the water barrel blinked like a pair of eyes.

"I am sure he simply wants a girl like you to warm to him and be an advertisement of his strength," Adakichi asserted.

Mitsu was perplexed. "No clients have mentioned this, nor have the papers."

"These stories are always far-fetched; don't let them rattle your ears," said Adakichi. "Kira said they were baseless. And I'm apt to believe the palace, for I've never seen a yokai."

"Neither have I," Maru said as she aggressively scooped the glasses into the barrel, sending away the eyes that looked up at her.

Mitsu looked at her, hands plunging into the water. "No ghosts? Not even your mother?"

Maru's stomach tensed at the direct question, and she volunteered nothing.

Mitsu continued, "My ancestors have appeared to me. We hear of yokai everywhere, under our steps and in the shadows up in trees. But snatching maidens . . ." She shook her head.

"Our ancestors are always close. Even closer when we pray. Visit the shrine before Obon, and they'll come when death's gates open, even if we can't see them. But as for yuurei—placing morijio outside your door will do fine," said Adakichi.

Maru wasn't so sure. She had no interest in superstitious routines like placing a small pile of salt by your door to keep spirits out of your home. She often went to shrines, but prayers for protection seemed to make no difference. This didn't particularly bother her since she wanted to believe in the possibility of seeing her mother again, even if it meant accepting that demons were real, too. Frankly, she already had a long list of issues she was combating. There wasn't enough room for yokai.

"Take these scraps to the backyard. Make sure not to bring bugs inside," Mitsu instructed.

Maru put the remaining pickled ginger and nibbled pieces of lotus in a bucket and made her way down the hallway, listening to the soft patter of rain.

Outside, she sidled beneath the awning in the alley to avoid getting wet and made her way toward the communal garden. Reflections of gas lamps and red matsuri lanterns hung upside-down in the pools of rainwater, rippling with each step and disturbing the small windows to other worlds. The stench was stronger where old lanterns filled with fish-oil ran down with the rainwater and collected in dips. The darkened shoji of the okiya surrounded her; she was quiet so that she would not disturb their slumber. She emptied scraps into the designated plot of steamy and rancid land, and turned back.

The fox! It was sitting there, as clear as day.

She gasped, and dropped the bucket.

"Please," said a voice. The fox's mouth moved.

She tried to scream, but no sound came out. Her knees threatened to crumble and send her into the compost.

"Please," said the fox, leaning forward, its yellow eyes staring. The fox raised its paw tenderly, bending it in a funny way. *Just like the statue.*

This time, she wasn't imagining anything. It was no trick of Raijin's stormy light. This was happening. Her chest heaved.

She frantically tried to move backward. What about the neighbors? Were they awake? Could they see her? Would they save her, or would she die here at the hands of a yokai and be an embarrassment to her clan?

"Please. I'm hungry." There was no mistaking this. The fox was talking. She looked at it steadily, rain dappling its face, unsure if she should respond or run. She had to choose.

But she was alone with nobody to tell her what to do.

"Please."

Maru was quiet, but couldn't move. The fox stayed put, sitting calmly.

"How do—" Maru stammered. "How do you talk?"

"I need food," said the fox.

"No, I—no I can't—this is—" She couldn't think of an excuse.

"Please," the fox said softly. It didn't move. Its eyes stared at her. One of its paws hung limply, and its shoulders shook slightly.

Maru's heart was replaced by a taiko, a bell chiming in her head. She tried to think of a way out, fearful of someone seeing her, wondering if she was seeing or hearing things.

"I need food. My injured paw makes it hard to forage or hunt."

Her feelings of empathy eased her worries. She hated this attachment, these great urges of hers to please others. The fox hadn't moved. It wasn't threatening. It was just, well, *talking.* The softness in its voice was soothing. She felt calmer and didn't fear for her life or the neighbors' safety.

"I have no meat," said Maru, suddenly not even sure about what foxes ate.

Why was she wondering what foxes ate? She couldn't be considering *feeding* it.

The fox's eyes brightened.

"Anything, even tofu. It could be rice. Just an egg. Any vegetables or that ginger you discarded."

Maru shook rain off her face. She was regaining feeling in her fingertips and looked back at the pile of soggy food. Her drenched hair clung to her collar. Adakichi would be upset.

"Adakichi will be worried about me. Give me some time," said Maru cautiously.

The fox said nothing but moved aside, bowing its head.

Maru's heart raced. It was giving her permission to leave. Or was this a trap? Kitsune were tricksters. But she took her chance and rushed away, avoiding eye contact, shutting out the image of its sullen face. Her hands weakened; she wavered and struggled to grab onto the slippery bucket. The rain felt cold against the goose bumps on her arms.

She took a gamble and looked back. It was still there, in the rain, one paw hanging limply as it watched her go. Her heart jolted. She didn't know the fox, but she already knew what she'd do—suddenly, and resolutely.

•••

Maru took a deep breath at the front door, basking in the lantern's glow. Something stirred inside her, like she knew the secrets of the world. Ghost stories sprang to life with each step she took. If there was a talking fox, a wild demon *could* be hunting maidens in Tokyo. Takeda's stories now seemed like a warning, instead of a silly way to pass a casual evening. Although in a state of disbelief, calm washed over her, bringing her into a trance, unaware of the rain still hitting her neck. She straightened up. She couldn't let them know something was amiss.

Sliding the door open, Maru was careful not to let it have an unusual tempo or shut too abruptly, especially if it would disturb the yanari. After methodically putting away the scrap basket, she tidied up the back kitchen.

Adakichi came to the doorway. "Oh, you *are* here." She felt a smack on her back.

Maru composed herself, obeying the urge to make herself less suspicious. She quickly looked down at the cup she polished and filled the silence with a little chatter. There was a warm tingling inside her, and she didn't want to share it with anyone—this was all hers.

"Working on these dishes. Listening to the rain. It's nice, having nothing else here." A twinge in her gut made her feel Adakichi could cut open her stomach and find the truth spilling out.

Adakichi gave her a prolonged stare, then retreated down the hallway. Maru watched her, already starting to put down the cup to fold a cloth and place it inside her obi.

And then something took hold of her.

She lunged for the pantry doors, searching for scraps, old rice, left-behind eggs. She wasn't sure where the surge of determination came from. It was exciting, nerve-wracking, unexplainable—something she'd need to seek help with. Nobody would believe her. She wasn't sure if she believed it herself.

She realized the noise of her rummaging could drift to their ears in the sitting room. She raised her head, blood rushing to her cheeks. She heard only soft murmurs of chatting. She was safe.

She returned to the cupboard, moving aside jars of pickles and old bottles of vinegar, ceremony dishes, and boxes of crinkly tea leaves.

Food. Food. Food. *What did the kitsune say?* Vegetables! Eggs!

But where did they have eggs? They usually bartered for enough to last days. Would a fox eat leftover vegetables? It insisted rice was fine, but she couldn't boil a new pot of rice.

She was overthinking it, blinding herself in confusion. But the stocks of leftover vegetables were already counted. It was a risk to take from future portions, but if she took a little from everyone, and evened it out—or replaced them before anybody even noticed, it could work.

That was a battle for tomorrow. She would have to salvage something to replace them or go short. She would offer to swap cooking duty with Mitsu or call in the maid or a cook.

Chopsticks! She needed them to fasten a brace for the fox.

Abandoning the food search, she went to the cabinet filled with ornate pairs of chopsticks, some made of metals, and a precious jade pair. She wanted an old pair that nobody would miss.

She muttered aloud as she read accompanying tags indicating senders' names. She shifted boxes. *How many chopsticks did they have? Were any of these clients dead?*

Then she saw a box labelled *Hosokawa.*

Her clan name? When had someone given her these? She pulled it out. The box had smooth wood with gold ink.

She slid it open, just as she heard Mitsu ask:

"Do you need help?"

Maru dropped the box, bumping her head as one of the chopsticks rolled out of sight. She grabbed the remaining one and stuffed it into her robe before putting the box back.

"What do you need?" Mitsu took a step toward her. Maru put her hand up, and Mitsu stopped.

"No, sorry, you—I'm sorry. I was counting them," said Maru.

"I counted them earlier."

"Yes, sorry. I was curious."

"Did my numbers read as letters?"

"No, no. It's just that tomorrow is my day to cook."

"No, it's my day," Mitsu replied.

"Oh, I didn't know. I had a new recipe in mind," Maru hurriedly added.

Mitsu folded her arms and said, "Oh? A new one? That's . . . really. . . that's quite delightful." She said this in a way that made Maru feel Mitsu meant the opposite. "Would you share it?"

"No!" said Maru forcibly, suddenly, then retreated and softened. "No, sorry, I . . ." Maru started shoving the vegetables back in haphazardly. "It's a family recipe that's private . . . I was thinking of making it tomorrow."

Mitsu was studying her. "Yes, sure. Let's see how it turns out tomorrow."

Now Maru had more problems than just a relationship with a talking fox.

A new recipe? Family secrets? She should curse herself. Now Mitsu suspected something. She knew Maru couldn't cook. Her family had no recipes. She didn't know how to cook anything special—but wait a moment. She had her oba-san. She had a solution! Oba-san was a clever woman, a friend of her clan, and her stand-in grandmother who could produce something inspiring.

It was a steep order, and not a desired option. But Oba-san could save her. She would try to visit her before sunrise; but it still left the fox hungry.

It was time to join Adakichi and Mitsu in the sitting room for night tea.

Adakichi cried, "Why, you're soaking wet! Go upstairs and go to bed before you catch a cold."

"No, ma'am, I am fine, I just—"

"Go to bed. I insist. You look like a stray animal. You need to look after yourself as a maiko or geiko do. Though you are neither, you could still let our habits rub off on you."

"Augh! I'll have to dry this," said Mitsu, dramatically pulling a soaked pillow out from under Maru. "Unless you want to take this chore from me too, tomorrow?" Adakichi said nothing to defend Maru this time.

Her heart raced. The fox was waiting for her, it wouldn't know she wasn't returning.

"Mayuki," Adakichi said."

How would she give the fox the food *now*?

"Maru, answer me."

She would have to wait until they fell asleep . . .

"*Maruya*!" She felt a sting on her cheek. Adakichi was ablaze.

Without a word Maru trudged to her room. In the mirror she saw her hair was tangled; the black lines beneath her eyes foreshadowed her adulthood. Her eyebrows, described as caterpillars, needed combing. Her forehead was red from bumping it and her cheeks were flushed. Her skin seemed blotchy like a child's, no semblance of maturity on her face—and little bearing to her parents.

The disguise of shikomi was creeping over her face, erasing the one she used to recognize. A tsunami of pain rolled in her chest, and a numbness gripped her arms.

Sparks flew in her eyes, and nausea wriggled in her stomach. Her brief bout of excitement had been so suddenly snuffed, as she was overwhelmed by consequences.

How did she get into this? How could she fix this—where was her father—why did her mother's ghost never visit? Why was she here in this strange ochaya, trying to be something she wasn't and tolerating intrusive men? Why had the presence of a kitsune conjured these feelings?

Darkness breathed into the window's wooden frame, and daytime evaporated from the glass edges. An energy still fueled in her that she needed to pour out. Adakichi. Her mother. Ghost stories. The fox. These edges of her reality were leaving new scars on her wobbly legs.

Her hand shook too much to allow her to write, so she felt for one of her few books she brought to ground herself. She selected Princess Kaguya, born inside a bamboo stalk, who discovered her true place was the Moon, where she returned after years of searching the world, even turning down the emperor's hand in marriage.

It was a tale her father would read often. It transfixed her—a girl from the moon! But tonight, beneath the fragment of a crescent moon, her eyes clouded. She heard the sound of her father's voice in each word, hushed prayers in between. Calm clawed its way through her ragged breath, but resisted her desired embrace of peace. She wanted to part the dark curtain and step through.

There were creaks of someone coming upstairs.

Mitsu took her nightly steps before going to bed. She went to her closet to disrobe, then to her mirror where she would always light her lamp and first undo her long hair. In between thin gasps for air, Maru listened to her brush her hair and sigh as she carefully wiped her face. Eventually she unrolled her futon.

Maru shook as she slipped beneath her blanket, but had lost her urge to cry. The heat in her chest dissipated, the last of the boiled-over emotions left the shore of her heart, which bobbed in an ocean of calamity.

I am no samurai daughter.

Her eyes drooped as her impatience brewed, lying there in wait. Maru heard Mitsu comb through a book. She heard her plump her futon and pillows, then shuffle around until a page turned. Then there was a more peculiar sound.

Cracking? Yes, clearly something was being cracked.

She heard more cracking, the sound of something soft splitting open in the air. Eggs! Mitsu had eggs! She heard her munch on boiled eggs, slurping up gooey, golden centers.

So that's where they were. Mitsu had her own secrets. Did she have more? It was just what the fox would want to eat.

She heard her drop shells into a ceramic bowl. She wondered how much earlier Mitsu woke up to sneak them from the cabinet downstairs.

As she listened to Mitsu's cracking and munching slow down, Maru studied the banisters through her mosquito netting. Cranes and ribbons hung still. A grey light came from the window as the stars tip-toed out to their vast stage with the sliver of moon. Suddenly, it was quiet.

Her eyes sagged from carrying the weight of her ragged heart, her eyelids threatening to close and take away her pain. She fought the need to sleep and willed herself to sit up.

Obligation inspired energy. The fox needed her. She slid open her door and was met with silence from the rafters. She pivoted toward Mitsu's room, dreading she'd see an odd shape or strange eyes staring at her. After a few cautious steps she was in front of Mitsu's door. It was already ajar. She slowly pushed it halfway open and slipped in.

She half expected Mitsu to be up, but her silhouette was still. She wondered how Mitsu could sleep through the sound of her pounding heart, and prayed it would not give her away.

Maru held her breath, straining in the darkness to locate the eggs. She stood between Mitsu and her window studied her face. Her mouth was slightly open; her chest gently rose and fell.

Maru was terrified. What was she doing? Why had she felt compelled to come here? Was she being tricked by someone? Why was she so readily robbing Mitsu?

Maybe I can act like a samurai daughter.

Something sharp beneath her foot grabbed her, pulling her legs apart. She yanked her foot back and fell with a soft thump.

She sat on the floor, staring at Mitsu's body, waiting for her to wake up. There was only silence, as she slept, her head propped on her takamura to keep her hair in place.

For a moment she was unable to breathe. She strained to see what was under her. She saw eggs! And a bowl filled with discarded egg shells.

Energy vibrated through her fingertips; she didn't care how many she took. Mitsu had done something against Adakichi's rules. She wouldn't be able to blame anyone without admitting to pilfering the okiya's stash.

She stood up and carefully placed them in her scooped robe and was tiptoeing to the door when she heard screaming. The chilling sounds rattled the building's bones. Her heart galloped.

Mitsu stirred. Maru hovered between the room and the hallway.

There was another bestial scream and a flash of light. Mitsu sat up, yelling "AHHH!"

Maru dashed back to her room listening to Mitsu shouts until Adakichi ran to her room.

"Yokai, yokai!"

"I'm sure it's nothing."

"I saw it in the door!"

Maru pretended to be asleep, and Adakichi worked to calm Mitsu. As she lay there, listening to her hums and reassurances, she thought about the terrible scream.

Was it the fox? The howling yuurei of the widow who haunted Hanamachi? The woman she had seen at the palace? A maiden being taken by Shuten Doji?

When Adakichi's door closed, Maru got dressed and tucked the eggs into her sleeves. She looked out the window. It was nearly dawn.

She slid quietly out of the house, running as light as a rabbit to a mossy grove. Everything was still.

She had done it. The eggs were her victory.

She sat down among the tilted pots, leaning barrels and crates, a crooked broom. But there was no fox. She rested among the tall, silvery cedars draped in starry droplets of rain, as the morning stars closed their eyes.

"Ssss," she hissed and paused to listen.

"Ssssss," she said again, a little louder.

"Don't be so loud," someone said. Maru jumped up, her tight throat, keeping her from squealing.

The fox sat before her in the soft blue-yellow light, its eyes brighter than the moon.

"You returned," it said calmly.

"Sorry," said Maru, unsure if she was apologizing for being late, or for almost not coming at all.

"I am grateful."

"I—here. Eggs. It was all I could bring . . ." her voice trailed.

The fox stood, its limp front paw raised, and sniffed the eggs. "Boiled, how kind."

Maru opened her mouth, but then thought better of it. She watched the fox swallow the eggs whole, one after the other, shattering the shells in its grip—the yellow goo of the yolks oozing into its bristled hairs.

Why was she here? Sheer curiosity was getting the best of her. Her caution was waning.

"Do you have a name?"

The fox finished munching. "It has long been forgotten."

Pity came over her. Something familiar panged her.

"How did . . . how did you get hurt?"

"By a Man," said the fox steadily, gulping down another. "A monster. They become more and more violent. Humans anger the kami and nature with their rumblings. Things change shape and there are new dangers. This one was large. I tried to fight it."

What monster? "How . . . what did it look like? Where did it come from?"

"You have a lot of questions."

"I—I've never heard of such a thing. I cannot see what you see. Tell me about it."

"My memory has faded. It was a bad attack. Dark and Loud."

Maru could not think of anything that would have fit that description. There was no monster, no loose animal, nothing gigantic that took over the city. Someone would've seen it.

Feeling dizzy, she tried to regain her balance. Was she talking to an oni?

"I am sorry you're injured," she said softly. The fox finished the eggs and flicked its tail. Its eyes looked pleased, its face softer, although Maru couldn't be sure how she knew.

"I can help you with your paw, too."

The fox presented its paw. She wrapped the *Hosokawa* chopstick and cloth around it, feeling the bones sift between her fingers. She cringed, praying she wasn't further harming it.

"One night you run away. Now you feed and bandage me. This is curious," it said.

Maru bit her lip. "I want to help you . . ." she said quietly.

The fox tilted its head. "That is good. Because we could help each other."

Maru looked inside her empty basket. "Help each other?"

The fox turned around and around before it lay down. "But now, I must sleep."

The stars had disappeared; a soft yellow light appeared at the mountains' edge. "I can return later," she said.

"I will be here."

Maru stood, feeling awkward about leaving a talking fox behind; no amount of Adakichi's conversation training prepared her for this. Was this real or a dream? She only knew that this was the first event in a long time that sparked excitement in her heart and chased away the clouds behind her eyes.

On her way to ask her Oba-san for help in covering up her good deed, her mind ran wild in its new horizon. She had seen the shining hairs on the fox's back. She had smelled last night's rain in the mud trapped in its fur. She had heard it crack open the egg with its teeth and saw the goopy yolk staining its mouth. Its voice was soft, neither feminine nor masculine. But it was real.

Out of the corner of her eye, Maru kept seeing movements and shadows. The periwinkle sky was quiet. Grass moved without a breeze. She heard whispers in the maple trees, rustles in rocks. Did she feel eyes watching her? Was the world manipulating her vulnerable state? Was there a yokai laughing nearby?

She turned as many corners as possible to lose any yokai that trailed her. Her mind wandered to the girls she had seen in the market and at the matsuri.

Soon the cobblestone road turned to dusty trails, crowded blocks softened into dew-dappled rice paddies, and the tiled roofs changed into straw-thatched tops. She was almost home.

At last, the white stone wall beneath the cedars surrounding her clan's dwellings emerged. The fresh forest air was cool and welcoming. As much as she wanted to push through the wooden gate and rush inside, she feared being reported by clan members who knew about her father's orders.

Across the way, Oba-san was yanking fresh daikon from the garden outside her leaning shack. She beamed at her. "Your clan has been so quiet! I was hoping you'd call."

"Oba-san, I know it has been a while," Maru felt guilt flood under her tongue. Though she only called her "grandmother" to be affectionate, the short woman with the greying bun had befriended her parents long ago and behaved like a relative. She looked in on Maru when her father left their home after her mother passed away. She secretly wished she could live with her and escape the ochaya; but knowing how destitute she was, Maru knew she would have been a burden to her. *I should have brought a gift.*

"No formalities here! Abandon your manners. Do you need something? Does Adakichi feed you?" she pinched at Maru's elbows, inspecting her skin's elasticity.

She smiled widely, at least until Maru pretended it was Mitsu's birthday and she wished to celebrate with something special and offered to pay for it. Oba-san shook her head.

"Nonsense, you are mine. I promised your father. How can Adakichi not adore you?"

Her tilted door swung open with a bang as she scuttled across the stone floor scattered with trinkets, clothing, and parchments. Knickknacks were strewn about in the musty clutter. She had too many dressers for one person. Clanging came from where she had disappeared.

"Are you cleaning?" Maru called to her.

"Eh!?" she exclaimed. "No, no dear; I'm selling! This emperor—" She came huffing and tumbling back. "I can trade something for a coupon or even pinch a coin out of this junk. Such a chance! The market is so expensive. Throw me out and get a new grandmother who can treat you! The train is ugly, but it brings things from Europe an old hag like me would never see otherwise. Have you been there? I have a sales-something—what do you call it—oh!, here—"

Maru wanted to sit and bathe in her endearing chatter. It made her miss the mornings in misty temple gardens gossiping with her. Guilt came over as she handed the ceramic vase with the twist-and-lock wooden top, its handles straining to hold its weight. Oba-san was offering a stew she had prepared. It would have lasted a week. She was filled with shame.

"You'll need to simmer it to bring it to life, but it'll do the trick! It even has meat." Maru stood helplessly, vowing to never ask her for anything again. The meat must have cost her a fortune.

"Have you received word from your father? I check every day. You know, your caretakers don't smile at me anymore."

Maru shook her head, her lips locked in humiliation.

"He must be doing something good. It is a hard fight to change careers and upend one's life. He's a good man, I saw him raise you."

Heat roared through her body at Fujiwara's dirty words about her father that had consumed her in worry. The ease Oba-san offered was worth a hundred traipses home. She wanted to bottle up the feelings and carry them around like she did with the fireflies. Surely they'd keep the demons away.

"I wish I could live across the way again. I could help you here."

Oba-san put a crinkled hand to her cheek. "Trust in your father. It was a hard decision, and many weren't so kind. You remember? It's a dangerous business around here, mind you. Some of the old samurai families have vanished—the word is they got a little too mouthy."

"Father isn't like them; he helped the emperor. We haven't done anything wrong."

"It's best not to give them any inkling of a reason for his leaving."

As sunlight crept over the tea fields and the warm steam rose, she had an impulse to tell her about the talking fox that weighed so heavily on her mind. But the okiya would wake soon and find her missing. She curtsied and said goodbye, showing her remorse.

"And you be careful, the rains these days bring blood. There's something in the air, and I don't like it one bit. There's a girl that's gone missing, did you hear? And Ogawa—the farmer family down the street—has taken a turn for the worse; they are in a sorry state. Pray that Meiji will protect us. You be sure to visit." Oba-san urged her onward, pressing bony fingers into her back.

Maru nodded absently, marveling at her luck and confused by the warning.

Ogawa. Did she know that name? She frowned, too tired to summon a recollection.

The pale dawn glow was disappearing. She stepped over misshapen cobblestones beneath the familiar trees of Gion. The creek was bloated. Willow branches graced its surface, lush leaves fluttering with the pulse of the city's veins, the streets' bends flowing. The red bridge's frog residents sang their morning *keru keru*, as white rabbits in the quiet alleys retreated to the shade.

She remembered what her grandmother had said in an overheard conversation.

"Send her to Adakichi? The ochaya? Your daughter is tender; they will feast upon her." Oba-san's voice came through the wall.

"You doubt me? You sound like my late wife. You told me to find her work!"

"Because you have been protective to a fault. She is an innocent."

"Maru is mine. You forget your place outside the clan. Your judgment is misplaced."

"She is indeed your daughter. It's why I caution you. I fear she will bring down the ochaya."

A power surged in her heart. She breathed in the moist morning—there was no hint of blood. No shadows lurking. No ghostly movements following. Chimneys empty of smoke were still for the day. The excitement of more summer matsuri in Kyoto, the fox's voice, and the problem-solving stew bubbling inside pushed away her worries about her father and her anger at Fujiwara. She bowed at a small stone statue that was draped in a red apron beneath a shrine at the crossroads, and thanked its kami for good fortune. She would figure out everything and make her father proud. She was humming as the ochaya door abruptly slid open.

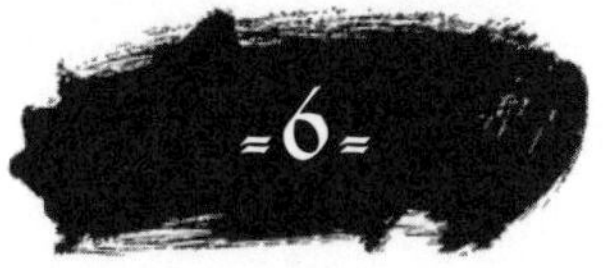

"We have been worried!" Adakichi said loudly.

Maru put on her slippers in a rush, dread pouring over her, and steadied the heavy vase.

"What is the meaning of this?"

"Okaasan, I am so sorry. I promised to make my family recipe, so I wanted to prepare it at home." She braced for another slap. All she wanted was to make things right. And she was still about to be punished for it.

"Are Adakichi's not good enough for you?" shot Mitsu, her arms crossed.

"Yes, of course they are, I—"

"And you raided our cabinet; you said she had everything, including extras!"

"Yes, that is true—"

"So, you sneak off without a word to either of us and—"

"Yes, I did. To cook."

"You can cook?" asked Mitsu.

"Girls!" Adakichi said.

"Yes ma'am, I am . . . I mean when I was going through the cabinets, Mitsu said those foods were rationed, so I went home to use my own stock. Nobody there is using it. It would have gone bad. I left without being dismissed, and I'm sorry." She lied more easily to them than to Oba-san. It was not a habit she wanted to adopt.

"I need the fire to stew my dish longer. May I?"

"It's already cold? On a day like this?" Mitsu said darkly.

"Well, there's meat in it."

Both looked shocked. Adakichi slapped her knees. "What a surprise. We certainly do not have meat in *our* cupboards."

Mitsu had nothing to say, so Adakichi threw out her arm, snapping her fingers, and said "Tea."

They returned to their routines. Adakichi was reading about ikebana, Mitsu was reciting poetry, and Maru was trying to recover when there was a knock on the door. A young boy held out leaflets of printed news; an image of the train bound in black ropes jumped out.

Adakichi scoured the page, trying to decipher all of the words. It wasn't often that news was delivered, but important announcements called for door-to-door handouts. Geiko subscribed so they could know rankings of geiko, the graduation of maiko, and keep up with political events for conversations with their clients.

Both Maru and Mitsu refrained from seeming too eager as they waited for Adakichi to summarize her reading. She frowned while she read. Maru's impatience grew. She was nervous about what this concerned. The train stared from where it hung suspended on the page.

The door opened again, and in came a whiff of patchouli. "Good morning, birds!"

Tomosuke! One of Maru's favorite geiko, one of the last two males in Gion running their own ochaya. They hadn't seen him since Tanabata. He was already in full makeup for the day, sporting turquoise robes covered in waves. His appearance was dreamy, and she desired to be swept up in the fantasy.

"Aki, Aki my charm." He nestled in and helped himself to tea, fanning himself with his own paper, using Adakichi's casual name with ease.

"You are early!"

"Am I usually late?" he acted offended. "Look."

He opened the pages, and words floated into the air; a sudden swirl of announcements, movements, and new words they attempted to sound out together.

"Such news! More train tracks will be laid, and they'll introduce a longer schedule of trips. It seems Kyoto is building a large home for them. *Home?* That's not how to read kanji—they misplaced its pronunciation guide."

"Interesting word. I don't recognize this one either," said Adakichi.

"Its grand opening coincides with the Gion Matsuri!" Mitsu cried. The matsuri was the pinnacle of Kyoto's matsuri season and was coveted by all. Maru caught her breath, visualizing hundreds of painted geiko and maiko dancing on huge floats carried through the streets with bells ringing everywhere. "It says here they will be installing something called 'wires' to prepare for – ele – ck – tri – shi – tee?"

Adakichi squinted. "They said it's quite a feat, and Tokyo has been using them for a while—ah! This must be what the decree was about: lamps that won't need oil!"

"A light that never goes out. Messages sent between two homes without a scroll. Talking instantly to someone. Such a foreign concept," Mitsu said.

"Instantly! Right! Can you imagine? Isn't it a marvel?" cried Tomosuke. "Now, don't listen to ol' Satori or Mihiro, for they think the wires curse us."

"Curse us?" Adakichi tilted her head.

"There are rumors that the sickness spreads through the wires. It's why whole towns fall shortly after the wires rise," he said in a hushed voice.

"Well, Satori and Mihiro are both foolish geiko. You remember how they treated me after my maiko damaged our good name with her behavior. This makes me even more enamored with the idea of a non-flammable lantern," said Adakichi.

"If that is how you feel, then I am pleased to share this news: The emperor is asking for notable families or businesses to put their name on a list if they wish to have it installed early on in their place to lead their wards," said Tomosuke.

Maru stirred her soup; none of the words were making sense to her.

"Why not us?" said Adakichi finally.

"Why not you?" Tomosuke said, and clapped.

Maru and Mitsu's eyes met, sharing an understanding in misunderstanding.

"What does it mean for us, madam?"

"Fame!" burst Tomosuke.

Everyone looked to her, and Maru changed her mind, not wanting to risk her privilege to represent the ochaya at the palace today.

"You two will take this opportunity to comb the roots of your differences. Visit a temple and return in one piece, and at peace."

As Adakichi and Mitsu slurped their soup, Maru served some to Tomosuke, Adakichi murmuring "Steady . . ." under her breath.

Plop, plop, plop went the skinny mushrooms and the soaked, crinkled cabbage.

Tomosuke leaned over and said in a hushed voice, "Did you hear about the missing girl?"

Plop, plop, plop went the eyeballs—splashing into the bowl, rolling and staring at her.

Maru screamed and threw the soup across the room. It splattered, sending reddish liquid down the wall.

"Mayuki! What in the devil—!" Adakichi bellowed.

“Stop eating! Stop eating!” Maru lunged for Mitsu, who yanked herself away from her, sending Maru into a heap on the floor, bashing her knees.

Tomosuke jumped up and down, lifting his feet as if hot coals were beneath him.

“Sit, sit! Mayuki! What called for this?”

“The—the eyes! They aren’t—I’m sorry! They—” Maru pointed to where she had seen the eyes rolling away, only to find a small chunk of reddish meat resting next to a piece of daikon. The soup trickling down the wall was yellowish-brown, bubbles of fat bursting in the silence.

“I advise a cleansing at the shrine, too,” said Tomosuke.

• • •

Maru usually didn’t mind Mitsu’s company. But to embark on an important mission—after she blatantly stole from her and created the soup fiasco—was not ideal.

It was true that Maru sometimes envied her coworker. With her beautiful round face and delicate nose, Mitsu was the ideal image of a geiko. She was feminine with a softness that announced her youth. Maru felt both proud of herself and embarrassed for Mitsu when people suggested they could be real sisters. She couldn’t see the similarity, especially when Mitsu seemed so poised and self-confident.

They both enjoyed the attention they attracted as they made their way down beneath canopies of maples, past tunnels of wisteria and walls of clematis; on this morning the dragonflies’ wings clicked as they spiraled toward the swelling grey storm clouds. Maru tried to ignore the watching eyes.

Fanning themselves, Maru sensed Mitsu was relaxing beneath her adorned face. Without Adakichi, Mitsu was in charge, something Maru didn't relish. She was also relieved to be in hitoe robes and without a painted face today, while Mitsu had to lumber about in many layers, wig-to-geta, for their outing.

But they had time to admire the newer fashions—men wearing more slender pants like those seen in the market and at the palace more women were wearing the bigger dresses.

"They all look so silly. And did you see the man sweating yesterday? Adakichi is too polite, but they are all horrid. All of this is so they can keep in style and pretend they're in Edo," Mitsu said after she tried conversing with them.

"Tokyo."

"Whatever people want. Who could think those fat dresses or skinny legs are better than these robes? At least I can breathe under here."

Maru wasn't sure about that: her robes were stifling around her obi, the towel at her lower back soaking up the sweat felt heavy, and she had just a small draft up her legs. She remained quiet, but she was curious and eager to try on the luscious dress Ai donned. But a thought came to her. What if they were doing away with robes and would wear those "bustles" from now on?

"Doesn't it all feel different from when you were a child?" questioned Maru, forcing some normalcy in their day. Men nearby were throwing fish from a cart onto counters of an open-air restaurant.

"What a smell!" Mitsu wrinkled her nose. "Yes, it is all different. Though my childhood was short. Sometimes I'm afraid to leave the okiya, for fear everything will have changed again."

Their geta hit the stone road in unison.

"The train, the food, the capital changing—and now an eternal lantern!" said Maru.

"Sometimes I want to play like I did as a child, ripping petals off flowers."

Maru laughed in surprise at the idea of Mitsu displaying any child-like qualities.

"You give me such a laugh."

Mitsu chuckled in return, and then silence fell between them. "But why are you also gifted with such stubbornness?"

"I don't know what you mean."

"Sure, you do. You do things your way, controlling the story, as you will. Think of your outburst earlier. Yet here we are being compatible, and I find your character tolerable."

"What is the story?" Maru tried to hide a furrowed brow.

"You were told to hide here, I know. And I've been respectful about your past, which I'm not privy to. But it will do you no good to test Adakichi's generosity. Someday the tales will turn, and fate will take back the ink you steal."

Maru said nothing, stepping aside for a line of school children to pass. Her comments were not as artistically veiled as Adakichi's; an art form she was still chiseling away at. She wasn't sure what to think, except to hope Mitsu was bluffing her way to learn a secret.

"Do you miss your family?" Maru asked, moving past Mitsu's comments.

"I've been here over half my life. Adakichi is as good a mother as I could hope for."

Maru couldn't relate to this with her father being away so long; his absence was more apparent than ever. She longed to go back to when the maple leaves were bright against the new snow and follow his footprints before they disappeared. "But surely they miss you."

"It is not my job to miss them. You should get used to it."

Maru hardly thought that was fair; she didn't ask for her mother to die or her father to leave. She didn't mean to become friends with other girls of high status who would turn her over and show her bare behind to the world if it bought them a single copper. There was an ocean between her and Mitsu and between her and Kiku, Ai, and Tane. Their paths were pristine and well-trimmed. Her path was full of fledgling weeds as she lumbered along, languishing, tugged by everyone, unable to follow her own heart. But a desire to be on Mitsu's good side prevented her from wanting an argument.

Mitsu continued, "I'd rather focus on playing hostess to my paying clients who can afford to help me make my future, rather than prolonging a past that's no longer mine. And I would not want to think I had to change my name to hide my shame about my family's loss of social standing."

Maru did not dare to acknowledge Mitsu, who spread gunpowder over her words. She was inciting a fight, and Maru wouldn't light the match.

At last, beneath apple and cherry tree limbs bowed overhead, they turned down the wide Koji street leading to the palace. She was in awe of it all over again.

With no new decrees posted, only a few lingered. Trees along the pathway were stout, shading the courtyard. She peered inside the grand archway for a glimpse of his throne but couldn't see into the dark entry under the green copper roof.

People waved fans and kites. A royal procession walked down a carpet beneath banners. Her father's strong hands clutched her sides as she sat on his shoulders, biting into a candy apple.

Her robes scratched; she was cranky from the noise, but she loved the hair-dos and scarves representing clans. Through the parting crowd, a pale face looked back at her, eyeless. A thunderous voice, echoing across the courtyard, red tapestries flowing in the wind, reaching further: "*Ma* . . . ru . . . ya."

The voice faded. She looked over her shoulder and heard only cicadas.

Maru ascended the steps outside the Gosho, careful not to trip. The staircase was regal, reminding her how tall she felt that day on her father's shoulders. Today it was still and solemn.

Nevertheless, she hoped her father would be proud and excited by her frequent visits, finding them a new venture of opportunity. The thought made her stomach flutter.

But it was Kira's tone the other day that made her nervous. She was annoyed with those who seemed to doubt her, who implied her father harbored ill will toward the emperor. He wasn't fighting; he was embracing the new ways of business. He didn't agree with everything, but never suggested violence. And what could be so evil about some silly pants or a lamp? Nothing worth fighting over. Her father wouldn't betray her over that . . . no, he was taking his time, bettering his business.

"Ladies," said a frail man, bowing. It wasn't Kira, but he looked noble all the same.

"We are here, sir, on behalf of House of Adakichi to answer the call for volunteers from Emperor Meiji for—"

"For electricity," he finished. "Ah, wonderful, the House of Adakichi. No doubt the emperor will be pleased to have such an esteemed ochaya receive the first light."

They followed him past panels bearing cranes, reeds and ponds, castles on foggy hills, and battles of shogun on horses. High on the sloped beams hung tapestries, bright red, as she remembered from the coronation. Doorways to other darker rooms piqued her curiosity.

Inside a dingy office the man moved aside scrolls of maps, shelves of books looming behind him. Maru gasped. Even her school didn't have any maps, and in books she found so few beyond Kyoto. Pieces of news and copies of decrees were stacked high, some in foreign characters she had never seen. Images of strange black figures were on top of another table. Bottles of ink, pens, feathers, and utensils were in open wooden cases.

Maru couldn't help herself, as if the papers were calling to her, demanding to be caressed. "Could I please look at your maps?"

The man was taken aback. "They are quite complicated for a young lady."

The room darkened; black clouds took over the sky as thunder roared.

"Her character needs constant distraction, but she's harmless," said Mitsu with a bite.

"If you must, you could pull the one of Kyoto," he conceded. "But they are proprietary."

Lightning cracked, startling them. "The joys of tsuyu," said Mitsu, horrified as Maru reached forward. She felt the burn of eyes on the back of her skull. "Ah, Kyoto. Our city."

Even under the darkness of the sudden storm, the detailed map showed every corner of her city. To the southeast, the shoreline with Fushimi's peak was marked. Temples were outlined throughout with the gold and silver pagodas painted with ink. She saw the marketplace in the west, and prominent shinise along the Koji street surrounding the palace were labelled. Schools and university campuses were drawn in, canals lined with restaurants and brothels were in the north. And there, in the east, was her beautiful ward and its cherry trees, willow trees, and a small, red arched footbridge.

"There—here is ours!" pointed Maru, breathless with excitement.

Mitsu released a short spurt of air, signaling her distress. Another lightning bolt flooded the room with light. Out the window, the courtyard was concealed by a tapestry of silvery cymbals.

"Yes, indeed, such precision goes into them. We have auditors check measurements and names many times before they become official." He moved aside, pulling out a scroll of names. "House of Adakichi—the same address I suppose?"

"Yes, and I am her head maiko. I'm Maiko Adakichi Mitsuki," she said with pride.

Thunder bellowed, bearing the lion's teeth.

"Ah yes. So Mitsu's name ceremony will be soon no doubt?"

"Yes, this fall, I will have a ceremony, sir. How could you think—"

"We hear many things around here. And your katsuyama hairstyle gave it away. The emperor will send his regards when it's the right time." Mitsu's face flushed under her paint.

"And you? I did not know the house of Adakichi took on a new apprentice. It's unreported."

"I am Shikomi Adakichi Mayuki."

Lightning danced in the courtyard.

"Madam required help recently to prepare for the matsuri season. She never meant to keep it from the palace," Mitsu hurried to say. "Her role is temporary, as I understand it."

Maru perused the maps of varying wards of Tokyo, old ones with Edo crossed out, some of the Ainu territory in Hokkaido, the farms and shores of Shizuoka, and spotted one labelled "Satsuma." Her heartbeat surged. *"Ma . . ."*

She took a step, and the man put down his brush. "Satsuma—wah! I haven't been there. Is it mystical, being a port city?"

The man, growing impatient, did not offer his approval this time.

"And tell me about your clients. We will cross-check with our records of businesses. This is customary, nothing to worry about. We want to ensure everyone is abiding by the rules."

"Ru . . ." Maru peered into the map, an acute need to open it gripping her. She took hold of a corner. As she peeled it back,

she saw the southernmost coast outlined, with the southern palace labelled on the beach aside the "southern Mt. Fuji" and old temples on seaside cliffs. She peeled more, and closer to the center she saw something that strangled her breath.

"Samurai camps," she said, loudly. She heard a gasp and drop of a pen. In the distance, thunder lashed its tongue, taunting its sharp, white-hot mistress.

Maru couldn't believe her eyes. She saw labels of what appeared to be clan clusters, labels of "emperor" and drawn, organized figures. There were Xs through some streets, a circle around three buildings, and a shoreline with ships bearing names in other languages.

The map was snatched away as beads of rain pounded the window.

"This is the business of emperors . . . a lady must not bother herself with such drudgery. No touching of these materials." The man glowered at her.

Maru's mind was skipping beats. No, her heart was. "But what was that about samurai?"

"It is nothing, simply an old map of old quarrels I'm afraid. It was out for archiving."

This made sense if he was referring to the old wars with former shogun. But he wasn't. The ink was a rich black, as if freshly inked. The rumors . . . the words of Kira . . . seemed to breathe on her neck.

The rain started to taper. *"Ma . . . ru . . . Ma . . . ru."* A soft thunder hummed over the hills.

"We certainly like to know the current news; it makes for better conversation. But Satsuma is indeed very dull!" chirped Mitsu. "Her tea is better than her conversation."

"That I would need to taste to believe it," he said darkly. "A second interview will be conducted at your ochaya. Undoubtedly the emperor will show interest in your application. I do think that with some sway, we can secure this grand opportunity to grant you this gift."

Maru said, "I was just looking for news of a girl who—"

But Mitsu bowed and grabbed Maru, ushering her outside, as the tall, white clouds drifted back out to the blue, rain-soaked mountains.

• • •

Maru struggled to keep up with Mitsu, who gracefully glided through the moist, earthy air, carrying her darari obi and churning her own wind in the noise of early daytime—the rolling wheels, rice-pounding, and wind chimes and temple bells that consumed the city.

"And what was that all about?" Mitsu asked as she reprimanded her. "Now there is a chance we won't be selected! Imagine what they must be thinking! Can you refrain from being so selfish for just a moment? Is this possible?"

Maru was silent. Her cheeks looked scorched.

"You make every conversation about yourself—Please stop it!" Mitsu bared her teeth. "If Adakichi finds out about this, she could have me removed! I will not take risks for you again. Improving your behavior will lessen the constant burdens you make for us."

Maru dropped her chin and tried to step away. Mitsu flung her arm out, her long furisode demonstrating she could put up a wall to Maru's freedom.

"For once, be respectful and recognize this event is for our ochaya! We don't do this just for you. Without this invitation, we lose our chance to maintain important things in our lives. We could lose our jobs—and who would take in a spoiled brat like you?"

Maru felt naked in front the older men and anxious apprentices who were watching her curiously as they swept away the muck that had come in with the rain outside their store fronts and shanties. She tried to disarm them with a little shrug as she picked up her robes to chase after Mitsu.

"Mitsu! Wait!"

Mitsu headed to the bridge and slowed her pace only when she arrived at the marshy river, cicadas humming louder in her wake. Maru trailed behind to give her the leading position and when she caught up with her said, "I didn't intend to be disrespectful. They seemed to accept our application—all I did was—"

"All you did was act childish. You threw out everything we've learned. I felt I was watching someone possessed!" Mitsu stopped. "What have you done? What if they tell the emperor about your behavior? Imagine what will happen!"

Maru couldn't explain why she had fixated on the maps. It was her innate curiosity that she should have controlled. She longed for her father, remembering his tales about places he visited and the gifts he'd bring home. She missed his excitement when he described the different cities, the funny masks he saw and the eerie folklore—and eating purple potatoes. Today she was wearing the omamori protection charm he bought at a far-away temple.

Mitsu continued to berate her. "Are you imagining what might happen to you? The way I might end your life if you do something like that again? I cannot be asked to cover for mistakes as egregious as these." Mitsu's youthful, flirtatious demeanor had evaporated.

Mitsu leaned in closer, "I do not know why you have chosen us, but I will find out who you are before you ruin us. You will not destroy fifteen years of my life over silly trifles with swordsmen. Don't doubt me. Others have tried to ruin me; I've stopped them before, and I'll do it again," She whispered in her ear.

Even along the river the heat was relentless, offering no respite from the overbearing sun. Mitsu had her reflective oil-coated aburagami parasol to reflect the sun's rays, but Maru had naturally forgotten hers because she was always carried away in her river of overwhelming thoughts.

She tried to listen for sounds of the sea that were powerful but soothing. But here the small waves of the river sounded nothing like something that could swallow the earth. The river was simply a vein that divided the city and guided her home, not a place that the kami seemed interested to play in.

"I'll do it again." Mitsu's threat echoed though her mind.

She squeezed her eyes shut, but there were still too many sounds. A man passing by with a cart, two haggling women, someone coughing, children crying—nothing was tranquil here. She sought to make sense of it all—why had the maps gripped her attention? Could Mitsu alone bring her down and shatter any hope of a future? Something didn't feel right—she wanted to seize the map, to see if it had answers. The truth alluded her.

Her mind drifted back to the fox, and she was filled with a sense of dread. Nothing fit—this winding river was branching out; the banks were overflowing. She wanted to stop the flow and climb out of its way before it pulled her under, but the bank was too slippery.

They silently crossed the bridge, slapping at mosquitos, the stones hot beneath them.

"We'll go to the temple first," said Mitsu gruffly. "Though peace may be a hopeless ideal."

They walked beneath willows next to pale buildings with bamboo fence fronts, rice-paper-covered shoji, and sun-faded lanterns. This led them to Yasaka Shrine, the bright red and white temple on a slope overlooking Gion, where kami protected geiko and their patrons.

They bowed at the gates and walked through the tunneled green-gate entrance surrounded by pink hydrangeas. Inside the garden were cicadas celebrating their arrival. A smattering of smaller shrines stood along a path that wrapped around the hill and pond, where weeping cherry trees bent over the koi and cattails.

Maru took Tomosuke's advice and bathed at the temizuya, methodically washing each limb in the appropriate order, praying to be cleansed. Perhaps a priest would bless her.

They made their way to the biggest shrine: a massive hall hoisted up on wooden columns atop smooth stone. The sides were covered in hanging lanterns beneath an imposing deep brown awning painted with red and gold designs guarded by a short bamboo gate. A bell adorned with ribbons hung from the ceiling over the prayer steps. A garden in full bloom replaced the musty street air. Mitsu rang the bell before they clapped and bowed in unison, closing their eyes to pray.

But Maru's mind was immediately abuzz.

The fox. She tried to shake it from her head.

Her father. No! She tried to empty her mind.

"Ma . . . ru . . . fight . . ."

But the fox and her father came in waves crashing behind her eyes. The map again tugged at her mind. Everyone around her was whispering about blood, the missing girl, the woman's wails—*why did they plague her when this had nothing to do with her?*

She squeezed her eyes to shut out her intruders.

"Thank you," she willed herself to say. She heard, *"Tell me who the fox is—I don't understand—what does it mean?"*

Suddenly yellow eyes found her behind her eyelids. She opened her eyes and tried to calm her heaving chest.

"Maru?" said Mitsu, her voice soft. She tugged on Maru's sleeve and led her away from the shrine. "You have been strange. This morning . . . what you did was embarrassing."

Maru rubbed her eyes. Maybe Mitsu wasn't the demon she had imagined. "It's just the heat," she said unconvincingly.

"We are all hot and tired," said Mitsu. She felt defeated. "But we have no choice. You must hide your strange curiosities. They get in your way . . ." She took Maru past the Noh stage where statues peered from beneath a blue hydrangea.

"How do you do it?" asked Maru earnestly. She was unsure how to still her mind when she seemed to be always harried with worries and doubts.

"I've had a lot of practice," Mitsu admitted. "My parents were strict. It is natural for me."

They followed the path where a lion head stood guard by a pair of stone lanterns. A sound of rock crunching made her turn around, and Maru thought she saw the lion blink.

"Your state is caused by the worry about your father, isn't it?"

Maru tried to focus on Mitsu's words, pushing down her sadness. They passed a pond where small orange fish tasted the air with their gaping mouths. A larger, green, hairy thing plunged into the water. Was it a Kappa oni, the reptiloid, lurking to seize her? She couldn't make out its form through her tears.

"Listen. Everyone is curious. I admit I also have a tendency to be too inquisitive, but I suppress this weakness. Adakichi is kind and shields you. And I follow her. After all, I protect you as my assigned imouto, and younger sisters always look up to their older sisters at the okiya."

Maru saw how dusty her tabi were.

Mitsu shifted impatiently. "But we can only help you so much. So please don't do this again; I don't want to be mad at you."

Maru sighed deeply. She was uncomfortable with Mitsu making her case before her. She wanted to push it all aside and not worry about the ramifications if her father was against the emperor's code or someone revealed where she had fled. She and others would be in danger. And she knew, deep down, it would mean she'd have to face the fact that he had lied to her.

Mitsu seemed remorseful; her eyes were pleading.

Over her shoulder, Maru saw a young girl listlessly walking around the corner. A sadness shadowed each of her steps. She looked like the girl she'd seen in the kimono alley, except, now she was horrified to see that the little girl was naked.

"I can't help thinking something is very wrong," Maru said to Mitsu as she watched the girl, who stared at her with her arms hanging.

Mitsu said, "There is no reason for something to be terribly wrong. The kami will watch out for you."

The girl pivoted toward them, her tired eyes staring through Maru. She looked sickly and weak. Had she been stricken? Had the Tokyo plague reached Kyoto?

"And so will your father," Mitsu added.

Maru tried to smile. She was grateful but unable to tear her gaze away from the pale girl. She asked her, "Do you need help? Where is your mother?"

Mitsu backed away, looking down the path. She turned her head left and right, then back to Maru. "Who are you talking to?"

"Are you—are you alright?" Maru asked as she took a step toward the girl.

"Maru? What is wrong with you?" Mitsu asked.

The girl lingered, swinging slightly. Maru noticed she had red-stained hands.

"Maru, what is the matter with you? There's no one else here."

"You're hurt!" Maru approached the girl faster. She saw her suddenly put her hands up, and bent her head backward with a *CRACK!*, opening her mouth wide as if she was about to scream. Her skin blackened in front of them. She stretched taller and taller, her neck reaching higher and higher. Her pale face turned bright yellow.

And then she vanished.

Maru heard a cry echoing, and bumps crawled on her arms.

"What—?" Maru called out. "Where did she go!"

But even the cicadas had stopped humming.

"Come. It's just the heat." Mitsu's voice was louder. "Let's go. We need to get ready for tonight's guests. I think we may see Fujiwara again."

Maru looked for the mysterious pale girl as they passed the sitting statues of emperors of old before crossing beneath the red and white arched gate and down the slope back to Gion. She thought she smelled blood piercing the hot summer air.

• • •

Instead of Fujiwara as the expected guest, it was Kira. He had sent a note to Adakichi that he was coming by sooner than they expected. It would be unusual for a guest to not have the accompaniment of a long-term patron of the ochaya, but as a member of the palace he would certainly be welcomed. However, giving a warning of more than a few hours would have been much appreciated, regardless of the client's rank.

A rush of chores began, and Mitsu hurried to uninvite Fujiwara, one of the most sacrilegious things an ochaya could do. But faced with the event of entertaining guests from the palace, they had no choice.

Maru absentmindedly washed down the house, prepared fresh minazuki, and rolled a barrel of sake to the kitchen for cooling. Her mind couldn't let go of the girl's empty eyes, something she saw in her own mirror, all the while on guard for an appearance of the fox.

"There's no time to call a proper hairdresser!" Adakichi huffed. "Switch to the gold one!" she ordered. Maru put the green and pink scenery partition away, pulling out the gold one with white cranes.

"No fresh flowers? Were they never delivered?" Mitsu glowered when she saw the vases of sprigs of cotton and dried reeds.

Maru shook her head and Mitsu groaned, "Fujiwara—Ugh! He never sent the roses, did he? It's too late. We are not ready in the slightest—what were you doing while I went out?"

A lot, Maru thought, but knew better than to retort, and mumbled an apology she didn't think was warranted.

"I'm so hungry," muttered Mitsu. "Mind the door."

Maru glanced out to see the street sweeper lighting the lamps as the sun dipped beneath the rooftops. She liked to pass by the houses' pink and orange-dyed facades that stood quietly beneath streaks of high blue clouds in the summer evening. She coaxed in a breeze, creating a draft that smelled of damp bamboo with a touch of apple blossoms from the trees across the way. The appealing odors would soon be replaced by sake and sweat. Maru instinctively put rice paper under her arms to soak up perspiration, and dread. She couldn't pinpoint exactly what she feared. Terror stalked her like a predator, and she didn't know what it looked like.

Thud, thud. Maru had forgotten again to replenish Mitsu's egg stash. She would be the maiko's prey tonight.

She heard a rap at the front door. It must be divine intervention.

Kira threw his arms wide before giving a spin to show off his dark blue suit with bright gold buttons. He was grinning from ear to ear.

"Fit for a teahouse?" he inquired.

He was indeed wearing what Maru could only assume was the latest style, which still had not grown on her. His grin seemed too wide. Clearly he was unaware of the chaos he had caused the house or the curling of her stomach when he made his comments about her father. But she had to swallow any doubts and feelings of disdain for the sake of the ochaya.

"I fear you make the rest of look underdressed," she replied.

"Kira! Apologies for my shikomi. You look magnificent!" Mitsu thrust herself forward, bowing profusely and pushing Maru aside.

"No reason to apologize for Maruya; she and I can have a little banter," he said.

"Ah, I am the 'shikomi' here," Maru interjected, panicked by Mitsu standing over her shoulder.

"Using her name pollutes her mind; she's in a fragile, youthful, and impressionable state," Mitsu explained. "Her title is preferred."

"I can play along," he responded to Mitsu as Maru poured his drink. "But it gives me a rather peculiar feeling to be served by her." Maru's throat was tight as Mitsu closed in on her.

"Our paths cross in strange ways," said Mitsu stiffly. "But let this not cloud the night. The tobacco will do that enough! You have brought our house joy."

"I put up with pleasantries all day," he lit a pipe. "Why don't you have a drink and loosen your collar."

Maru hoped he meant figuratively, but she also got the impression he wasn't entertained too often in teahouses, which was strange for a man of his class. Dignitaries usually reveled in spoiling geiko in teahouses with customary lavish gifts, boasting about their evenings to their peers who held a similar affection for the Gion district. But not Kira.

"How about a game to start our night?" Mitsu asked.

"Only if Hoso—Shikomi-chan—joins in too."

"This can be arranged," said Mitsu in a voice so quietly curt that it was only Maru who caught her disdain. She lit the first incense of the night, a thick, spicy smoke erupting.

Mitsu decided to be assertive. She pulled out the cards and began dealing without asking for his game preference. She split the deck, then stacked it high again, relaying rules until he lost patience, "These are games for a gambler, and I'm an old man. Let's play something simpler."

Mitsu tilted her head in agreement and switched to Kitsune Ken.

"Shikomi will act as a mediator and keep score." Maru accepted this instruction with tight lips.

"Kitsune, hunter, or villager," Mitsu said, demonstrating the signs for each one. "Follow my beat, and on the drop, choose your role—the kitsune will best the villager, the hunter kills the fox, but the villager will defeat the hunter."

"My, this game is also complicated," he said, laughing to cover up his hesitation. "I'm afraid it will reveal my proclivity for paper and ink rather than—" He waved his hands.

Adakichi appeared with her painted smile, looking elegant in her brightest robes and gold chrysanthemums in her hair. "I shall assist with a song," she said. She sat down, and began strumming her harp.

Kira clapped out of rhythm in boyish delight, swept up in Adakichi's magic. Her notes were flying, his hands reaching out to slap them like they were mosquitos. At the sound of the final, drawn-out syllables, followed by a louder silence, Kira drank the rest of his sake.

"You have made a man delirious! You have even disarmed my heart."

Adakichi nodded for them to continue with the game as she strummed a beat.

Mitsu and Kira faced each other, any fragility on his part vanishing as he made formations with his hands. He chose the hunter first; Mitsu chose the kitsune; Maru tallied one for him. His forehead was beaded with sweat. He had an impish grin when he triumphantly cried out with each of his wins.

Mitsu suffered three more defeats before Adakichi rescued her and concluded the game.

"Would anyone like sake? Kira, why don't you share your life's strife with us."

"It's too much of a burden to unload onto someone else. It wouldn't be very masculine."

"We could let the cards speak for you. We can offer guidance. There would be no prying ears, only the kami."

"Ah, the riddles of a geiko. My problems are easily solved by a good meal."

Adakichi laid out her fortune-telling almanac and asked Kira's age and birth.

"You aren't still consulting the lunar calendar, are you?" Kira crossed his arms, leaning back.

Maru knew Adakichi was uncomfortable but concealed it with a thoughtful tone. She said, "We have adapted to Meiji's, but there is still value in using the former for calculating auspicious days to anticipate."

He sighed. "Will the almanac tell you when I shall perish, too, as they all do?" He pointed to her chart, indicating his month and year, frowning at the zodiac printed on the page.

"We do not specialize in morbid predictions," she said. "But I could assess your taian. It does seem there is turmoil there. You seem to be battling a foe who is familiar. Does this ring a bell? The cards insist you have an opportunity to heal the wounds of your past, but must find clarity first. You will face this foe, but I have no doubt you'll let wisdom guide you to the higher path."

He seemed unmoved by the reading. He just nodded along. "Ringing bells bring snakes," he mused. "Do all your clients listen to the conclusions of your books?"

"We can't help having your best interests in our hearts," insisted Adakichi.

"Fujiwara has taken to them," offered Mitsu.

"Fujiwara? Of the greater Meiji family? He is wealthy if he is from the prosperous branch."

"Ahh . . ." Adakichi tilted her head. "I'm afraid it's privileged information, but he has an air about him. He has a lot of charisma to help him succeed in business; as for his other talents, they remain a mystery."

Kiri gave her a genuine smile for the first time that evening and said, "Then what about another game—is that in my fortune too? And what about food?"

"It is always in the stars. How about Tora Tora Tora?"

This was Maru's favorite game. Each player would stand on the opposite side of the partition as a contestant sang. When prompted, the rivals would jump out and reveal the character they chose as being more powerful than the other. She loved how it could escalate into a tizzy more than Kitsune Ken could; the anticipation of the big reveal of the talented winner appealed to her more than the front-facing hand games.

Tora to-ra to-ra tora!

The boyish Kira appeared, darting behind the partition, his vitality coming through again, but Maru found herself hopping in and out faster than him.

Tora to-ra to-ra tora!

She chose the old woman. He picked the samurai. She won.

Tora to-ra to-ra tora!

Maru appeared as the samurai. He was the tiger. She won.

Tora to-ra to-ra tora!

He chose the old woman. Maru chose the tiger. She won.

"I am beginning to think I am not so apt at this game! Your shikomi lets an old man get his ego checked. Yet, receiving it from a fair-faced girl is more of a pleasant experience." He collapsed on the floor to sit and regain his breath. "You know, Ho—Shikomi, if you wore more makeup as does your maiko, you would have a radiant beauty like her. It's uncanny," he said as he patted her.

Maru was flushed with pleasure. She took an unabashed risk when defeating a client in a game, but his smile suggested they both won. They took their seats, and she served bean cakes.

"But there are traces of your father, too. When I look at you, I fear you'll open your mouth and scold me with his voice," he laughed. "Say—have you had any news of him? Since we—" Maru shook her head.

"Ah, it's a shame, I prayed for him. Can you tell me what he imports, again?"

"Sake," Maru said quickly.

"Oh, I thought for sure you said porcelains. You know, Koshida's koi porcelains—bowls and such—are catching on fire. He'd make a decent salary if he sold those up north. But if sake . . . surely my old-man mind can't be collapsing yet. But alas, the day comes for us all."

Maru wanted to clutch her chest. *Hadn't she meant to say bowls? Sake . . . why did she say that?* Because she wasn't certain. She was so determined to keep her family identity a secret that she was forgetting the truth about them. She looked to Mitsu, who had a subtle raise of an eyebrow.

But Kira opened his own flood, lamenting in veiled terms that there was a conflict within his walls. He explained that some doubts were cast about the current policies, and the policy writers were wrestling with the finessing of their words. Discussions between Kyoto and Tokyo were embroiled in conflict about the interpretation of papers received from abroad and how to implement their rulings. "It's a matter of wanting to preserve our foundation by listening to the views of all prefectures, but we must also rival our neighbors in a way that is just."

Adakichi responded with simple reactionary phrases that solidified his thinking, encouraging him further.

Kira went on to say, "Disagreements in how policies should be prioritized are a danger, and we have seen flaws in inviting poorer ranks into the court. Their perceptions are duller, and it takes quite a grinding to sharpen their senses. Maybe not all of them should have traded their thatched roofs for the cerulean tiles of the Gosho."

"There must be value in each voice, an underlying alliance," Adakichi responded.

"Everyone is eager to avoid war. This is indeed a road forward, save for growing pains," he remarked brightly.

"And it must include these new wired trees?" Mitsu asked cautiously.

"You mean the electricity, I presume. We usually speak in more technical terms at the Gosho as opposed to metaphors," said Kira. Maru wrinkled her nose at his demeaning tone.

"Wasn't there a tremendous fire in Tokyo?" asked Adakichi patiently.

"I think the fire you are referring to was caused by a gas lamp that was not well kept, as we understand it. This outdated technology is what we were first sold on, but electricity can course through a whole city without the need for something to be lit and unlit. It is much less tedious and more efficient, and much less prone to cause accidents."

"We've heard people become sick from the wires," Adakichi pressed.

"The sickness is not real . . ." He waved the end of his sentence away.

"It's really safer than getting light from gas lamps?"

"You doubt the emperor's decisions?"

Adakichi moved back slightly, an indication of her indignance that he would be sharp with her. She said, "Not in the slightest, I am just aiming for a deeper understanding."

"And is what I also pray for. Any disrespect leaves cracks in the foundation and allows poison to seep in. We must unite to have true order and establish these precedents of strength; it will be essential for all ranks of society. All facets, even the frivolous and artful, must share a vision."

"We are marveled by the transformation the train has brought to the city," said Mitsu gently. "But I am curious about how it can be so powerful."

Kira brightened up and said, "We have a vigor, you see. It's a great machine that requires its own fire. It needs a heart to pump it, and we have devised it to do just that, giving it the vitality it needs."

"Streets that smell of blood in the morning . . ."

Maru shook her head, and the memory of the pale girl went away. Kira didn't mean what her mind jumped to, which was the rumors. He was surely just speaking poetically.

"It is thanks to our careful negotiation with allies. China was the center of the world for centuries, but by sharing power with friends across the sea, we'll overcome them. We ally ourselves with the Europeans. The shogunate kept us from harnessing their capabilities, but we can grow into our full, destined potential.

"It's the reason I abandoned my daimyo position readily—even the salary!—to join the Emperor's Court. It's important that we vanquish the romance of the past in order to detach us from turning to ideals of comfortable simplicity. The world is finally ours to grab, but we must be ready to seize it together as a united nation."

Maru shivered. Her father once shared the excitement that Kira exhibited when speaking of foreign powers with technologies and culture they had known nothing about. When she was younger, a tutor tried to teach her Latin and English. But she became overwhelmed, so the lessons ceased. Her mother reminded her father of the fears the shogun had long warned of were lying in wait overseas beyond their horizon. Their borders were closed to protect them from teeth-gnashing violence over an infiltration of the worship of idols blamed on reading books published in the West. Maru had seen depictions of George Washington battling snakes and tigers. She admired the art and then tossed them aside with the other fairytales. Her father, however, embraced a future of coexistence, certain the true enemy was within their borders in the leaders who abandoned their morals.

With voices of her mother and father in her ear, she had little chance to determine her own opinions. Was she afraid to face what was foreign or afraid of missing out on such wondrous things?

Hearing Kira's rabid enthusiasm now sounded off-putting; she was uncomfortable with his assertions and wished her father was there to discuss the implications. She feared disappointing him.

"Do other men who have the privilege of seeing inside these walls also feel the internal strife, or are they as enthusiastic, ready to spill their own blood for advancement?" He laughed at a joke he didn't share. "Only the iron stomachs will survive." He beamed. "Let's have a song!"

The room fell silent; Maru went to the hall to wait for Adakichi's music and Mitsu's dance to begin, taking deep breaths during her respite to still churning thoughts. She wondered if the fox was waiting while she was inside a cage of her own, constructed by her father, Adakichi, and the stories she tried to keep straight. The candle on a shelf nearby seemed to sweat with her.

The first notes were plucked. From the hall, Maru saw Mitsu count:

3, 4 and slowly stretched her arms wide,
one north to the sky,
the other south to her feet,
7, 8 She opened her fan
below her eyes
spun once, twice,
the notes plucked, the tempo intensified,
3, 4 Mitsu raised her fan high,
Then back low
Stepping across,
And back again
7, 8 folding the fan
crossing her arms,
her hands a butterfly,
opening her arms to drop her sleeves,
3, 4 she was brought to her knees,
one by one her hands covered her face,
then outstretched before her,
7, 8 she rose, gracing her lip with her fingertip,
hand on the fan,
to open one more time,
3, 4 she touched her ear,
and the strings cued her spin,
folded them across her chest,
7, 8 she knelt, hands before her,
fan at her feet,
and forehead to the floor.

Across the darkened street she saw shadows from the moon stretch, and a familiar silvery glow appeared across the compost boxes. And there, on the side, she saw a pair of yellow eyes emerge.

The fox! She whipped around. It was back. She wondered how long it would wait. Its eyes were undeniably mysterious, unnatural in a way, as if they were looking directly into her.

"... should be here soon, in time for the Gion parade." Maru's ears perked up; she leaned against the doorway to listen from just outside their sight. She heard someone say "the emperor?" and other fragments of their conversation.

"... should be in attendance. He will make a rather important announcement..."

"... telegraph to be demonstrated ... longest message ... telephone..."

"... no, no fires with ... the plague is suppressed ..."

"Impact is distilled as such announcements become more frequent!" Adakichi said as Maru re-entered the room with a rushed step, carrying a tray of pickled plum, cucumbers, and rice crisps. Kira chuckled, appreciating the secret alliance he had with a geiko.

"I heard you had quite an interesting visit with the Scribe," Kira said, as she placed a plate before him. Maru's face burned.

"Ah, ah, it's fine," he assured her. "I was tickled when he mentioned your fascination in the maps."

"Maps? Of what?" asked Adakichi, a horrified expression crossing her face.

Kira said, "The emperor has access to all kinds of information. Alluring, sure, but certainly not for everyone, especially young women. I trust you'll resist these temptations, in future visits."

Maru bowed her head sincerely. "I apologize."

"You are your father's daughter at heart."

Adakichi flinched. Maru knew she'd feel it later with the underside of a geta. Mitsu looked like she was ready to cut off her ears.

Kira continued, "My visit here is, admittedly, a partial insurance, we shall we call it. As I've reported, the palace—here and in Tokyo—is in a heightened state of apprehension about the steady stream of people engaging in diplomatic relations, but I won't lament over these doldrums. It would be a shame if someone breached our trust."

"Kira, my girls are better behaved than this. I shall assume responsibility and represent the ochaya on palace visits," Adakichi said steadily, knowing her application for the lamp, and possibly even their participation in the Gion Matsuri, was in jeopardy.

Maru wanted to be a candle and melt herself away. Had Kira been waiting to pounce? And here Adakichi had to defend a shikomi, of all people. What if someone, another geiko or another client knew what she had done. Maru felt ashamed. If she left the house, she'd have to work in a factory or await marriage with a ragged, penniless merchant. Her few choices humbled her. These walls suddenly seemed closer.

"You have the privilege to choose your path." The optimism that came from her father flickered.

Kira waved his hand and leaned back with his palms—indicating he was a man who knew he was in control.

"Frivolous curiosities of women are charming to a degree. In actuality, I owe her gratitude—for if someone who was a real threat to our empire made their way inside in some insidious disguise, that would certainly have worse consequences."

"If she's a thief, she's a clumsy one," laughed Adakichi. "A geiko can balance on a bamboo in a river during a storm. I'm not sure she could tell a river from the riverbank."

Mitsu made eye contact with Maru, who took it as a cue to start cleaning. She knew Mitsu meant to get Maru out of their sight to punish her, but she was grateful for permission to leave the room that was thick with something more than summer air and incense smoke. Her body was weary from needing to sit so still to remain unseen.

It was something she had craved to be a part of, but it was also a curse she wanted to shatter and break free from them.

She made her way to the pantry—the moment she had been waiting for.

Sliding the door open, she sighed with the rush of air that stroked her face. The fox emerged from the shadow. Its fur was bright. He was wearing a healthier coat.

"I haven't much time," whispered Maru.

"Good evening to you, too," said the fox. Maru smiled, feeling awkward about greeting an animal. She reached into her robe and dislodged a clump of rice and natto.

"This is what I was able to scrounge up."

Maru watched in fascination as the fox ate with gentle mannerisms that gave her a new perspective, seeing it as nothing more than a harmless stray in need of scraps. But when it lifted its head, staring at her with piercing eyes, her apprehension returned, bringing back her speculation that it was a demon. She clenched her fists in quiet defense, afraid of it turning on her.

She had fed the fox and bandaged it. Her work was done. She stood, ready to be released from this strange relationship. Kira's words ricocheted in her bones, reminding her of duty.

And believing in fairy tales wasn't her duty.

"Well, I hope you don't regard me as rude, but I need to be on my way," said Maru. She decided just then that she needed to mind her head and avoid Adakichi's wrath. She had to help her father and keep her identity safe. And the fox had made it difficult to keep her focus on this. It needed to be banished.

"Thank you," said the fox. "But I'm afraid I still need your help."

Anger rushed through her. "Sorry . . . I can't do any more for you. I hope you can find a new place."

"I can help you in exchange."

Maru wavered, but then said, "I'm sorry, but I don't need anything." She didn't want to negotiate with a talking animal, and recent ghost stories lingered in her mind.

"Not even fulfilling a wish?"

"I don't have any wishes." She lied. She was guarded; all stories of demons told of the traps laid out for unsuspecting victims.

"Says the one who is haunted by both past and future."

Maru raised her head and stepped back.

"No wishes? Not even for the return of your father?"

Blood drained from her face. She wasn't sure how the fox knew, but she was becoming more convinced she didn't want anything to do with the fox. All excitement she had harbored for him was departing and replaced by discomfort and fear.

"He is on his way back. He said he would be here soon." Her words poured out, and she couldn't explain why she continued responding and defending her father to this creature.

"Before the leaves bleed into gold and red," repeated the fox.

Maru froze. "How do you—"

"I know more than you realize. I am not an ordinary fox. I may not remember my name, but I know this and need your help."

The moon was sitting above the rooftops, ready to sleep before the sun rose. She couldn't steal more time. Kira would be on his way, and Mitsu and Adakichi expected her. She suddenly felt silly for talking to a fox—a fox that was clearly evil.

"I don't know how else to help. I can't sneak around."

"The large and dark beast that harmed me must be stopped. And then your father could return."

Her breath was suspended in the air. Reunite with her father. Leave the ochaya. But at what cost?

"Stop what, exactly? Stop who? How can I help you if I don't even know?"

"It harms not only me, but others. You hear their screams, you smell them. You saw its victims yourself. There is something in your midst that is hurting all of us. It's taken many of my own. And it will hurt you and your world, too."

The girls. The fox means the girls.

Maru paused and looked at the closed windows, wishing someone was near who was able to help her. It knew about visions she was having. Could it restore her sanity? Or would it kill her?

"You attacked it, on purpose? How do you know—? Why do you not remember what it was, then? How do you know that—" She stopped short of saying *that I've seen things?*

The fox replied, "It hunts my own kind too. It's luring them in. You've shown you can see me; you must be able to see others too. You can help us. And I'll help you. You made a wish, didn't you? I can grant your wish. You won't see them again if you don't vanquish the beast. Your city will fall to it if you don't stop it."

Kyoto. Kyoto was in danger.

"No, I couldn't, I've never seen others." Her words fell flat: They were a lie. "Besides, I could never—I couldn't ever stop something, especially a kami, if you couldn't! I'm not like you. I never wished for this. It's—it's not for me to do. This would be impossible!"

"I could perish without your help."

"And I could, too, if I stay," Maru said, voice shaking. "Leave. I can't be bothered with this anymore. Find someone else." Rushing inside, she slid the door shut on the one thing that gave her hope—all extinguished in a single moment.

7

The sky rolled beneath her outstretched arms. She flapped her arms and found they lifted her like the wings of a bird. The sky was cloaked in the sunset's spectacle, with creamy clouds suspended beneath its starless expanse. There was no land in sight—but she had no fear, an exhilaration she could never recreate in the waking world.

She basked in the disappearing glow among golden-red clouds. A koto strummed.

One cloud darkened; lightning curled around its edges.

The sun was shutting its eye—something was wrong—the koto's melody stuttered.

A terrible blackness burst. Yellow eyes and screams barreled toward her.

A gust of wind pushed through her chest— she was falling as the strums rose to a crescendo.

F a l l

i n g

She was falling into the deepest blue, running her fingers through water—she reached higher water—she was kicking waves in the water.

She couldn't find a light—or a surface—she flapped her arms, but she was sinking. A girl reached for her, but her hand broke off. Maru screamed—the koto abruptly stopped.

Another scream cracked open her ears, but this time it was her kicking away the tangled mosquito netting, gulping down as much air as she could in gasps.

She rubbed her collarbones, straining to remember, telling herself it was a dream. The stars outside were dull; the rooftops were no longer illuminated by moonlight—the shadows of night muted as the sun fought to awaken.

Nothing stirred, not even the birds. After a few moments of soothing herself, Maru closed her eyes to chase away the pale hand that curled over her window frame, ignoring the face with dark eyes that peered in; she was certain she was already dreaming, her hardened tears caking her cheeks.

• • •

When the birds chirped, ribbons of light hung in the air between the bamboo shutters, soft and slow, juxtaposed to Maru's racing heart. Her fears from last night hung like a lump in her throat she couldn't swallow.

She sat up, listening for movement, worried she was late to do chores, and then recalling:

It was their day off!

One of her few days a month she had to herself. It was time to think through what she needed to do. She fumbled through her thoughts of the fox. Nothing seemed right; but was it the fault of the fox—or had her reaction of shutting the door to it been a mistake?

She rubbed her face, feeling tender places where Adakichi bruised her after Kira left. Maybe she'd bathe today. Or ask someone about the fox. But she couldn't come out with this. She still wasn't entirely convinced the fox was real. Maybe she was delusional. Seeing the girl in the garden—perhaps this was how myths started: one person imagined something and everyone believed it.

Maybe she could ask her friends.

She shook her head. They had been acting strange all summer, treating her differently ever since her father left home. It left only her Oba-san who she could trust for an opinion.

Oba-san!

She owed Oba-san for saving her with the stew. Hunger rumbled in her stomach. Or maybe it was guilt. No, her stomach was too tight for her to eat. She kicked off her blanket. The morning was slipping away faster than last night's sake.

She needed to get answers about the fox, the scuffles in Satsuma everyone was afraid to talk about, and the pale girls that kept appearing and disappearing.

She lit incense to clear the smell of night sweat and dabbed her forehead with rice paper, discarding oily remnants and pressing fragrant flowers into her sheets. She then pulled on a yellow hitoe kimono. With Mitsu's help, it would be tied together with a pale blue obi.

Maru's nose wrinkled as she remembered how the rest of the night had fallen. How Adakichi, after Kira left, retired to her room to burn a candle into the night for writing notes in her book. *"A good geiko retains best relations with clients when she remembers the finer details."*

But this morning Adakichi was already clutching the emperor's paper, titled "Parade Lottery Announcement," without an inkling of seeming bothered by Kira's visit.

"Did we—Were we—?"

She held the paper up. It had a painting of a line of geiko holding fans over their shoulders parading through Hanamikoji. Stout men in white robes carried a grand palanquin with a priest inside, lanterns lighting the way. Below was a printed list of those awarded a place, and at number five was "Adakichi's Ochaya." She clapped. They were high on the list!

"We passed Kira's interview," Adakichi put the paper aside. "There's more."

Maru held her breath. Would she be part of it? Her favorite matsuri? Adakichi was beaming, holding back something.

"I was dismayed. The words to express my shame aren't coming to me in regard to Kira's remarks. Perhaps having the night to think about your behavior has taken root. However, this news brings me peace. It seems that long term damage has not been done by your stray tendencies."

Maru hung her head apologetically.

"Can I be assured there will not be another incident? You know that disciplining you is not pleasurable to me." The enthusiasm in her strikes contradicted her tongue's insistence.

Maru gave as much assurance as she could, combined with a low bow.

"Okaasan, I'd like to share the news with Oba-san. May I do this?"

"The teahouse is closed today, so the day is yours," said Adakichi. "Oh, I forgot your wages."

She pocketed them into her knapsack, noting it seemed lighter than usual, but not daring to raise it. She instead submerged herself in the heavy morning air, a bright light cascading over the tiled roofs. Cicadas hiding in zelkova trees sang their summer song on her way to market.

The copper gave her freedom she didn't have last night, though she was still unable to afford her dream. Adakichi declared that wages were harder to come by. Most clients, former daimyo and shogun, had fallen into difficult times after the war years. They lost their footing and source of income—arriving at teahouses as poor people but still demanding to be entertained as they had for years. Adakichi was obliged to rebuild her clientele.

Being part of the Gion Matsuri was the pinnacle of their career for many geiko, and for her, a shikomi, to be adjacent to them was good in many ways. Maru remained hopeful she had a chance of advancing herself and prove to her father she could do what he envisioned.

Along the river, she watched the fishermen casting their lines out. Her thoughts drifted to her family enjoying fishing and her father explaining how samurai scrounged for anything they could find on the road, exempt from rules feudal lords imposed—when even salt was a luxury.

Why would it be so bad if he was still one, when he brought so much good to so many?

The question made her halt, and she considered its ramifications as she perused rows of delicately-painted cakes and selected one with strawberries for Oba-san. After thanking the baker, she admired the shiny tiled roof that had replaced the thatched one of the Edo era.

Smokey spices blew as families prepared meat on outdoor barbeques, their chimneys churning as if it were winter. Everyone was infected, gobbling up the "new" permission they had, a façade that painted them as equals, the type her father fought for.

Along these roads, merchants resided alongside daimyo's prominent homes. Beyond them new factories rose, offering jobs and churning out more goods than ever. Shinise crowded temples. A few years before, feudal lords separated districts, barring even foreigners from stepping onto their shores without permits or some form of a bribe. Arbitrary laws allowed them to skim prices, taking change until there was nothing left for citizens, leaving them destitute.

These streets were once awash in blood; air thick with bats, darkness hiding the sun. She recalled leading up to the

Boshin War when the Tosa clan swept through, assassinating Tokugawa sympathizers instead of awaiting negotiation, which her father had called for. Revolts knocked shogun walls and burned daimyo roofs. The feudal lords rebuilt them using tiles and banned anyone else from using them, returning the fire tenfold, and calling on samurai to silence naysayers. Her father had complied until he snapped. He was tired of fighting those who simply wanted a fair chance.

Cicadas hummed a welcome as she approached Oba-san's home. The stone torii in the middle of the yellowing rice field, framed by a grove of tall, old blue trees, beamed at her. Her heart softened, and her knuckles hardened to knock on the door. As she waited for an answer, she drifted into a dim memory from years ago.

Her mother was sound asleep behind the night's blue eyes. Maru swung her legs onto the stinging cold flood and let in a pinch of warm orange light pouring in. Darkened figures sat cross-legged, bracing chins into palms.

Her father's eyes were bright. "Sakamoto, leading the campaign, sees hope in this vision. Listen to what is rooted in 'all men are equals.' It opened my eyes to another life, one for all of us."

"But it is not a vision the Tokugawa share with other shogun. There is no room for them in this plan," said a man with long hair. The fire crackled. "Sakamoto is a rebel to them. They'll never forget the pain his friends the Tosa are causing. They will orphan many children. We should consider moving forward without waiting for Tokugawa to come around."

Her father had stuck to his word promised in that conversation, and opened his door to Westerners and found allies in them. They armed merchants and peasants to fuel the urgency for new leadership. They were the first voices in centuries who promised not to backstab them.

Hope caught on faster than the plague. Whispers of the changing tides became fire, and the daimyo rushed out as their homes filled with smoke, the shogun conceded, Emperor Meiji rose, and the gates were thrown open—her whole life Maru had known change.

Maru wondered if she had ever truly known peace.

"Maru-chan! Your face is a blossom in winter."

"It's summer, Oba-san," Maru laughed. Oba-san's cold palm touched her cheek, and she brought her inside the cool shanty and put on a kettle.

Here was the closest she felt to peace.

"You brought me something too pretty to eat!" Oba-san held up the cake with her brittle fingers, admiring the plumpness of the strawberries atop the golden dough.

Her shaking hands reminded Maru of how close she had been to never having Oba-san. The end of Tokugawa's reign brought the most chaotic years: bodies strewn in gutters, left to rot for weeks. It had been easy for their coalition to bewitch citizens to follow the Western fable.

> *"The Tokugawa play commoners like a tiger playing with a field mouse," her father had said. "With an emperor, we can crush their power."*
>
> *"And who would this emperor be?" inquired an older samurai. "It is traitorous—they would have our heads for breaking oaths.*
>
> *"Tokugawa broke their oaths first, rattling the gates of morals, bellies void of courage. We live by bushido, but cannot when we war with our own. It's up to us to restore hearts."*

"So, you have been to market! Tell me, isn't it bustling? You can feel its soul."

A soul that had been asleep for years, caged. There had always been doubt, fearing the demons they did not know.

"If we maintain our borders, we can remain at peace," grunted a square-jawed man.

"Nay, partnerships overseas will bring new opportunity. Their ships carry machines that put us to shame," her father assured. "I have already spoken to the Meiji family. They are poised, and ready for the fight to reclaim their rightful place."

The fire sputtered and interrupted her recollection. "It does feel different," said Maru quietly.

Oba-san stirred leaves into her pot, gasping with delight when they sputtered back.

"Is something the matter?"

Maru wasn't sure where to begin. She had been rummaging through memories, loose pages of thoughts, trying to remember when it all went wrong, listening to old conversations she had overheard between her father and his allies.

"Meiji? They twiddle their thumbs—Tokugawa serves them," one man exclaimed.

"Hypothetically. You know the Tokugawa paint lies. Restore Meiji as a true leader, and we will grant him the berth to implement the justice we claw for so bitterly," assured her father.

"And who? The old man? He would be no better. He sits on a throne of gold, waiting to collect the taxes to buy his next meal," an older man protested.

"His son—" her father began.

"A child?!" someone shouted.

The kettle whistled, and Maru lifted herself from the memory to pour the hot water for Oba-san, who waved her hands in protest, surrendering when the tea kissed the cup's rim.

"No word from father Hosokawa?"

Maru looked down. She wanted to come out and ask Oba-san if she knew of his loyalties, thinking back to when her own father was drawing lines in loyalty between the shogun and samurai.

"He has been studying global politics. He wants Sakamoto's constitution. They can send word to clans in the north and south. They can convene an army of loyalists to take on feudal followers."

"Calling us 'loyalists' to a defunct throne will rile the shogunate, who hold the power. We will die on this foolish journey. Takechi, their leader, will evade capture only for so long."

The flames painted new streaks of orange on faces creviced by furrowed brows.

"I was hoping I could find a friend in you, Kira," her father said.

She left her memory and piped up suddenly to Oba-san.

"I saw father's former friend at the ochaya," Maru said. "Do you remember Kira?"

Oba-san clapped her hands, knocking over a tower of miss-matched pots.

"I do not want to be made a fool. Besides, what is to become of us once the shogun falls and we can no longer receive income?" replied Kira.

"Inexcusable! Think! We are hired by commoners for help. They are the ones who have fed us and housed us. When was the last time a shogun lined your pockets with a sliver of his wealth?" her father cried out.

"I wonder why Kira was so adamantly against the idea of the emperor but now serves him," said Maru, recalling his exchange with Kira.

Oba-san's eyes widened. "Your father is persuasive. He must have found the right words."

"But father himself never took a job under the emperor."

"He wants to be with people! Not in a stuffy palace," Oba-san laughed. "He could never give up his travel and savior spirit."

She knew this about him all too well, as he strategized over many late-night fires with friends.

> *"We cannot solve all our differences tonight, but I urge you to consider that this is our time to strike. We must unite, rid ourselves of plagues," her father had pronounced. "I will trek south and find allies. When I return I hope to have friends at my side. I do not want to put my sword through your hearts."*
>
> *Hosokawa's eyes swept the room, locking on Maru.*
>
> *Her mother grabbed her shoulders.* The memory faded.

"I thought more people would be willing to look out for us," Maru whispered. "His travels have become cumbersome. I worry he has a new focus."

"You can rest assured that there isn't another daughter claiming his attention!" Oba-san pinched a piece of the cake, grinning. "This is better than the onsen during snowfall."

"I've been in debt to you," Maru murmured, thinking of the streets bustling with families shopping freely and enjoying the matsuri while her father was away, continuing to pay his own way.

"Family members are never in debt to one another," chided Oba-san.

The emperor's ascension had brought a surge of hope. And surprises. When Meiji enforced conformity "in the name of equality," bodily autonomy and arms went wayside. Her father, covered in stark black depicting mythical battles of giant sea creatures, had to shroud himself, now that it was a crime to be different. He insisted he was proud to relinquish art and his sword in the name of denouncing a violent past and forging a peaceful future. It eased the minds of those who never held a sword. Others followed his lead, and the samurai, as they once were, existed no more.

Meiji then handed swords to farmers and boys: anyone who wanted to be in his army. She remembered how her father had reacted to the news.

> *"No better than ashigaru," her father said, scoffing. "Samurai have skills, but he wants an army loyal to him." He laughed. "Who can blame him? He has no debt to us, no qualms."*

Maru stared at her own cup, still undisturbed.

"Ada-whoever must have instilled in you some lessons! I've never seen you sit so still!"

Maru smiled weakly and took a sip of plum tea that brought her back to life.

"Has the emperor done something so egregious?"

"Eh-what?" Oba-san spilled tea onto her own lap.

"Something that would make someone fear him. Or rebel."

"Ah, the rebellion," Oba-san loudly sipped her tea, almost swallowing her own tongue with it. Seeing Maru's remorseful face made her shake to attention.

"No leader can escape his share of controversy. How can you make any single family happy? Much less a whole land? Meiji's reign is in its juvenile state; men will act accordingly."

A new, nervous energy emerged, as once-peasant neighbors wielded an equality they had never known before. Commoners became scouts who reported to the emperor were once beggars in shanties kicked aside by the shogun, now had respect and trust from an emperor. The people were emboldened; and everyone seemed happy.

And when Meiji built his palace in Edo, renaming the city to Tokyo and claiming Kyoto no longer served him, everyone agreed. Edo had been the seat of power for shogun, and he must take up the throne to prevent them from the returning in a fury.

Tokyo, therefore, became the rising city of the East, the dawn of tomorrow.

And Kyoto unraveled. Maru hardly understood what was happening diplomatically ("Oh Ma-chan, nobody knew what was happening in their palace," said Oba-san), but felt people were tense in the markets and had heard the ebb and flow of movements from her father. She knew their way of life was being overcome by outside ideas threatening to undo the ways they'd always known. But it was for a greater good, an investment, he kept saying.

For her future.

Then Meiji had declared that all must practice Shinto and did away with Buddhism. In school she learned the emperor descended from Shinto sun gods, so the change felt natural.

> *"They need to slaughter the cow, but first they need permission from different kami," her father explained in her memory.*
>
> *"But father, we eat cow already." Her mother made a strangled cry in her throat.*

Maru was afraid to ask what the consequences were to her mortal life of being allowed to eat cow. At night her parents had heated discussions. Maru was unsure why something intangible could worry people. They remained silent as the sky filled with smoke; her favorite temples were charred beyond recognition. There were whispers and pointed fingers everywhere they went. Her mother hid away the symbols of Buddha from their home.

"There are new shrines to pray to. A kami is a kami. They all do the same thing," said Oba-san, putting a bite of cake between Maru's lips, to coax her to eat. She should have been grateful for its sweetness; and could hear her father scold her for not finishing her supper: "We never had such full bowls; we were lucky if our rice didn't have bug legs."

Sweeping away the ashes, the prefectures were stitched together to weave an empire. He was willing to work with his former enemy and shogun. Though leery, her father saw the joy that the prospect of unity brought and remained quiet. Any distrust of leaders dissipated as commoners became grateful for full bellies, roofs, and steady income. That was an exhilarating, addictive power that ceased whispers of revolts.

No dissent had been allowed under the shogun. Now, nobody dreamed of dissent.

Except for the rumors of Saigo's betrayal of the emperor in Satsuma. What would make him so disdained?

"Do they have kami across the ocean?" Maru asked.

"I suppose if they have a boat," said Oba-san.

Her father had excitedly told Maru the emperor promised to retain Japanese beauty and share with the West: fashion, ceramics and traditions were wildly popular abroad. But nobody Maru knew had seen any riches or popularity as the papers had declared would be the result.

"Everyone is enthralled by us. We brought our art to the World Fair, and everyone wants to be us, and to know us."

"Where, Papa?"

"A place called Paris."

Maru remembered he couldn't find it on a map.

Modeled after the West, there were new rules of business operation and employment rights. There was new banking and commerce. A locomotive train. Electricity was coming. Messages that could travel without a horse. Now, voices between homes shouted into a device held by both hands.

"Father once said we were 'behind' the world. Why would our kami hold us back?"

"Because if we were unleashed on the world too soon, we would have burned it down."

And what had been the release down, down, down—when had the arrow been flung from the bow, an unstoppable force, aimed for the target?

And what, or who, wondered Maru, was the target?

And did it have anything to do with Satsuma? And what the fox warned of?

She bid Oba-san goodbye and made her way back to market, idling before returning to the okiya. A shriek made her pause, and a shiver went down her spine. But it was coming from two small children playing at the edge of the river where their father was watching them while he fished.

If her father had gone back to his "samurai ways," as Kira had suspected, it would carry deeper complications. It would be against all she had known of him when she was growing up. To throw away life-long ambitions and rebel against the very emperor he helped to rise to the throne, and all of this—the way the city was building around them, food filling the plates of all, the way she was allowed to go to school, the names her friends bore, were all a gift from his efforts and the daring risks he had taken.

There was no reason for her father to retract all he had determinedly fought for over the years. The rumors of the dangers of the train would become normalized, just as he had dreamed.

And Maru knew she must continue to support him, for the alternative—that it had all been folly, that he had lied to her, was too heavy to bear. He had been her harbor, her lighthouse, her sails. He would have warned her if she should fear all that was around her, as too many commoners did.

> *"But you bankrupt her instincts to have fear when you shut your door," a woman protested.*
>
> *"Because there is nothing to fear. We may have fewer options, but building a new world takes time. Have faith in our emperor as I do."*
>
> *"I see your candle burning for a long time. You cannot yet afford the new gas."*
>
> *"Candles are old friends. Your nose will blacken with curiosity when you get close."*
>
> *"Do you intend to shut me out, too? How will she know who to trust if not her own father? I see the way she looks at the door, unsure if this is the time you won't return."*

Neighbors would destroy him and her family if he turned his back on them.

She would be in danger, even at Adakichi's. She would need to flee, marked as a rebel.

The fisherman flicked his wrist and pulled back on the string, giving something in the water a tug. He was too impatient, she thought. Her father taught her to have an abundance of patience in fishing— "or find something else to do." *What if I am the kitsune's fish?* Maru thought her father would know the answer, and felt her longing for him grow stronger.

She missed his gentle spirit, his endless knowledge, and the safety his presence brought.

"What an unusual name," she heard Fujiwara's voice in her mind. "So masculine, you'd think her father played a joke on her, wishing for a boy."

She was accustomed to people raising their eyebrows. She stuck to her family name in school to evade detection and jokes about being a boy. Her family name was something powerful that overlooked all her flaws. When the emperor held a national Name Day, granting all commoners the right to formally use or change their names publicly, she had wished for a new one. Her father insisted their name gave her power she would need one day. She remembered Kira scoffing, saying people were stealing names they were unworthy of, something her father waved aside. "If anyone wants to be a Hosokawa, let them. May it give them opportunity."

So today she couldn't escape it and hid to avoid questions about her father still being a samurai and feudal sympathizer.

"We have received much from our name, let others choose their fate."

"But what about me?" Maru wailed.

Her father squatted. "Maruya, do you know how your name came to be?"

She wiped her eyes. The other girls had pretty names. All she wanted was to blossom.

"On the horizon, years before you were born, black ships with the tallest sails appeared where the amabie play. They struck fear in the steeliest men and sparked fire in the darkest hearts.

"And you, Maru, are my ship who shares their name. When you were born you arrived at my shore, and shook my life. You drew a final line and closed my circle.

"You will bring a world of change. Your name foretells it."

"Careful! Watch it!" A rickshaw rushed by, with the width of a horse hair between them, nearly sending her tumbling. A young man earnestly shouted "Sorry!" as a stray dog chased its dust.

Maru hurried on, refusing to dawdle more in memories that did nothing but disservice.

She first passed by her favorite bookshop, nodding to the older lady, and a row of men chopping wood aside a leaning building with a circular window that revealed a maple garden. Further on, she approached an art shop selling ukiyo-e made from woodblocks and studied the window to see their new prints.

Pressing her nose to the glass, she saw pieces lined up depicting parades in Edo, new wires crossing across cities in the shadow of a mountain, and another enormous dark machine of some sort.

The sleek black object with a dozen wheels, flanked by horses, rested beneath a red roof with skinny red columns near a lush green riverbank. A castle was in the distance.

"That's the train," the bent-over shopkeeper told her. He was an old man with deep wrinkles in his face. "It's a new one."

Maru stared.

"Impressive, isn't it? The train at Edo Station." He used the word Adakichi and Tomosuke had tried pronouncing! Something about the train seemed eerie. Its yellow lantern stared at her.

"Come in. Looking doesn't cost anything."

She followed him into the damp shop. Its bluish shade was cool. The walls were perspiring, smelling of musk and wet tatami. Tracing her fingers along sheets of curling paper, she waited for one to catch her eye. The man, quietly watching from afar, encouraged questions.

She passed over Kuniyoshi's portrait of three giant, thieving frogs gazing over a landscape of pagodas and ginkgo. She lingered by a series of prints of ghosts, yuurei, and ancestors passing through a torii at night, lanterns on the hillside of Kyoto on fire.

"Obon," he said promptly. She looked up, startled. He nodded toward the woodblock print.

"As we approach the late summer Obon season when we honor our ancestors, yuurei are frequently seen. Whether it is yuurei of their spirits, or dim lights of another shape, or just sheer delusion, we can't be sure. The closer we get to the matsuri when we open up the gates between our world and theirs, we will see the spirits caught in between reaching out. They mean to tell us something; we need to listen."

She studied the rows of silvery-blue figures, limbs limp, passing down the reed-lined stone path. "We will see the spirits reaching out." *Why wouldn't her mother do this?*

She crossed the aisle to a long telescope that stood in a corner, amused to think that the old man, bent perfectly to fit the level of the eyepiece, gazed at stars like the geiko of Gion. On one shelf were prints of star signs and clusters representing the new season.

Her eyes drifted to the another corner, where some prints caught her attention. She walked over and picked up a small portrait of a white fox outside of a shrine gate. It was unusual; she rarely saw kitsune depicted in art pieces, and this one was darkly painted. Most had gold, green and red colors, but this had a dark brown and black wall with the white fox standing in front, wearing a small red collar with something silvery in the collar.

"Pearl," she said suddenly. The man leapt to her side.

"What do you see?"

Maru pointed to the fox in the print. "That thing around its neck that looks like a collar."

"Ah, the pearl of the kitsune. You see them at Inari Shrines."

Maru nodded, although she could not recall this. "What purpose do they serve?" she questioned, realizing her kitsune did not have one. Was it not real?

"Ah, the kitsune like this one is white. You see, this is indicating that it's disguised as something or someone else—but this is good! I don't mean to frighten you," he said. Maru realized her eyes must have widened.

"And the pearl is its soul that is contained. A shapeshifter like the kitsune-fox must keep its soul separate so that it doesn't get trapped in another shape. This is for its protection in case a transformation from one being to another goes wrong."

She frowned. "What about foxes that are golden or orange? And have no pearl?"

"Sounds quite ordinary."

"But they are not evil?"

"We all have a little evil in us," he laughed, nudging her. "Kitsune might not be much different. They're generally auspicious. Maybe this one lost its magic," he mused. "If that is the case, it must not be very powerful. Or it's storing its pearl in something else."

Maru studied the fox, her ears ringing. It seemed alive, like she could stroke it. Feeling braver because she didn't think the man was likely to gossip about the plain girl who walked in to made inquiries, she pressed him more. Maybe the battle with the machine or kami had taken its pearl.

"But they are always mischievous. You must remember this from childhood stories."

"What or who could take its pearl? Where else would it keep its powers? And what kind of power do you have?"

He laughed. "A bombardment of questions! Do I need to call a priest? This kitsune could have something mighty, some power that could outwit the best trickster of them all. I fear what it fears." He stroked the stubble on his chin.

"Have you ever seen one?"

He laughed again. "You are curious! Foxes are common here."

"Have you ever heard of a talking one?"

"No. I would be put down out of mercy if I told someone such a crazy thing."

Maru covered her mouth and smothered a laugh.

He leaned over and whispered, "Your secret is safe with me."

Maru had no response.

"Don't fear this, dear. A kitsune must have chosen you. Many coax someone to make a wish, but few are granted. You must be a marvelous soul indeed."

Maru felt as if her mind had erupted. He patted her on her lower back.

"Please take it with you, as my gift," he said. "It seems you have many things to consider. Perhaps this will help you."

She left his shop, her hands shaking as she clutched the portrait. Outside it had become even hotter. She felt dizzy as she searched for a yatai offering melons that would quench her thirst.

Heading down one of the main roads, she was taken aback by the view. She saw what looked like tall, naked trees lining the road and jutting into the sky. They were as black as night, and odd looking black and silver strings hung from each one.

Throngs of people passing by eyed the tall columns and grimaced, making an effort to avoid walking beneath the long strings. An impassioned woman shouted, gesturing frantically at the columns and warning of plagues. Nobody paid the old woman any mind, but a policeman approached, waving his finger in her face until she quieted down.

Maru looked along the yatai of vegetables, the river at the end, small houses beyond, and a torii nestled in some nooks. It was the Kyoto she had known. Ahead, the scenery changed, as if she had walked into another city. The symmetry of the buildings was dismantled; stone clashed with bamboo. The river forked into several disjointed paths. Darkened factory towers leered closer.

Something—a smell like sour meat—twisted her stomach, pushing her away.

She heard a hammering ahead of her. Men were moving sand; others sloshing barrels of water with their many arms. She leapt out of their way. They were singing along without a single care about the towering poles with the strange black and silver strings that blocked the sun.

Protestors shouted and held banners saying in red: "*Wires choke Kyoto in sickness.*" Maru stared at the wires strung up on the foreboding poles, and remembered the rumors of the plague. Was everyone falling ill because of them, as the protestors claimed? Satori and Mihiro had said so, as Tomosuke had relayed to their ochaya. But Kira had waved his hand away . . . she knew who she wanted to trust: her family friend, once-upon-a-time.

She pulled the fox portrait closer to her chest, staring in amazement at what was unfolding and fascinated by the men's conversation.

"It's an absolute disgrace. It will send everyone into a tizzy."

"The emperor must help us."

"How can he help us, when people inside his own palace disappear?"

Maru started to hear other voices of middle-aged women in their iki kimono frowning at the road and tilting their parasols so they could get a good view.

"The price we pay! We fear for our daughters!"

"Such ugliness will destroy our city."

Fear crept into her heart. She wondered what her father would say—if this would excite him or if he would be critical of their opinions.

The men methodically drove their wagons and wheelbarrows, attaching bricks to walls, digging big holes, hoisting the columns, and stringing the silver from pole to pole. Transfixed,

Maru heard her father's voice echo in her head. This was the change that would make them equal with the world.

That memory wrapped her in warmth, assuring her this was supposed to happen. Still, she shuddered, smacking her lips, tasting something tangy, sour, bitter and sharp. *Was it the blood?* Did it have anything to do with the kitsune's beast?

Whispers broke her memory-wandering. Eyes of passersby looked away. Did they recognize her? Had Fujiwara spread a rumor of her father across the city? She felt as if something was throttling her, and as she tried to leave, she spotted delicate Ai, twirling her aburagami parasol.

"Ai!" she rushed to the familiar face, seeking solace in the confusion that gripped her.

"Mm? Ah, Maru-chan—you shouldn't run like that. You don't want to catch their eyes."

"Oh . . . yes." She made herself smaller.

"I say this for your sake." Ai smiled sweetly.

They lingered in each other's gaze, a quiet judgment holding their conversation hostage. Maru took the plunge first.

"You bought something new today?"

"Ah, this. The emperor is supplying prominent families with their own telegraph." She uncovered shiny silver pieces inside her crane-painted box and scrolls of messages alongside them. Maru could not make sense of the scattered pieces.

"How does it work?"

"Well, this doesn't work in its current state. It needs to be assembled, of course."

"Ah, of course," Maru echoed, without the slightest clue of what she was talking about.

"Then, we can send a message through taps to another shrine or to the emperor himself. We are privileged to have direct access, naturally."

Maru managed to nod through her daze and discomfort.

"Wasn't this what the emperor was hosting a lottery for?"

"Ah, yes, for commoners to apply. And for telephones which were imported this summer, which we applied for. You could, too, but there may be more winter before you."

Telegraph? Telephone? She couldn't tell the difference. But she didn't want to appear to have the intelligence of a rock in front of Ai. Her heart pounded, and she stumbled. She wondered if her clan might also be granted such machines.

"Yes, that is impressive," she said.

And then she saw them.

In a doorway over Ai's right shoulder, peeking beneath a noren, was a pale face of a small girl with her mouth agape. Her eyes looked black. When Maru opened her mouth to speak, she saw another girl closer to her own age. She stared at the black-eyed girl who looked very frightened.

Maru instinctively made a move to approach the girl to pull her away, but her steps were unsteady.

Ai asked her, "Have you fallen ill? There is a contagious cough going around in the East. You should have said something if this is what is wrong."

Maru pulled away from her. A putrid, stinging smell was filling her nose.

The older girl opened her mouth as if she might scream. Maru saw a blackened, toothless mouth. She began to run to the bridge where she stood.

"Ai, watch out!" She screamed.

Ai called out to her, "You shouldn't act so strange; it's scaring me."

"Look at her!" Maru shouted. The older girl grasped the bridge banister as Maru rushed toward her. The small girl peered over the ledge. A whistle screeched on the horizon.

"No! Stop!" Maru reached out to hold her back, but the little girl leapt, flinging her body into the air. She was immobile, suspended like a puppet and held up by the wind until a blackened arm jutted up from the water, grabbed her ankles and pulled her into the river. She disappeared beneath the ripples without so much as a wave stirred.

"Help! Help!" Maru rushed to the bridge's ledge. Several men rushed forward, throwing off their robes and suits. Maru pointed to the river, flailing her arms helplessly.

"She was taken away into the water. Please help her!"

The men dove in, frantically diving below the surface Maru had pointed to, searching the depths of the reeds. From the bridge Maru watched intently, looking for signs of her. Some men in the river were waist deep with their nets, shouting at each other, pulling river weeds, and chasing children away so they could search.

The other girl with the blackened eyes was also gone, and the shop's noren was undisturbed. Maru kept her eyes on the water, hoping the young one would emerge. But minutes later the men in the river hadn't found her, either. For a while they continued to look for clues with the the help of Maru and the onlookers, but it seemed the girl was lost.

Maru slowly retuned to Ai, who was unconvinced by what she'd seen. Had she steered them wrong? What if nobody had been there at all?

It had seemed as real as Ai standing behind with her telephone box.

"I saw them," Maru told Ai absently. She was trying to convince herself of her truth. "I saw the girls behind you."

Ai turned around, then back to Maru. She was perplexed. "Do you mean that fox? Is there something wrong with you?"

A fox with shining fur bounded behind a warm-slatted shinise.

Ai told her, "It's best if I leave now, but do take care of yourself." Her box clanked as she passed by.

It was just as well. The men who were drenched from searching the river were glowering at her. She hadn't meant to send them on a fruitless search, but she needed to leave before the terrible truth came out—one she could barely admit to herself.

That these girls would do such a thing—

She pivoted back to the road to Gion, staying off the main path to avoid detection. She almost ran into Fujiwara, who was drunk and apparently boasting about some business venture to anyone who'd listen as they basked in the steam of a corner noodle shop. Her bones began to jitter.

Was he on his way to antagonize a girl?

She stayed to watch him repeat a story in wild gestures as if he were performing a kabuki all on his own. The audience was entertained, even enamored with his tale. She couldn't possibly relate to it. She was always exasperated by his exaggerated tales and his inability to fulfill his promises.

She saw him check a pocket watch and suddenly turn down a street. Maru felt she must follow him.

As the girls had followed her.

He was a peculiar man, after all. Maybe he would know something of the missing girls. With all the business he did and people he knew, why wouldn't he?

She remained a good distance back from Fujiwara. Crowds with their hair done-up for the evening passed between them. She kept her eyes fixed on the way Fujiwara swayed. His whistling made her skin tingle; old nightmares roared into her vision.

Perhaps he could be conjuring her terror. He fit the part when he terrorized their ochaya.

The girls' empty eyes gripped her heart.

But he headed for Shimabara, the side of Hanamachi she never visited. Oiran, gambling houses, and groups rumored to be cults met there. How fitting. She was glad that Adakichi did not allow her to go there; one of the few rules she agreed with. Her mind was on fire.

The wails of the mothers.

Maru saw the golden hue of billowing clouds and realized the afternoon was aging. She had to hurry! Disembodied shouts accompanied her as she rushed to the ochaya; each cry was a reminder that she might be losing her sanity and was frightfully alone. When she felt a stitch in her side, she slowed her pace and realized she'd discarded the fox ukiyo-e at the bridge where the girl jumped. There was a frenzy ricocheting in her body with every step.

There hadn't been a splash.

But it was already evening, and she hated the idea of waiting to see what lurked in the shadows. In tales when yuurei were bold enough to emerge in broad daylight, the night would bring even worse horrors. She wouldn't fall a victim to this. She regretted that she couldn't chase after Fujiwara and couldn't help the girls this night.

But they're not girls, Maru finally admitted. She slowed to a stop.

They're ghosts.

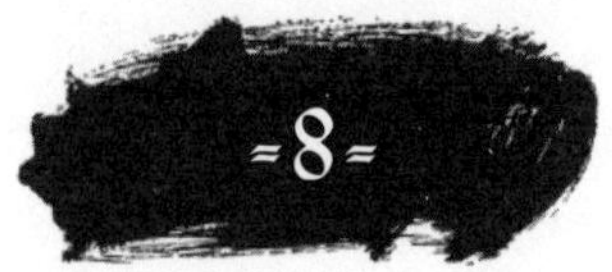

8

As the moon waned into rebirth, Maru was unsure of how to describe all she had seen. She put ink to her pages and tried her best to leave her emotions and the ghosts on paper, aching from the burden they bore in her mind. She was afraid of the consequences of relating her experiences to her ochaya companions. Adakichi and Mitsu were excited about their choreography and were absorbed in the promises of the emperor—all of the good things that were to come and might be announced at the matsuri. She had to keep her problems to herself. She tucked her pages between folded robes in her closet, lest Mitsu find her deranged rants and have her cast out and left destitute.

At one particularly ambitious dinner, Maru chewed slowly. Instead of feeling proud of her cooking talents, she felt a sadness rooted too deep to grasp and yank out of her soul. She should be excited to see the future unfold, but realized that imagining her father would receive the news well was unrealistic. After all, she was seeing ghosts! She feared if she brought up the subject, the outcry would tarnish the upcoming celebrations. And eventually her father would need to find out she had encountered demons. Imagining his reaction consumed her.

She couldn't help thinking she had rejected the fox too forcefully. The man in the print shop had tried to quell her fears. But if she had been chosen, and turned her back on a trickster, would it guarantee she'd have bad luck and misfortune? Was the yuurei who entered her life part of the trick? Was it really a disguise for somebody else?

But maybe the fox would never return. He might receive help from someone else. Even if it approached her again, how she could help it to defeat a demon or save others was beyond her.

And if the ghosts are around forever, she would need the fox's help.

"Rice doesn't need to be hunted," Adakichi told her. Maru straightened her posture and tried to shake her consuming thoughts.

She had pangs of envy when she was with Mitsu and Adakichi. They were allowed to be focused on their roles. Everything about their lives seemed so simple. The maiko was set on her path to becoming a geiko, and Adakichi, by retaining her status, had a lifelong history of entertaining the highest caliber of men. Neither of them struggled with the tragedy of missing family members or fears about politics and the transformation of their neighborhood. And neither of them had a strange relationship with a talking fox.

But she couldn't shake the feeling that everything happening all at once meant she was missing something she couldn't remember.

Maru finished her dinner, but her hunger remained.

She berated herself for being too scattered. She was a bag of marbles rolling everywhere. She needed a time of calm. Stepping into the back pantry with the washing bucket, she let the darkness of the room soothe her. Here she was away from the chatter and her fear of the flurry of arrows aimed at her.

Washing the dishware gave her something methodical to busy her hands. It helped to wash away her thoughts.

under the cool surface of the water
submerging her arms deeper and deeper . . .
she heard a call to dive in
as if she was plunging into a void
blocking out all sound and sight

A yellow eye opened. She heard a whistle. No, it was a scream.

"Mayuki!"

She came back to life. The water scared her, the way it flirted with her, trying to pull her in, and how she almost accepted its invitation.

She walked into the sitting room and saw that Mitsu had her fan out. She was kneeling beside Adakichi, mimicking her slight twists, rippling it through the air like the surface of the water.

"Smoother, gentler; yes, start the tilt as soon as you're ready. That's right, now slower, slower . . ."

Maru watched in silence as Mitsu perfected her technique and then stood and suspended her limbs, rotating on covered feet like a doll. Maru could never do that, regardless of Adakichi's knack for training talent.

"Bring your arms up sideways, the same time as your back. You're coming up with your back first. Your arms look weak. There. There you go."

Mitsu followed Adakichi, sweeping her arms wide, side to side, as if she were helping grass grow taller. Maru thought they must be taking one of the spring dances and adding in elements from the Ocean Day dances.

"Then stand at the end and put your arms up with the fan. Hmm, maybe it would be better if the fan is in front, not too high."

She asked Maru, "How does it look?"

"Well, it is mixing two styles, Kitano and Kamogawa, but—"

"Is it no good?"

"Not at all. I was trying to explain—" She flinched, afraid of being bruised again.

Adakichi seemed too distressed to raise a hand in violence, waving her words aside instead. "With her naming ceremony this fall, this should be a prelude to attract interest in attending."

Maru responded, "Then maybe something more unusual would be good, something they won't expect."

"These dances are predictable, yet some audiences may not realize it is replicated from the spring dances," replied Adakichi with disdain in her voice.

Maru looked out the window as if she expected the fox to be peering in and tilted her head, trying to exude cleverness.

"What about the Kitsune Dance?" she whispered.

Adakichi answered, "But then her face would be covered by a fox mask: This would be bad for business."

"What if there was a twist with a reveal?" pressed Maru, not giving up.

Adakichi knit her brows. "It could be enticing to have the anticipation of wondering who it is."

The two immersed themselves in the routine until Adakichi was comfortable enough to add music. "Mayuki, could you take the shamisen?"

Maru paused.

"I forgot. Mitsu, can you please do this." Adakichi brushed off her mistake without another thought.

Maru's chest released her tension, but she remained still, staring at the place where the instrument sat long after Mitsu picked it up and brought it to Adakichi. Her body tingled. She was dismayed that she almost reached out willingly. With one small move she would have surrendered the disciplines she had respected and abided by her whole life. It was as if she faced the same battle her father did when he relinquished his samurai sword. Yet, in the back of her mind she couldn't help hearing Mitsu call her "spoiled" and wonder if it was time to disregard some of her traditions.

"Would you fetch the leaflets?" asked Adakichi softly, breaking Maru's trance. "And the mask."

Walking into the open foyer, Maru passed a display of Adakichi's most prized robes. She then entered the large dark den with her dim lamp. Maru held a candle flame to the shelves until she found the Kitsune sheet music.

She knew the exact number of steps to take across the floor before she reached Adakichi's mask collection.

The mahogany case had row after row of shelves with notable faces from all types of stories. Some were Noh or Kabuki. There were laughing men, snarling demons, curved grimaces of feudal lords, childish grins, bulging eyes. They always gave her the shivers, even in their lifeless silence. She sensed they were carefully watching her.

Shining brightly at the end of the rows was the fox mask.

When she picked it up, she thought she felt a small sting. When she held the flame over it to gaze into its empty eyes, a pair of yellow eyes blinked at her. She gasped and dropped the mask. She heard it scamper across the floor as if it had legs.

"No!" she screamed. This wasn't real. She had just imagined it. It was the way the flame flickered that confused her. It was only a mask. *Masks don't move on their own volition,* she told herself.

She held out the light carefully, trying to ignore her shaking arm. She was afraid to look.

But there, facedown, in the middle of the floor it rested. Sighing, she tenderly picked it up and turned it over.

She saw nothing.

The room breathed with her. She rushed out to the foyer, no longer willing to wait for something else to happen. She had always hated that room that was perpetually in limbo. As everyone carried on with their lives, it remained stagnant and neglected, collecting dust and attracting spirits who knew they wouldn't be disturbed.

In the sitting room she polished the fox mask while her mind drifted in and out, mesmerized by the fluidity of Mitsu's dancing and the steady chords of music. She hardly noticed when they concluded their practice, but she noted the worn-out gas lamps were giving off puffs of sea-air. They used the cheaper fish oil when they had no patrons for the evening, saving the expensive aromatics for their guests.

"If only we had that 'infinite fire,'" Mitsu chuckled. "I could have danced and danced."

"We can pray for good fortune to have it soon," said Adakichi. "Proceed with caution. A few years ago we only served clients in the daytime to save oil; let us adjust step by step."

Maru mulled over the reality of the blackened barren trees jutting into the sky and the silver strings crossing through the air, weaving through the streets. She wondered how soon they'd be right outside the teahouse, changing their landscape forever, all for the purpose of turning on a light inside. And how often would all of their lives change, once again? "May I step out?" she asked her okaasan.

"Yes, but do not go out of sight of this window," said Adakichi sternly.

She'd never been asked to stay in her sight but didn't dwell on the matter.

The street was still and soaked with honey under the lamplights, and she was an imposter, unwelcome in this section of Gion at night. She crept to the brush that lined the creek and leaned against the bamboo fence to gaze at the gentle waters below, their quiet, comforting laughter awakening at her appearance. The gossip of frogs and cicadas resumed once they grew accustomed to her presence, and before long she felt she was just another statue trying to survive the night.

She folded her arms. She would wait to see if the fox arrived. It was beginning to dawn on her that she *did* want it to reappear. She felt she had a received a call to something. It seemed unexplainable, but undeniable that she received signs from the movement of the stars above.

But nothing had moved; no eyes appeared again. Had she been too abrasive? She was not entirely convinced that she hadn't made it all up. She had wished so much for something to give her hope.

Pointing her nose to the air amidst the damp earthy tones, she caught a scent of a pungent floral perfume—something she usually smelled near Ponto-cho or when older men passed by on their way home under the moon. She glanced about, ready to rush into the teahouse if she saw unwanted company.

But there near the bridge were two small figures in deep conversation. One of the girl's faces was obscured by her long hair hanging over her face. The other looked pale and worried. Their sudden appearance made her nervous. They couldn't have been there longer than her. Were they yuurei?

She crept closer, trying to catch what they said. But they spoke with their lips barely moving. She was meters away when one of them abruptly turned and floated away silently. Maru's heart quickened when the other noticed her.

"Oh! Kiku!" she said, greeting her friend who reeked of perfume and tobacco.

"It's so late," cooed Kiku. "I feel damp and sticky, like mochi is stuck to my armpits."

Maru laughed. "Who was that girl?" She gestured toward the alley where she had vanished, feeling both curious and jealous of the company she kept without her.

"Hmm?" Kiku shrugged. "Oh, just another working girl. From our school actually."

Maru moved on. "The candles are still burning at Adakichi's. We were selected for the parade."

"We saw the announcement. My madam is furious," said Kiku, grumbling.

"Aren't you selected to march in it, too?"

"Yes, we are, which is part of the problem. Not all geiko want to be associated with Adakichi at the parade," Kiku said. "It's petty, if you ask me."

"But really, is it so bad to be provincial? It was good that she threw out the maiko who caused the trouble last year."

"Oooh, don't let others hear you say that," said Kiku, almost laughing. "Don't worry. You'll soon recover your business. Gion just needs a new scandal to talk about."

"Fujiwara is one of our only clients. He's so, you know, uncouth and loud." Maru scrunched her face.

"Any man who pays is a good client."

"That's one of our predicaments. He barely pays what he owes. The vases are dry and the fabric account is being run up; it often goes unpaid except in words. He's not a good client if he isn't helping our income and status and drags in his degenerate friends."

"Everyone is a leech," sighed Kiku. "Even the nobles. What are they performing, anyway?"

Maru paused, knowing geiko always proudly guarded their secrets. But Kiku was her best friend, and her eyes were inviting a confidence, her lips sparkling in the starlight. "The Kitsune Dance," she conceded.

"Ooh, interesting," said Kiku. "So that's what has been keeping Mitsu so busy. And you'll be in the performance?"

"'I'm an executive assistant of the ochaya,'" Maru said proudly, wanting to impress her and make her laugh.

But Kiku scoffed at this. "As if Adakichi could hire other help. Most maiko are already booked by other ochaya." Maru's heart fell.

"Have you heard from your father?"

"No. But I've been wondering about his situation. I met one of his old samurai partners, who—well—cast some doubts. What if he's not stopped—" Maru took a deep breath. "What if the rumors are true, and he's still acting like a samurai?"

"And working against the emperor? After he helped him ascend to the throne?"

Maru twisted her lips.

"I don't know. It doesn't make sense. It's rather a feeling I have. Don't you think the city has been strange lately? People mention they notice a rancid smell. And everyone is always whispering! My gut tells me something is very wrong, but I can't discern what it is."

"Our gut informs us of things all of the time."

"Yours, too?"

"Naturally. Where do you think our regrets are born?"

Maru became quiet.

"Listen, your father said he'd return. He's now a reputable businessman. Sure, there are some rumors. Our speculation was in jest. I don't think he's doing anything to harm you. He's making a name for himself without a sword. Is there reason to doubt he wouldn't continue fulfilling his contracts?"

Maru shifted uncomfortably, waiting for the creek to whisper an answer to her. "No. It's not that I think he's involved in something terrible."

"There's nothing to worry about. Your imagination runs wilder the longer he's not around. He used to go away when you were younger, remember?"

"The circumstances seem different now."

"Oh, you mean in the south? Don't mind them; it's old men wanting life to be exciting again."

Kiku seemed so confident that Maru couldn't help feeling more positive.

"Do you trust your father, or do you trust slimy old men who always have an agenda born from their pants?"

Maru almost smiled, thinking perhaps she was being silly.

"The war ended years ago," said Kiku, shifting. "He has his head on straight, unlike some who live in the memories of their past years filled with bloodshed. Your father conceded that he wanted to change. Remember how excited you were on the day the war ended?"

Maru did recall going to bed with Tokugawa in charge and awakening to the news that the Meiji family was on the throne. Her father had triumphantly come home, scooping her up, saying their lives would be different. They would be on their own with the freedom to choose what they wished to do instead following orders at the whim of the shogun, and paying taxes to the daimyo.

Happiness radiated from him. When he picked her up in his strong arms, she felt as if nothing in the world could hurt them again.

"Don't overthink this. Keep your determination."

"I'm not sure how to summon any now."

"No one is given the recipe, but we all find the ingredients along the way," Kiku swatted at a mosquito, triumphantly grinning at its squished body.

Maru was in the mood to surrender her doubts. Her heart soared into the night air, flying up to the dark tapestry dotted with stars. *But did she deserve it?* Mitsu's bitter words, bruises by Adakichi's hand, and whispers in the street pinned her back down.

"Kiku . . . am I . . . spoiled?"

Kiku gave out a snort, but when she saw Maru's pleading eyes, she sighed and offered, "You are many things, but I'd call Ai spoiled before I'd say that about you."

The embers in her chest glowed, and she dropped the subject. The pages of poetry she had written, mulling over those feelings now felt silly as Kiku snapped her fingers and made them disappear in a few reassuring words.

"Listen, did you hear about that missing girl?"

"Which one?" Maru thought of the woman at the palace, the girls wandering alone. She wondered if Kiku knew of them. "Have they found them? I think I saw one." She couldn't mention that she thought they had once been girls and were now yuurei.

"They suspect a kidnapping, so you should stay close to home."

"I can defend myself just fine," said Maru, instinctively touching her flower-cutting tanto under her obi. She thought about Mitsu and her threats. She would need more than missing eggs to hold over her head. She intended keep her distance from Mitsu. "Uhm, what do you know about Mitsu?"

Kiku looked ready to respond, but something caught her eye. "Unless your second floor is haunted, I think Adakichi is watching us. You'd better go."

Sure enough. She saw Adakichi standing in the window, looking down.

"You'll return too?"

"Night isn't over yet," said Kiku with a weak smile. Maru wasn't sure what she meant but knew she wouldn't get any more details at this time.

Just on cue, the gas lamp in on street went out and unleashed a darkness Maru remembered from childhood when her mother kept her inside after sunset. "*You cannot trust beings that rely on the dark to hide*," she told her.

Her father had argued, *"The worst are those who pretend to be your friend in the sun."*

The door opened. Maru paused. Was Adakichi beckoning her inside or about to threaten to hit her?

It was neither. It was Mitsu. She quickly slid the door shut and rushed away, barefoot and carrying her geta, with only illumination from the stars to guide her. She was like a rabbit.

Maru's nostrils flared. Who was Mitsu to run out the door under night's hot breath, while Adakichi kept her within sight of the window?

Another panic surged its great wave against her cliffside: had she overheard her and Kiku speaking of her father? Would she run off and sell the information outing her identity?

If Mitsu was to be a rabbit tonight, Maru would be the fox.

She abandoned her fear of being punished by Adakichi's hand or the iron kettle. She tucked her geta under her arm and raced after her. Her robes seemed to turn into wings that carried her on a summer breeze over the dewy streets.

If girls are being kidnapped, I'm doing this for her safety, Maru rationalized. Mitsu can't be the next victim.

This determination must be born from a protectiveness instilled in her.

The star-dusted trail kept Mitsu's heels in her sight; the long hikizuri of her kimono and a glittering print of a dragon breathing petals on her darari obi flew behind her, catching the eyes of shadows that awoke.

Maru felt her senses ring alive; the shadows slithered, snakes in pursuit at their flanks. Somewhere, a temple bell rang, signaling true nightfall. She ran faster, now fearful about what would happen if they caught her or Mitsu. The tanto pressed into her robes, jostling with each beat against the stone, reminding her it was there.

They were taking the alley where the backsides of ochaya faced them. Scenes of drinking, loud music, and games were flying by—stories unfolding as the night wore on—glimpses into worlds that weren't their own and the lives of people unaware of the chase ensuing out their covered windows.

But at last, Mitsu turned in front of the small shrine on the road that forked at the end of Hanamachi. The moon's smile grazed the statuette's eyes inside, following Maru as she tore after her, silently judging her decisions.

Shield us, she prayed.

And Mitsu took her down a surprising path, past the leaning-shanty teahouses and ryokan where travelers rested weary bones and right into Shimabara. At the red gate, where the bright lanterns cast their bloody light into the alleys and up the darkened doorways guarding the pleasure chambers, Maru came to a screeching halt. The shadows on either side scampered up gingko branches, leering down at her. Mitsu made her way around a corner and was now out of sight.

Wasn't this Shimabara, where the oiran worked? It never occurred to her that Mitsu would go there. Adakichi forbade it. The emperor didn't allow inter-district fraternizing. She could be ostracized and exiled for this.

Was she visiting a lover? It wasn't unheard of for a maiko to have a lover until marriage or public love forced their retirement. But meeting someone here was shocking. *Was she moonlighting as an oiran to earn more wages, as the maiko before her did, who was then pushed out and ruined? Was Mitsu really risking her career and involving Adakichi in scandal again?*

She realized it was not worth knowing her secret. She was afraid her association with it would cause her to be cast out, too.

But she had to watch over Mitsu.

She took a few steps further, acutely aware that creatures were gathering on the rooftop; faces with darkened eyes were lining up on the edges of the roof.

"We will see the spirits reaching out." Maru recalled the shopkeeper saying. *"We need to listen."* What were they saying, by being there, watching her? Were they warning her? Or perhaps protecting her, as she had prayed?

Focusing her gaze on the way ahead, she brought her robes closer. She heard the squawking of cicadas, and a dim candle in a window was flickering.

She was sure the chochinobake was there.

"Ma—ru!" someone called out.

The cicadas stopped their rhythmic ticking. The pounding in her ears beat louder, and louder.

Mitsu needed her help. She drew the tanto from her obi as she approached the corner.

She heard voices.

She pushed against the edge of the handle of the tanto. The red lantern's glow was on her left. The darkness on her right seemed to hover over her to protect her naivety and conceal the truth.

Clutching the tanto handle in her palm, she closed her eyes and counted Three, Two, One, spun around the handle edge, and brandished the blade into the darkness. But in the light of her lantern, she saw she was in a small alley littered with crates, old tools, discarded vases, and broken lamps.

No one was there.

But when she recovered her tanto, she heard someone whisper *"Ma . . . ru."*

She stepped into the whispers and held the tanto out in front of her.

"Fight!" she heard someone shout.

The voices were getting louder. She crept by, looking inside a row of windows. The sound of a strangled scream came from her left. She heard a woman giggle and the voice of a man hushing her. The woman teased him back. Maru breathed deeply.

"Ma—ru!" she heard again.

Shadows and sounds of footsteps scampered on roofs overhead. It seemed a trap had been designed to catch her.

She stopped at the end of the block, facing a building without lanterns. She hesitated before carefully taking one step after another until she was almost at the edge of the row of windows where the voices spoke words she couldn't discern, in a tongue she didn't recognize.

The last window was broken. She'd be able to see inside. Her heart was beating loud enough to give her position away. It was now or never; the shadows were turning into a small army poised on the roof, watching her in anticipation.

She spun to face the window and pointed her knife.

And there was a woman. Mitsu! And a man. Fujiwara!

Both stared at her in shock. A thin, silvery crescent of light showed the curves of their noses. There was no mistaking who they were.

"Ma—ru, fight back!" she heard.

She saw Fujiwara's mouth open and keep opening. It stretched wider and wider until his entire head was a huge mouth. His teeth were growing longer and longer and oozing a black substance that dripped onto the stone road.

Mitsu's piercing yellow eyes blazed at her, blinding her. She stumbled backward, crying out, as long, white, spidery hands grasped the edge of the windowsill and the creature pulled itself out, reaching its arms out for her. But Maru was frozen in place.

In a burst of light, an orange shape leapt from the shadows. It was the fox!

It sprang on the outstretched hand and bit it. The demon recoiled in a mangled cry, its skin melting from its face into a fleshy maroon mess before it evaporated into blackened dust in the air.

"Run!" shouted the fox.

She ran without looking back with the fox's golden tail leading the way and the shadows jeering as she sprinted to the ochaya. Her geta was left in a heap under the demon's window.

Apparitions rose all around her. Voices came from above. Her father's mangled cry echoed from the mountains. Arms reached out, grabbing at her sleeves. She saw the shapes of the girls when their black shimmering figures blocked her path. But she pressed on, racing through the ghosts of time, waving away the luring voices and shapes before they consumed her.

At her door she bent over, gasping, before turning to talk to the fox. But it was gone.

The indoor lamps were out, so she put herself to bed alone in the darkness. She was too tired to wonder if Adakichi would punish her for wandering too far, and without permission. She gathered the courage to open her bamboo shades to let in the last rays of moonlight and attempted to find peace in the remaining hours of the night. She thought of the story of Princess Kaguya from the moon and breathed out the pain and sadness that wound around her body like ivy.

What if she became the next ghost?

Maybe a few weeks before this, the idea would have been inviting. She had longed to float away, to be where her mother was if she could not be with her father. But now the embers in her chest had ignited into a flame, spurred by Kiku's encouragement on the heels of encountering the yokai.

She had been so close to finding out the truth about the beast that harmed the fox and was possibly the reason for the girls' disappearance and bringing ghosts out of shadows. But all she did was dismantle her beliefs. Her father's words swirled with the other voices harping on what she should do—stand up straight, hide her real self, become a different person, behave properly, conceal her family name and her past. She had bent closer to the earth, her face in the mud, drowning from the pressure to be someone else.

In between hearing the echoes of their opinions, she whispered prayers for the safety of the fox, thanking it again and again. She became enthralled with a driving ambition. Although she had sent the creature away, she wanted nothing more than to see it again.

9

But in the days that followed, the fox did not visit her, and Maru's hopes diminished. It was a familiar pattern; the letdown pulled her under, and the current was stronger this time. The loss struck a nerve even Adakichi couldn't find a way to hurt.

In between the shock of the encounter with Mitsu and Fujiwara—or the shadows of themselves—and coming to terms with the possibility of residing with a demon, she was forced to go through the motions of daily upkeep. She swept in the morning, washed down the floors, took more lessons from Adakichi to learn the practices of serving tea (riddled with raps on the back of her unsteady hands), and put in requests with Chiki for new robes.

"Are you using Fujiwara's account?" Chiki asked.

Maru affirmed that the ochaya was using it, wondering if he was who he claimed to be. Chiki shook her head, muttering something about the unreliability of man. She handed Maru the latest "magazines," the loose booklets cycled each season to present new kimono styles. Maru was avidly leafing through them and recoiled when Mitsu came and snatched them away.

When Mitsu appeared after her night near Shimabara, she looked like her normal self. And when Maru's eyes lingered on her too long, studying her to find cracks to reveal her disguise, Mitsu shooed her away.

Maru knew kitsune were tricksters, but to what end? If Mitsu was a demon herself, what would she have wanted from her or done to her if she had stayed with her? She was embarrassed how hastily she had followed Mitsu somewhere that turned out to be dangerous. Why had she been so foolish and reckless? If Mitsu hadn't been there, she wondered if she would be a shadow lingering in a temple garden today.

She was certain nobody would believe her if she said she had seen a yuurei. She needed to take greater care about what she told people. There was a chance the kitsune was truly counting on her.

Day after day, more electricity poles were erected, blackening the sky and replacing the beautiful juniper bonsai. As Kyoto evolved into the progressive city her father defended, many were afraid of what the future would bring, expressing their fears both in hushed undertones and loud protests outside Koji's gates. How could people be so upset with the emperor that they would take their grievances to his gates and risk retribution? Amidst the commotion, red buildings rose brick by brick, and a train screamed into Kyoto almost every night.

In the early fog, there were fewer deer and tanuki. She remembered the kitsune's words about the increasing violence in their world. But perhaps the animals were all avoiding the heat.

She didn't forget her conversation with Kiku, either. She prayed for the fox and her father—and for everyone.

Tane visited a shrine with her one misty morning under a peach-colored sky. Maru couldn't help observing the cicadas and frogs were fighting to be heard over the churning and clanging of the factories on the other side of town. The sun was orange behind the smoke.

"Kiku said you were showing interest in taking revenge. We believe a banishment of such thought might help," Tane coughed, covering her nose with a handkerchief. The smell of blood was strong. "We know a good shrine to go to for such a ritual," she added.

Mitsu. Maru had to concoct a defense against the maiko. But now she saw Tane's fear in her eyes—and hurried to explain herself.

"If you're worried it was something I would have done against you, please understand—"

"Oh, of course not!" Tane said quickly.

They crossed the boardwalk through the pond covered by giant lilies. Frogs were leaping from one flower to the next. Maru couldn't help imagining pushing Mitsu beneath their massive leaves, her body not to be found until winter when her shocked face was frozen behind nature's glass, and she'd never worry again about Mitsu telling Fujiwara her secrets.

Out in the markets, dozens of girls ambled through the shops, baskets under arms.

"Why are there so many outside today? Where are the boys?" asked Maru.

"Oh, Maru! The decree board said it was necessary to remove some girls from school," Tane replied.

Maru had checked the decree board daily, only to see more boasts of progress and nothing of Satsuma and nothing about missing girls. There were never any answers. But everyone in the city was talking about them and how none had been found—not even a trace. This gave her reassurance that the emperor was finally taking action.

Maru asked, "Was this done to protect them?"

"No. It was to . . . well, to encourage motherhood," stammered Tane.

They both knew it wasn't common for people to go missing, but sometimes people moved away to start a new life, often to escape from abuse or avoid paying a debt. But it was unusual for so many young girls to vanish in a short span of time.

"Some are being recruited to work for the factories," Tane added quickly.

But that didn't explain the wails in the night that kept her awake.

Maru was certain there was a perpetrator. Fear of being ostracized, especially when she was trying to conceal her identity, kept her from speaking up. And she had visions. If people knew she could see the girls, perhaps the very girls who were disappearing, she would become suspect number one.

Fujiwara, who Maru was beginning to suspect was a ghost because of how often he came to their teahouse, stopped by as a slim crescent moon appeared in the evening sky. This was the first time he had visited since she saw a yuurei shaped like him. When she jumped up nervously to greet him, he laughed and pinched her behind. There was certainly nothing different about his behavior.

Flanking him were two elderly gentlemen nearing the end of their lives. She assumed they had stepped down—or had been overthrown—from the former shogunate and wanted one more ceremony before their spirits departed.

Fujiwara and his company enjoyed Mitsu's stories, laughing uproariously at all the right times, thanks to her cleverly calculated cadence and rhyming. Maru thought their intimacy was something she never wanted to know. Her blood simmered at the thought of Mitsu getting away with sneaking out at night and getting all the attention. It was a demonstration of demon behavior.

"Kami will use their power to bring us daylight at night," remarked one of the balding gentlemen.

In true Maru fashion, she couldn't recall his name, and found this unfortunate. Two former daimyo would harbor great resentment toward her family for being Imperial sympathizers who helped dismantle their power a few years ago. The Boshin War her father led resulted in their fall. She would have to tread carefully as they spoke of the electric lamp.

"But what if it means we never sleep well?" remarked the other white-haired man. He looked dignified in his dark robes as he sipped his rice wine.

"Matsuma, we already hardly sleep because the train interrupts our slumber!"

"But imagine this, Fujiwara, if you will. When will the city rest if the sun never sets and man changes the very form of nature itself?"

"You overthink this. How ridiculous to say man will keep working because they have an eternal flame. You always think of work. Electricity would grant us longer hours for pleasure!"

"I think this is more existential than you realize," said Matsuma gently.

"Shikomi, what do you think? Will men now work longer into the night, never returning early enough to lay with wives or play with their children?"

Maru paused, still unaccustomed to being solicited to join. "I think that if men cannot work past sundown, that is what women are for—to do the work men are too tired to do."

Mitsu sulked while the men laughed.

"But women don't work as we do!" cried the daimyo. "Have you ever seen one put in a good day's work?"

"Do you talk to your mother with that tongue?" teased Adakichi, entering the room.

The men scrambled, several falling over from the wine.

"Ah, Adakichi, my mother rests eternally and cannot hear me."

"She needs it after raising the likes of you, Gotemba," she said with a smile.

"He's a great fellow," Fujiwara said. "I reckon you'll be enamored with him in no time. Pump him with drinks as you would at the well, and he'll lead the charge in a he-gassen before long." Fujiwara shifted and made a noise.

A thunderous reaction by the guests to Fujiwara's pass shook the room. Mitsu and Maru held their nose but Adakichi gave him a stony glance.

"I'll hang you outside as bait." Gotemba's face reddened when he said this.

Fujiwara laughed nervously. "He's endearing! And isn't it good to be a king? Even if it's being king of . . . fine, fine!" he leaned away from Gotemba, who made a gesture that he was ready to hit him. "Look, I can feel him loading his barrel. He'll be contributing his violence in no time—Maiko, light more incense!"

Mitsu pretended to rise, getting even more laughter and an approving nod from Fujiwara.

"She is working for her wages tonight." Matsuma declared with a chuckle. "Good thing she's so pretty. You know a girl like her probably can't boil an egg." Mitsu's obedience kept her from retorting.

"Listen, she's honmono. You're not on the cheap west side. Not only could she boil an egg; she could cut off your toes and boil them, but you'd be too drunk to notice," said Fujiwara in a rare defense. He was paying for the entertainment and requested recognition. "This is harder to come by, gentlemen. Don't be fooled."

"Shall we hear a ghost story about *Nekomota,* or would you prefer more your cup of tea, such as the *Waraime*? Isn't she your mistress, Gotemba?" Matsuma changed his demeanor after a few sips.

"Bah!" Gotemba lunged to punch him. "May the emperor drive out these horrendous yokai that lurk in our alleys." Maru was startled. Maybe she wasn't the only one who felt them around her.

"You aren't assuaging any fears when you say you've been pestered by the kerakera-onna."

"The yokai just aren't the same anymore. There are real demons out there—far worse than the toothy oni our grandfathers warned us about," Gotemba said darkly. "The gates to Fushimi are being rattled."

Maru envisioned Fushimi and the thousand gates. She hadn't stepped under the red torii since she was a child. She remembered pulling her robes, careful not to trip up the steps. She was tired but wanted to make her dad proud. He paused every few steps so she could follow him.

They had been chasing fireflies, looking out at Kyoto from a ridge. Thick leaves glowed from the setting sun. She had cleaned her feet in a small creek, stepping on stones in the clover to reach the thick moss under ancient guardian trees where the beds of fireflies lay. But they had evaded every grasp. She bit her tongue until it bled and tried not to cry.

A chill fell over her. She remembered the shopkeeper's words about the gate opening for Obon.

"I've heard the plague is sweeping Tokyo."

"The plague is here, in fact," said Fujiwara. "Takeda passed away the other night. He enjoyed Aki's company so much in his final days."

"Adakichi, he was in a state of constant coughing fits, the poor fellow."

Maru remembered his retelling of Shuten Doji in between coughs. *"Have a vegetable!" Adakichi had suggested that night. "I had one. They come from Ogawa!" he had beamed.*

"He had Ogawa's plague," Maru said suddenly. The room quieted. Adakichi squirmed, and Maru dropped her chin as if she had a rein tugging on her throat.

"The plague comes from the wires," growled Matsuma. "It's carried town to town."

She felt a strike in her mind; yellow eyes flashed before her.

"Plagues come at nighttime if you let the demons catch up to your tired feet," offered Fujiwara, tucking in his feet.

"Which is why the emperor's lights will be essential to protect us from shadows," Adakichi chimed in.

"The emperor is replacing the yokai of the past with his own terrors. I pray one of these uprisings finally prevails and brings us peace. The one in the South seems promising."

"Oh, Matsuma, you are a wet blanket."

"No, no! It's true. Unmarried girls are being snatched by the emperor for this dirty project," he snapped. "He's making them a dying commodity." He swirled his drink.

"Please share your information. What does the emperor need of maidens, besides keeping his bed warm?" Fujiwara demanded of Matsuma.

"He wants their blood, of course. Those machines, those god-awful trains, run on their blood. He wants blood from the purest ones so the trains can run faster. It's very slick on the tracks. You can see the blood glisten. You smell it, don't you? Such an awful thing." He took a swig.

"The machine needs a heart to pump it full of energy," Kira had said. But was maiden blood purer? It was the first she had heard of such a notion. Maru looked around to see if anyone was uncomfortable and looking to reveal a truth that had been buried beneath stones in a riverbank of lies.

"I do not think they use blood to slick down the wheels, Matsuma," said Fujiwara. "Mingling with gamblers is taking more than your money. Have you slept well since your wife passed?" Fujiwara laughed. "Why don't you look for an oiran and enjoy yourself."

"I too have heard of this," Gotemba murmured. "It's whispered among the men who bravely drive the trains. One engineer. . . I shiver when recounting what happened."

A silence fell over them.

"Demon trains," Gotemba said simply. "They appear at night. They leave blood in the morning. The smells are all from the entrails they leave behind."

Maru sat up straighter.

"I shot at one the other night after a conductor told me of his encounters. He was plagued, not by disease, but with the failure that poisoned his mind. A fox tried to bite me," Gotemba finished.

Fujiwara burst out in disgust, "You fellows! No wonder you were toppled with the Tokugawa. There are no such things. Bah! Ghosts and ghost trains! You're as bad as Takeda, who said Shuten Doji was here."

Maru relaxed as the laughter grew, relieved he wasn't a yokai. But still, she found herself wanting to say "fox."

Gotemba said, "It is dangerous, I tell you. You readily forget that the engineer was found headless. The emperor is hell-bent on wiping out people like me, and I try to protect you out of kindness!"

"But he has brought us so much and delivers on his word," said Fujiwara.

"You aim to reach the pinnacle by believing *what's new is best*, and this is not necessarily true," Gotemba said.

"Not all of us could buy our name," Matsuma spat. "He drove Takechi and the Tosa to death and took away samurai to become a god he is not. His choices besmirch us and undoubtedly do not protect our women, whose blood stains the roads in the name of *progress*.

"I barely recognize Kyoto. But there are noble allies fighting to restore our capital. They have woken up to Meiji's atrocities—his unbridled changes that addle our minds and cost lives."

Maru stared at Matsuma.

"And I believe in our allies' ability to overthrow this despicable tyrant. Otherwise, next year we will speak another language of some foreigner he welcomes so readily. They sleep with our women and dirty our beaches and infiltrate our city. And our reward for allowing this is that they kill us!" he said, and spit into his cup.

"Matsuma, your shouting has my hairs standing on my neck," said Adakichi.

"Please, dear, tell him he is mistaken about our emperor," said Fujiwara.

"You have asked the wrong woman, for you know I place music above all."

Maru thought this an odd time to be joking. She understood the anger about dormant daimyo—how they resisted her father and the emperor but hated the idea of poking a sleeping bear.

"What does concern me, Matsuma, is what you say about young girls," Adakichi said. "And you know this from the papers?"

"How could they print such a thing when it's the emperor's hand who scribes those very words? No, this is directly from daimyo in Tokyo, trustworthy sources who have nothing to gain but keeping our girls safe. I will deliver verified letters to you, ma'am, for I see this as urgent," he replied.

"But our Gion Matsuri this year celebrates the train and the opening of the station," Adakichi said.

"I, for one, won't be celebrating," scoffed Matsuma.

Maru was conflicted. Their presence, though she had yet to see the trains, worried her. Their force, an unshakable sign of future opportunities her father had gloated about for years, was right at their door front. Yet here, a man who was a shriveled leader of the past, spoke with a terrible look of fear on his face at the thought of these trains. But why was her heart ready to abandon the belief in her father and cower alongside this man who was once her family's rival?

"Matsuma, where does your family come from?" Adakichi asked gently.

"Gunma, ma'am."

"I can attest that Gunma has the best hot springs. My family from Tohoku passed through there back in the day," Fujiwara asserted.

"And the horses, the wild horses in the yellow mountains: they are a sight to behold."

"Won't it be nice to see us as one nation, all one people?" beamed Fujiwara. "Such beauty is for everyone to enjoy, free of feudal land-owners who kept it themselves."

"Nationalism? I haven't given it any thought. Doubtful that—"

"I have a song from Gunma, but please pardon our Kyoto dialect," Adakichi said.

Maru fetched a new bottle and mugwort cakes while Mitsu positioned herself on the stage. The lyrics were unfamiliar to Maru, but all that mattered was the happiness of the listener.

"Ah, I have a tear in my eye," Matsuma said. "I have not heard this since my mother weaned me before the wars when there was such tranquility. Then the roads weren't ripped up. You didn't hear females shouting in the street like banshees, the shogun minded our business, and the emperor was nothing but an old myth. A truly fine nostalgia calms my heart better than a fresh cup of tea."

They drank their wine. Maru's cup of patience ran out first.

"You said you hunt foxes?" she asked. She could hear the burning of incense sticks and tobacco leaves.

"You are asking this for what reason?" Matsuma asked.

"Shikomi is not actually asking; you may excuse her," Adakichi informed them.

"No, no the apricot is asking!" howled Fujiwara. "What he won't tell you is that it's bad luck," roared Fujiwara.

"I'll tell you what. When any blasted demons get in my way, the rules are off, especially ankle biters," Matsuma said.

"A demon? You think those things are demons? You've never seen one."

"I hunt demons all the time!" boasted Matsuma. "But as far as Yamauba—you don't hear of them!"

"Nobody goes into the mountains!" cried Fujiwara.

"And tengu. The skies are void of them. Have you seen one lately? That was me!"

"Listen, my dear friend, the ghost stories and ghost trains are a delight. They tickle the senses. But machines aren't alive. Tengu haven't been around since Nanboku-cho," Fujiwara told him.

"You're mistaken; we're safe because of the nobility of good men who risk their lives for us."

"You're a petty hunter who takes care of vermin?"

"That fox wasn't ordinary! It was a demon in disguise, I tell you. I got myself a souvenir," Matsuma responded.

A pearl, Maru thought.

"I daresay, these days the geiko houses lack a certain deviant allure to them," Gotemba said. "And I think I'm starting to see why I go straight to the other end of Hanamachi."

"There's a difference in service," conceded Adakichi with a small bow.

"That's the thing. There used to be joy and freedom within these walls before the emperor interfered," Fujiwara said darkly. "There's a change, and it happened fast—you can sense it."

"Are we not having fun?" inquired Matsuma.

"We could be romping like free birds, unburdened by our robes, but instead we pretend to be inspired and intrigued by each other."

"Well, oiran are not exactly artists, either."

"It would seem you are seeing the wrong girls, then." Fujiwara chortled. "The best I know is Hone-Onna; you could offer her a bone before she's too old."

Gotemba glowered. "All the same, Adakichi. It's a shame, and I realize it's not your fault that it's so dull around here. I mean no offense to you when I say the emperor's stink is everywhere. here."

"Then, good friend, I invite you to brighten the mood with a song of your own!" declared Fujiwara. "You are full, aren't you? Warm us up with a good trumpet melody."

Gotemba dove at Fujiwara, throwing back a drink that hit the floor. Maru hurried with a cloth, before it seeped into the grain, staining into it a memory.

• • •

With her sleeves rolled up, Maru scrubbed the dishes furiously to remove the stench of wine. Her mind was spinning. The conversation was ripe with information.

Allies fighting to restore our capital. Oh, what exactly did he say? Maru heard the words over and over, neglecting her sleeves, which kept dipping into the water. She rolled them impatiently, wiping her brow. The humidity and deep scrubbing were wearing her out.

Who was an ally of the old daimyo? She tried to think. They weren't names she recognized, but they could have ruled from a northern prefecture, meaning their information from Tokyo would make more sense.

Her father couldn't be an ally of the daimyo who had become his enemy. He was from Kyoto, the west, not the north.

These allies of Tokugawa would look down on him. Unless he had a change of heart toward the emperor. Then he would say, "They have awakened to the atrocities of this emperor."

"It is best not to dwell on this. The work will be done faster if the mind is clear," Adakichi told her. "How about my sending in Mitsu."

But I'm still scared of her, Maru wanted to say.

Mitsu appeared and began polishing in silence. She heard soft chirps of singing outside. Maru used the shadows of night to excuse herself from catching Mitsu's eyes.

"Do you think it's true?" Mitsu whispered when Adakichi was out of earshot.

Maru jumped.

"About the girls," Mitsu whispered more urgently.

"Oh! I'm . . . I'm not sure," Maru said, trying to conceal her deep fears. *The cries and screams, the ghostly girls . . . Mitsu and Fujiwara . . . shadows of yokai, straight out of fairytales.*

"That's what I thought. His insistence made me doubt what he told us."

"You've been downtown. Have you smelled or seen what he says exists?" Maru tip-toed around the subject.

"The construction areas smell . . . but it must just be turned dirt."

She sensed Mitsu was more afraid than she let on.

Maru agreed with her, saying, "It smells like the soil my father used to dig in our garden. It was earthy, with odors of clay and worms or moss. He said it was rich in nutrients from lives lost, buried, and reborn in the flora. When it was shifted to make room for new vegetables, we could smell the freshly turned soil for days. But there was nothing ominous about it."

Mitsu polished the porcelain slowly, fixated on a spot that didn't exist; rubbing it over and over. "Suppose they're making a big deal out of it just because they are trying to negate the emperor."

"Adakichi won't let anything happen to us," said Maru quietly.

"For the rest of our lives we might fear for the safety of maidens, and if the emperor was behind it, who would protect them? Or us? We wear their hairstyles, too."

Bumps rose on her arms. Maybe Mitsu *was* telling the truth. Maybe Maru hadn't seen her the other night but saw a demon disguised as her. Should she say something about this?

She longed for her father to return, and to feel intrinsically safe. But it was becoming apparent that she was alone and needed to fend for herself. If the emperor was truly hunting maidens, she would be in great danger if she couldn't protect herself. Her tanto wouldn't be enough.

She must not become the next victim. The fox had to show itself. She knew her answer.

"Maybe it's just a silly story," Maru tried to elevate her voice to sound optimistic.

"Yes," said Mitsu, with a small smile. "Either way, I will be glad to have a light in our room. At least it would be easier to find eggs."

Maru didn't even notice what she said at first, but then she gasped, "Oh! I—" Her mask had slipped on Mitsu's third attempt to tell her she knew the reason for the missing eggs. She must have been the one who tailed her relentlessly.

"I thought so. But please ask next time."

She felt a sickness in her stomach and her cheeks burned from shame. She found it too painful to apologize.

"You know, as your assumed older sister, I push you to be better," Mitsu told her.

Maru's eyes stung.

"Mayuki?"

She let the bowl drop to the bottom of the water bucket. A tear ran down her cheek.

Mitsu touched her elbow and said, "Adakichi won't let anything happen to us. We *are* safe here," Mitsu told her.

Maru nodded, her heart changing toward Mitsu. The doubts and her vision evaporated right there. She never had a sister, and before this, she thought her school friends were as close as she could get to other girls. Here, she had something close to a familial, more than just a stage imouto. It meant she couldn't be a demon.

Her guilt over wishing for knowledge to hold against Mitsu pinched her spine.

"I need to un-paint my face; I trust you can finish up?" Mitsu went off with the candle.

Maru's mind wandered aimlessly to Satsuma. The maps in the palace that held secrets, the fox, the train and the whistles and screams in the night all seemed stagnant in the summer night's air.

She picked up the food-scrap bucket, thinking of the fox, just in case it needed food. It would have to settle for mashed plum and leftover mugwort. Maybe it had run off and could fend for itself now. Maybe the fox found someone else willing to help it.

Or maybe she had dreamed all of this.

When she finally heard Adakichi's footsteps upstairs and her door sliding shut, Maru slid open hers. She stepped carefully into her slippers, leaving her geta behind, and went quietly into the alley.

Once in the courtyard she looked at the split in the universe high above. The homes and teahouses encircling her seemed to hold their breath in the absoluteness of the night. When she placed the lantern down and felt she had gathered her courage, two glowing eyes appeared in the shadow before her.

She was surprised at the words that escaped her throat. "I wasn't sure if you were hungry again."

She placed the bucket down, and the fox carefully hopped toward her. Its golden-red fur emerged from the dark looking exactly as she remembered it. She hadn't been dreaming.

The fox was lapping up some of the slop.

"So, are you an evil demon?" The words had just spilled out.

"There's such an unpleasant connotation in your question. Would you trust something evil and feed it?" the fox asked in return. A bit of rice was on its nose.

Maru thought about it. "I don't think I trust you, but I also don't want anything to starve on my watch. I'm sorry I ran from you." She tried not to sound breathlessly excited.

The fox continued eating. Its bandage was dirtied but still tightly wound.

Maru said, "I am—I'm glad you're back. I have some questions. You left before I could thank you for saving me the other night." Her heart thumped.

The fox threw a lump into the air and snapped its jaws. "You also helped me; I will answer your questions."

The ends of her fingers pulsed with excitement, sending her mind rushing.

"How can I learn to trust you?"

"How refined are your instincts? Is 'saving you,' as you claim, not enough? What good would it do to betray your own instincts? Holding a fear of even those closest to you isn't such a bad habit to hold."

But wasn't it? Where could she be safest, if not with her father, or those she knew well?

"You ask for my help because you doubt you can trust him?"

The fox had read her mind! She was guilty. Dumbfounded.

She said, "I'll never get used to you answering before I even ask you something."

"I trust you enough to know what you will ask."

It should have been unsettling. However, she found herself baring her belly, allowing this creature to know her fully, relieved to be understood.

Excitedly, Maru said, "Listen, tonight, I heard something. Maybe it's what attacked you. It sounds, well, it seems incredulous. And the yuurei. You were there. But—"

"Mayuki?" She heard behind her.

A cold rush of air chilled her right to the bone, although it was the middle of summer. There in the pale night light, stood Adakichi, as silvery as a ghost in her nighttime robes.

"Sorry, I was dumping out the scraps."

"I heard your voice."

"Yes, I was talking to myself," she said.

"Hurry inside. Don't catch a cold like Takeda did."

Adakichi moved to let Maru through first. Maru hesitated and turned around so that she could not see the fox.

"Mayuki, please come with me," she commanded.

Maru saw that the fox had vanished.

Relieved that Adakichi hadn't seen the fox, she buried her frustration and followed Adakichi back into the ochaya, bracing herself for punishment. Her mind was embroiled in her thoughts, mining excuses that would be most viable. She was ready for a blow.

Instead, Adakichi said, "Have tea with me".

Maru brought out a fresh pair of cups as Adakichi pulled the kettle over the dying fire, and they rolled up their sleeves to avoid singing the silk. Dim lamps cast long shadows against the painted dividers in the soft yellow light. Pops in the embers filled the room, louder than the cicadas outside.

Adakichi kneeled, staring into the kettle spout, as if she were trying to coax it to boil faster. For the first time Maru noticed the delicate wrinkles beneath her eyes.

The spout blared, startling both to the present. Maru reached out to pick up the pot, but Adakichi shooed her hand away, a mark of respect rarely shown to Maru. Maru admired Adakichi's precision as she served tea with her delicate cups perched on the black lacquered tray next to a book.

"There's a lot on your mind, isn't there? The spotty cups tell me so."

Maru clenched her cup. It felt unbearably hot.

"Those men said some strange things tonight," continued Adakichi.

Maru tried to sip her tea, but surrendered to its heat. The wide room, mostly a barren space for guests to fill, felt claustrophobic in the dim light.

"Did they upset you?"

She normally reserved her thoughts, as was the normal practice. But now it was tempting to tell her what was on her mind, but was it appropriate? She feared a scolding.

"Men bring tall tales," she ventured to tell her. "It's not unlike being with the company my father kept."

"That may be, but something in particular has you bothered."

Maru wanted to find solace in the shadow of the lamp's flame flickering on the wall. It seemed to be calling out to her, but she couldn't interpret its message.

"In my beginning days, when I was a maiko, I took the guests' words at face value, and they played me easier than cards." Adakichi's dark eyes were gentle. Her relaxed hair, rarely out of a bun, drooped to the side, making her appear matronly. Even as an okaasan to the ochaya, she seemed almost motherly. Maru had forgotten what this was like; a warmth rushed through her. Her shoulders dropped, and her jaw slacked. Her mind stilled.

"Had they told me they were born a fish, I would have believed them," she continued. "My okaasan never warned me about them. Once she closed the door during their visit, she closed it to their stories and emotions. She closed it to everything. She had snapped. She shed her real face and became someone else."

Adakichi took a sip and Maru mirrored her, careful not to make eye contact. It was rare for Adakichi to open up like this, and Maru was nervous about ruining their quiet, intimate conversation.

"I didn't realize I was meant to do the same. That since I have my geiko face, I'm assuming a role, and it would be best to keep myself sealed behind it."

Adakichi seemed so energetic and eager to converse or dance or play, that Maru often forgot she was aging. She had watched the city change hands and had faced the same dilemmas her family had. She had to remind herself that Adakichi, who seemed infinite in all her being, was also mortal.

"And one man kept showering me with the most gorgeous words. Usually, I was the one who read poetry, but he recited it back. At the time, I saw it as a gesture, a proclamation of something beyond our roleplay. As it turned out, he was a poet who merely enjoyed having an audience.

"But it escalated. His poems spoke of far prefectures and unrequited love. He brought gifts to me. I interpreted this as a profession of love. I thought he could be my danna."

Had she been in love? Adakichi was reserved and good at building walls. She pictured the gifts tucked beneath unworn robes in a back corner of an armoire.

"Of course, he did leave one day, and I packed a small burlap sack and chased him. I found a rickshaw that could catch up to him. It was so expensive to take it out of the city it became a debt I never finished paying." Her sharp cheekbones emphasized her fatigue.

"And when I caught up with him, he was horrified. His wife was sitting next to him, and I was a wild, brazen, woman with illicit intentions chasing a man who belonged to someone else. She didn't know he visited teahouses and took up with oiran, wasting their money and breaking her heart."

Adakichi sighed and sipped her tea. "The rain began, and I trudged through the ankle-deep flood. When I reached the okiya, my okaasan opened the door and closed it on my old ways. I then understood that men flirted only with the idea of me as a perfect woman, not with me as a real woman like their wife."

She placed her cup before her, cradling it in her lap, her thumbs stroking the sides.

"The wild tales of Satsuma overthrowing the emperor, of girls being snatched from beds," Adakichi waved her hand aside, expressing aloofness, "is merely men enjoying holding the power of a presumed knowledge. And when they know nothing, they invent something.

"They seek a reaction, a type of validation from practiced geiko who know how to comfort and encourage them. My asking him for a letter is not because I expect one. I imagine it doesn't exist. But if he believes that I believe him, it makes his experience valid. He can feel like a man," she concluded. "If I let each detail affect me, I could not be a geiko."

Something dawned on Maru. "Like when they agreed women shouldn't work?"

Adakichi gave her a half-smile.

"Because they must know it's not true: Oba-san earn wages as laborers in rice paddies; you earn wages here. That's what a job is, right? And my mother did when father would leave us."

"We know our truth. Their perspective is theirs, and if we disturb this we can shatter it and risk going without our wages.

Then it certainly would have been a waste of everyone's time and work."

Maru relaxed as a sleepiness came over her; her feelings of nervousness from seeing the fox had dissipated. She thought about all of the girls barred from school that were bound for motherhood instead.

"You are not a maiko, but this lesson can still be imparted. Do not get caught in the stories told by a desperate man that are a result of childhood fantasies; you risk losing sight of your own truth and knowledge of your worth."

Maru ruminated on a thought, feeling as if she could open up to Adakichi in exchange.

"What do you make of the ghost stories? What if someone has seen the ghosts?"

Adakichi didn't lift her eyes from the fire. "Seeing ghosts are remnants of our past regrets that haunt us. Ghosts are not always physical things that are outside us, Maruya. They are feelings within us. Some people need to convince themselves that they are good people. Acceptance of ourselves and our behavior vanquishes them."

The clock chimed midnight, and, as if her legs were temple bells swinging, they swept up her feet and swung her up the stairs, leaping over the hands that tried to grab her under each step, thinking about the *Hosokawa* chopsticks she'd found in Adakichi's cabinet.

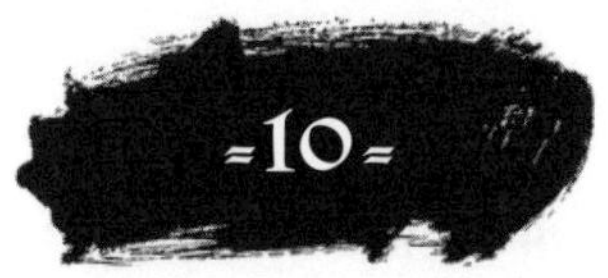

Leading up to the Gion Matsuri and the grand opening of Kyoto's first train station, relentless tsuyu storms struck the city, keeping people housebound. The *pitter-patter* on the roof at the ochaya was drowned out by the continual music and dancing as Mitsu practiced the Kitsune Dance for her upcoming performance. Few wanted to venture outside, relying on contracted boys to knock doors on their behalf. But the hairdresser still came at the beginning of the week with new wigs in tow.

It also meant they relied on pantry stocks since Adakichi didn't let either of the girls go to the market "or everyone will be sick by nightfall," showing her constant worry about the plague. Days of chores and making rice created both monotony and comfort that suspended time.

All Maru wanted was to have contact with the fox. The jarring interruption of their last meeting strengthened her eagerness to see it again. She was no longer afraid. The fox had answers to questions she couldn't ask Adakichi or her friends.

Maru stamped her feet to reverberate with the rain.

Tick

Tap

Tock

Tap-Tap

It was her metronome, reminding her of how much time had passed since seeing the fox and her father.

At least being holed up in the okiya meant respite from the realities outside their door: the sense of being watched, the wails and protests in the streets. Everyone and their grandma had an opinion about the rumors of a samurai rebellion or the emperor's policies.

It was her dreams she couldn't escape.

Again and again, the pale missing girls appeared in a dream. Faceless boys encircled her. In another dream she was pulled under water, where animals bared their sharp teeth.

She wanted to rid herself of the imagery and asked Mitsu to help her meditate. They lit incense and sat on the floor, but Adakichi's humphing over unfinished chores interrupted them.

Ruminating about the fox's riddle was useless. She didn't know how to help it defeat the beast that tormented him. She didn't know if it was the same beast who was abducting girls. Perhaps a being smaller or much larger, such as a man, was doing this.

Could it be Fujiwara? He was annoying, for sure, but hardly seemed capable of taking away young girls. He spent so much time at their ochaya, it didn't seem possible.

What about the police? That would make the emperor complicit. And her father would never have wanted to ascend a man to the throne who had such a terrible ambition.

Or Kira. But remembering their times together when their clans were side-by-side, gave her such fond memories that brushed away her suspicions.

The beast had been described as *"large and dark."* All she could think of was the river. And she couldn't fight a river.

The excitement of the stories shared by the daimyo had diminished, even as the streets flooded. Adakichi and Mitsu carried on as if they weren't true. It was implied Maru should follow suit. When the streets dried out, she resolved to ask Obasan, unless her father returned sooner.

When she was finally in her futon, she closed her eyes. The rain was dark against the bright white clouds like ink spilling onto a blank canvas. The streets were empty of life. She breathed deeply in and out, creating her own peace inside the shelter from the rain.

It was on the third day as their stockpile, including the sake, was depleted, when the clouds broke. At first they didn't notice the pelting sound had disappeared from the roof. But they couldn't ignore the warmth of the sun peering through the rafters. They rushed outside to fill their bodies with the gold rays. Others hurried from their confinement to hang their robes in the sun and order fresh goods.

And then they smelled it.

An undeniable sharp odor cut through the air.

It was blood.

She remembered when her father had come home smelling as such. His robes were badly stained. Her mother had shooed her into the loft, but she had seen enough to know the smell and imagine the limp bodies it had come from.

Had they been attacked? Had Matsuma's ghost run through town? How did it go unseen? Maru's mind wandered, and she fell silent.

Adakichi waved her fan, grimacing. "Rain is meant to wash away muck, not bring it in."

Standing at the stairs waiting for Mitsu to finish her hair, Maru absentmindedly listened to the sounds of Kyoto coming to life—a sense of normalcy emerging as a horse plodded by until the hooves slowed to a stop. Maru listened carefully as she peered down to see four dark feet poised outside. She heard a rap on the door.

Maru heard Adakichi greet two men with gruff voices. She strained to listen from the top of the stairs, her mind running like a thousand horse hooves as she waited.

"Mayuki," Adakichi summoned softly.

Maru found her knees were wobbly. What was she so afraid of? News of her father? Her Oba-san? What should she do—try to find the fox?

She met Adakichi in the hall. Her face didn't reveal any hint of why she was being called, making her feel worse that Adakichi concealed her true opinion.

Maru curtsied before two emperor's men in black uniforms with red trim. The emperor's flag was attached to the horses' saddles. Neither smiled but gave her a quick nod.

"Hosokawa?"

Maru nodded.

"We have questions regarding your clan member Totohiro and his whereabouts."

"Might you know where he is?"

Maru was frozen but knew she had to answer fast or they'd doubt her.

"He went southwest—and then south."

"South?"

"Yes—I think he went for the purpose of trading."

Oh no. Had she gotten her stories mixed up? Pots, sake? Would they ask? Did they care? Were they here to catch her in another mistaken lie? Who had she told?

"Where in the south?"

Maru knew the truth about this. He went to Satsuma. As southwest as you could get, but she was certain it was also the wrong answer. Mitsu was lingering behind Adakichi, grinning.

"Past Osaka," she started to explain.

"Sah, west?"

"He mentioned he went to Satsuma for Portuguese trading, just briefly, I think," she said.

"What is his business with them?"

"Needlework." Maru's memories clashed. His friend, a spunky samurai named Sugihara, had retired with him, swapping his sword for swaddling blankets, finding joy in childbirth and choosing the bloodstains of birth over the dreary spilling of blood in war. His father's friend taught him how to mend and sew blankets for babies—but was that his real work now?

"It's better if you show us your clan dwelling."

Maru almost keeled backward, knowing she'd failed to convince them.

"The Hosokawa have caretakers for the home who could assist you," Adakichi said.

"They may be informative, but it is best for us to interview the family members."

Adakichi's unease showed at the corners of her mouth. "All right. Be back for our evening guests."

Neither man spoke in the street where the sun seemed too hot, the rancid smells compounded by the rising humidity. Two hands grabbed her waist and hoisted her onto the sweaty horse. She gripped the saddle while the man gave a shout.

Children watched in fascination as she mounted the racing the horse. Their giggles calmed her. But parents looked at Maru in apprehension. They narrowed their eyes, trying to memorize her face to later ask who she was and why she was taken away by the emperor's guards.

Riding horses with her father once brought her such joy, giving her the strength and speed that she wished she had on her own legs. She had yearned to be something beyond an ordinary human—someone who was a warrior like her father—a person admired for the ability to tame wild beasts with ease.

Instead, she was trapped with these men stiffly riding the horses clumsily with their reigns. She wondered what they could be investigating and what information they'd need from her to leave her alone.

Before she knew it, they were in front of her clan's gate, already opened by the few caretakers remaining who barely noticed their arrival. Maybe it was a normal occurrence.

She led the way, unsure of what to say or if she should call for help. She had nothing to hide. Her father hadn't done anything wrong. He had just been away taking long trips that were normal when you are trading. *Yes, everything is quite normal,* she told herself. There was no reason to assume otherwise.

If anything, it seemed the palace should be answering questions about the mystery of the missing girls.

The men clicked their tongues at a nearby gardener, motioning for her to tie the horses up. Maru bowed but got barely a nod back. She observed two men standing outside the side houses; Maru waved, only to see blank expressions returned to her. Her heart sank: These were extended family members, now appearing to have no recognition of her. Something was terribly wrong.

The men flanked her as they walked to her door and waited to go inside; even the cicadas' paused their song. She fumbled to pull the door open, finally spilling inside to find its stony interior cool, dark, and still, the way she'd left it long ago.

"You have a mother?"

She shook her head.

"When did she pass away?"

"During the last mikka korori," Maru whispered.

She despised thinking about it: how she had been so well one day, only to be blue and empty the next day. Sometimes she could still smell the death in this house lingering like a jaguar in the rafters, waiting to pounce and seize her throat.

Her stomach churned, thinking of Ogawa and Takeda, how they had been close so recently. She was brushing death's hand.

"Many perished," said one of them without emotion.

"Did you recall any other business your father may have in the . . . South?"

Maru shook her head. "You can see, there, on the cabinet and dresser some of the pieces he has returned with." She pointed to vases, ornate gold flowers bursting off the handles, realizing now this had nothing to do with needlework. Would the guards have forgotten? Everything seemed to be watching her; her home held its breath in anticipation of betrayal.

"Fine piece. He didn't bother selling it?"

"He has sold many; this was a gift for mother." *Had he picked it up after she passed?*

"Sellers keep receipts."

"Sure, they might be at his table." *Or were they in a cabinet or with an accountant?*

They stood there, eyeing her, the dim light concealing their expressions, burrowed under heavy eyebrows and thick mustaches.

"Bring us those."

She rifled through the drawer of her parents' things, digging for leaflets that looked anything remotely like a receipt, or a license for trade or business her father would have received from the emperor. What would it look like?

Letters, old paintings, a marriage agreement, casual correspondences, distant family or clan announcements, business proposals—and a license! He was a licensed trader for goods, as backed by the local government of Kyoto, with the seal of the emperor. She sighed with relief.

She presented it to them in the sunken sitting area. They inspected it quickly.

"This is nearly a decade old," said one finally. "When was the last time he paid for an updated license?"

Maru hadn't a clue it was outdated.

"Any more receipts? Or licenses?"

She quickly abandoned the search for receipts upon finding his license. She hadn't realized it wouldn't be enough.

"We will have a go at it. We know where men keep their business matters."

She didn't have a chance to protest. They pushed by her and ripped open drawers, revealing folded tapestries, old robes from her mother, her favorite yellow one with irises, and her mother's handwritten poems. They flipped through the pages and rifled through the trinkets from their travels. They then moved to the pantry and rummaged through the cabinets. Upstairs they knocked over the table with a crash, dumping contents on the floor. Tears welled in her eyes. Why were they in her house? What would they find? But worse, what would happen if they didn't find what they were looking for? Her life was being shredded before her eyes.

She looked over her shoulder at the open front door: the gingko, maples and white walls contrasted with the solemn cave she stood inside. She wanted to run into the sun and keep running. Maybe she could take one of the horses. Would the clan help her? Or were they her enemy? Her Oba-san's warning, the criticism of her clan, came rushing upward through her body, and she heaved.

"Ah!" The clamoring came to a standstill.

The closet was open, revealing her father's old samurai armor.

"You," he called down to her. "His armor was not taken?"

Maru frowned, trying to recall what he meant.

"The emperor recalled all swords. This armor—he kept his?" The dark eyes beneath his heavy brows stared at her.

"I—I think he surrendered his sword—," she stammered.

"And not his armor?"

"It is sentimental. He was allowed to keep it—he supported the emperor," she said. "It's not for bad faith or a sign of disloyalty—" her voice cracked. She was relieved, too. It meant he was not wearing it in Satsuma for any sort of fight. "Sword's not here," muttered the other, sidling up to him. "Look at these," his voice lowered, and he showed a booklet of papers to the other man, who leaned in.

Maru couldn't tell from the distance what the papers were. Had he left something behind she wasn't aware of—some secret document or a love letter? She cringed to think of her father's private words being spoiled by these two rotten grunts.

Change was coming at a cost that her family could no longer bear. They were already stripped of their rank, their wealth, their community they'd built. And now it seemed their home would be demolished, plank by plank, stone by stone. She couldn't imagine having another dinner in the house. All that was left was their kamon; and these days it stood for nothing.

"Receipts," said the heavy browed man, waving the papers like a fan.

They stomped across the loft and strode downstairs with steps that threatened to cave it in entirely. She kept her head low, waiting for their verdict or a sword to be brandished.

"We need to confirm they aren't forgeries. They're old."

"Forgeries! We aren't petty thieves. He is bushi; he wouldn't break an oath!"

The younger one spoke up. "There has been an increase of illegal licensing. We are assessing the voracity. Disenfranchised samurai get into dangerous business situations out of desperation."

"Here are some letters," muttered the other man, handing them to his partner.

"No, no!" Maru said. "Those are private."

"Do they contain anything the Imperial Palace shouldn't be privy to?"

They started to stride by her, when the younger one spoke. "When did you say he left last time?"

"Before the first snowfall, at the turn of the year," she said.

"And with no word at all?"

Maru was frozen.

"If you hear of anything, please report it to the Gosho," said the older man.

When they went to the door, she burst out, "Why are you inquiring about *him*?"

"You haven't heard?"

Maru wasn't sure she was expected to hear whatever it was.

"Trouble in Satsuma. We need a census of city residents, to make sure they're not caught in the crossfire," said the bearded man carefully.

"It would be unfortunate to lose a prominent businessman over a misunderstanding. Or to see him turn to other means to keep busy. You don't think he'd hurt a child, do you?"

"Crossfire? The missing girls?" Maru stepped forward. Were they implying he was the reason for the disappearances? He took down evil men—not girls—and would never harm children.

"Keep the content of those letters to yourself," he told the younger man with a bow.

The door shut, and she was left inside her family's home, clutching the license in her hands that was sealed and signed by *Hokke*. She looked around the room at the mess, unsure of where to begin to put his property back in order.

Her mother's book of poetry was laid haphazardly against one of the dressers. When she picked it up to smooth out the bent pages, it fell open to a haiku she had written years ago:

Fireflies light, dark
Door opens and door closes
And the heart flutters.

Across the way, a door shut.

• • •

A chortling rooster woke her out of a stupor, prompting her to tidy up. Some cracked dishes were strewn about and there were papers everywhere. She was desperate to put the papers in order for her father to easily find them when he came home.

Looking around, her home no longer felt safe. It had been violated, and the slivers of empowerment she had gathered in the recent days was smashed to pieces, too. Her hands trembled as she placed the vases and knickknacks inside the cabinets, relieved that the men had left her alone, but frightened about the reasons they had pursued her.

Could it be because of the current census?

She knew they were conducted every few years, but she wondered if perhaps they were doing a sweep to see who was here because of the conflict in Satsuma. She had been certain he wasn't caught in the battle. Did she now need to consider the terrible possibility that he had been killed?

But the frightening and absurd accusation that he took children to stave off boredom made her shiver.

His papers had been in order. His armor was here. If he was involved in trying to be a hero again, he would have taken his armor, Maru decided. He wouldn't be hiding in shadows, stealing young girls.

She rose and saw the armor in the closet, standing proud and protected, without a speck of dust as if he hung it up yesterday, excited to leave behind a symbol of violence in exchange for unity. She remembered what she had overheard one long night:

"We have enough allies; our plan is in motion—we move North to meet Tokugawa head-on. Within this season, we will have a new leader."

"Whatever does it mean for us? How long will you be gone?" her mother had asked breathlessly.

"As long as I need to make a future for us and Maru. She can be more than who she will marry—she can be taught many things and go to another land and do anything she desires. And no more lords will tax us out of house and home."

"We are no commoners."

"I have fought for them and seen their struggles. To be united under Sakamoto's eight proposals is our mission. He will bring it to allies with Tosa. We have been downright barbaric to one another. All for sacks of rice. There will be a diplomatic, nonviolent future. Reason will return."

"And what will our leadership be?"

"The rise of the emperor supported by a whole parliament. One body with a thousand heads thinking about a unified future, not ranking any one over another. It is effective in other lands. It's democratic. It's the epitome of equality."

"How will we manage—it will be dangerous." She was frantic.

"There is a plan; you'll be safe. This conflict will be over quickly. I promise."

"Maruya is so young. What if there is a suicide?"

"My servitude to you will never tire. It's why I will go to fight the cowards."

Maru didn't understand where her father had to go, and why so soon, but knew her family was on the brink of the end—and also a beginning.

She thought her father's eyes blinked beneath the helmet, and her belly warmed.

He had been fighting *for* the emperor. They wouldn't find anything they were looking for that would say otherwise. He had retired, opting to work in business, setting aside his samurai ways and galloping his way forward to a more hopeful future.

The dust was finally settling, the bones of their home returning to its composed state. Once Maru confirmed that all was in order, she left the home less reluctantly than she had a year ago. She saw dwellings with their doors open revealing families sitting for dinner. Nobody invited her in.

Shadows were growing in length, their blue tinge darkening. Hurrying with her mother's poetry book tucked under her arm, Maru felt lighter than when she'd been on horseback with the policemen. The street seemed safe. Nobody was paying her any mind and seemed unaware she was the girl who was almost whisked away, never to be seen again.

She breathed the free air as the evening birds chirped under the golden-yellow clouds. It was easier to feel she'd never been in danger now that she was on the other side of her interrogation.

The smells of the approaching market was a welcome distraction: There were fresh bites from the sea grilled over coals, peppers and bamboos leaves wrapped around minazuki, rice and beans, and a whole cartload of the largest fish she'd ever seen. Would Adakichi like to have these? Picking some to take home to her might help to smooth over any terror they felt at Maru's sudden summoning.

Without ever having gutted a fish before, she bravely pointed to one thin, red fish with a small mouth and short teeth. It had a friendlier face than the other larger fish, whose eyes looked at her begging for mercy.

"A good choice. He looks less likely to bite," said a man who sidled up to her. He wore a strange, floppy, cotton hat and a Western suit, but it was brown instead of black.

Taken aback, she passed a coin to the merchant, nodded to the man and backed away, swaddling the new fish in her basket.

Nearby, older men chattered.

"It's growing bigger in the south. Soon it'll be out of hand."

"More should join."

"This scuffle won't be over quickly."

She tried to shut them out, making her way through the thick of oiled parasols and straw hats until she was stopped by a figure, stark and black, standing before her. She felt the wind sucked out of her. What kind of normal being would be enshrined in such darkness with everyone moving around it as if it were a rock?

Was it staring at her? She couldn't see any eyes.

She took a step toward the figure. It didn't move. Voices around her became indiscernible.

The figure raised its head, a glint in the being's eyes revealed a familiarity.

It was her father.

He was darkened; his eyes were glazed and looked as if they had been hardened by something. There was no fondness in his gaze. He stood, still, waiting for her. Why wouldn't he soften up? Did he even see her?

"Father?" she whispered. Her eyes fluttered. She'd been praying for so long, and now perhaps she didn't need the fox at all!

His eyes found hers. He gave her a grin that was toothy and sly. His nose was crooked and seemed broken. His hair was sleek and oily, dripping something bloody. A rotten smell emanated from him.

She stopped. There was silence, and she saw it wasn't her father. But as she realized it was a trick, the figure stretched out its hands into claws, braced them and took off in a run, leaving a wind rushing into her chest.

She felt it would knock her over or blow right through her, its wind whistling in her ears.

"No! You are not my father!" she screamed.

Its hair was growing higher. Its horrible grin was stretching wider and wider, and it was coming faster.

"Stop!" she yelled and spun around to protect the fish and herself.

She felt a wham from the monster and heard someone cry out, "Maru!"

"Tane!" Maru answered. Her friend was in iki robes clutching a basket of rice and a large summer zucchini. She was not a yuurei.

The shock of seeing her father had ripped her heart. She panted in relief but felt on the verge of collapsing, having been so close to her dream coming true followed by a cruelty she couldn't have conjured up in her darkest nightmare.

Tane stood there, gently lifting Maru up. Her hair was curling in the heat—something the other girls were always envious of—glowed in the golden evening haze, her smile lighting up Maru's torn and grateful face. Tane must not have seen the apparition, Maru thought.

"Whatever is the matter, Maru?" Tane murmured.

Maru shook her head and said, "Two men from the police stopped by today . . ." She watched Tane's face give away her opinion as she recounted her story, except for the part about the presence of a ghost.

At the end, Tane clutched her elbow and said, "But you're in good shape, aren't you?"

She had to tell her she was not. "They took our papers. Has anyone come by to ask your family about a census?"

Tane shook her head. "But we have always been . . ."

Maru stopped herself from offering the word "commoners" to finish her sentence and instead nodded quickly. It was what made her friendship with Tane unusual. They were able to be friends solely because of the emperor's order that all children must attend school, removing this restriction only for the samurai or higher classes like Ai or Kiku's families. Otherwise, she would never have met Tane.

"I wouldn't worry," she said quickly. "They took the papers. If this was wrong . . ."

Neither knew what to say. Maru put her hand over her heart to feel if the loud thumping had ceased.

"The emperor may be bored," Tane suggested.

Her words didn't encourage Maru as she had hoped. She wondered if it was worth mentioning the other fears; that her father was a suspect in the case of the missing girls. Or that that she had just seen an apparition of him. Or that some ghost was just using his face for a disguise. But Tane interrupted her thoughts with a new subject before she had a chance to muster the courage to explain all this.

"Say, did you hear from Ai recently?"

"Did something happen?"

"Her parents finally settled on a match. She is going to be married!"

"Oh, this is much happier news! We always knew she'd be the first." Maru was heartbroken to be the last to hear the news when she had seen Ai just a few days ago.

"Yes, she is so pretty . . ." Tane's voice trailed, her round face suddenly solemn.

"Cheer up, there is a suitor out there for you. Your family has a great restaurant; anyone would be lucky to eat so well the rest of their lives," Maru mustered her enthusiasm, soothing herself too.

Tane smiled, showing the light on her face before she finally swung her basket, saying she needed to get back before her mother worried. Maru agreed. She saw the sky exploding in the pink and orange, stretching horizon to horizon, the rooftops lined with gold, their white and bamboo fronts flushed in hues that would make any geiko envious of nature's palettes.

"The train! The train—it's the demonic machine! Bringing us evil!" a voice hissed, breaking her thoughts and startling her.

The voice continued, "Girl—girl and girl go! In the night! And the train comes."

Maru held her breath. Was it true? And not a tall tale? Maybe it would absolve her father since he was incapable of shape-shifting. She felt relieved that it was inhuman.

"And nobody sees it except me. I see it! It screams before it eats!"

The woman lunged at the air and fell forward on her face. A policeman, out of nowhere, helped her up and started to say something to her. Maru quickly left, suddenly wishing to be back in the okiya after such a haphazard encounter.

People turned up their noses at her as she hurried away. Did they know she had been the girl with the emperor's men just a few hours ago? Did they all think it was her father's fault? They looked at her, their heads moving faster the more she hurried; she broke into a run.

Passing through the east, she went by the great pagoda. It was five floors high, thrusting lit lanterns into the pink-water-canvas as white stars emerged. The crisscrossing streets were quiet. Most field and factory workers had already retired to their shanties where cedar needles nailed their crooked straw roofs. The mess of outhouses and wells was carved into the land, and night soil boxes were full and ready for pillaging. She limped to Gion, looking up at the sturdy eaves of neighboring buildings and heard kettles humming as the evening bells tolled.

"Ma . . . ru."

The hairs on her neck tingled. Someone called her name. She was afraid she'd look behind to answer the voice and see a charred, eyeless figure take the shape of her father again.

"Ma . . . ru."

She didn't wait another moment. She tore away, rushing, beat after beat until the embrace of the willows reached out to comfort her.

She was in familiar streets! Could she breathe? She closed her eyes and inhaled sandalwood incense and wisteria. She had to find the source of the voice.

"Watchit!"

Suddenly Kiku bounced off her, and both girls gasped and laughed at the coincidence.

"Post-storm market run too, eh?" Kiku jabbed her in the ribs, but her smile quickly drooped. "I actually saw Tane. She told me of your, um, circumstances today. How are you? Say, you look winded, like something gave you a fright."

Her neck almost broke from how quickly the mood shifted. *How fast did that word travel?*

"Tane maybe said this already, but I doubt you have anything to worry about. You're a Hosokawa! Can you imagine the palace daring to question you? Though why would they waste their time if something did not seem fairly credible?"

"What do you mean?" Her heart clenched; the palace men had sounded certain they would drop the matter.

"What do you think they're going to open there?" Kiku nodded toward a tall red tower.

"I don't know, but why did you—"

"Oh, I saw your Oba-san, she asked me to let you know her kettle is always hot."

Maru's cheeks flushed.

"It's easy to let our familial duties slide away," said Kiku with a tone of sympathy. "They're the ones who'll forgive us for our faults."

Her words didn't make Maru feel any better.

"Oh! And Ai is getting married."

"Tane told me. I haven't received an invitation yet."

"It's coming; I'll remind Ai." Kiku was always in the center of everything.

Some shouting caught her eyes—men in flowing, dirtied robes were accosting the suited crew members, shouting about how they were desecrating traditions. As the shouting escalated, Maru became less sure about what they were fighting about.

"Come, before anyone gets out their sword." Kiku tugged on her elbow, and they headed for the river that would take them back to Gion.

"All of this. There's something unsettling about them. Can we stop by the shrine?"

Kiku nodded. "We need all of the help we can get these days."

They picked one along the way, having pledged no allegiance to any of the thousand shrines. Kiku kneeled next to Maru as she prayed aloud for her father and prayed that the palace wasn't hiding anything from her, that girls would be protected, that her father wasn't the villain others thought him to be, that the Parade would go smoothly, that Kiku would take her to one of their secret gardens to hide, and that Adakichi would—

"Don't burden the kami! Your ancestors are worried enough," Kiku said.

Maru rose sheepishly. She was about to ask Kiku her opinion of her father, but realized she didn't want to know how Kiku regarded him.

They passed through the lantern tunnel lit for the upcoming Gion Matsuri, crossing the bridge to the willows bending in delicate beckoning. Maru had thought about confessing her fears about the ghostly girls, but Kiku's effortless, unfazed charm, and the reassurances she gave Maru several days ago had changed her mind.

Kiku said, "I haven't forgotten your question about your maiko problem. Don't give me that look, I read between your lines," Kiku said with a laugh, as Maru looked at her in surprise.

"I tracked down your ochaya's former maiko, the one you replaced. It seems, if I've understood this correctly, that Mitsu may have had a hand in banishing her."

"Did she tattle on her to Adakichi?"

"Yes, and the former maiko claims it was a fabrication attributed to their competition."

So, this is what happened. Mitsu had lied to Adakichi to get ahead. She was holding the key to get Mitsu banned before she had a chance to sell Maru out.

"Alright Maru, I've been trying to be polite, but what is that horrendous smell coming from your basket? Everyone is staring."

When she was on her way to the ochaya, the wind was at her back, bringing with it incense from shrines. This is where she belonged. The smells from open yatai, smoke and steam pouring out windows, children fussing. This world felt so alive, and she felt happy to be in it, certain that a nothing could not touch her, casting a boundless, wild hope that all would be well.

But maybe she was lying to herself.

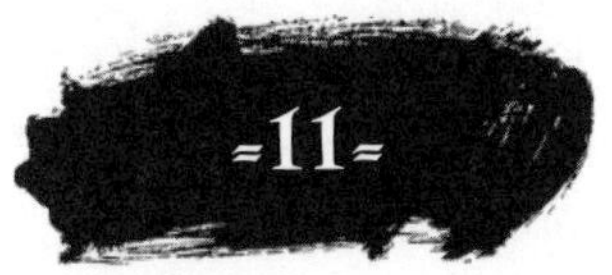

11

Adakichi initially expressed concern about their recent encounter, but Maru assured her everything had been taken care of. The police would only come back if they had more questions. Maru was euphoric after learning about Mitsu's secret and was eager to help the teahouse get ready for their first guests since the storm.

The presentation of the fish and her offer to prepare it—although she wasn't sure yet how she would do this—also helped to smooth things over. Food was always a way to someone's heart, especially with the famine still fresh in the minds of the earlier generations.

It took only a few moments before the presence of the fish was a burden. "No amount of ginger or incense could mask that smell. We'll have the all the strays of Kyoto here by nightfall on top of the other stink we have," grumbled Adakichi.

Matsuma had brought by his letters while Maru was out, barely able to contain his grin, Mitsu explained, as Maru flopped the fish onto a counter, ready to cut it open.

He vowed to protect them— the "precious commodities" who will "make fine wives someday," which Adakichi accepted with a straight face.

"There's no telling if he forged them, though," Maru replied, thinking about the accusations she heard earlier from the emperor's men.

"We must think of our guests as men of honor," said Adakichi. "Have you figured a way to cook the fish? Should I put the kettle on? Do we boil it?"

Maru had a handkerchief wrapped around her head to cover her nose as she held the fish down with her slimy hands to tug out the bones. She was feeling defeated. This had been a popular dish in her household but didn't think now was a time to boast, especially when she wasn't sure how to prepare it, having always left this to their clan's maid. She was never trained in the duties of a lowly cook; all she knew was the proper cutting of vegetables and fruit.

"In the market they were eating it fresh," said Maru. "I remember eating it dried."

Adakichi looked disappointed but said, "We can hope the guests tonight will overlook our shortcomings. Nothing is amiss. Remember that even with Matsuma's letters you are not worry."

Maru hoped she was right and proceeded to push her finger through the scales of the fish, feeling the soft, warm flesh part ways, as she went down to the bone. She grimaced and yanked out the brittle bones.

"Don't fight it, Maru," Mitsu instructed. "It's already dead."

Was he also fighting something already dead?

She bit her tongue and tried shaving off the scales before cutting it into small chunks, but found her knife wasn't sharp enough—the chunks shredded into flakes, and flesh splattered.

Adakichi stayed in her room, claiming she needed to prepare for the evening, but Maru believed she was avoiding the fish smell.

Mitsu said, "The red chunks look like melon." She touched a corner of the fish. "It's a little cool! Might be nice on the rice."

"We have no way to keep it cool once it's on the hot rice."

"Imagine, if instead of magically turning night into day, we could make warm food cold and cold food hot! Or change our seasons on a whim! I would like to be in winter now."

Maru smiled. Winter was her favorite. She recalled sipping barley tea inside, crossed legged on the tatami, she would watch the snow fall onto the hibernating garden, fur blanket draped over her shoulders. The stillness, a smooth cup, a coldness as she pressed her hand against the window, crackling fire in the irori, boiling mushrooms, persimmons drying in the eaves—it was all she wanted. She remembered being tossed into snow by her father until their toes froze, her mother rolling mochi, the stickiness that caught in her fingers.

"You're in your head again!"

Maru snapped out of her daydream, finding her fingers deep in fish guts.

Mitsu said, "If I had your imagination, I would be a storyteller."

And if I possessed your ability to lie, you'd be out.

Maru replied, "There isn't a job available that pays for my imagination."

"If you could carry a tune then you'd be more useful," Mitsu called down the hall.

Maru heard Fujiwara's voice fill the room and her whole body groaned. He came with an old friend they'd seen before. Both were content to drink and play games and content to have Adakichi and Mitsu show them the routines and explain the rules. The men, of course, either had no idea what to look for or wouldn't dare criticize Adakichi. They praised the women throughout the night.

Maru seem relaxed and revealed a new self-confidence. She finally answered questions about whether her father was safe and in a legitimate business. She said he was doing well, and their fears had been misplaced.

She appeared to welcome Fujiwara's teasing and allowed herself to be braver. She encroached on Mitsu's territory, stepping back only when Adakichi's eyes warned her. Fujiwara didn't know about her family's home welcoming scrutiny from the palace—at least, not yet.

The fish helped to keep sour conversations away from the table. It got a hearty laugh from Fujiwara when he saw it: "A great battle was fought here. Did you call Hokusai to capture it?"

His friend offered his opinion, "Consuming it wouldn't bring any solace to a tortured spirit."

The conversation remained light. There was some excitement about the train ("I've seen it. It is the grandest thing you'll ever see; It could carry elephants and hardly as sinister at Matsuma will tell you. It certainly is not a ghost."), and Fujiwara told his latest experience of trying out a telephone. ("I could hear a voice on the other end! I'm not sure what they said, but I heard a voice!") Maru found herself picking at the scabbed thoughts of her father all evening.

The best part was the night ending early—the incense was only half-used, shown by the measurement Adakichi used to determine success—and they were able to clean and finish their chores early. Mitsu stole upstairs to brush her hair before going "out" while Maru finished cleaning the pantry. She wondered if she was pushing her luck by wishing for the fox to appear when she went outside.

That wish came true, too.

The fox was sitting beside the compost pile and an old barrel disguised as a small flower bed.

It said, "You're here."

"Yes, I've been hoping you would be too," Maru said breathlessly.

"Did you bring food?"

Maru held her empty bucket and tilted it forward. "Fish bones, and some—"

The fox pounced. "Have you given thought to my offer?"

"I have some questions. Can we go somewhere else?" Maru whispered.

She had knots in her stomach from feeling she was being watched. The image of her false father bolted through her mind.

Maru led the way, spotting people leaving a rowdy sake bar, and others on their way home from noodle shops. She wanted to warn the fox but saw it slip under the bushes before she could say anything. Maru made her way, carrying herself as if she belonged in the neighborhood.

Drunk patrons shouted happily in nearby teahouses and izakaya. She was grateful Fujiwara and his guests had not stayed late, pitying those at the mercy of those who needed vices to find comfort.

She crossed Gion bridge to the road took her past ochaya. Their elegant noren bearing their kamon was suspended in the hot, windless night; their tall gas lamps were blinking. She'd heard it was because Abura-akago, a ghostly boy, was addicted to lapping up oil that spilled over the edges, causing a stir in the light.

She averted her eyes as she passed by a torii, praying she wouldn't spy otorishi, the creatures she feared the most. She shuddered, wondering if one of the hairy creatures was sitting there, ready to pounce.

At the end of the street was a cluster of bushy trees. The dark leaves shrouded the entry way. She found the pebble path in the shadows; she slipped through the narrow passage and stepped into to a small clearing. A garden was lit with statuettes and stone lanterns, revealing flat stones in a circular shape. A small white and brown tea house, surrounded by a short bamboo fence, stood behind hydrangea bushes, their pink and blue bouquets bright in the candlelight.

It was quiet, as she had hoped. The tea master lived in the building across the way, leaving late night visitors alone to meditate and pray.

She bowed and softly whispered "thank you" to whomever may be listening, feeling the earth breathe after stirring at her arrival. She called out to the fox who sprang from the shadows, with his wrapped paw extended. Maru felt shy during this moment she had been waiting for.

"Does it still hurt?"

"It is on the mend. I haven't known a human before who helped me."

"Nor have I helped a fox before. Much less, seen one so closely."

"We are always closer than people suspect."

Some frogs began to sing their night song, startling her. "Sorry I'm so on guard."

Maru tried to get her mind straight. "So, I've been thinking about you. And your pearl. I thought kitsune like you had one. And me. I mean, how you came to know me. Sorry, I'm nervous. How did you find me? And what—what do you think I could do about the beast? Because my father, well, I think he needs help—or maybe it's someone else who needs help." She stopped short of saying "I'm the one who needs help." Personal desires were frowned upon; she should be considering the clan's reputation and society needs.

The fox coat was gold under the light. "It's an orb, something that possesses my soul."

"Your soul?"

"In humans, your soul is in you. When your body is struck mortally, the soul slips through the wound, and is released into the air. For me, it is protected in the orb to easily pass to another shell."

"Hence your shapeshifting."

"You learned about this."

Maru smiled proudly. It was an unfamiliar feeling but she gladly accepted its embrace.

"Yes. It's a power I have. I can transform back and forth if I have my orb to call home. My soul lives in different shells, changing shape from time to time for protection. If my shell were to be damaged beyond repair, I'd need to find a new one."

"If your orb is away from you, how are you still able to be yourself?"

"I am slowly losing my abilities as it gets further from me. I cannot remember my name. Before long, this shell will break down. It will weaken and die, and while someone else is trapping my orb, my soul cannot have free reign to find a new shell to occupy for my spirit to keep on living. I could cease to exist if I never find another body to inhabit."

"That sounds rather dark."

"Does your kind not believe every object in your world possesses a soul?"

Maru was uncertain. She hadn't paid much attention to the monks and their lessons. But she knew kami and spirits could take shape of different persons or creatures, figures or objects. Perhaps this kitsune was another being in disguise of a fox, concealing its real identity. What other forms had it taken? Would she recognize it if it were in another shape or form?

"Most answers are beyond our reach," it said, as if answering her.

"So, you have some intuition," she remarked.

"You're picking up on this nicely," said the fox.

"I am far from being like you."

"If you so choose, it's a path you have an option to pursue."

Maru frowned. "If I choose? But I'm already me."

"Not yet. There are many crossroads yet ahead of you." The fox flicked its tail, looking at bats flying over. Cicadas singing, competing with frogs filled Maru's ears, clouding her thoughts.

"Could something be born without a soul?" Maru paused. "Can you see a human's soul?"

"Can't you?"

Maru shook her head, but then slowed, as a thought dawned on her.

"You are not looking hard enough."

But the ghosts would be souls, she thought with a start.

"The other night, when you rescued me—"

"There was no rescuing happening."

"But you came to me when the thing reached out for me. It would have hurt me."

"You asked for help. I answered."

"They're yuurei, aren't they?"

"Are they yuurei to you?"

They certainly weren't Fujiwara and Mitsu. And that wasn't her father. It wasn't.

"Are they what attacked you, too?" she asked. "It's nearing Obon, and spirits are meant to come out. I thought they seemed evil. Unlike what we celebrate for Obon. Our ancestors."

"Are all ancestors meant to be good?"

The answer hung limp in the damp summer night.

"I haven't thought of that. But how did you find me? Why me? You know my father somehow. How and where? Why did you mention something coming—something foreboding. Is it those demons or yuurei? My father? Could he be part of this?

Many suspect the emperor, but you said you suspect a machine. And palace men said it was perhaps a man. But you or someone said there was such a thing as ghost trains?" She felt breathless when it was finally said out loud.

"A *train*?"

"It's what we call it. I wanted to tell you last time. It's a big, black thing, but it is run by man, not by anyone I know. It's a machine."

"So that's what man named it. This is familiar. I've seen it." The fox seemed distant.

"One came in the other day, bringing treasures from the north." She was relieved it didn't seem shaken by her question about ghost trains. Another unfounded fear that is now gone.

"I cannot imagine any 'treasures' that are worth such a monstrosity. Man is selfish, and thinks everything they own that looks gold or handmade is a treasure and worthy of the efforts it takes to move them. But that train stirs creatures. Many are unsettled. The kami are displeased by it. It's ugly, and rumbles the world."

"The river shakes and brings in things too."

The fox looked amused. "My memory is fading. If I had my pearl, I might remember how I was drawn to you. I relied on *intuition*."

"Oh, the pearl! Someone has it. The person said they hunted oni and found it. Could it be yours?"

"I would have to see it to know. Each of us has their own."

"Someone told me you may find other ways to store your power while you are weak."

The fox was quiet. "This person is familiar with our kind."

"I feel weak too," Maru confessed.

"You merely perceive weakness. It doesn't need to define you."

A cricket leapt onto a stone lantern.

"But Adakichi strikes me, and I stand still. My father is gone, and I can do nothing to find out his truth. They ransack my home and rob me, and I let them. My friends whisper, and I have no retort. I face a yuurei and call for help. I have no control. I don't know who I am."

"You are a patient hunter. Turn your hesitancy into your power," replied the fox matter-of-factly. A toad emerged from the iris stalks. "Strike back at the right time."

"How will I know when that is?"

"When you decide you can't accept it any longer."

The toad's tongue grabbed the cricket, silencing it.

"It's as if I can't see the truth. It's cloudy. I have no idea what to believe. It renders me incapable of making decisions. My father used to do everything for me. Now he is replaced by Adakichi, who tells me everything to say. I have no idea how to do anything. All I feel is a sadness everywhere I go. And I have been accused of being selfish for feeling this way."

She gulped. It was the deepest confession she ever made aloud. She hadn't considered it her truth until it came spilling out. But through the summer, it stared her in the face: even in the sun, during the matsuri, or nibbling on strawberries, something was missing. A darkness, a constant storm overhead, frothing now in the form of ghosts spilling onto land.

"You were raised with certain expectations, only to have your life rearranged. Adapting a new path requires courage. Grief is the most worthless emotion a human can have. It does not create the life you desire, but consumes the light you already possess, and darkens your path. I do not envy mortals who bear pain of invisible diseases," said the fox.

"You do not know it?"

"It will be a battle you must fight on your own. Praying to kami will do you no service."

She dropped her head. "If everything went right, I wouldn't feel it anymore."

"And how would everything going right look to you? A boring, content life without change?"

"If only everything could slow down. I cannot keep up."

"Then you can stay behind and choose inaction."

That wasn't what her father would do. He would always stand before others and lead them to clarity. Their future was here because of him. She faltered, thinking of him, wondering if one day she would see his yuurei too, leading her into a trap.

"He is not here with us, so he is still alive," surmised the fox, reading her mind.

She felt chills. "You can see him? And wait—you can see others who passed? Is anyone here?"

The fox didn't answer.

"Will he return?" Even with her vulnerability, she didn't break her gaze.

"He has many paths before him, too."

An invisible hand let go of her throat. "And you can see this. He's not in trouble, is he?"

The fox paused. "That is subjective."

Her face grew hot. She didn't want to be direct. "He told me he was doing business, he wasn't in trouble, and today the emperor came for me. He wouldn't lie to me."

"Then if that is what you know, so be it."

Her chest heaved. "How can you be so sure he is alive?"

The fox flicked its tail. "You are before me, here with me, conversing with me, fueling my energy, and helping me focus, so it is easier to hear someone's thoughts. Without you, it is difficult."

Maru's heart leapt. She couldn't rationalize her caring for it and why she longed to help this creature in front of her—a creature she harbored fear of being a demon.

"Are there more kitsune like you?"

The fox looked around the garden. "There are. But I cannot find them. I cannot remember where they are. There is a shadow . . . it's threatening us . . . we cower . . ."

A forlornness pushed her into silence. "I'm sorry."

Its eyes were full moons rising. "The world is changing. Each day you wake and part of the world you knew fades, and a new day emerges. I can offer protection. But you need to warn your world of the consequences they build. Eventually, I'll need your help to stop the demon."

She was on the brink of accepting, but there was still a doubt that this was all too good to be true. Had someone heard her on Tanabata?

"I will do my best. I still don't trust you. I need more proof, something that proves you are what you say—that I'm not being tricked."

A scream broke the air. The land was stilled. The cicadas were silenced.

Maru said, "My father. Show me proof of him being alive. I need to know where he is. This what I need to help you. I must know where he is."

The fox bowed its head forward. "And you will believe me, no matter what answer I bring? And you will help me to save your city?"

Her heart pounded, ready to erupt. She feared if it burst from its bony cage, it would be seized by the fox and swallowed whole, proving it was a trickster all along. Betrayal was everywhere. She still didn't trust the fox, but she wanted to be able to prove everyone was wrong about her father.

She couldn't think about the alternative yet. "Yes."

A whistle broke the silence. The sign of a demon. She shivered, half-expecting to see a charred figure burst through the brush. *No, it's not real.*

"Kitsune, is it a—"

An ugly, brutal laughter cut through the air only steps away, and Maru jumped to her feet.

Beyond the brush, the tops of two heads passed by. She ducked out of view beneath shrubbery to peer at two middle-aged men, their robes open, one without hair on his head, the other with a lopsided hairbun swinging under his shoulders.

"And then I said to her, well then, why don't you come with me?" The men laughed, cutting down trees, putting her in danger of being discovered.

"Besides, I may not be great looking, but it's better to be with my wife than slaughtered to grease the emperor's toys!"

Maru's blood ran cold. The fox vanished.

She was left to fend for herself. Something scurrying came from the shadows. She heard another cry further in the distance and the sound of heavy breathing over her shoulder. Breaking into a run, she tried to shut out the yokai and yuurei that encroached, hissing into her ears, licking at her ankles. The tengu guarding the temples turned their heads as she ran by. But this time, she felt brave and strong enough to deny their temptation. She had something to live for.

"Maa . . . ruu . . ." a voice called.

A horn blared in the distance, like a piercing scream. She ran faster. She was nearly at the ochaya front when she turned, hoping she would see the fox one more time.

Instead, she glimpsed Mitsu's unmistakable garb draping over the red bridge leading out of Gion and heard heels disappearing into the darkness.

12

A warm glow in the distance disappeared as smoke flooded the night sky. Held in her mother's arms, Maru watched the fire rise, orange faces appearing against the engulfing blackness—evil faces wagged their tongues, concealing the stars.

"It's war, it's war!" shouted a maid. "Enenra! It comes with fire! It comes for us!"

Her mother was firm, watching from the courtyard. Cries, clashes of swords ricocheted through the air. Chaos swirled; her mother fearlessly stayed a rock amidst the wind.

A limping figure stumbled through the gate.

"You're back—oh—I haven't stopped praying—Takechi died. I feared you wouldn't return!"

"It is done. It is done! We've come so far from the small room at Akebono. And we've done it. Sakamoto led us to peace." Father embraced them, burrowing her forehead into his sticky, charred neck that smelled of something sour.

"The tides have changed. We're riding into our new world. We've been asleep for so long."

Her father's face beamed and beamed until his teeth stretched from ear to ear, consuming his face, his eyes melting into one bright orb that came closer, backing her against a wall.

His mouth opened wider as black smoked seeped out, curling down his chin, and the bones of his face pulled upward, hardening into a blackened skull that crept forward.

There was a scream, and a tower of smoke swallowed her whole—and a laugh turned into a whistle.

• • •

Mitsu was already practicing her choreography when Maru awoke. The rising sun painted her room in red, still too early for it to be crystal white. Chimneys and shouts from the factories were already heard from across the river; men were at work building more poles. The soft *thump-thump* of Mitsu's steps, and Adakichi's gentle coaxing and directing—it was Maru's least favorite part of being in a teahouse. No matter how beautiful Mitsu appeared, how perfect her motions seemed, there was always something to correct.

"Flatten your hand."

"Keep your shoulders back."

"Lower your fan."

It went on and on. Many of the orders were contradictory, and she wondered how many strikes from Adakichi it had taken to create her depthless patience.

Maru rubbed her eyes and said a quick thank you that she was not a maiko. She dressed in yesterday's hitoe kimono, saving her best for tomorrow, and made her way downstairs, as they took a break for the news and rice.

"Mitsu, it's your turn to have today's paper—a good geiko reads thoroughly and often to be ready to discuss current topics. The palace mentions more constructions—as they call it—a show of strength. They also discuss a scuffle in the south, so pay close attention to the generals they mention who are navigating the turmoil."

Scuffle. There was that word again. Maru choked on her tea. The rumors were now formal news comments by the palace. The wound in her heart festered from her worry.

"We can pray for his safety," said Adakichi suddenly, softly. "No matter what his status is, under his rule geiko could choose their own names and leave their families behind. And remember, geiko abandon their personal identity during business, so the guests feel your full attention. Take care to remember that when choosing yours. Mind the news today."

Her father wasn't the one holding her back from choosing her path. He had pushed her on to it. Adakichi was exhibiting a lack of trust that put Maru on edge, that gave her the bravery to ask a question that had been on her mind.

"You don't think samurai are why girls are missing, do you?" Maru blurted.

Adakichi, stunned, leaned back. "I am unsure how such an idea would be conjured."

There was a heavy knock at the door.

"Ah, Adakichi, I apologize for the sudden intrusion, but I believe one of your girls is missing these?" The man held a pair of geta. Hers. Their ochaya's kamon was burned into the sole.

Adakichi looked at Mitsu, who looked at Maru, who looked up and saw the man was Kira. Was it perhaps *he* who haunted the back alleys, taking girls? At the thought, she wanted his blood spilled there on the tatami. Was he here, emerging from his cocoon in the aftermath, as a triumphant hunter?

"I certainly don't mean to cause alarm or—ah, a disturbance in your relationships. Everything is so precarious lately. I thought it best if you knew someone spied one of your girls sneaking around Shimabara, hm? If someone saw this, others will whisper—and I'm doing my best to deny anything happened before the palace visit, so it will not affect your applications.

Rest assured; you have my word. It would be unfortunate if this affected your plans for the Matsuri the day before."

Adakichi sprung to her feet. "Kira! My, a visit about finding a pair of geta—I will see to it that proper reprimanding happens. Thank you for confiding in me first."

He bowed and took his leave, eyeing her before shutting the front door.

Adakichi struck Maru across her back until she seared her skin. When she was out of breath, Adakichi stood and smoothed her hair and threw the geta into a corner.

"The fish stench—or maybe it's just the sight of you—fills my stomach with dread. Get yourself to the onsen. I don't want to look at you."

Maru gasped, clutching her ribs.

"Be back before sundown."

She made her way to the door and said quietly, "Is it because of the missing girls? Did they ever find them?" She whispered with the smallest hope.

But Adakichi didn't reveal any new information. "Just don't become the next one."

Mitsu asked, "Could you bring me back some onsen eggs?"

Maru could hear a sly smile in Mitsu's voice. Had she already ruined Maru's name?

Outside she bathed in the warmth, gulping as if she had been starved for nature for days as she left behind the tension that made the walls ache. The roads appeared less familiar. New buildings made of red rock had been erected nearby, and more of the naked trees with silver ropes were standing tall. Maru feared the day she opened her door and nothing looked the same.

"How is the soup these days?" the man before her asked.

It was Tomosuke, the good-looking male geiko wearing dazzling gold robes today. He was laughing, recalling the day when Maru thought she had seen eyeballs splattered on the floor.

"Ah, I haven't had any lately," she said sheepishly, concealing her pain. If only he had shown up moments before, she would not have been bruised: Adakichi had never before hit her in front of others.

"It's just as well. It's too hot. Are you on your way to the train?"

"To the onsen, for the matsuri."

He smiled at her. "You take care, Maru. Don't let shadows fool you into becoming an enemy," he said and went inside, leaving her free.

She continued her walk, drifting into memories of her father and mother's conversation the day he left with other samurai to support the ascension of Emperor Meiji and defend him from the shogun.

Her mother had asked him, "When will there be peace?"

"Peace takes time. People are more resistant than anticipated. The shogun hired samurai willing to be bought to defend the old regime. They are fearful of a future. They see others gaining equality as their loss. We and the Choshu will heal this splintered land. Tosa retreated after Takechi."

"The Choshu? Who burned fields and cattle in war?" her mother sounded tired.

"We met Sakamoto and discussed terms. Allies can be found in rebirth. Shinsengumi, the strong clan we hoped to join forces with, opposed it. But I'm more convinced than ever: Meiji is ready. The shogun will surrender. Nobody wants to be embarrassed."

"And this is the only path?"

"Our feudal lords will all fall. And I won't stand in the way as nature devours her children." Her father was earnest, but Maru remembered him avoiding their eyes, donning his armor, and going out the open door as they said, "Kishikaisei."

A desperate man finds success after being burned.

• • •

Kicking pebbles and ideas away, she climbed the slope past the exclusive shinise as the sun was curtained by a thin haze. Near the towering pagoda, women balanced fabrics and children with pin wheels. Men sitting on top of barrels took swigs, laughing over a plate of what looked like monster legs with little white suckles on red, curvy legs. She stared a little more, trying to figure out which creature was being maimed, but avoided being caught looking ("Which is the rudest thing," she could hear Adakichi say. "Avert your gaze at all times unless it is meant for a man with whom you have relations.")

Restaurants were adorned with dainty summer flowers, and the scent of fresh ginger wafted into the streets. It was too pretty for there to be any yokai or yuurei around today or to have thoughts of sour men.

When she reached the peak and passed beneath a torii, two women in bright robes approached her.

"Many of our customers today have smelled like you," one of the ladies told her and laughed. Maru followed them under the canopy of maples.

"Like an old fisherman?"

"Yes, that's the smell. But the fish are so divine. Perfect on a hot day like today."

Maru would have to take her at her word.

They led her to a small wood building with a low brown roof with rusted hooks holding large lanterns. Stepping into the bathhouse, steam from the onsen blanketed her face. In the open-air rock patio, above-ground wooden tubs and sunken pools under a bamboo cove awaited the guests.

"Be careful. The stones are slippery."

Adakichi praised the bathhouse for giving protection to working women, and it was certainly unlike those the commoners used, which were no more than a shared tub of mildly warm, murky water. Geiko often came here to be in safe company and exchange news of available bachelors, families drowning in scandal, or which teahouse was embarrassed by an unruly guest with wandering hands.

Several geiko were already bathing, their hair tied up in a tenugui wrap.

In the back she spotted an empty bamboo tub sitting under a painted landscape of Mt. Fuji on blue tiles. She dipped her toes in the water before sinking in.

Sighing deeply, she stretched her legs, leaning back to float, draining the worries from her shoulders and feeling her mind detach from her spine. The hot water washed away the odors and dust caked on her skin, shedding with it the weight of recent events. Her bruises and welts stung, but subsided as she gently massaged away the pain.

She had some guilt about being there, feeling safe while her father was away, possibly fearing for his life if he was caught up in the trouble in the south.

Adakichi's dismissal of the rumor that samurai were causing recent terrors released a deep-seeded fear. She pondered whether a demon was to blame. *Could they shapeshift? What if the hunter was right?*

Lessons from the temples told her a fox could have a proclivity to be an evil spirit, but she was growing warmer toward the fox, and she trusted herself not to bond with something inherently dangerous.

The fox was going to help her. It would get her the answers she needed. It was peculiar that she had sent it away, commanding an animal—a wounded one at that—to leave, but she assured herself such a mythical animal could protect itself. It bought her time to think through the next steps.

Wiggling her toes in the water, she gazed at the painting of the holy mountain, transporting her to a pilgrimage her family had taken. She had insisted on collecting fistfuls of leaves, her small purse stuffed full. Her mom encouraged her to return them to nature, while her father challenged her to find the perfect one. On top of the mountain they prayed and paid respects to monks who once defended the mountain in a bloody battle caused by Tokugawa stealing their land.

In the misty fall mountains with pagodas of shimmering reds and oranges, she mused that life was long, and she had time for exploration. Every day brought her new wonderment and was crammed with new knowledge. Her father clutched her hand, giving her a sense of safety as if she would live forever. Her mother gifted her a small talisman from the shrine with gold stitching of the word "family"—the embroidered white silk guarding a prayer inside.

She had turned it over in her hand, racing down the path, scattering leaves to the wind.

But that was so far away. She no longer believed she'd live forever.

Danger was everywhere. Maybe it had always been there, and she'd had the privilege of not seeing it, having been told it was kerakera-onna laughing, or ubagabi causing another ruckus in the river, or noderabo lurking in the temples, mischievously ringing bells. And with each day heavy with new developments, towers rising and clanging in the night, she couldn't fathom a long life of peace without scandal or challenges if anger was brewing. Maybe the fox's anger toward humans wasn't so misplaced. But to suggest blaming her father . . .

Even Adakichi, despite denying the validity of Matsuma's claims, insisted Maru be home before sunset. Something was stirring. The unease in her tone required Maru to look over her shoulder, to be wary of the emperor and worry for her father. She wanted to leap into the painting.

And where, then, were the girls? If *they were taken by a demon, which seemed unlikely*— she couldn't think how it could be feasible—*where would they have gone? To Tokyo?*

Perhaps it wasn't meant to be evil but to take them some place better.

But where was better than Kyoto?

Overwhelmed, her eyelids grew heavy from the steam and the weight of her world. She spied a nearby horse-hair bristled brush and methodically scrubbed her body. Her mind wandered to the women of other okiya who were huddled near her, trading stories.

"Girls in Edo are not nearly as disciplined," one scoffed.

"So, naturally, they would wander into the night. Fools. Pretty little fools."

"This emperor would do good in Edo. Maybe his presence would set them better."

"I heard *he* turns into machines," said a woman with a high bun.

"But how—how could that be?" stammered a round-faced, pillowy geiko.

"The machines' faces open, and their black tentacles come out to take girls, even from far away. They are inhuman, so of course they will take what smells the strongest."

"And their perfumes! They are so strong these days. Influenced by France."

"They want to be anything but us! We have no pride anymore in who we are. We wear dresses that cost outlandish figures. They let others in and immediately lose sight of themselves. Clients want us to speak foreign tongues because they want to imagine being with one!"

"Well, my house will never speak anything but Kyoto-ben."

A pause. "You heard about the one new brothel girl? It's a shame."

The news of girls snatched had reached the other geiko houses. Maybe Matsuma had made his rounds? But claiming that the emperor could shapeshift? Pure blasphemy. *Could it be true?*

"I fear how hideous Edo must be these days."

Maru wished she could recognize their faces. It was hard to distinguish them without their features painted on them. Adakichi would have undoubtedly known them all.

As the discomfort snaking in her heart refused to let her relax, she slipped under the surface and let herself be consumed by the silence the underwater offered. At first all she knew was heat, a comfort that only the very core of her recognized from the imprint of a deep, faraway memory. Something innately familiar and maternal.

Peace. But only for a moment.

Something yanked her ankle and tugged her farther below the surface.

She reached her arms out in desperation, gasping for air and choking on the boiling onsen water that burned her belly. A hand, webbed and scaly, clawed her leg, yanking her to the bottom.

She was going to drown. Her chest burned. She had no more air. She kicked in the darkness, waving her arms, splashing frantically—surely someone would help.

It pulled harder, refusing to let go, digging its nails into her sides. No one was coming.

No one.

She writhed and twisted, reaching for where it was, desperate to fight it and save herself.

Help, she mouthed as her vision darkened.

A scream pierced through the water, and the fox's eyes appeared before her.

She was released. Her body floated to the surface, her eyes awake and alert as she panted. Through the steam, faces of horror stared at her in silence.

She lifted herself out of the tub, her elbows weak and shaking, and found her robe. It smelled of jasmine.

Her hair was stubborn as she ferociously tore out knots with a borrowed kushi, grunting through the pain. She wanted to rid herself of the demon that groped her, seeming to want to force her to join it in the depths of death. It had nearly succeeded; nobody had aided her. Her head grew hotter with each tug, as if yanking off the heads of the foul women who refused to help. She tugged on a particularly nasty one, when she heard something snap

Oh, no!

Closing her eyes and grimacing, she pulled broken pieces of the kushi from her hair. Bad luck. It would be expensive to replace. She tucked it under a zaru of towels and abandoned her hair and tried to settle her jitters by rubbing cream on her face and scrubbing a waxy yuzu on her lips, her stomach rumbling at the teasing flavor.

With her hands shaking from the misfortune, a maid helped her dress and tie her obijime before she went into the sitting room where women sipped tea, some staring at her in distress.

"We will have to close ours; we don't have another option."

"I cannot face it—the thought of a man overseeing us."

"It's not so bad. My father could have—"

"It won't be the same now that many traditions have been discarded."

These words flew by her. They were small sounds dancing around her head. She tried to piece them together. Something about them sounded familiar; she could almost grasp their meaning.

One of the onsen ladies rushed to her stool with a cup of cloudy tea.

"Jasmine?" asked Maru.

"Pardon?" the lady responded.

"The incense. It's not too strong, is it?"

"Why is there a cause for worry?"

"Oh, nothing. No, it's fine, thank you. I didn't mean anything . . ." Maru's voice trailed off. The lady disappeared behind a hanging tapestry. Maru flushed. Would her odor attract danger? Would she be snatched off the street?

Others watched, trying to assess which house she was from; she kept her gaze averted.

"Aki?" whispered the round-faced geiko. Was that Satori? One of Adakichi's reviled gossipers?

"We left her here," said the thin-faced woman Maru recognized from the matsuri roof.

"She has only just begun. She's too old."

"Aki is too kind, risking another scandal to take her in," said a woman Maru thought to be called Mihiro, Satori's known sister-in-arms. They were never far apart. It made Maru uncomfortable to see those two conversing with Adakichi's closer friends. She turned her head away to listen, and couldn't tell which voice belonged to whose face.

"Someday there will be trouble."

"Alas, not all are meant to be admired, for the prettiest pastry goes stale if it merely sits."

"Well, I wouldn't have taken her in!"

"It's because we are sensible."

"Keiko saw her carted away by police . . ."

"That father of hers—something is wrong."

Maru sipped her tea loudly. How could they say such things? How could they, touting traditionalism, forget the sacrifice of the samurai so readily because it was convenient? They ridiculed her as if her father was a barbarian.

"They would fit in better in Edo, far from here."

"Supposedly samurai fight in Satsuma."

"He will assuredly kill them in battle or kill them for being traitors."

"And to suddenly abandon their daughter! For an act of suicide."

"Really, it says so much about him as a father."

Maru stood up. The women stopped their chatter, unanimously sipping their tea noisily. Their eyes followed her as she passed by the wide patio and made her way under the arched pines and cedars. She said a quick prayer before leaving them behind. But the soothing effects of the bath soon faded away. Her rational thoughts evaporated in the sweltering heat and anger coursed through her.

In her wandering to slow her racing mind, she found herself near a quiet, ancient temple. The moment seized her, and in desperation to find peace, she ascended. At the top of the stone stairs, beneath the torii, she gazed over Kyoto. The sun's heavy rays through the treetops sent tingles down her spine. She felt the cool drops of dew from their thick leaves on her face.

The dark rooftops reflected sunlight in soft crevices of purple shadows in between the pale shanty walls. Much of the city looked the way she remembered it, except for having more smoke and clusters of buildings on longer streets. The tall dark pagoda remained in the foreground, where it stood for a millennium as a reassuring landmark and guide.

More than ever she needed a guide. Was there something wrong with her, as the other geiko implied? They were just gossipmongers, but she couldn't swat their chat away.

Kyoto seemed to smile back at her. It was a beating heart of gold cascading across the town and her home. The city would always offer protection here and a way to belong here, somehow. While she might never know what the next day would bring, finding beauty here was always a certainty. Energy from the ground radiated up her spine, fueling her onward.

These views were the only souvenirs she wanted. Chiming music sounded in the distance, signaling the middle of the day. She descended, making sure her toes clutched her geta so they wouldn't slip off.

An orange animal crossed in front of her.

Was it a fox? Was it back already?

No, it was a stray cat diving beneath a shop's stoop. A mother and her children picked out tea leaves at a yatai known for serving the best matcha that was brought in from Shizuoka on a donkey.

Older ladies fanned themselves, leaning into another. Men pulled rattling carts of meat toward the pagoda.

Stretched down the cobble road before her was one of her favorite paths—one her family had wandered down many times. The long, curving road was lined with beautiful shinise. Here, there were no ugly, barren, iron trees with crisscrossing silver ropes, no blocky red buildings or long walls. These were creamy, with slotted fences and yellow-brown frames over rice paper windows. The path sloped past potted geraniums and statues of mischievous deities, a gutter of petals rushed down to carry away muck. The road followed the sun, so no matter where it was, it formed a tunnel of light.

Around the bend, a merchant's cart was stacked tall with apples, cherries, and melon too beautiful to eat. She picked a jar of ume. A nearby flower shop had massive orchids, blooming kikyo and suiren, bushy ferns, tall palms and long reeds—all waiting to be taken home.

When did the market become so varied? Galleries advertised unfamiliar names. A pastry shop stood on the corner. Were these commonplace now? She had a pastry once on the emperor's birthday and remembered sinking her teeth into the soft bread, the crush flaking off her lips, dissolving it on her tongue. One time her father offered her a spoon of honey behind her mother's back.

Peeking through the window, she saw small melon breads and small, flatter bread. It smelled so warm and sweet. She wished her father was with her. He would grin and pull her inside.

"Don't tell your mother," he'd say, even after she passed away.

"Ma . . . ru..."

The voice interrupted her daydream. She looked around, but nobody seemed to be there.

"Ma . . . ru..."

There it was again. It was coming over the rooftops. It wanted her.

"Ma . . . ru, we need it."

She wanted it.

Instinctively, she turned off the curved shinise road, searching for it.

"Ma . . . ru..."

Where was it taking her?

The voice was insistent, and she needed to answer. Would it lead her to the girls?

"Ma . . . ru, come fight."

The pace was picking up. She hurried after it. Was it the creature that pulled her under? Was that how the other girls had been grabbed? Her feet were urging her to go faster and faster—the shops, the shanties flying by, barely an apology when she pushed past a child—when a voice caught her.

"Maru?"

Tane stood in her way, her basket askew. They clasped hands, grinning from ear to ear.

The voice vanished.

"Don't you need to be getting ready for the matsuri tomorrow?"

"Ah, I stopped by the onsen. Then I found myself here," she said, confused and frightened that she didn't remember how she found her way to Tane's side of Kyoto.

"Come, have tea. My mother has a fresh pot."

They squeezed down the alley. The bustle was fading. Maru heard trickling water as they approached a shop nestled beside a pond with a spout spewing. Two bright koi were spinning to greet her. She admired the fat fish, envying their simple life.

They stooped to enter a small building with unstained wood walls. The far wall opened to a lush garden. It made her feel like she was having tea inside a forest. Tane's family distinguished their way of preparing cold noodles by running them through bamboo shoots with mountain river water before plopping them on a zaru. Their shop had become popular with poets and philosophers who filled the corners to write in a cool, beautiful setting.

Sitting on two pillows, Maru and Tane dangled legs over a ledge that dropped to the mossy bed of the pond. Tane called for her mother, scrambling to her feet. When she didn't get a response, she went to get the cups herself.

Maru stared at the garden out, trying to ignore the echoes of poisonous conversations in the bathhouse.

He will assuredly kill them in battle or kill them for being traitors.

"Sorry. Here, try this—it's new. What do you think?" Maru jumped at Tane's resurfacing and took the cup, peering over the edge and saw a pale, viscous liquid.

"Royal milk tea, as it's called."

"Sorry?"

"Apparently the Europeans take their tea with milk and sugar, so we thought—"

"Sorry?"

"Maru, I don't understand, either!"

Maru took a sip. *Too sweet!* She grimaced, forgetting her manners.

Tane tightened. "It's not my cup of tea. I think everyone is pretending around here."

Maru snorted and tried to conceal it with a cough. She couldn't let go of her feelings of despondency.

"Are you alright? I'm sorry about Ai's wedding, I really don't think she meant any harm."

"It's fine, I've already forgotten," said Maru stiffly. She hadn't forgotten, but she had far more important things to worry about than whether or not Ai was being petty and rude.

Tane gulped. "Well, Kiku and I don't feel any sort of different way about you. We're always close. Ai is funny about these things. I wasn't sure if I should talk to her about this, or if she was waiting . . ."

"I understand; I know you were in a complicated place."

"Yes, you always are so understanding—it's why you'll be a great geiko."

Maru wanted to believe her. No matter how many times she had explained it to them, her friends couldn't grasp that she wasn't on track to be geiko. She was in fact worse off because she seemed to be forever in an apprentice role, to observe and fetch and clean and serve without any glory or professional name that she could claim. There would be no ochaya bearing her kamon, no danna looking to be her lifelong patron. She'd always be a shikomi.

"Have you heard from your father? Or more from the palace?"

Maru shook her head.

"I heard there was some commotion recently in Satsuma. You don't think he is in trouble? Some of our visitors yesterday were talking of heading south to be part of it. It's scary."

That was the last thing she wanted to hear. The women gossiping, that was second nature, and expected, but her friend telling her made it seem more real.

"Being questioned by the emperor's police is scary. I was worried about you. I thought about it some more, and I think they may come back."

This was not what Maru wanted to hear.

Maru closed her eyes. "I was thinking of writing to him." The idea had suddenly dawned on her. She had to know. Was the fox near? Was he angry at her? The demon pretending to be him haunted her mind.

"It's so strange for us to send something through the post that Tokyo could have by dinner the next day."

"The emperor is doing a lot of good," said Maru carefully, recovering a sliver of dignity.

"Yes, he's something," Tane said sheepishly. Tane had done poorly in history and politics classes, Maru remembered. A feeling of confidence was coming over her.

"He's going to choose the house of Adakichi to get the first eternal lantern!"

Tane's eyes tilted downward. "What? The electricity? Mom and pop applied for it—"

"It's a secret. We will be presented with it; this will be announced soon. Adakichi is honored."

Maru didn't know why she was saying this. Maybe Tane would tell Ai and help to rescue their friendship. She'd be less likely to be left out if Ai knew how special she and Adakichi were.

Tane nodded, looking paler. "That's wonderful."

Maru jerked her head. "Do you have paper and ink by chance?"

"Poets constantly leave some," she said, dipping behind the tapestry where there were several large fires and kettles boiling and shelves full of glass jars of tea leaves steeping. When she was younger, they fascinated Maru, but now her curiosity had faded.

Other shop goers were stooped over cups, summoning fortunes from tea leaves and paying no attention to Maru. It was exactly what she liked. Here, she wasn't from an ochaya, and she didn't have a famous father. She was a customer stopping by for tea and some peace and quiet.

Sitting at the kotana, she looked through the thick leaves and over at the largest, oldest shrine in Kyoto, built atop massive wooden trestles with a long bridge connecting each prayer hall that wound through the treetops. Squinting, she could make out a gold statue surrounded by candles. A line of red-cloaked monks crossed the bridge to the shrine that disappeared into the greenery; branches rustled, and a monkey was climbing nearby. On mountain walks when she was younger, she had longed to be up there with the monkey defying the rules of being human.

They threw nuts up at the monkeys, trying to coax them to play. She remembered being disappointed by their shyness and her father assuring her that "the fruit is plentiful. They have no use for our seeds." Maru remembered her mother being worried that they'd carry her off.

"Paper and green tea," Tane said and passed them to Maru before checking in on other customers.

This tea was much sharper and bolder than the sweet "milk tea," and much more to her liking. She pulled the paper close to her and prepped the ink.

GHOST TRAIN

• • •

It was a cold, dark night, before the start of the year. They were awakened by the smell of smoke. A bell was tolling.

"We must get out! Now!"

Her mother's arms seized her, rushing her through walls of smoke and raging flames. She clutched her mother's body. Ashes were falling as thick as snow. As they escaped from the building, men carrying long guns and others with swords were shouting.

"Sakamoto is dead! This is the end!"

"No! Stop! He's not here! It's a child!"

"To the death of all who defied him!"

Another scream and a rush of figures, a hand covering her eyes, and more shrieking.

"Run! Run! I've got them!"

Suddenly her father ran toward the forest, disappearing from view.

Her mother pulled her into a run on the path, frightened that every sound they made would expose them to the enemies. She ran along the river until the blood red sun rose against the grey sky. Her feet were so blistered they had to stop. At the river's edge, they waited for a boat.

"We're safe; we're safe now," her mother told her over and over.

They found their way home. When her father came back he was filled with rage. He could barely talk. He put fear into her heart. He paced awhile and then was out the door without any reassurance of when he would return.

And her mother cried, holding Maru tightly and waiting for him.

• • •

Readying herself to write, she found she had lost the words to explain the sadness of that time. When her mother died it was hard on her father. He no longer communicated well with his daughter. The jokes between them waned without her mother to warn them when to toe the line. He spared her the details of business and spoke less about his travels and trades. There was a growing cavern between them as she began to know him less, and he asked fewer questions about her school and friends and other interests.

When the emperor made changes to impose more restrictions, it altered her family and clan. The emperor now asked more of her father, and it took a took a toll on him. His praises for the emperor lessened, and the shadows on his face deepened. Before he left for his journey, his nights grew longer, and he slept more into the day.

Maru tried to say something about his erratic patterns and a seeming frustration and unhappiness. But each time he insisted that business was complicated with new policies and international relationships, and he was just learning the role of a merchant and shedding old habits to get comfortable in new routines. But he continued to fidget.

The day finally came when he knew he had to take her to Adakichi and ask for the favor of her help. She was afraid, but knew there was no use in fighting it. He had been himself, chipper and trying to joke along the way, saying it was for her own protection. When he walked away, it felt as if she had lost both parents and had no reason to believe he knew what was best for her or himself.

Adakichi had calmly taken her in, claiming to know nothing more than what they had been told that day and never pried or speculated how long she'd be staying with her.

Maru went back to her paper, putting ink to it.

> *Such news these days, wave after wave and I can't swim. It's not just rules that change every day, but the game itself. I am not even sure which cards I'm supposed to have. I surely hope you are successful with your trades, for I wish to play with you instead.*
>
> *Home is fine. I eat well. Visitors are kind and I am becoming better. Fireworks are nice from rooftops.*
>
> *The city will look different when you return, but the sun sets and rises the same. Adakichi told me about a southern volcano that never stops talking. It's like the birds here, with their endless chatter, from faceless sources. I hope you are safe. Some are missing, and I hope you do not suffer their fate. You know how the hungriest bird screams the loudest.*
>
> *I pray for you.*

Maru twirled her pen, unsure if there was any need to say more, if she needed to mention the fights breaking out, or the police who visited her, or her visit from Kira and ask if he remembered him. She feared going into too many details in case it worried him.

She had to be subtle enough to get the truth from him. It was the simple answer. Maru put her letter away and prepared to leave.

She said to Tane, "I forgot. When is Ai's wedding?"

"Oh, I think it's in the coming weeks. They'll put it in the news. You don't have to go."

Maru's bent her head. The feeling of isolation was creeping in.

"It seems unusual. She of course knows my geiko house. It's so prominent in Gion."

"Yes, of course it is."

"Is she embarrassed about me?" Her cheeks flushed, but the question spilled out of her readily, like a full cup of tea that burned to the touch and jumped uncontrollably from her hand.

"I don't think it's you, it's just—"

"It's what? She's embarrassed by knowing geiko?" Tane was silent. "What then? That I'm not married?" Maru's voice rose, daring Tane to tell her the truth.

"Definitely, no. None of us are."

"Then what?"

"It's the rumors about the guards and other worrisome things. She said you are strange."

Maru clenched her fist.

"Look, Maru, your father and mother were both so nice to us."

"Yes, they were! Always giving candy and letting us play on the lakeshore. Her father never took us anywhere. We just stayed inside and listened to priest stories."

"Her family has the highest-ranking priest. Stature is of importance . . . those stories . . ."

"Her family is important? And mine isn't?" Maru snapped in retaliation.

"Not that you aren't a person of stature. But samurai are—well, they're outdated. And we think you know that. We aren't sure what he's doing in Satsuma, and there's trouble there, and you were visited by guards who investigated you. It's a little controversial, don't you think? If it were up to me, you'd come with us. Of course. But it's their decision."

Maru nodded.

"Your father is a good man, but they are afraid." She whispered, "Samurai are up to something against the emperor. It's not a rumor anymore. In the paper, he was calling for any information to be shared or it would be traitorous. I wanted to be the one to warn you."

Adakichi hadn't told her about the paper mentioning that. Tane hadn't betrayed her. Did she know something else? She felt sick. Her blood was boiling, her heart whistling like a kettle.

Tane asked her, "Are you truly fine? Please tell me if you know something that puts you in danger. I know the police scared you the other day"

Maru shouted, "My father is a good man, and it is despicable you'd accuse him of such a thing! You tell me he's fighting the emperor and telling me I'm a traitor. *You* are betraying our friendship! They destroyed our home, the only place I ever wish to be. And I can't go back now. He risked his life to raise Meiji to the throne. He is a tradesman, as I've told you; yet you believe strangers rather than your friend!" Maru snatched her things and abruptly moved to leave.

"Please, shh, the guests; this isn't the place for this."

"Don't insult my father."

"Let me talk to Ai. She'll change her mind. You obviously are distracted. Calm down!"

"My mind—" Maru raised her voice, feeling herself redden, as if she had a fire ablaze on her scalp.

Tane's scared expression cooled her rage.

She dropped her voice. "My mind is all right. You think I care about her wedding. I don't. How could you? I come here because you're a friend."

"Yes, please, sit. It's been a while. I'm so sorry. I'm confused, too."

Tane held her arm, and Maru reluctantly let her, then yanked it away.

"I always say the wrong things. You remember me in school," Tane's voice was shaking.

Maru's heart stilled. Tane had never been considered an outgoing or confident student. One time she was teased for being "mousey." When she did speak up, she was often wrong or expressed an odd opinion. Although they were apart in social ranking, Maru befriended her, sometimes feeling sorry for her. Ai and Kiku welcomed her too, unabashedly enthusiastic about her sweetness and distinguished family. But now her shy friend was bearing the brunt of the Hosokawa tiger roaring at her.

"I have a letter to mail," Maru told her.

13

Maru cut through the city until she pierced its heart. Carts darted left and right like dragonflies; people loitered and flicked through newspapers with images of that blasted train and cartoons of foreigners, and drawings of the stoic emperor.

Her mind was filled with Tane's words. Nobody knew the extent of her turmoil.

She claimed that her father is a good man, but the authorities have heard rumors that he's planning something against the emperor.

She was repulsed that Tane dared to say this out loud. Kiku had said "It was always in jest. We don't believe the rumors." Timid, shy Tane who had little to her name, now wielded a sword.

Tane had informed her, "In the newspaper, Emperor Meiji was calling for any information about a conspiracy to be shared or it would be traitorous."

This she would have to see for herself. Not that it mattered. She had cleared his name when the guards attempted to ruin her reputation and left her home in a rubble.

Friends joining in the destruction hurt her in a different way by believing something is wrong with her.

Thinking of Ai gave her another pang. She had enjoyed swinging arms with her friends as they went up and down Gion carrying their bushels of dried flowers, nibbling on dried fish, picnicking on the riverbank, whispering about the attention-getting kimono.

Now, she could only orbit, basking in their sunshine as an outsider.

Someone on a corner was shouting at people passing by, and making wild claims about the emperor and protesting some new change. Maru didn't look twice as police swarmed the protestor.

Should she go back to Tane? Maru was justified in her hurt and eagerness to be away from her challengers. Tane had reached out, brave enough to say what was on her mind, her feelings she held toward samurai. But Tane was wrong. The image of her face made Maru dig her nails into her palm.

Laughter from a group nearby rang out, reminding her of running through the Tanabata matsuri, giggling over their wishes and their jovial dancing. It seemed like it happened years ago.

Kiku! Kiku would be the answer. The ever-present, forever-pleasant Kiku could be the peacekeeper. She'd simply reach out to her and explain her side, and then surely Kiku would be able to get through to Tane. She would see it her way, as another defending her family's status. Her heart softened thinking of sharing salted watermelon with Kiku by the sparkling riverbank.

She felt some confidence creeping up her shoreline.

Dodging the day drinkers and girls scouting for day work, she began to look more fervently for the post office, which she knew was near Tokaido road "where Edo meets Kyoto." She hardly knew how it worked or how much it would cost her. Adakichi's paper announced the southern postal route opened a few months ago; before it only connected Tokyo and Kyoto, with exceptions for foreign mail in Hakodate and Kobe—although she had no idea what foreigners could possibly be sending back and forth to each other.

The idea of a public postal system made her itch. Was it a risk reaching out to her father in any way?

A bell chimed, concealed within a shrine hall. Her heart leaped. With clock towers erecting all over Kyoto, it had been years since she heard a shrine's bell signaling the time. They had been considered archaic, replaced by faces with moving hands. This shrine must be one of few still carrying on the tradition; and now its nostalgic tolls called her home. But she turned her feet toward the city center and continued on her way.

A family along the riverbank caught her gaze. The adults sat cross-legged on their cushions cracking scallops out of wooden boxes while their children splashed in the water. This was their little empire. It would have been ukiyo-e perfect if her family had been there.

The bells chimed again. Their second ring meant evening was approaching. Where had the day gone? She needed to hurry. As she passed the shrine's wall of lanterns, each had a family kamon painted on it for the next day's matsuri. No Hosokawa this year. She reached out and ran her fingers along the sun-lit parchment lanterns, stacked as high as the buildings. There were so many more names than last year. Ever since the Name Day, families had emerged, proudly allowed to bear theirs. She smiled, thinking of the gift her father gave to so many. A young girl rang the bell. Maru wondered what she was praying for until her father rushed out, pulling her away and bowing to the monk who peered out the door.

Her reaction to Tane had been too extreme; she had to mail her letter without doubting her actions. If her father was innocent, why wouldn't he accept her letter and reach out to her?

The smell of blood filled her nostrils, and she searched the crowd, feeling afraid, but then realizing she'd only bitten her tongue.

The new buildings here were never dainty like the nicely framed, flowers-out-front kind of places in Gion. These were stone or red square rocks. Solemn and intimidating. Their formidable size blocked the sun. Some were even larger than the palace or the Kabuki Hall. She wasn't sure how they were built to be so firm, unlike the soft wooden curved homes that blended with the forest.

The change made her queasy. It all looked so unfamiliar and asymmetrical. She tried to suppress a cramp, gently rubbing her belly hand near the bump of her tanto.

She had to be close to the post office. Signs for routes directed people to schools or the palace. And the people—she couldn't believe her eyes! Even more were wearing pants here and displayed the most peculiar tops and dark outer wear she'd ever laid eyes on. Even women wore them! They were carrying leather bags, headed to and from important looking buildings, which read "office this" and "office that." Was this part of the emperor's expansion?

This wasn't like Kyoto at all. Maru was a foreigner in her own city.

She was looking upward in disbelief when she collided with someone.

When she stepped back, a middle-aged man with a smooth face and bright eyes wearing pantaloons and a floppy hat was smiling at her.

"Did you enjoy that snapper you picked out?"

"Oh!" It was the man in the brown floppy hat from the fish vendor.

"Are you lost?"

"No. No, sir, I just need to mail a letter."

"Excellent, because I don't know my way either, so I was afraid you'd put me on the spot. It's a new city, very different from when I was a boy. You'll see yet another new monument here tomorrow."

"Tomorrow?" His accent was thick, and she had trouble catching his words.

"New faces are coming and going here every day, and new buildings going up. It will be like Tokyo someday."

Unsure of what to say, she relied on her training, creating a reactive question based on the one word she caught: "Are you from Tokyo?"

"Tokyo, Tokyo yes, I'm from there and here. From everywhere, when I read a lot. I find Kyoto delightful." She understood half of what he said. Some of her father's house calls were to men from prefectures where accents differed, but having to listen on her own was difficult.

"Kyoto is delightful?" she repeated.

"It's good, it's good! Beautiful." She nodded and smiled. Of course he would find Kyoto charming: he was in the better place of the two, no matter what their former lords had to say about them. She saw that in the papers he held there were strange markings in the corner, indicating "Tokyo."

"Is that to Tokyo?"

"Ah, it is to go *from* Tokyo, yes! It was delivered to me today by the post office. Quite a good eye you have. I'll accompany you there if you like. It's around here somewhere . . . I found it earlier, but the day wasn't so hot and I wasn't as tired then. Maybe we will get lost together." He smiled.

Maru nodded awkwardly, politely accepting whatever it was he had just offered. They continued to walk by the bland, grey buildings with funny names that Maru didn't recognize.

"Where did you come from, if you don't mind telling me?"

"Where? Oh, Gion, up the river."

He laughed, cutting her off. "The day a Japanese person doesn't know what Gion is—that truly is the end. So, are you a maiko?"

"Maiko? No, though I am in an ochaya." Her plain robes apparently didn't give it away.

"You are a beauty, and you're polite. You will surely make a fine geisha someday."

"Geiko."

"We'll have to compromise," he said with a soft laugh. "My upbringing."

"I have never been to Tokyo," Maru said carefully, her ears adjusting to his beats and predictability. She gestured to the taller, dark buildings. "Does it look like this?"

"It's even grander." He proudly threw up his arms. "Thirty cities in one. Expansive, ever-bursting at the seams. Kyoto is a spring rain and easier to cover on foot. But if it ever stops resisting, it may transform into a grander metropolis than Tokyo."

Maru smiled absently. Some of his words were too ambiguous to decipher through his accent. She turned to admire the sweeping roads heavy with the wired trees and lamps. They were also full of rickshaws piled high with burlap sacks and barrels of supplies. She thought of a way to focus his attention.

"How did you get here?"

"A wagon. I'm not rich enough for the train," he said and laughed. She wasn't sure what was funny.

"The train can carry people?"

"Why yes, and someday it will undoubtedly carry a hundred. You will be able to go to Tokyo in the morning and be home here in time for dinner—someday."

Maru thought she was hearing gibberish. Maybe his accent made it too difficult to understand him. She couldn't imagine moving at such a high speed or being in a vehicle where many people traveled together. Tokyo was far away. Her father would describe his aching joints for weeks after trekking across the old Tokai-do road that ran between Kyoto and Tokyo. This was the first time she was told that the trains also transported people. She thought of the fox's warning of the emperor ruining nature.

"But how does it work, exactly?"

"How charming! You have an engineer's mind!" he said.

She had no idea what an engineer was. "You seem to know what's happening. All I hear is from visitors, but they're usually trying to impress Adakichi, my madam."

"What have you heard?"

"I—well, I don't know—some peculiar stories," she said.

He waited, and she finally stopped staring at her feet and asked, "Do they run on blood, sir?"

"On blood?" he tilted his head back and laughed. "And dare I ask whose blood? It would take an awful lot of it to push a machine that big."

Maru was too nervous to laugh and wondered if he thought she was stupid.

She said, "Sorry, I don't know. I haven't ever seen a train close up. They say maidens' blood is best."

"You've never seen one? Well, why not watch the next one arrive? In fact, the Kyoto Station is having a grand opening. I'm sure you've seen the announcement. It's actually quite nearby."

She nodded, eager to dismiss the rumors about blood.

"I've never had to answer a question about the train's fuel. I can reassure you that trains are run by using the elements of coal, fire, and water. These three elements produce steam that's the force that keeps the wheels of the vehicle churning. I am simplifying this, mostly for my sake. That's why a train is called a steam locomotive. There is no blood involved. I don't know what they teach you here, but I have never heard anyone else talking about such fuel."

Maru was lost. She was too nervous. She had been about to ask about the wires and if they required blood, too. Or if the train had tentacles inside of it that could grab people like the women claimed in a hot tub at an onsen. The man patted her shoulder, and she flinched. She realized she was fully aware he wasn't paying to touch her.

"This sign says the post office is this way," he said, gesturing. His wide eyes looked sad. She hadn't meant to offend him, but she wasn't sure how to tell him she felt uncomfortable when he touched her. She couldn't articulate it herself. Adakichi had never taught her how to rebuke a man politely for unwanted physical contact, except to urge them to visit a brothel.

She was surprised to see him slow his pace so she could keep up with him; men typically rushed ahead, wearing looser clothing and shorter clogs.

"Are the trains awfully large?"

"Ahh, they are the size of several wagons. According to the British, the trains we have are only a quarter of the size of the ones they produce in England. But their boats are not big enough to carry them here."

"A quarter? British?" She was puzzled by more strange words. She hadn't kept up in foreign affairs, and she could not recall any school lessons that would have offered answers.

"Ahh," he sighed, scratching his chin, "It's ah, an island off Europe similar to ours, where they've ruled for a long time. Many live in Tokyo. I have met a few myself."

"The foreigners?" She shuddered, imagining someone coming from so far away to live in Japan.

"Yes, there is quite a community there. There are thousands of them!"

"Thousands?" *Had she heard that right?*

"Yes, they are helping us implement the telephone wires from Hokkaido to Nagasaki. Some of their great minds combined with our prowess, is something to behold."

"Oh. About the wires. Do they do bad things to—?"

"Before you finish, let me say no! No maidens are harmed during the establishment of electricity. Our system will strengthen our infrastructure across all prefectures, as destined."

There was now something familiar about this. When her father talked about foreign lands, even while praising them, he diminished their size and wealth. To her, Japan was the biggest country in the world. Imagining another country rivaling them with bigger trains helped her to understand the fear the shogun must have experienced when foreigners flaunted their strength and machinery.

"They must be so powerful." She wanted to ask him the difference between a telephone and telegraph and how sewing machines worked, and if the train could fly or hunt like a hawk, and if there was a beast he suspected was taking away girls.

He said, "Yes indeed. With the new technology, we are on the brink of being our strongest self."

She paused, thinking over his words carefully to ensure she understood. "But it seems Kyoto is fading away."

He tilted his head, pondering this. "Nothing is fading away. We are discovering the best parts of ourselves. Japan is only now seeing our true potential emerge. It had been hidden away."

They walked in silence for a few paces. Maru was proud. She considered his words and what the future held for her family.

"There it is!" He pointed toward a humble stall with a stable next to it. "Good! It looks like they haven't left yet for the day. There is a counter at the side where you can purchase a stamp."

"A stamp?"

"Yes, the sticker that goes on your envelope certifying you've paid for your letter to be mailed."

"Oh please, come with me! You know everything." Maru was beginning to like this man.

"But you seem to handle yourself just fine. You are young, and your curiosity will move you."

She was a little perplexed but grateful for his help and wanted to express her gratitude. "I'm sorry, sir. I have taken a lot of your time. And I was impolite, badgering you with questions."

He laughed again, so easily.

"I am—ah—it's a little difficult to pinpoint. Let's say I'm a lifelong student studying society to find ways to preserve our culture, and I record what I see."

Maru gave a little shrug to indicate she knew no more about him than before she asked what he did in Kyoto.

He continued, "I help the government and our emperor, namely by sharing information about our ways with our new allies. There is a cross-cultural exchange happening, and we need to preserve what we can before it disappears." He gestured to the tall buildings. "Kyoto is the place to do that. In fact, we are searching for ambassadors to travel here to study our culture and represent us. You could say I'm interviewing people for this job."

She wondered if they so afraid of Kyoto vanishing, they needed to write it all down. Who could remember what happened every day? And who would ever want to leave their home to go somewhere unknown?

"Things are changing fast," he smiled, as if reading her mind.

"You're here in time to go to the Gion matsuri tomorrow," she said hurriedly.

He smiled. "That's one of the marvels I have heard a lot about and have seen on postcards."

"And the yokai here—you must have heard the tales about them, too." Maru felt nervous, worrying that something wasn't translating correctly. "Well, they are integral to our matsuri, you know. We need to respect them and their ways." She thought about what the fox said about mankind chasing them away and wondered if this man was part of what the fox warned her about. Or if he was aware that he was complicit in this.

"Oh, the Yokai!" He laughed. I know those are just stories. Yokai aren't real. They are part of our country's folklore. You might say Meiji killed them all," he said.

Maru wanted him to stop laughing and explain what he knew.

"What about the blood odor. Where does it come from?"

"The smell of blood?"

"Yes, it rots in the morning after it rains. Don't you smell it? You must know that girls are missing. They say there's a new Shuten Doji taking them—or maybe—something else is doing this."

"I'm afraid I am a bit lost. If you mean the smell of metallic wires on electricity poles after a rainstorm, it's a chemical reaction that could be confusing people. A type of rust, if you will. Ha! I suppose it would look like blood. And, a new Shuten Doji, you say? Isn't its head in a temple? Well, something is there, at least. I doubt it's anything but a painted goat head."

Maru felt frustrated that she unable to explain this to him in his dialect. She shook her head, only trying to spare herself. She was ready to dismiss the subject with him.

"But then, how are the girls harmed? How are they taken away?"

He stared at her with no expression. From Adakichi's lessons, she knew she had to intervene before embarrassing him and keeping him from having to answer "Never mind."

"Oh—you're talking about the girls reported to be missing? Ah, there were two in Tokyo that went astray, but I believe they were mistresses caught in a bad business." He shook his head in what Maru perceived to be a false sadness. "But I can assure, there is no Shuten Doji wreaking havoc on the town. It's usually a man with a gripe."

Maru didn't know what he was saying anymore. It was time to part ways; she curtsied and told him: "The day is getting away from me, but it was a pleasure."

He touched his hat and went back down the wide street they'd come from, when she heard, "Oh, Miss! A teahouse is the center of Kyoto, and it would be the perfect place to study."

Maru stared at him expectantly. Then the pieces fit together.

"Oh!" she said. She pulled out an old card holder Adakichi had given her, slipping a hanameishi from it, and presented it to him with both hands. It smelled of incense and pea flower.

He took her card and bowed. "Thank you, House of Adakichi."

Maru blushed.

"I'll call on you and your house! Or if you run into me tomorrow, I'll take to the station. It has the best view of the train!" And he vanished into the crowd.

Maru stared after him for longer than she wanted to admit, snapping out of it only when an angry old leathery man grunted at her for standing in the way of his rickshaw. The post office was a yatai that was stacked with papers, envelopes, twine, burlap sacks, and colorful squares stuffing the shelves to the brim. She was taken aback when she saw open it was to the public. Her father had relied on secret networks that transported letters by bribing cavalrymen to be their couriers. She knew that at one time formal letter-sending was reserved for only the court and feudal lords—or for jealous concubines disguised for the purpose of sabotaging a former lover. Here, in broad daylight, was a place anyone could send a letter without using any bribery or sabotage.

A small young man snapped his head up. “Where to?”

“Sorry?”

“Where to,” he waved impatiently. “Tokyo or Osaka?”

“Oh, to Satsuma.”

He glowered as if he were trying to judge if she was a member of the so-called resistance. He seemed to have figured out his answer because he relaxed his face.

“Ah, Satsuma. That is extra. Very far.”

“Sorry. How much?”

“Three!”

“Sorry?”

“Three copper!”

It was expensive. She had barely a few yen to her name.

“Actually, make it five. In case it requires a contractor.”

“Five! You said—”

“There is a military conflict going on there; haven’t you heard? I can’t walk into a battle and risk my life for paltry wages. It will cost five. Or ten if you keep lingering here.”

She clutched her letter that now seemed diminished in its meaning. She defended her father to Tane and worked up the courage to come all this way with the coins hot her in purse.

She heard: “Hosokawa, life continues to bless me.” The mail man scoffed and ducked behind the counter as Maru stepped into a man’s shadow behind her.

“Kira!” she exclaimed.

He said, “You are so skittish! Are you alright?”

Maru folded the letter tightly.

“Yes, yes, apologies. It’s not you. There was—ah, it is a surprise.”

“I do step outside the Gosho walls now and again. You are mailing a letter?”

“Yes, I thought I would write to my father.”

“Any word from him?”

"No," she said slowly. "Is that bad? Is it something to do with what my trouble caused? Again, I am so sorry—it wasn't my place—"

"You are the daughter of a samurai," he said teasingly.

She felt bashful. "Two palace policemen visited me."

He raised his eyebrows but didn't say anything.

She continued, "They were asking about him. I thought it was my mishap at the palace or something I'd done to interfere with his business."

"No . . . no." His slow response was too doubtful, and he repeated more urgently, "No, no, everything is fine. We heard some rumors, something rather childish, of some traders partaking in a rather black-market business. The Gosho is concerned about making sure traders are, ah, not importing anything illegal that isn't licensed."

That wasn't what the policemen mentioned yesterday. Neither did Tane or the newspaper.

Everyone was lying to her.

"Maru, your father is okay. I know he is a fine man. Though sometimes we receive information that warrants caution. These days are fragile, and we all must protect our empire," he concluded.

Maru smiled weakly, his opinion causing her knees to bend.

"Well? I need to get a move on if I'm going to Satsuma."

The postal worker waved a wooden sheath in her face, waiting for her to slip the letter inside. Kira smiled down at her and gestured for her to pass it to the mail man.

She was holding it over the counter when a flash of yellow blinded her. She heard Tane's voice rose and saw the threatening guards bursting through her family's door. Fujiwara tilted his head and said something vulgar to her—the same way Kira had leered at her—who was once a trusted family friend. And here she stood, as frozen as a hunted deer with the fox baring its teeth at her. Her doubts flared.

The gentle man in the funny hat had smiled at her and told her it was all for naught—but who was to be believed?

"Ah, right, here's copper!" Kira broke her stream of thoughts and set down some coins. "There you go. Enough for Satsuma, correct?

"Let me help you. This heat is terrible. Yes, it's quite hot today. It will peel anyone's skin." He pried the letter from her hands, and the mailman snatched it away.

"Not so hard, eh? We all need to take that leap sometime," he chuckled. "Say, shall I accompany you home? I may be heading that way."

"I have to go. It's dinner time." Maru could only shake her head and run from there.

He called after her, but she didn't look back.

• • •

When she was out of breath, Maru slowed down. She had scraped her foot, and a few drops of blood were on the hem of her robe. She rubbed and rubbed, trying to get it off. She must not be hunted and snatched by a yokai—not now.

"Move, move!" barked an angry voice. She jumped as a horse cart narrowly made it past her on the road. The smell of hay and horse sweat burned her throat.

She was wary of everyone who grimaced at her, the careless girl who had stopped in the middle of a busy road and was lost in her own world. She ducked behind a shop's noren. Her heart was jittery, her stomach growled in displeasure, and her mind couldn't stop the tsunami of images of Tane, the guards, the strange man, and her missing father.

In hindsight, the words in her letter seemed unnatural, hastily written under duress. Her father wouldn't think there was anything normal about this; it would only worry him. She trusted him, so why had she wanted desperately to reach out to him? What if it was intercepted by the emperor and the police came after her again, accusing her of false statements and blasphemy against her clan? Tane's warning cast doubt about her reliability. She couldn't understand all of the things happening to her at once. But it was now out of her hands.

She rubbed her eyes. She needed to keep her head: father would want her to keep trying to remain safe, and this was no time to put them in needless danger. The fox promised it would answer her. But she had no idea how to keep her end of the bargain. She felt her hidden tanto pressing into her ribs.

She passed a well-lit restaurant with queues waiting for bowls of soy noodles with steam pouring out the front. She could smell onions and meat. To rid herself of her cravings, she plunged into the street's shuttered store fronts, passing a lady who carried woven baskets full of eggs across her shoulders.

Eggs! She had forgotten Mitsu's onsen eggs again!

The lady caught Maru's eye and hurried to make the sale: "Ten for one sack; it's a good price."

Not everyone accepted coins or coupons; some merchants were still so poor, they preferred to be rice since they could not eat copper. She would boil them while Adakichi and Mitsu worked, although she couldn't replicate the taste of the onsen eggs. Mitsu would know the difference.

"You'd better hurry; you know what they do to girls who are out and about," a woman with missing teeth told her. She had deep lines on her darkened face.

Maru asked, "Exactly what happens to them?"

"Young lady, you will die! They take you and you die! You go away, cut like a chicken for its blood. Go home!"

"Who does this? Or, *what* does this? A man?"

The lady shooed her away. "It calls you! It's the emperor's shadow! Next time, come here with a male escort."

Maru ran. She turned down an alley and tried to win a race with the sun.

Why couldn't she find an empty rickshaw? Her feet ached. They were covered in bulbous sores. The geta weighed her down. She knew she had to walk slowly or risk breaking a leg trying to escape an invisible danger.

The man had laughed at her when she asked about the blood. Matsuma, men in the streets, the woman who sold her eggs, and Adakichi had all warned her about dangers after sundown. There were rumors—no, there was something stronger than rumors about the trains. And even if blood wasn't used to fuel the train as the man said (a mere stranger, she reminded herself) there were other reasons someone might be on the lookout for a girl like her.

She listened for footsteps or the laughter of a yokai waking up. Each step was more painful than the last. The city was emptying as early darkness descended on the summer night. A storm was coming.

She continued on her frantic search. Patrons who spied the ominous clouds ducked into a teahouse, brothel, or sake garden to wait out the storm. Faces looked at her disapprovingly; older women raised their eyebrows. Did they know something but did not dare to help her?

The bridge swaying in the wind made her fearful that a monster was rising from its slumber.

Across the way, she limped toward Gion. The gas lamps were already lit, and she spotted maids outside the Kabuki

Hall beckoning last-minute clients to come inside their brothel: "Come in for an hour, gentlemen! Have fun you can't remember having with your wife!" and "We have fresh wine tonight, fellows! You look parched. Come join us."

From what Adakichi told her, the side streets she was passing through were for the up-and coming geiko. Their storefronts didn't have the long hallways with fresh flowers, bowls of water with lilies, or thematic tapestries. She knew they had a harder time making money.

Inebriated men were already coming out of restaurants and sake bars, loudly discussing where they would go next.

"I'm going to see Kotake!"

"Nah, you're too ugly for her."

"And you think you look better, you fool?"

"No! I learned that when my mirror broke. But even yokai don't want her."

She had heard that horrible joke before. Her chest tightened. There was something sinister about the joke being told everywhere and repeated so casually, as if everyone knew a something she didn't.

"Hey, there's one! Hurry missy, hurry! He's gonna GET YA!"

Maru almost shrieked and ran by the men as they bent over their knees laughing at her.

Was any of it true? She felt silly about being even briefly comforted by the stranger's unfounded reassurance.

When she crossed one of the last streets in her ward, her feet were about to give out entirely, and her robes were drenched. Waving her uchiwa brought no relief, and her throat was parched.

Finally she recognized the old buildings at the edge of Ponto-cho. The wooden walls were stained black at the bottom from rain and years of wear and tear, their grounds otherwise pristine. The doors had plain iki noren hanging, without indication of any kamon or name. She knew that visitors' appointments were by invitation only. Everything in this district had an aura of mystery and secrecy, with their windows darkened and streets clean of clutter.

Two figures were standing near her in the twilight. One was tall; the other was a girl who had a bow at her waist. It was tied unlike Mitsu's darari obi, so she wasn't a senior maiko.

She crouched behind a hydrangea and inched closer to get a better look at them, afraid of the repercussions if someone saw her in the oiran district at this hour. *Why had she wandered off her path?*

The taller figure moved into the light of a red lantern.

It was Kira.

She pushed deeper into the brush, feeling branches stab her back.

"What was that noise?" the young girl asked in a shrill voice.

"No more delays," Kira growled.

She said, "Maybe it is a yokai. You heard the others are missing. We should stay at madam's place."

"Nah, you're coming with me. With no company."

"It will be higher rate, then," the girl said. She giggled nervously.

Maru held her breath and watched them through the branches as their steps come closer and closer, until their faces passed under the lamp. It was clearly Kira and a young girl.

She locked eyes with Maru.

A thin scream came from the distance, followed by a deep bellow that seemed to hollow out her insides. Kira pushed the girl behind a noren of a darkened home.

Maru didn't wait another moment. She ran.

As she ran around a corner she saw a group of young men bearing their scrawny chests, swigging drinks, and pushing one another playfully.

They're always the same, she thought. She instinctively put up her chin and made a point of standing up very straight herself and looking very confident as she veered past them.

"Oy! Oy!"

They weren't talking to her. She knew they weren't.

"You! Girl!"

No, there was another girl nearby, Maru told herself.

"Egg head!" Maru closed her eyes and slowed obediently to a stop.

"That's right," hissed one of them. The boys were starting to circle her. The faceless boys from her haunted dreams were coming into view. These young men had eyes that bore into her.

"Good evening," she said carefully, trying to sound strong, if not curt.

"Ohhh, yes good evening. We have a little lady here, not a girl."

"Girl, don't you know what time it is?"

Her eyes remained focused on where she was headed.

"Yo! He asked a question."

"It's rude not to answer. You're not really well-trained."

Maru bit her lip.

"Where are you headed?"

"Home," she said firmly, as they leaned against one another, towering over her.

"No work for you? You aren't open for business tonight?"

"She doesn't look pretty enough to work." One particularly tall boy came closer. He had sweat on every inch of his skin and smelled strongly of barley.

"You know what happens to girls like you? Who don't work and are worthless?"

Maru stared back at him. Any idea of what to say in this situation evaporated quickly. She was feeling her soul would surely vacate her flesh.

"Or you could take us home with you, and you can be out all night as much as you like," laughed a boy behind her.

"What, you've never been with one before?" A boy reached out to touch her hair. Maru moved to the left of his hand. He widened his eyes and laughed.

"She is alive!"

"We thought you were deaf or dumb," said another.

"Both."

"No wonder nobody wants you."

"No, she's got spirit. She would be fun to break in."

Maru stiffened, looking for someone, anyone, who could help her, but the ochaya doors were shut with many patrons inside. Music was rising from the chimneys, the silhouettes she saw on the shuji walls were laughing, drinking, and strumming their shamisen. Anyone she spotted outside was already on their way somewhere and averted their gaze from the group. Maybe they couldn't see her in the middle of the boys.

"So, which one do you like best? Any of us will do. We'd all be of service."

"Pick fast, or we'll choose someone for you."

"Or we can all have a go."

They were like hawks surrounding her. She couldn't get out. She thought of her father, and how unlike him these boys were. Of Mitsu, who had wit. Of Adakichi, who wouldn't tolerate this behavior. She thought of friends who might even tease them along and go with them willingly.

Then, she remembered what the fox said. *"If you ever need protection, think it or wish it."*

Maru clenched her jaw and tried to quiet the heaving of her chest. Her head was burning.

She was on her own. Should she try to summon the fox?

"Choosing which of you is 'best' is difficult when you're all equally the worst possible."

A few of the boys made noises indicating they were surprised and mildly impressed, but the ones nearest to her moved in closer.

A boy said, "You're no geiko. None of them would ever talk down to a man."

"I don't see any men here," said Maru darkly, putting her hand over her hidden tanto.

He raised his hand and Maru turned her head.

She heard the sing-song voice of a female she thought she recognized say, "Boys, boys, boys—finding fun is so troublesome, isn't it?"

The boy put down his hand, and the group broke apart.

"Aren't you boys getting into trouble because you're bored?" the woman asked.

"We aren't bored!" said one boy indignantly.

"Doesn't look that way to me! One girl and six boys? Come on. You need to have balance."

Maru recognized her. "Sakyou!" she cried. It was Kiku's ghost, the one who had floated to her and Hanamachi a few nights ago. When she was close to her, she realized she knew her once upon a time. Her moon-shaped face was adorned with pink paint on her cheeks, and she wore a loose kimono with loud-colored patterns.

Sakyou gave a wide smile and bowed her head toward Maru. Sakyou's beauty radiated even in the darkness. Maru's heart thumped.

"You can't possibly know this rubbish," said one boy, spitting at Maru.

Sakyou responded, "We're best friends from school. She's better than me. She works in a real ochaya."

"You're way prettier than this one."

"Where I work, I can have more fun," Sakyou said. "Don't you boys have somewhere you should be?"

She stared at the boys who seemed to be standing down. Getting a better look at her, Maru saw that her eyes had dark rings. Her skin was dewy with a thin layer of sweat, her fingers lifeless as they twirled about her hair. Maru tried to find something in Sakyou's eyes that would reassure her.

A small parting of Sakyou's lips—*a request? An invitation?*—was a moment of entrancement that transfixed her.

Then she broke into a small, sly smile and told Maru "This is no place for someone like you. You know what they're saying about maids these days. Now boys, the rain is coming fast."

Maru ran off and soon found herself among the familiar willows over the red-painted bridge. The evening lanterns were on. She collected herself, aware that her eyes betrayed her agitation.

When she was finally inside the ochaya, she peeled off her geta and was relieved to hear Mitsu's warm voice as she chatted over cups of sake with Fujiwara and Matsuma and another person she didn't know.

"Shikomi! Welcome home! Ahh, my eggs! Gentlemen, she has brought us delights."

"Show her! Show her the jewel you picked up."

"I always knew I'd come into riches. My fukumimi—look at how big they are!" Fujiwara tugged on his ears to elongate them.

"It's best not to tantalize her." Mitsu laughed. "It will blind her with jealousy!"

Maru hardly knew what she had interrupted but gave them a smile before going to the kitchen where she threw down the basket and fell to her knees. Her eyes stung, but she had no tears. Her soul came back into her flesh, pressing itself into her bones and aching as her soul was awakened. She leaned against the cool wall and closed her eyes.

When she and Mitsu were out and about, they were usually harassed by men. Especially when they were dressed up, men mistook them for oiran, unaware of the difference in ribbon ties. How was Sakyou's obi tied? She couldn't remember the distinction since Adakichi always showed them how to "do it the right way." It hadn't looked like Mitsu's, either.

She hadn't learned yet how to handle aggressive men. If Sakyou hadn't interrupted him, the boy might have carried her off.

An egg was cracked and spilled, the consequence of her rushed escape.

Maru listened to the dull chatter. The room wasn't filled with the normal ruckus. The tide was pulling out, and she feared what it would bring in return. She wiped the splattered egg, placing the remaining egg carefully inside a kettle with soy, boiling them one at a time. She stared into the glow of the fire, lulling herself into her thoughts and hoping she wouldn't be summoned.

Her wish didn't come true; Mitsu's shadow crossed the doorway, and Maru obediently followed her into the yellow light of a world transformed with joy and drunken pleasures.

The night was a blur. She was caught thinking about Tane, the man with the answers to questions she never asked, the letter, and her narrow escape. The rippling effects of the day put in perspective the fact that pouring wine for a couple of older men, in comparison to her recent experience, was quite tolerable. She would have taken any number of slaps from Adakichi in exchange for not having to relive this day.

In the meantime, Mitsu performed a dance calling for relief from the rain as the thunder bellowed and the rain clawed at the roof. Adakichi played her harp, giving a pattern for her steps, and Maru's feet instinctively curled and twisted along with her. She knew she was supposed to replenish their cups throughout the night, but she was looking right through them. She wandered through her mindscape searching for a truth in the thicket as she wondered where Sakyou went.

Adakichi joined them and helped Maru serve the delicious fish—cut to perfection, unlike the butchering they suffered earlier. Fujiwara elbowed Maru in jest.

The night began to end when the moon was high. And as Maru's heart settled, it leapt again when Mitsu strode into the pantry for the eggs, saying, "Let's send them off with a treat," only to stumble into Maru's open fire and boiling eggs. She whipped around with her nostrils flaring.

"You can't even get eggs right, samurai girl," she hissed.

She'll sell my secrets as punishment.

Maru picked up her robes and dashed after her, seeing Mitsu take Fujiwara's arm and lean in to whisper to him. Their two faces were contorting and elongating. Their skin was shedding, revealing blackened shapes, and their eyes became four lanterns in the night. Their salacious laughter scratched the back of her skull. Blood rushed to her head. She had to save herself.

She burst out, "You can laugh at my samurai father all you want! But Mitsu is the demon! She tricked the last maiko, and lied to Adakichi to get her banished! It's *she* who is the evil one who lies to claim her place wrongfully!"

Their faces turned back into human forms. Tatami was soaking in the silence. Only her heavy breathing could be heard. Even Adakichi lost her ability to stitch words together to save face.

The delirium, the heat of the night, and the incense clouding her thoughts took hold. Maru saw that Fujiwara was standing over her. Would he reach out to strike her? Adakichi was swooping in, her sleeves stretched out like wings.

The door opened, and air swept out the foul stench of betrayal; a door shut, and piercing screams bore into her ears:

Adakichi told her, "You know nothing of what you accuse another of doing!"

"I never did such a thing!" Mitsu protested behind Adakichi.

"I saw the girl steal our wages and indulge men outside this ochaya with my own eyes," said Adakichi coldly. "You choose to ruin us over a moment of misplaced pride. Selfish. Spoiled."

And it was then that Maru realized Kiku had made a fool of her.

No amount of apology or knee-bending could stop what was brewing. Adakichi grumbled that her lotion-filled gloves had fewer hours to soothe her hands, finding ways to blame Maru with each breath she drew. She let her hands express her anger.

"You will not be seen with us at the matsuri. Your pathetic tenure is ending."

When bruised and dismissed, Maru retreated to her room and held her mother's poetry book before a short candle that melted into a slow, mushy death, its waxy drips—each another secret, another foothold, another grasp on life—were dripping away.

Fixated on the blue center of the flame, she slipped back into peace, revisiting the words her father told her over the years that became her mantra:

"Nothing is amiss. Everything is fine. I'm fine—there's nothing to this rumor. He's telling the truth. This is all temporary." But her voice broke. Nothing was good, nothing at all.

Her eyelids were heavy. She found herself in a lull in front of the fire, hushed voices whispering, the yokai lurking under her floorboards, the voice of a fox from far away.

It all melted away, and Maru found herself in

f
r
e
e
f
a
l
l.

"We were promised equality! We have a new emperor and no more shogun in this new world. But it was all for naught. I have yet to reap what we have sowed. We made sacrifices. He would rather have a farmer's hand than one of us." Was that her father?

"Join his Court; take his offer: it was a good one." Was that Obasan speaking?

"I will not be a servant! We disavowed that under Tokugawa, bearing the battles. We always had to be ready to die!"

"Then you must be diplomatic." The woman's stern voice rose. Adakichi?

"And they need to keep their word!" her father sounded like himself, but was different. Frantic.

"There is time," the woman's voice was gentle.

"And this is not independence," the man spat. "Sakamoto was executed. We will all live in fear. You were almost killed. If not for Kira, storm water would rise from the earth and return."

"And Maruya?" the voice shape-shifted; was it her mother? She was dead.

"Put her in school with commoners. Hide her. Be ensured that she protects herself. I'll fight."

"But you surrendered your sword."

"I cannot break my oath when we are on the brink of another civil war. I will do business in peace, but I will never stop hunting. He cares

little for how we are treated after we clinched his power. We will fight a familiar enemy over and over: the enemy of ourself."

"When?" Who was crying? Was it a girl?

"I need to make Meiji see the danger he put us in. He owes us a debt. I need to believe he will fulfil his word," her father hissed, his body a tangled snake with one yellow eye that searched and found her, his body lunged.

Maru awoke abruptly to her memories blurred with her dreams, waves of voices erasing and clashing, inspired from rumors and projections by enemies. But the early morning moon filled her room with a soft light that put her back to sleep, pulling away the heavy doubts and covering her in a cool blanket that kept her mind from running away.

■ ■ ■

Although exhausted from the seven-stick incense-night, they all diligently rose.

It was time for celebration. But not for Maru.

Nightmares of the boys' faces blending with Adakichi's and Mitsu's kept her up most of the night. She was fearful of waking up to find them dragging her out of her window and she feared the possibility of Kira—and an army of his boys—collecting victims. What if Kira had led her to believe her father was at fault and was covering his own sins?

And none of the missing girls had been found. She couldn't stop thinking of Sakyou being next victim after her mingling with the boys.

As she was getting the courage to ask Adakichi of the news in Hanamachi, Chiki and her assistants tumbled into the okiya to dress and ready them for the day. They had big smiles on their faces and did not inquire about Maru's solemn, pale face.

"Say, are you pulling funds from the Fujiwara account? It hasn't been replenished lately, so I thought to see if there was a mistake and made an inquiry."

"No, continue using it. He insists he will remedy it."

They took an hour to dress Mitsu. She looked like a fox. The gold threads of her robes caught the light and the sparkling in her eyes. "You are so lucky!" she heard Adakichi say. She was dazzling as she moved so easily with her body, at one with her own skin.

"You do look beautiful," Maru said when Chiki left to join Adakichi for tea.

Mitsu carried on with readying for the day, minding her stacked, decorated hairdo as if Maru wasn't in the room. She turned to leave her, but the doorway held her back enough so that she could release what she wanted so much to tell her.

"I am sorry, Mitsuki," Maru whispered, using her full name for formality, a blade of grass bending in a breeze. "I just wanted to protect my family." Mitsu didn't take her eyes from the mirror, but her hands stilled.

"Your performance will surely recapture the hearts of many." And with that, Maru left.

"Did you hear an oiran ran away last night?" an assistant whispered to her downstairs.

Adakichi insisted she had not known, saying "Those girls, I don't blame them for running off. What an awful life." They all nodded in agreement before moving on to their tasks.

It couldn't have been Sakyou. She wasn't an oiran. Or was she? The other girl with Kira certainly had been one. Her bow had been tied differently, but maybe it was a new style. She could ask Chiki. But when she opened her mouth, Adakichi put her hand up.

Although she felt compelled to ask Adakichi if she knew of Sakyou or her Okaasan, the fear of seeming guilty for gallivanting with a possible oiran stopped her. The ever-revolving doors at the brothels kept them anonymous, unless they somehow obtained legendary status, were never stricken with disease and married or found sudden wealth. She had to protect her ochaya. If it was still hers.

Sakyou and the girl Kira clutched both had sullen expressions, unlike the typically mischievousness painted faces of oiran. She was convinced Sakyou's large dark eyes, softened by her pink cheeks, had sought Maru to help her. She felt she would always be wrought with guilt, wondering if she should have stayed.

"Must you occupy the table? There must be a chore to attend," snipped Adakichi.

Maru went to her room and carefully knelt before her mirror, wiggling back and forth with her knees to preserve her kimono ties. How she longed to go to the Matsuri with them! And see the train at last. Looking in the mirror, her demeanor and determination reminded her of her mother's stern expressions toward her father. Donned in her summery kimono with her stiff and, unyielding manner she kept Maru in a tight routine, focused on the everyday life in their clan below the clouds where her father lived. It reminded her of a poem her mother wrote:

> Yellow, purple blur
> cranes take flight, feet lift up high
> Sky falls as eyes close

Reciting it to herself, she brushed her hair methodically, pulling it into a tight bun. Even if she couldn't go to the matsuri, she wanted to feel presentable, as if she were. She brushed her eyebrows and pressed lotion on her lips—enough to be seen.

And fool herself into believing it was deserved.

She looked in the mirror and screeched.

Sakyou was there, looking back at her.

Maru kicked away from the mirror.

It was Yuurei.

No. She had seen Sakyou last night. She wasn't a yuurei. It was Maru's reflection staring back at her, looking scared.

Her feet padded against the road through rice paddies to school, under a blue sky. She went into the stout building, filled with her classmates.

"Whenever I want Ren, it is as close as the palm of my hand," she hears a teacher say. His voice rattles the walls but does nothing to get the students' attention. "If you wish to be established, help to establish others. If you seek to enlarge yourself, enlarge others first.'"

Maru sat with hands in her lap, empty as she played with the lines in her palms, tracing her past and future, her mind drifting to the pond near her house, thinking of how frogs splashed.

"To love a thing means wanting it to live," the teacher continues.

Others idly flipped open books, letting their eyes wander to neighbors' notes and the sun peering through the window lattices.

"Hosokawa, read about righteousness, and explain how one can become?"

Her palms offered no answers. Her book was at home. She sought mercy, remembering his stern eyes, his teeth lurking beneath blemished gums.

"Hosokawa, can you read it?"

"Take my book," Sakyou's soft voice had told her.

A soft knock downstairs broke her stupor.

"Shikomi of House of Adakichi!" It was a voice full of optimism and confidence.

"And you, sir, are whom?" said Adakichi.

"Forgive my manners. I'm Yamanobe Satoshi. I met your wonderful apprentice and have been warmed by her presence. She is gracious to have shared how I may find your ochaya."

Leaving Sakyou's memories and mirror scattered in pieces, she thumped down the stairs, risking the possibility of undoing her obi and dropping her tanto the moment she saw his face.

"Ah! You are here. I was afraid you wouldn't show up or had forgotten me."

Maru flushed. It felt serendipitous; something inside her soared.

"It would be such a pleasure to accompany you to the Station Opening. I happen to have Grand Hall access that may elevate your experience. Even the emperor won't have that view."

Mitsu now appeared at Adakichi's elbow, curious; her dark cloud threatening the man's invitation, as he eagerly held their hanameishi Maru had given him as a souvenir. But there was a kindness and authority in his eager voice that Adakichi couldn't refuse.

Maru was going to the matsuri.

A rickshaw carried the four of them as far as it could before the crowds became too thick. Each passing step became more of a glide as the knots in her stomach unfurled to become sails catching wind. Strange faces wearing pure elation that she wanted to, but couldn't relate to.

Children traded berries, grinning at each other between monstrous bites, juices dribbling. In trying to focus on them, further from their joy, she was oblivious to the shadow that passed their way. She longed to be that young again, but now she couldn't summon images of her youth, as if it was something she never experienced, born only days ago in a very different world.

"Your accent, it is not Kyoto-ben," Mitsu said to Satoshi.

"No, it isn't. You are observant. I'm from Tokyo. I am here on business, a researcher, a kind of amateur historian."

"Ah, I see" said Adakichi, her eyebrows arching.

Adakichi adamantly refused to look at Mitsu. She was obviously already in love, and smiling childishly. The politics of all three of them accompanying him made him appear to be every bit a man of status, while it made them seem as if they were desperate – and Maru knew Adakichi was being put in a situation Satoshi didn't fully grasp. She had an internal war between her reputation and her desire to be part of what he was promising.

A heavy discomfort held Maru back from feeling ready for what awaited them. The teal roofs looked duller today, and the usually warm light streaking through the tight alleys seemed to have disappeared. The lattices looked dusty. Sounds blurred and passing faces were unrecognizable. Sleepiness and heat were compounding her uneasiness with the throngs of police in her vicinity,

The crowds thickened into a human wall. Maru felt watched all around, unable to shake the eyes that were studying her or escape the knives Adakichi drew with her conversation.

Mitsu and Satoshi were conversing with ease, while Maru's stomach was worse off than last night when she thought she wouldn't be coming at all. If most of Kyoto was here to see the train pull in, then surely, that group of boys and Kira would be present too. And maybe the police. She had so many enemies that made her uneasy, but she was determined to see them again, almost willing it to happen to see if they seemed guilty of what she suspected. But if she saw them, could she confront them?

Or better yet, would she see Sakyou with her madam today? And see that she wasn't the one who had run away, thus absolving her of failure to protect someone in need?

She touched where her tanto was, imagining her father's disappointment in her behavior.

Swallowing hard, she blinked and pinched the back of her hands to help refocus, as they passed into central Kyoto. The strong, taller, dark electric poles were spilling little pools of water from last night's storm. Young boys were tossing a small white ball to each other, their bare feet splashing through mud. The scent of blood seemed to move through the air. What had he called it? *A "chemical reaction"?* She shook her head in confusion.

The tall boys, forcefully pulling their arms back and snapping them forward to throw the ball, were laughing so heartily, it reminded her of the nasty smirking boys who had insulted her and Sakyou. Something bubbling rose in her, and the hairs stood up on the back of her neck. The way they planted their feet to pivot and twist their body, ready to take control and overpower them, how they had stood their ground before her with their taunting and daring.

"Watch out!"

A ball was flying toward her head. Her mouth opened to shriek but hung motionless and soundless as her hair blew in its wake. Her body froze, her feet rooted to the ground as she braced herself to be hit.

A boy ran in her direction. He was a tall silhouette against the sky and had a wild look in his eyes.

"Pardon me. It didn't get you, did it?" he stopped in front her, his chest rising up and down dramatically as he tried to suppress his laughter.

"Are you hurt?" Satoshi asked again.

"No, no, I'm fine. It missed me," she gasped.

It hadn't been thrown by the boys from the night before. Their images reverberated in her mind.

"What game are they playing, anyway? They're all over the place chasing that thing."

"It must be one of those newer sports that we read about from Yokohama," suggested Adakichi.

"There's always something new," murmured Mitsu in response.

"Yes, there's always something new," Adakichi echoed.

"It's called baseball," Satoshi brightly answered. If they heard, neither woman acknowledged this.

Shops were grilling their meat. Smoke pouring out of windows along the way clouded her vision and stung her tired eyes. She tried to find relief by covering her eyes with her sleeves.

"Be careful. Apply pressure to the edge of your ear lobes for a few minutes, and the pain should soon pass," Adakichi said. Her eyes were stern.

The harder she tried to force herself to take in the scenes and feel the joy everyone else felt, the more she recoiled, backing herself into a dark hole. She couldn't rid herself of the memory of the boys' taunts and Adakichi's hand slapping her back.

A flurry of people rushed by, shouting as they pushed through the billows of curling grey smoke, kicking mud on her robes. The shouting finally quieted down, and there through the parting fumes she saw a gold-orange shape.

It was the fox.

It seemed as if waves of a tide had left her standing with the fox on a harbor's shore. They stared at each other through the coastal fog. There was a gentle breeze. The world slowed down until it was holding its breath, sucking the warm air out of the sky and leaving a peaceful clearness in their small world.

Mura saw that the two yellow stones burrowed in the fox's face of golden fur were unwavering. She was intertwined in a bondage she didn't want to escape from. She walked through the sand to the coolness of the sea to quench her desire to bring her back to the love of life.

She took comfort in watching the eyes of the fox. It was as if she were being guided by a lighthouse beckoning her to a dock that would drain her of the dark waters that had flooded her ship, dooming her to sink. The glow emitted from its eyes sent away the demons before it turned and ran.

She blinked, and the real world spun back to her. The first to come was the suffocating heat: It was a hot pillow pressing onto her face. She wanted to talk to the fox again.

But the fox was not beneath the storefront. She peered down the alley and saw some friends running from an older man who was shouting at them. But there was no fox. She thought she smelled the scent of blood

"Ugh, what a horrid smell. Must be Nuppeppo nearby," said Mitsu, waving away the smoke with her uchiwa.

"There is no such thing, thankfully!" Satoshi laughed. "A compost must be overflowing."

Larger stately buildings came into view. People here were bustling, most heading in a stream to their work. As the buildings downtown became taller and tightly knitted, she found herself missing the sun. The sound of chimes was replaced by horses' hooves and creaking wheels.

She kept her wits about her, trying not to feel on edge from the boys' laughter, indelible in her brain, and her sighting of the fox. And the girls and her father. The images that wouldn't leave her. The pale girls seemed to be lurking everywhere, asking for help in a way that said, "I told you so."

The crowd was getting tighter, and Maru wrinkled her nose at the smell of warm beer.

"Come, we are near now. Let's break through this crowd quickly." Satoshi put his elbow out for Mitsu.

"Your elbow? Is that a Tokyo thing too?" laughed Mitsu, touching it. She made the decision for Adakichi without consultation.

"Ah, it's a Western thing. A man offers his arm to lead a lady." There was a flutter in Maru's heart. He led them through the crowd against the tides.

"Everyone clamors to visit these sights without really thinking it through. Not everyone has the mind of a scientist, but more of—"

"An animal?" offered Mitsu.

He laughed.

"You are here only for the Gion Matsuri?" Maru heard Mitsu ask.

He was her acquaintance, but Mitsu had already taken control of their relationship. How could she interrupt them when Mitsu was the one hanging on his elbow and Maru was now disowned? Maru didn't know him well, either. Mitsu's radiant smile caught the sunlight, and Maru was filled with a gloomy defensiveness that was becoming familiar. Why did it matter that they were laughing together? Mitsu was always the center of attention.

"I'm a historian," he was proudly telling her.

"Eh?"

"I want to capture our lives as they are. And the beauty in the every day. I want to know the details and track the progress of our cities and lives. And study how the decisions of the emperor affect us all. Those sorts of things."

Mitsu said, "You Tokyo men are not as impressive as you make yourselves out to be. It is a wonder you found your way at all on the Tokaido."

"I wouldn't have without the well-worn path. We have gone off-track."

"Off-track?"

"A delightful phrase born from the trains. We will be there soon, and you'll see how beautiful it is."

"Many blame them on the disappearances of the girls," Adakichi reminded him.

"Ah, the pesky blood rumor," he grinned at Maru. "I heard they found one girl drowned in the riverbed and another's body was lost in the woods after a matsuri. All with their blood intact, by the way. Another unfortunate end befell them."

They knew all along that the bodies had been found? Why hadn't the palace shared the news?

"You speak so casually of the cruelty that took their breath," Adakichi said.

He tilted his head. "It's the historian in me. I cannot absorb the stories or my skin would become too heavy to wear. I merely share the information that's available."

But why don't we know why their lives were taken?

They came to the center of the city, which opened to a grand circle where rickshaws and palanquins spun as a brassy instrument sounded from a balcony. Hundreds of flags hung from awnings, each facing a large display of tessen flowers in front of the largest building she had ever seen.

The brick building with white trim and a clock in the center was wide. The sparkling windows had the brightest, clearest glass she had ever seen, and a grand porch with white columns led to a huge entrance. People were lining up along the train tracks.

The excitement she had sequestered burst; all doubt and unhappiness washed away as awe took over. She had the sense of receiving a secret from a friend that couldn't be taken back. She was about to see something that couldn't ever be "unseen" again.

Maru wasn't sure Adakichi or Mitsu were as moved as she was. She couldn't take her eyes off the grand building and wished her father could see a culmination of all he fought for.

"We all need some guidance. Step carefully; we're going in there."

"Into there?" cried Mitsu.

"If you're taken by the exterior beauty, I can't wait for your reaction when you go inside."

He pulled them to the side wing, where a slimmer door stood. Inside, a long staircase went up to a long hallway that formed a bridge where Maru could watch people stream in beneath bright red drapes. The clear glass windows were framed with brown shutters. Clusters of lights caught the colors of the jewels that hung from a large chandelier of candles hanging from the ceiling. Maru was scared to walk under the huge lamp. It looked too heavy and too precious. A red carpet stretched beneath her feet, leading to what she learned was the ballroom.

Any suspicion of Satoshi evaporated. A man surrounded by ornate things like these couldn't be harmful.

"Wah!" said Mitsu. "Is this real? It's like a home of a princess!"

He laughed again. "This train station is a future welcome gate to the West.

"Look here," he smiled, and gently tapped her elbow. She stepped to an unoccupied mosaic glass window that created odds shapes of light on her outstretched hand.

"It's the effects of a prism," he gestured, pointing at the triangles.

Maru moved her hand, smiling at the rainbows in her palms.

"It occurs when light passes from the windows and hits the chandelier. It's from France," he boasted.

It was a richness beyond what Maru had ever visualized, and she'd seen gold woven into kimono of barons' wives, Hokusai paintings on palace walls, and the finest vases from China. She tasted sweet oranges, smelled the most lustful jasmine, but the hundred jewels that hung above that could feed all of Kyoto, were something she couldn't summon any words for.

"And where does the train come in?" asked Mitsu.

Satoshi went over to her and leaned in, saying: "Follow those—the black lines—yes, the tracks. It will come from that way, the east, and will stop here where that raised platform is. Down there on that box with the curtains is where the emperor will greet it."

Mitsu asked, "Meiji is here today, too?" Maru closed her eyelids. Mitsu was going lame in the head over Satoshi. Of course, she already knew the emperor was here today.

"And there are so many fine ladies in dresses," remarked Adakichi. Women in cinched waists and strange buttoned petticoats, and men in pants flocked to the front crowds near the train outside too. Many men wore tall, black hats that were more intimidating than Satoshi's brown and floppy flat hat.

"See the flowers down there, too? They are gifts for the engineer."

"The who?

"Engineer. He is the man who runs the train."

"Ah, never a woman, I suppose."

"I'm afraid not, only men so far."

"They haven't chosen to take the job, or is the job reserved only for men?" Adakichi asked.

He paused. "A law currently stating the job should be filled by a male, does not diminish a woman's capability," he said calmly. "Although a string of accidents may persuade employers to prefer one sex over the other."

Adakichi's lip stiffened. She was critical of being with this man she considered without heed for fairness to women, and her defense mechanism was to find ways to put him down, whether it was reasonable or not.

Satoshi looked disturbed, biting his lower lip. "The dignitaries will be in here soon. I hope you all enjoyed this respite."

"Ah, the men will come soon, you mean." Adakichi smiled.

Maru was perplexed by the animosity. She didn't feel Satoshi said anything wrong.

"I believe it is mixed company," he said, excusing himself from the hall.

"How did you meet him?"

"Oh, at the market. I though his hat was funny."

Adakichi was silent. "Regardless. He is a government employee from Edo. He is no friend of ours. Be careful of him; he does not know the ways of Kyoto."

On the contrary, Maru thought. She wanted to shout he was a historian and was here to preserve their stories and study Kyoto, that he had been gentle and honorable, and was no enemy. Instead, Maru was quiet and watched the crowd gathering at the platform. The emperor had not arrived. She could have thrown up in anticipation.

"He seems nice," said Mitsu in a high voice, meaning she could be convinced otherwise.

"*Wa – kon – you – sai*," said Adakichi, matter-of-factly.

The voices were audible before their faces appeared, but soon persons flooded the hallway dressed in the funny Western suits and fancy dress that Adakichi despised and filled the hall with clangs of glasses, pops of champagne bottles, and loud chortles. They were hardly recognizable as citizens of Kyoto. The spoke in different dialects and were from Osaka, Tokyo, and the countryside. Had they really come so far to see a train?

She stood far, far away from Kyoto.

Satoshi stood out from a crowd of nameless faces in his brown, floppy hat and suit, but no one was paying any attention to someone like her who wore a worn, outdated kimono. He rushed to her.

"It's on its way. If we could have a window open, we might hear it," he said with the excitement of a young boy.

"Is the emperor here?" Maru was nervous in a way about seeing Meiji. The man who kept her father away, the man the city thought was traumatizing Kyoto. The man whose face she last saw years ago, taking the crown for himself at his ascension when she'd been a child unable to grasp the moment.

She wanted to see his face, to see if she could measure his guilt and see if he was a criminal or still the man her father praised.

"Look there." He pointed at the velvety canvas with gold tassels where a small man sat with a smattering of soldiers and dignitaries in navy and gold. He was staring intently at the crowd. He seemed younger than she imagined, not too far from the child who became emperor, except for the thick mustache and longer hair flopped over his forehead.

"Why is everyone here?" Maru asked suddenly. "I've seen the smokestacks. We know the trains are here, but now it's as if it's all new."

He gave a nervous laugh. "Trains have been coming and going as you undoubtedly know, mainly carrying supplies. There have been tests, unannounced, unbound to public schedules. It's for liability in case something goes wrong. This unveils it for the public, opening of the station."

"Why so secret though?" said Maru. "Why not be more open to help lessen the fear I think many have. These changes are all so sudden. This station appeared overnight."

"Fear? No, there are just unanswered questions."

The uneasiness of the rumors was a dark cloud over the station opening: the way everyone reacted and had their own ideas of what its purpose was and where the city was going.

"Something the matter? No more blood talk, I hope."

"Oh, just town myths." She smiled weakly. "We won't all get sick, will we?"

"Sick?"

"I heard people are getting sick from the train," she said slowly.

"People get sick from one another. Not from a train; it's a machine! It can't catch a disease. You'll see for yourself. There is nothing to fear, only fuel for imagination of our future."

Satoshi passed her a glass. So bubbly! She hadn't expected it to hit the roof of her mouth.

A cackling across the room jilted her, taking her back to the onsen where the women had babbled about the tentacles. Although she felt like a fool when asking so many questions, and was moments away from embarrassing herself, if it was true, she had to know if the train could also be her enemy.

"So . . ." her voice trailed. Then her courage bubbled. "Do they not have tentacles on their faces?"

"Now, perhaps our dialects are too vastly different and I misunderstood you, but you said tentacles, right? Like on an octopus?"

She definitely felt like a fool.

"Oh!" He let out a hearty laugh. "The boiler! Yes, yes, I can see now, you must have seen the photograph in the paper of the steam engine exploding overseas."

She hadn't. She hadn't the faintest idea what he was talking about.

"You see, there are a number of long, let's say, pipes, in the engine. You'll see the engine soon, and how it looks like a cylinder. It's encasing gas and water in rotation as pipes churn out the steam to power it. But say there is an imbalance, and—oh, I'm afraid I'm losing you."

Maru felt herself tipping.

He bit his finger as he was thinking. "You know the feeling of pressure building, of being pressed again and again until you can't take it anymore? You've tried patience, you've tried listening, tried speaking, but you have no energy left to exert, and all you can do is scream? A train can do the same thing. And when it does, its face flies off, and the pipes—your 'tentacles'—burst out."

She was stupefied.

"It's coming!"

A collective gasp spread through the room, and everyone rushed to the window. He grabbed her by the shoulders and gave her a little push, so she could have a proverbial front seat, like the emperor. She cupped her hands against the mosaic to see better.

At first, she couldn't see anything except the crowd craning their necks, and she too couldn't help being nervous, staring unblinkingly toward the train tracks where the train would appear. The thing that was the source of smoky terror, that sang louder than any birds, scared everyone in her neighborhoods, and made the fox glower.

The floor rumbled. There were more gasps in the room. Some were startled and some laughed. Satoshi smiled and pointed out the window.

A black object, almost as large as a building, emerged, framed by the blue hills and the bright river along the yellow grass scorched by the summer sun. And oh, how the smoke billowed! It looked on fire! It was shiny and the darkest black she had ever seen. It looked solid as a rock and resolute in its direction with its rounded nose pointing towards the platform. A series of teeth were at the bottom, what she thought were surely scraping the tracks—and it had the largest wheels! Black and sharp, unstoppable. It was then she was properly awed by the grandeur of the train and in fear of its power.

And now an arm has appeared! Her heart stopped, but a man's head with a black hat followed. He waved to a crowd cheering rousingly, greeting him with their uchiwa.

She hadn't expected the train to be so mystifying and entrancing. Its allure was so unusual, so unlike anything she had seen before—the closest being the black pewter pot. But this machine had steam coming from it like waterfalls over jet-black rocks with a tower of smoke signaling to the kami, she thought, and its odor was both burning and tangy.

"Buuuuur!"

She gasped with everyone else as a large plume of smoke burst forth from a pipe. She found herself laughing, though she felt her stomach must have dropped right through her.

"Ah!" people exclaimed. Everyone was clapping. The emperor rose, arms outstretched. A door on the train opened, and a small man in all black stepped out and almost fell out, she thought, because it was so high, and turned to the emperor, bowing deeply.

Maru found herself clapping with everyone else, incredulous about the magic before her. How she wanted to touch it! It looked so smooth, so inviting, so dangerous and foreign all at once.

"What do you really think, then?" said Satoshi in her ear.

Maru jumped, clapping her hand over her heart, and laughed airily.

"Yes, I feel the same way. I'm speechless. It's always a marvel, and seeing someone else experience it for the first time has reawakened that feeling."

"It shook the floor like an earthquake; I thought it would come right through the building!"

"You are a storyteller too," said Satoshi. "Even more remarkable is that trains in Yokohama have carried people to Tokyo and back for five years, but it feels like the first time whenever I see it pull in. Ah, I believe the emperor will give a few words now."

She held her breath. Seeing him now, she saw he was hardly any older than her but was weighed down by gold adornments all over his chest that were held up by ribbons and sashes. They were magnificent and all surely carried meanings she couldn't understand. Men hadn't been awarded for wars in centuries, since killing a man was not worthy of gold, according to her father. Emperor Meji shared a new verse.

Unto the children,
Born in these progressive years,
At which we wonder,
First of all the tales of old,
Full of glory, should be told.

Uproarious applause broke out, fans and flags waving like the synchronized wings of cranes flying over the darkened sea.

Satoshi's eyes were glassy, reflecting the mosaic through which they stared so deeply. The emperor bowed his head and accepted hearty congratulations from his entourage.

She so desperately wanted to hear from him again about his confidence in the present—a power that catapulted her into fantasies of an extraordinary future. She felt a sense of great pride for him and felt shocked that anyone could defy him—a man who seemed so perfect and revolutionary. How could anyone think of him as a criminal who abducts girls? How could *she* doubt him. She saw what her father had seen in him: his stoicism, a poet for them all. There couldn't be any basis for those rumors. He *was* just a boy, and he had done what her father believed he would do.

The train whistled, ripping apart her thoughts, roaring into her mind, conjuring up nightmares and screeches that would plague her nights.

Admiring the medals, a new thought crossed her mind: Or was it true? Were those medals awarded for innocent lives he killed to seize the throne? Were girls killed for his train and a samurai's pride lost for his ambitions? Were medals awarded for every throat he slit, for the death of every samurai's daughter who would never be anyone?

The fox sprang to mind. There were memories of something deep inside that made her want to resent the emperor. Something evil that was taking over her life, despite the good, the joy, the urgency of the love of the life she had growing up with her father.

Sakyou's eyes glowed in the red-mosaic paint.

She leapt back, an angry sea churning. Where was her inherent fear coming from?

The emperor disappeared behind soldiers escorting him off the platform and down to see the train. She released a breath, not realizing she'd been holding it in. She was surrounded by people who dressed like foreigners in their big dresses and small glasses and skinny wool pants standing along the tracks of the train beneath this large brick building. She wanted to get out.

As if on cue, Adakichi reclaimed her, breaking the spell of modernity. "Thank you, Satoshi. We must be on our way; the three-day Matsuri begins today, and we must prepare for it."

"I won't keep you any longer. May I call upon your house if I find myself in Gion?"

Maru was surprised at his boldness, but Adakichi softened to his naivety: "Our door is always open. Please consider this an invitation for an afternoon of your liking."

He seemed to sigh in relief. "I was afraid you would rescind; this pomp and circumstance can be overwhelming."

Pomp and circumstance. The reference to this made her squirm. Her father had sacrificed it all, surrendered his sword, and might as well be on the other side of the world. He should have been here to see the festival, but instead here was this man in a funny hat touting things about his knowledge of history when he knew nothing of the fight her family put in to make today possible.

A hatred of him was forming. His stupid poem. Why hadn't he said anything about the samurai? Would he allow them to return, unharmed? Insist it was a misunderstanding? Or quell the fears of the mothers who lost sleep, fearful about the fate of their missing daughters?

And in the street, the ugly, spindly trees with their wires, the shimmering tracks, a wailing woman—"Don't look at her, Mitsu," Adakichi warned her—Had she stepped into a storybook? She wanted the peaceful surroundings of her willow, her favorite shrine, the matsuri lanterns, and the beautiful kimono the geiko and maiko of Gion used to play up their rivalry. She wanted dango and sake, not meat and bubbles. She wanted her father, not the gloating of Northern men with pockets heavy with coins and heads high with an air of superiority.

Maru pushed on past the onlookers, huffing and thinking a Tokyo man of the future like Satoshi may never fit into a place like Gion, a place as old as time itself.

• • •

Outside the station, Adakichi led the way. One of the first lessons Adakichi bestowed on Maru was containing her emotions in the face of panic. She tried to channel it, but found this difficult between the heat and noise, the annoying awe for the emperor plus her discomfort over Satoshi, the silence from her father, and her fear about Sakyou's haunting eyes. She felt she was outside her own body, flipping through her leaflets of complaints, hardly feeling where her feet were taking her.

A flurry of "Aki-san! Aki-san!" called out over the steady rushing waves of voices.

"Ah! Satori-san! Mihiro-san!"

A disdain for running into familiar faces kept her from returning sooner. Her obligations were always in the way of feeling comfortable. Her head ached from the bubbly drink; she was thirsty for something fresher and clearer. These two were a pair of newer geiko that Fujiwara admonished for being cheap. They wore flimsy fabrics and painted wigs, not genuine, traditional patterns and styles the way Adakichi dressed herself.

"Did you come from the station? Ah, it's so marvelous."

"Yes, we had to see it for ourselves. The terrible rumors really do us no service. It's all the oirans' doing, I'm sure, to reclaim attention or redeem themselves from whatever folly they have engaged in."

"And how ugly the rumors are! These ghost hauntings linger around every new proclamation and invention from our emperor."

"Bad luck. I suppose it follows any new leader."

"But what about him? He's so young, so influenced by foreign ideas; he's dissatisfied with his own home, so he takes from another."

Maru resisted the urge to frown; Satori herself was wearing a cinched-waist French dress with a huge pink feather sticking out of her hair—her lips so poorly painted she looked as if she was a walking doll, not a real woman.

"We could explore his stars and see how his decisions will shape the world—" Adakichi said.

"Aki! You must have heard the news. Don't let anyone catch you saying this." Satori took Adakichi's wrist and pulled her over to whisper, "They've restricted fortune-telling!"

It was because of Kira. Maru knew immediately what he'd done. Adakichi made an effort to recover her composure. She must not have known. She bristled as Mihiro changed the topic, waving her uchiwa with vigor.

"What an astounding machine though! Didn't you think it was wonderful? It was like a thousand horses!"

"Yes, it is quite a plaything for men," said Adakichi bitterly, leaning back to avoid contact with the dress that flounced unpredictably.

"Aki dear, nothing can replace Gion. This is to complement what we have. Don't you read the papers? The emperor writes gloriously how we shall finally rival the nations overseas."

"How we should bother with lands we'll never see, people who'll never come here?"

"Yokohama and Nagasaki are reportedly entirely run by foreigners ruling under Western constitutions, governed by policies that require everyone to speak Latin."

"You are speaking in riddles, Mihiro! Where did you hear such a thing?"

"A merchant who passed through told me. He made his way south from Edo, was pushed out by foreigners, and continued his way south to find out if there were any Japanese remaining. He couldn't recognize anyone on the way. The highways are taken over by pillaging foreigners."

"The face of our own empire changes shape every day," sighed Adakichi.

"We mustn't give in. That schooling teaches this new generation values, unlike how it ever did under the samurai. They are whining as they pine for their glory days."

Maru's blood boiled. People shoved behind her. She tried to steady herself, feeling herself reeling as colors rushed before her eyes. She couldn't lose her dignity in front of Adakichi, who had seen her slipping lately.

"There are noble men among the samurai," said Adakichi softly. "There is still a place for them in our society; they embody the values that were instilled inside each of us."

"Aki, you are holding on to the past more than we have understood," said Mihiro. "Have a bit of fun today. There's a train here in Kyoto! Get yourself some fresh yams and a new roll of silk. The best supplies will be the first to go, but you have some sway."

"W

Aaa

Ahh!"

A woman collapsed at their feet, grabbing Adakichi's ankles, startling a storm of dust:

"Get off! Get off me! Right now!" Adakichi was afraid and kicking her with her feet.

The woman screamed, "My daughter! My daughter! Please, please help me. Have you seen my daughter?"

Adakichi kicked the woman away from her and was motioning for help. There was a scuffle; a blur of colors blended with the dust and the grey walls that enclosed around.

"No, no, please stop! Meiji took her! Yokai took her! Help!"

"There is no such thing!" said Mihiro. "Stop with the nonsense. "Police!" she shouted, waving away the dust.

Maru ducked in fear. She saw the tops of dark hats coming their way, reminding her of the men who came from her clan to send her away. *They're not here for me,* she told herself, shaking off the ice that encased her heart.

"Up, up!" ordered a police officer. The woman was screaming worse than a yokai.

"Get up! You're a harasser. You need to scram!" They pulled her into an alley. Another officer was unraveling rope to tie her hands behind her back.

"What havoc!" the officer said.

"I'll say! Preposterous. I hope this won't become a pattern," Mihiro said.

"She was a belligerent degenerate," said Adakichi, straightening her robes.

"It's a shame the emperor pushes them into the shadows. I say we should do away with them."

Maybe that's why she's screaming, Maru thought.

A cold shiver ran down her spine; the train sounded its horn on the other side of the entrancing brick building filled with crystals. How could something so beautiful cause such pain? Everyone resumed their normal behavior; the excitement of the matsuri and the new station returned.

Was it madness? Had Maru been the only one to see the screaming woman? Was nobody concerned about what she claimed?

A laughter between the women broke out. A joke?

"I suppose you did hear that one of Hisa's girls is gone. Probably ran away with a gentleman, I reckon, as they usually do. Saka or Saki something is her name."

"Sakyou is her name," corrected Mihiro.

"Sure. I heard it was a newer girl."

The wind was sucked out of Maru.

She rushed into the classroom, the hard wooden floor tugging on her tabi. She sat on the floor, watching everyone open their books.

"And you, Maruya, can you please read—"

But her hands were empty.

"Here, take mine."

Golden light caught the round face of a girl whose eyes were dark bowls full of stars and had a smile from ear to ear. Her hands held a wax-bound book. Maru reached out to take it, brushing the girls' hands that were softer than petals.

It was Sakyou.

Statistically speaking, it was bound to happen that one of her classmates would wind up working in Shimabara as an oiran. Not everyone was lucky in their pursuit of a good marriage, and without skills or more education in Tokyo, there were few options for a female her age. Single women had to find a way to make a living.

"This could easily have been you. No father, no class to protect you. Only this house."

Satori was pointing at Maru.

"Not even a name." The girls laughed, enjoying their sinister remark to remind Maru of her situation. She wasn't sure what to do beside pretending to ignore the tongue lashing.

"Don't be sad, girl, things could be worse. You could not have the grace of such a merciful woman risking her reputation to take you under her wing."

Then, Adakichi nodded to Satori and Mihiro to indicate the conversation was over and made a motion for them to go about their day.

They hustled to keep up, slipping between the hooped dresses and groups of shouting men, vendors balancing baskets draped over their shoulders, and stepping over children crying over losing their parents in the crowd—a sound that gave Maru goose bumps.

Maru no longer had a desire to be closer to the train. The look of horror on the woman's face as she wailed, pleading for her daughter and accusing the emperor. It belied Satoshi's assurances that everything was fine.

Everything is not fine, and nobody understands.

Maru wanted to be at home, away from the overbearing heat and crowded buildings. But their day was just beginning. They passed by a shrine for a blessing, Maru's eyes wandering to the statues of guardians at the torii. She casually wondered what would happen if the tengu ever came alive and burst from their turquoise-painted gates that kept them inside their columns.

"Oh! Did you see that?"

"See what?" said Maru nervously.

"A fox! They usually come out at night."

"Let's hope it wasn't a fox, I don't think I could bear yet another terrible omen on this day."

Adakichi hailed a rickshaw.

"Seeing a fox isn't a bad omen, though, is it?" said Maru carefully, testing the waters.

"They are meant to ward off evil. You'd better hope it is working, and evil isn't lurking here."

"Then, shouldn't we be glad to see one?"

"I would rather live in a place that doesn't need protection from anything at all. Besides, many of them are shape-shifters—something other than what they appear to be."

They climbed into a rickshaw, and Maru took a nap, dreaming she was falling into a pond covered in lilies, a glorious cooling splash beneath dappled sunlight. Frogs ribbitting softly from their petal beds, the shallow waters cloaking her a plunging her into peace.

Then something snaked around her ankle. She flicked it away with her foot and saw it was a river eel.

A sticky hand slapped her leg.

She jerked her head up. Water-rush bamboo curved over her like a cage; frogs engorging them were staring at her.

Near her feet, a pair of eyes peering from the water. It was a kappa!

She kicked at the water as the bamboo and frogs reached for her, tugging at her skin. Was she naked? She tore away from them and ran from the pond, stumbling into a street where tall statues of guards stood.

Were their eyes moving? Did they blink in the sun?

She wrapped her arms around herself and walked slowly as if her ankles were chained. Something was encroaching. Yellow eyes were watching her from above, and below.

The path ended; a slope blocked her path. It was crowned with train tracks. They were icy to the touch, but this path didn't have statues. She took it, stumbling over rows of sleepers.

Something stopped her in her tracks. She fought to look, the suffocating feeling of being pulled down to the earth consuming her. She couldn't break free. She was bound go to her death.

"*Maaa—*" She heard a sound.

She kicked one of her legs.

"*Ruuu,*" and heard another sound. From behind?

And there, at the tracks near the bend, a lopsided bun rose, and two hands gripped the rails.

She clenched her hands.

The figure pulled itself up, bracing its elbows on the gravelly path –

She jerked in her seat.

A knee rose, placed itself on a sleeper, hoisting the bed upward, cloaked in bloody pink silk, heaving itself out of the ground.

She rolled into Adakichi.

It shook its head until it fell on the tracks.

Adakichi held her shoulders and shook her. "Wake up!"

A round, moon face, black tear drops rolling down its face, its smeared red lips and toothless mouth opening.

15

Maru stepped into the heart of her favorite matsuri. The factories were no longer clanging, chimneys were empty, and wailing voices were only a soft echo.

The matsuri was alive, erupting in smoke as shrine bells rang out. Champagne would soon be bubbling in Maru's stomach. The suffocating heat strangled their bodies, but people danced until the demons dripped out of their fingertips, retreating to treetops with the bats. Everyone was dressed in their best clothing. The shops and ochaya, and sake spots and restaurants, had hung matsuri lanterns. Flags were tied from building to building, and all the gas lamps were lit. When fireworks were shot off into the sky, a roar greeted every burst.

All the yatai in the city moved to Gion, where they crowded the narrow streets, funneling people from bridges to mountain shrines. And the smell! There were things she had never smelled before: blistered peppers sizzling over open fires, large barrels of eyeless fish, fermenting soy over zaru, sweet bean dumplings and spokes of twisted salted meats! And there were armloads of sunflowers everywhere.

Maru marveled at everything, wishing the rickshaw would stop moving too fast for her to get a good look. Everyone was waving and cheering, and Mitsu wasn't able to control a grin.

Adakichi made sure she elbowed her gently so she remembered to conceal her teeth.

They passed under the bright red and white arch of the Yasaka Shrine and ascended the steps lined with hydrangeas, giving low bows to the kami that invisibly guarded the gate.

She glanced at Mitsu and saw through the façade of her delicately painted face that her fear from the pressure to perform still lingered. She had the weight of the ochaya's future on her shoulders—something Maru, for the first time, did not envy. She sent a prayer of strength for the maiko.

There was no confirmation that Mitsu received it. She instead turned her lips upward, greeting other maiko and geiko with a smile and sharing their fortunes.

Maru turned to Adakichi: "Thank you for allowing me to join you today. I'm happy Mitsu will have her moment."

Adakichi didn't respond. It was time for Maru to be left behind as Adakichi abruptly ushered Mitsu into one of the performance halls to mingle with potential clients who would be taking drinks in the shelter of shade offered by the theater. The groups scattered into familiar cliques to eagerly reacquaint themselves with one another or initiate conversations with curious men who mustered the courage to speak to one of them.

Maru, without the marking of a maiko or geiko, and no place in the parade, was overlooked. She was ashamed she hadn't mustered gathered enough ability to graduate from being a shikomi. For months she had firmly believed her father would rescue her long before festival season; but now she was here, alone, and without anything to prove herself worthy of this company she kept. Almost no one knew she belonged to a teahouse, much less that she was anything above a maid or the daughter of one of Kyoto's most respected samurai.

Former samurai, she reminded herself. A tingle ran up the back of her neck.

She hoped to see a familiar face, wondering if Kiku would ignore her after her angry outburst at Tane. Kiku had undoubtedly heard about it by now.

Loneliness struck her. The women working at her teahouse were busy with their business matters, her friends were ignoring her, and she worried how disappointed Oba-san must be that Maru didn't keep her promise to visit her. She suddenly realized that she herself was the root of her problems.

What she wanted the most was to hear from the fox that her father was safe. Even if it meant she found out he was living in Satsuma. Why was it taking so long to find out? If the fox was truly a demon, it should take only a day so to locate her father. Why was her father so hard to find? Had he disguised himself? What if he had been maimed in the battles?

She tried to suppress her more frightening thoughts. When she passed by the emperor's guards nearby, she obscured her face. As she browsed for the matsuri foods, a child ran by her with a bug-catching net. She watched longingly as the child ran to her father to be picked up and carried on his shoulder.

Her fingers wrapped around a wooden handle of a black lacquered box, its net door open, as she scampered in the reeds to chase fireflies. A firework burst; the marsh lit up in red.

When she splashed, the fireflies rose.

"Try to enjoy yourself. There is nothing to be done tonight."

"There is always strategizing to do. You urge me to wait, but you know little about our urgency."

Fireflies sank into the grass. She crouched; a firework erupted, covering her land in gold.

"And what can you do then in the face of the insurmountable? Whatever happened to the parliament role, a seat with the emperor?"

"I gave it to Kira. His mind has been brainwashed by the emperor, but he deserves to have a position in his cabinet. It's the least I could do, after the tragedy of his loss of his son."

"Then find a way to get before him, speak your piece for us to have peace. Your ally will surely help. Tonight, rest and look at Maru. See how she hunts."

"And again, there you go."

"And what is the emperor doing on this night? Is he summoning an army? To convert everyone into ogres and goblins as you have read in those stories to Maru?"

She waded closer. Taiko shook the ground, their rumbles burrowing in the mud.

"You think of me as a poor father."

"I think you should be with your daughter tonight. She was your motivation for restoring the emperor, and now you speak ill of him. It spoils the evening. Find your heart again with her."

"It is in no danger of being forgotten."

She raised the box with her left fist, higher and higher, closer to the reed, cupping her right hand on the opposite side, bringing them slowly together.

"I am starting to see there is farther to go with this. We need to demand more. That is all."

She swung her right hand, pushing the firefly into the open doorway, and snapped it shut.

She heard a P O P.

Maru was jolted. When she jerked her head up, she was and face-to-face with a creature staring at her.

The fox!

"Oh! Fox!"

It was her height with a face frozen in anger, its painted mouth downturn, its eyes bright red. It wasn't her fox.

A small hand raised, grabbing the side of the face of the fox and slowly peeled it off, revealing a confused face of a young girl behind the mask. "Sorry?"

"Oh," Maru bowed her head. "My mistake, I thought you were someone I knew."

The girl tilted her head and put the mask back on wordlessly.

There was a sting beneath her ribs, as if her own body had rebelled against her, keeping her from thinking straight. Her breathing was strained. She snuck a finger under her belt to loosen it.

"House of Adakichi?" Maru snapped her head, seeing a face with a strange hat. She became aware of the flutes playing a twinkling song, rippling through the street, making her skin tingle.

"Oh! It's you!" She quickly yanked her finger out from under her belt, feeling a flush of embarrassment painting itself all over her face from being caught in an unpresentable position.

"Need some help there?" Satoshi gestured toward her belt. To her horror, it was lumpy and misshapen.

"Oh, no, no. it's fine," she said, clutching her side before her tanto fell out.

"I am delighted to find a familiar face in this crowd," he remarked, grinning.

It was as if he appeared to snatch her right out of her loneliness. But she resisted the urge to return the same enthusiasm. She was trying to follow Adakichi's advice to be subtle and humble. She had said, *"All women of stature know a man doesn't like a woman who is too eager."*

"Are you here to—" she tried to remember the word he had used "—archive the matsuri?"

He seemed as if he could barely contain himself. "Yes! I have never seen anything like this. Our matsuri in Tokyo are quite different."

"Oh? How so?"

"It feels like everyone takes part," he said. It was, indeed, getting more crowded with each passing moment, as the sun climbed higher and higher. "In Tokyo, the matsuri are relegated by each ward. The celebrations are more familial. Fewer geisha, sorry—geiko—attend them."

"Then who performs?"

"Men volunteer to honor their family shrine carrying the palanquins, totems, lanterns."

Of course, Maru had seen them do this in Gion, too, but she didn't want to diminish his pride. *"Let the man think he knows best, even if he is wrong,"* Adakichi's had said.

"And the fireworks will be the main spectacle. They go for hours. But here it seems the food and the geiko will be the centerpieces."

She appreciated his attempt at Kyoto-ben, but hid a smile.

"You are in Gion, after all. It's to keep yokai away."

"Yokai? There you go again." He chortled.

Maru frowned. "What is the purpose the Gion Matsuri if not to chase away the demons?"

"Yokai are scary creatures in our ancient folklore. The stories are meant for children, but this matsuri is a celebration of the season. No adult here actually believes having this matsuri will get rid of evil. They know that supernatural monsters don't exist." He shook his head, a glimmer of a laugh on his face.

"But when those girls disappeared this summer, everyone said they were taken by yokai."

"There is also a rational explanation. Unfortunately vicious, demented people could have taken them away. To blame this crime on a yokai does not give the victim the justice they deserve. Anyone doing something like this is a monstrous person."

But if the emperor was at fault, would Satoshi accept him as being a real yokai? He is too rooted in his mindset.

"So much is changing so fast, it's hard to keep up with," Maru said.

"And children will be the most affected," Satoshi agreed. "Adults can be blind and cause their worst fears to happen."

"Demon behavior of men," said Maru, thinking of the mothers wailing when they find their children are gone.

"Where is your house, anyway? I am not keeping you away from your duties, am I?"

He is considerate! He is aware I may have somewhere I should be. Satoshi, though he's stubborn, is fine company.

"No, I am happy to keep you company, as a guide, you might say."

The shrine bell rang out three times, and at the top of the stairs appeared the priest donning a kanmuri flowing behind his head, followed by a horde of monks – all in their newly-washed red and white robes, long sleeves floating in the wind like folded wings of cranes.

"It's starting," said Maru excitedly. "Come, we need a better vantage point."

She directed him across the street that was rapidly emptying to make way for the parade, to claim their own plot nestled between two families and a yatai selling roasted fish heads.

He asked, "Do you know where the emperor will make his speech?"

Maru could barely hear him over the shouts and the taiko that began their stampede. The desire to dance was distracting her.

"Presumably from here." She gestured at the shrine gate. She had almost forgotten about him.

He nodded, and Maru turned away to hide her shame, praying she could answer his next questions better and speak more eloquently.

"What's next?" he whispered, leaning in close to be heard over the drums. She wasn't sure how to answer. It was a parade! Did this Tokyo man not understand this?

She leaned back a little bit and decided she must be a better guide. "There will be floats. The monks and priests will lead, and some of the biggest tea houses will be performing. And then groups of dancers join the bearer of the mikoshi, the portable Shinto shrine and anyone can follow them. The group becomes bigger and bigger until it seems everyone in Kyoto is dancing."

The bells were ringing louder as the parade advanced.

Maru said, "I need more beer." She pinched coins together, and he asked, "You use the currency here, too?"

Maru wanted to let her heart beat along with them. She found his interruptions and questions rather jarring.

"Yes, yes, mostly for the higher-end merchants, such those who make kimonos and geiko houses, I think."

"Fascinating. And what of the commoners here? Stamps or rice? Copper?"

"Let's have a drink!" she shouted back at him. The drums beside them, they began their march down the hill. She took him to a small shop with shelves lined with brown and green bottles filled with yellow liquids that had never looked so inviting.

"I'll get the next ones!" he shouted over the drums.

Maru wondered why she felt so lonely earlier in the day. Now she was almost wishing to be on her own so that she could dance freely instead of uncorking bottles for a strange man.

But the cool liquid helped to quiet her racing mind. With each sip, the tension between them lessened. She realized she was waiting in anticipation of inviting him to the ochaya.

The monks were nearing the bottom of the hill, their sweeping robes cascading like deep red waves and carrying them through the heavy air. Taiko swung side to side with men in short white pants passed by. ("I wish I had their clothing," she said.)

"Those pantaloons are not appropriate for the occasion," the man remarked, causing Maru to sigh in exasperation.

The first colorful dashi appeared, ornate with jade and gold carvings, carrying an unfamiliar dignitary who sat in his seat, a thin curtain draped behind him. The float's bearers had giant callouses on their shoulders from the weight of years of duty. Dashi were heavy, laden with jewels and oak frames.

"Who do you reckon that person is?"

"The dashi used to be reserved for daimyo," Maru replied. "But since—"

"Since the emperor took the throne, you aren't sure they are giving us the proper blessings?"

"Why? Do you know who they are?"

His lips pulled back tightly. "Not at all." He laughed. Maru joined in, clanking her bottle, feeling her belly soften. Maybe he was the only man beside her father that she could tolerate.

The men in white who carried the mystery man, dressed in long black robes in his own temple, danced to the beat, their foreheads revealing their strain beneath the hot sun.

"How long does this usually last?"

Annoyed, Maru gulped of wine to wash it away faster. "A long time," she shouted, turning back to watch flutists in their straw hats twirl by and a tower of lanterns and bells swaying on top of a hill.

A few early onlookers started to stream into the parade, eager to ride with the flow, dancing with the falling sun down the orange-painted road. Maru laughed, feeling joy as they spun to the beats, rhythmic shouts filling the air as they hoped the kami—however far away they might be—could hear their feet pounding.

"Oh, don't you want to do that? When do we join?"

"Whenever you've had enough to drink!"

"I'll need some padding in case I fall. Let's eat. Food is the second-best thing at the matsuri."

She gestured with her arms wide as if she were the emperor admiring his kingdom. "Take your pick!" she shouted.

He acted like a boy, taking off his hat and letting his long hair free. "Let's try it all!" He said, pulling her by the elbow, ordering sticks of everything. She might have been mortified but knew she must eat if she wanted to last until sundown.

A mikoshi appeared at the torii, this one gold and red with tassels and shrine emblems. She nibbled on the dried pink thing, finding it chewy and tasting like the odors of the ocean.

"It's delicious squid!" he told her. His eyes were big, and he tore into it happily, as if he never had eaten before in his life.

"You like this that much?" she asked.

"Dried fish is very popular in Tokyo. It's a winter staple."

"But it's summer," she reminded him.

A new line was marching through. Their white and purple robes concealed much smaller drums that had sharper sounds that quicken like rabbit feet running through a meadow.

He said, "Come, I want some noodles."

She followed obediently as he bought a box of fried noodles. "It's, a style from Italy! Or from China! I forget!" he shouted. She had no idea what he was talking about. She was just happy to be eating.

"Ah, I see blueberries. They must be from the train."

I don't care! She wanted to say.

A harp strumming sounded with the first ochaya appearance. The women were donned in kimono of shades of blue to capture the essence of the sea. Silver obijime tied them together, as they sang and danced like fish cutting through an ocean of cheers.

Twirling red parasols followed as if they were in a field of poppies. Another geiko house right behind was performing a summer dance. They were careful to conceal their faces to drive the crowd into a frenzy as they played their breezy song on flutes.

Behind them, another dashi, depicted a giant fish flowing through the river of people.

Maru found herself with a second bottle of rice wine in her right hand, and a sweet sticky bun in her left hand, washing away her woes.

Mounted horses adorned in flowers rode by bearing men from the palace, monks, and Kabuki actors she recognized from posters hanging outside the Halls. They waved as they led a dashi of streaming tapestries catching the sun. Their robes sparkled, sweeping up petals and abandoned shuttlecocks. The colors swirled, and cheers erupted.

Maru was near her bursting point, but her duty to her ochaya kept her grounded.

Another dashi appeared, with nearly a dozen people in white on top of it, waving hysterically, grinning, and ringing golden bells in the air.

"Oh, I think I know him!" Maru heard Satoshi say.

And then more monks carrying towers of lanterns, taller than buildings themselves, like a flock of birds flying over the crowds.

The sun blazed red, diving toward the horizon, and Maru was spinning her way down the mountain with the parade, occasionally getting a glimpse of Satoshi's delighted face, his hands always holding a different food. A new color of wine stained his lips and the front of his suit, making her giggle.

And then she heard a soft drum, then a deep rumble and a quiver that made a guttural sound in the pit of her stomach followed by the sound of a single flute piercing the wind. And then bells began to chime.

She turned to see the sun had become a spotlight on a woman and the fox.

And the woman was Mitsu!

In her bright, fiery robes, she stood with her arms out wide, pouncing forward like a fox leaping over brush. Behind her, hired dancers were in white and solid gold. Their hair was tightly wound. Their small red lips and dark eyes were still as they were poised to let Mitsu turn and steal the attention of the city.

A dazzling geiko walked behind her. The geiko's elegance swept a hush over the crowd. Even the most inebriated were fixated on her as if she were casting a spell on them. Maru now understood why Adakichi had once been a favorite of so many men.

Mitsu was the single dancer while the others remained still. She was now earning her moment, her fan fluttering like a butterfly she had chased. Her fox eyes matched the rhythm of the flute.

Maru's breath was caught in her throat. She couldn't help rooting for her.

Mitsu remained suspended as the procession slowed, like a jewelry box dancer skating down the slope, their legs and feet moving steadily. It was the curve of the road that pulled them, rather than their body making the movements.

Mitsu bent forward into a cocoon like a fox diving into its burrow, and when she rose with the increasing beats of the drum and the swelling of trumpets, the sea of white and gold leaned like a field of golden wheat swaying in the wind, bending with the breath of the kami.

And Maru spun with them, feeling a pair of hands grab her wrists and spin with her. The drums quickened, flutes whistled louder, the bells clanged, and Mitsu's movements grew faster and faster, her arms and legs stroking the air, leaping back and forth out of danger or toward it. Her furisode and hikizurki spun with her as a whirl bleeding colors.

The hands pulled her closer. Her eyes closed and, the fox's face appeared:

"Open . . . open!" she heard.

She yanked her eyelids open. The music came to a dramatic halt. The crowd was erupting with cheers.

She saw they were cheering for Kiku. The crowd wasn't cheering for Mitsu at all. Kiku stood proudly, taking it in. The sun vanishing behind a cloud, drawing the curtain on Kiku's performance and breaking the spell she'd held on the crowd. Maru looked at the man who held her wrists and writhed away from him; he seemed to hardly notice as he took a healthy swig of a bottle, gasping afterward.

"It was so exhilarating! Do you know those dancers?"

Maru's chest was heaving. There was a ringing in her ears. Her mind was ablaze. Yokai were licking her ears with their poisonous tongues, lashing her earlobes with violent thoughts. Those eyes she'd fallen into time after time, entrusted her with secrets, held hands in temple groves. Kiku had drunk the poison and was like any other maiko.

The drums rose as Kiku passed her without acknowledging her, reminding her of her invisibility. Whether it a gift or a curse, the wine was muddying her thoughts and changing her opinion as quickly as the drumbeat.

"Ah, have you had yakitori before?" she heard Satoshi's voice ask her. "They season with onion, it's the best thing—" But she was watching Kiku stride down the hill, stealing Maru's dreams. Something peculiar was stirring, as a breeze rushed through her hair, coming loose.

That's my heart.

"No." She was angry, terrified at the idea of Adakichi finding out Kiku's house also was performing the Kitsune Dance after she herself had let them in on the secret. Her house would find out. She stuffed her face to distract herself from the pain welling inside, rising higher and higher. All around she heard were bells and screams, twisting into a tornado of dizzying sounds, clouding her vision, and blurring the voices around her. But one came through clearly.

"*Ma . . . ru...*"

She stormed away. Something was calling her. She had to answer.

"*Ma . . . ru...*"

Pushing through the crowd, she didn't know where she was headed, but something else wanted her attention:

"*Ma . . . ru...*"

A noren flew into her face, knocking her back in surprise; a body was nearby thrown to the ground.

"Not again until you bring something to gamble with!" a man with bushy eyebrows and thick, short dark hair shouted at the crumpled heap. Emerging out of his tangled suit and limbs, Fujiwara, who was red in the face, struggled out of his stupor.

"I have it, I have it! Yamauchi, please!" When he lunged toward the door, a foot pushed him in the chest back into the street, where he heaved, and saw Maru staring at him.

"Oh! Apricot! Please!" he grabbed at the hem of her robes.

She pulled away, disgusted.

"No, not you, too. Please don't tell Aki. Please help me—"

Her training kept her from shouting obscenities at him, from violently yanking away.

"Oh, let me help you, sir!"

Satoshi juggled his spears of yakitori, wrestling to get Fujiwara on his feet, their limbs flailing in an unchoreographed mess. Fujiwara, drunk and unstable, pulled Satoshi off his feet and into the crowd, receiving outcry from others. Maru turned from them, exasperated.

Then, out of the corner of her eye, she spotted Tane and Ai, their arms linked, laughing.

"Oi!" she called out, catching Tane's eye. A look of fear crossed her face. They picked up their pace and vanished into the crowd.

"You know them?" Satoshi said, reappearing and munching, his cheeks like a frog.

She remained silent. She felt as if heavy rocks were pulling her beneath the surface of the sidewalk as he tore violently into the chicken. She felt sick and turned her back to him.

She and Kiku had their differences. This was another depth of sabotage; she trusted her beyond any doubt—and here, the crowd hadn't an inkling why there'd be two of the same dance performances. It would be sloppy and reflect poorly on their ochaya for following it.

"My dear, my dear!"

"Oba-san," Maru whispered, ready to burst into tears. Her snow-haired grandma, smiling like a sunflower, was a welcome glimmer of hope. She fell against her shoulder.

"There, there . . . that's my girl. Have you gotten taller?"

Maru wiped her nose and laughed.

"My, there's such a flush on your cheeks. Where is your parasol? Mind your habits in sun, dear."

Maru noticed something in her hand.

"Why do you have an ofuda? What evil are you warding away?"

Oba-san had a terrified expression on her face when she said, "It's spreading. They won't tell you outright, but take care, dear, after Ogawa fell, one of your neighbors, Natsumi, became ill and left her child. It's a good reassurance. Shall I fetch you one?"

Everything Maru saw seemed painted in red. She heard applause and realized she had missed Mitsu's performance. Mitsu had taken off her mask in front of a less than appreciative audience. Confusion clouded her face, superseding all her diligent training.

Maru felt sorry for her. She wanted to apologize to her.

Oba-san motioned for Maru to come closer.

"You are so busy, granddaughter, and I know you have more important people than me, to turn to, but I thought it would be wise for me to tell you that your clan has been moving out of their neighborhood. It seems they are turning on your father. When the bells toll, the snakes appear. I have something to tell you about what I heard about him."

Maru wanted to ask more, to grasp her and demand answers, but the crowds pushed and separated her from Oba-san, casting her out into the wide expanse to be swept into her own guilt about her choices she had deliberately tried to avoid confronting.

The colors of the evening had begun, and the walls of Gion were lit with lanterns. Anticipation of the fireworks was on everyone's mind. The crowd seemed filled with a desire for debauchery. Many were covered with ashes from sparklers, and their hands were sticky with rice and soy beans.

Having long abandoned her clogs somewhere behind potted geraniums up the hill, she danced barefoot along with the crowd, forgetting all about her father, her friends, and Adakichi and the shame she carried on her shoulders. She cradled her deepest worries, doting on them all this time instead of letting go. With each step they grew heavier, and she longed to drop them to rid herself of the pain she had coiled around herself.

The drumbeats waxed and waned until they loudly pounded:

BOOM

BOOM

They were deliberately announcing something to shake the audience out of their stupor. Maru followed the voices shouting up on the hill as another yamahoko appeared. Inside it sat a man, a prominent figure that commanded gasps followed by silence.

It was the emperor.

She gasped too unexpectedly, a surge of excitement, a warmth of pride—*her emperor*—the man her father so proudly believed in years ago, was before her and now very close.

It was cut short when soldiers ascended the short steps to his yamahoko, head-to-toe in Western garb with no resemblance to noble samurai.

The joyous hope in her heart sank like a stone. They reminded her of the men who antagonized her days ago.

An angry sea churned, and heat rose on her neck. Warmth was replaced by burning hatred, an urgency to hear him speak and dare to face them. She wanted him to answer her, to tell her why her father's service had been in vain, that he could die in Satsuma as a bystander, stranded, caught in a war between groups wanting control, and that he no longer had nobility. It had been taken, and the police had knocked on her door. What was the meaning of this? Why must he scare her so? Her father fought hard for this day to come, and now may never see the train, such an expensive invention that kept families hungry to keep this man before her wealthy, in power, as he slowly found ways to corner those who had been loyal to him, repaying them with bitterness.

In the gas lamps that burned, she saw the yellows of the fox's eyes, and was reminded of a darkness that moved within her.

He stood there, a stern expression on his face, not even a hint of excitement for the matsuri; the discomfort in her rose, screaming, ringing a bell she couldn't tune out.

"*O-Kay*, I know who that is," Satoshi said excitedly, using a phrase she hadn't heard before, reappeared over her shoulder.

A hush fell and the men hoisting up the emperor's dashi shifted under the weight.

"On today's fine occasion it softens my heart to be at your side, celebrating our achievements to date, and commemorating our country's growth and steadfast commitment to our mission. I hold a resounding pride and keen appreciation for your good-faith efforts to trust in this world we are building, and I have nothing but the highest praise for your enthusiasm.

"However, I cannot refrain, at the risk of souring this delightful afternoon, from tempering some of your expectations and offering a cautionary word.

"It has come to my knowledge that there are threats seeking to undermine and dismantle what we are tirelessly working toward."

A rogue firework burst overhead. Adakichi, in the crowd, looked solemn.

"These actions are dishonorable. I call upon dissenters to immediately surrender and approach our tables with open minds and willingness to engage in public discourse, which has been encouraged since the beginning of my humble rule."

Her heart shattered. She wanted to reach out to Adakichi to confess what happened.

The emperor continued, "It is a shame that despite our forward approach, war has broken on our own lands, and will undoubtedly affect many of us. It is of grave disappointment we must respond; an atrocity of the heart that I bear with all of you."

It was true that there was war against his own.

"I wholeheartedly feel and take responsibility for being unable to meet the desires of all and am readily working with my council to resolve this discontent swiftly and with minimal price of harm to both livelihood and economy."

The wine boiled upward into a fountain in her body, and Maru bent over, releasing it to the gutter as people leapt out of the way with their clucking noises of disapproval. She heaved again, but his words clung to her no matter how desperately she purged herself of his lies. It was something she knew all along in her gut, suppressed until now—a violence she could no longer ignore or cover with daydreams of a truth she longed for.

"I implore then, with as much urgency as I can express, that we strive for unity, and hold an unyielding interest into our country. We aim to give transparent announcements about movements and clarity in our communications. To set a precedence of trust your instructions are simple: We come together and abide as such or the shared Oath will be futile and certain to fail and will bring us great harm from both our visible and invisible enemies near and far.

"Today is a beautiful day, and your faces are shining. Do not let these words dampen your spirits but, rather, use these shared feelings and come together and show a force of good in return, and peace will one day come to us again."

A brief applause followed along with a sudden crescendo of music and fireworks rapidly colliding in the air. Everything was a blur, seeming to move impossibly fast and unnaturally slow at the same time; voices were echoing; she was submerged in a sea of dread. And just when she couldn't take any more, the police, a dark shadow sweeping across the happiest matsuri, cloaked her vision. They had found her. They were coming for her. She whirled around, unable to run at all. Her legs were shackled to the ground. *Something was wrong. Why were they coming for her? Was it father? Had he been found a traitor after all?*

She tripped and collapsed.

"There, there, are you feeling unwell?" A hand patted her on the back.

She turned to find a face quite unlike the man she'd been with all day. It was Kira.

"Yes, too much wine," she said with a heave, wondering what he did to the girl in Ponto-cho.

"You sure it wasn't Meiji? It would be unfortunate if he was the cause of such distress."

She shook her head furiously. "Too many bottles." She coughed. The police were nearly over his shoulder. She kicked away from him. He smiled.

"Hosokawa, you need to watch yourself. Many eyes are loyal to the emperor."

"As are mine," she said, her voice trembling.

He tilted his head. "That is rather brave of you," he said. He caught her eyes and followed them to the police, nodding at them. They turned and left abruptly.

Why did he do that? She frowned, wanting to stand and have something to lean on. Where was Satoshi? Ah, she spotted him at a yatai, haggling over more buns.

"Why would it be brave to be loyal to the emperor?"

When Kira leaned over, she saw a small, folded letter peering out from the front of his robe. *It was her letter.*

"Then you could convince your father to relinquish these lofty dreams of his—surrender and lay his sword down, once and for all. Gosho would gladly accept his expertise and look the other way, but he must act swiftly, resolutely."

Something hot, and sharp as nails was clawing its way up her abdomen. *Why hadn't her letter been delivered? Was it returned?* There was nothing damning in it. Had he searched her house with the police and uncovered something?

"I thought it would be wise for me to tell you, your clan has been moving out. It would seem they are turning on your father."

There was something inside her roaring; she pushed it down, caging the beast.

"He has no sword to lay down. The emperor already reclaimed it; he is a trader."

"And at risk of being a traitor if he strays too far from his loyalties." Their noses were almost touching. "Old friends can protect each other only for so long."

"He is a trader," she whispered. "He's a trader." But the word *traitor* balanced on the tip of her tongue, the soft difference half a moment away from escaping her lips.

Why was it there? Why was it within reach? Then Adakichi's words came to her:

"Men who crave power will align themselves with its helm, regardless of the head that wears it."

She wanted to shout, but cotton filled her mouth; choked by a throat-clutching demon that licked her ear and taunted her about her inability to stand up for herself; she reached for his chest, but the letter disappeared, suddenly out of sight. When she reached for her tanto inside her obi he put his hand out. He anticipated her actions. He was evil. He had to be the one who was framing others for his evil deeds. The humming of the cicadas and matsuri bells were bellowing in her ears, demanding her to do something, say anything.

I'll kill Kira before he touches me.

"I know you are killing the girls!" she burst before doubling over. "For Meiji!"

The heave inside took form: it was thick, hot, and unavoidable—she purged it, releasing the poison all over Kira's feet, which jumped out of sight. He was long gone when she finally stood and found Satoshi happily eating the buns.

"You need one too." He handed her a meat-filled sticky bun.

She took it begrudgingly, looking into the crowd for Kira. But he was gone as fast as he had appeared, as if he were a ghost. Maybe it was her imagination, a gift from her wine.

"You look like you saw a demon," he said, his mouth full.

She peeled back, unable to shake the sickness permeating her stomach. The fireworks overhead sounded like gunfire her father once practiced with. The shouts from the crowds no longer sounded joyous, but angry, on the verge of a riot, as bodies mounted one another, arms flailed, and the drums deepened.

And further, a sanctuary: a stall of sasamochi; and Kiku, standing still, a contrast to the chaos that consumed the scene.

Maru left Satoshi for her friend—the coward who betrayed her in the most rotten of ways. She needed answers, to convey all she had bottled up inside, as her emotions began to overflow, seeping in anger and resentment, confusion and heartbreak all at once.

She pushed through the crowd, callously, ignoring the startled cries of people rattled by her rude behavior. She was reaching for Kiku, with her hand outstretched, needing a response. She needed to know her friend had not done it intentionally—that she had not meant to hurt anyone.

"You!" Maru grabbed Kiku's shoulder. "You . . . you!" she couldn't muster much more. Words she wanted to say were blocked by a dam of wine and food sloshing in her stomach.

"Maru!" Kiku's eyes widened. "You appear ill. Do you have fish fever too?"

Fish fever? She was too drunk to process this.

"You're swaying." Kiku tugged on her elbow and held her up. "A prime disaster, Maru! Whatever is the matter? Why were you yelling at the brothel man?"

Maru grinded her teeth. *Kira?*

"You have him all wrong. He's a regular, and protects the girls. Ever since his son died, he's been trying to figure out what's happening."

Maru ignored Kiku's soliloquy. "I saw you."

"Yes, we're all here at the matsuri today," said Kiku with exasperation.

"You stole our idea!"

Kiku cocked her head.

"You performed the Kitsune Dance too!" Maru raged.

"Ah." An aloof expression came over her face. Her eyebrows arched as she nibbled on minazuki.

Maru was stunned. "You betrayed me! I know what you did!"

"This is a bore. Anyone can choose to do any dance. Foxes are wildly in fashion. I saw one just today."

Maru screamed. "You've ruined it for us! She will have my head for this! You've abandoned me!"

"Nobody left you," she retorted impatiently. "You were haughty first with Tane. Don't you remember? She was crying all day long because of you!"

"You don't listen."

"No, *you* need to listen Maru! We have been worried, and you won't pay attention! It's all different now, and you need to get it together. Stand up!"

Maru was slouching, on the brink of collapsing entirely.

"No! No! I know things. There are things that talk to me."

"Oh Maru, you're a mess. Go home. Apologize to Tane. Then come back." Kiku pushed her into the crowd.

To Maru, it seemed filled with faceless ghosts standing listlessly. How long was she staring at them? It was time for her to find her ochaya to see if they had heard of her betrayal. Instead, the world spiraled around her. Her head was aching, and her heart longed for something she couldn't explain. Everything was spinning faster until she thought she'd collapse from dizziness.

A dashi rushed into her mind, and carried her away into a suppressed memory. It resurfaced and shouted a truth she had concealed from herself.

There was a fire and a group of men hunched over, swords laying across some laps, empty tea cups cast aside.

"We needed to industrialize. We cannot put the tiger back in the bag," said a dark man. "There will be no more clan wars. We have threats beyond our seas."

"It was a lie. We always had peace, thanks to us. Meiji is a boy; he forgets so quickly who was responsible for keeping order. We put faith in him prematurely," her father snarled. "You are buying into the fabrication that we will have prosperity and fairness. We have yet to see it come to fruition."

"He must know more than he is letting on. The Shinsengumi knew." said another.

"And the Choshu sent their spies to confirm their stories and couldn't!" said her father. "Instead, it was a betrayal. Samurai will no longer exist. The clans are stripped—it's happening!"

"You are a peacekeeper, Hosokawa. We do not dispute you. This is no fight for us."

"He is going to disrupt our way of life. His vision does not include us after all," her father insisted. "Now that we

foolishly aligned with him, we are not granted equality at all. We lost."

"Did you not go to him with your proposals? Did he reinstate you?"

"He would not hear me. He consults with advisors from other lands. He sends them ships but won't address plights at home. He believes he has won us over and seeks admiration on a grander stage, but it is one that'll turn their back on him." Her father clenched his fist.

"We ought to give him another a chance. Not everything can happen overnight."

"For years we have had our gates shut. For years we were stagnant, lacking ambition to overcome complacency and confront the snake. We have fought ourselves, plotting in the dead of night to carry his ungratefulness to a throne. For years we have sat like fools biding our time. Instead, he pits us against one another, the same grueling pattern as before."

"Hosokawa, you sound like Saigo. He warns to not trust these allies with such vigor, but Saigo validates himself by having a disciple. He has no doctrines to offer."

"Saigo is the man I have been corresponding with. He is leading the way but you doubt him, even though he used to command us as his brothers."

"And what do you propose we do about it? Clear intentions are needed."

"He has an academy in Satsuma with allied clans, readying for war. It will be just one more time, an investment for our future. We can rise and fight one more time." Her father stared at them, daring anyone to protest.

"Against whom?" someone quietly asked.

"The emperor."

Where was the fox?

She needed to find the fox.

She went past the mill to the torii at the end of the street. It was brightly lit with open flames. She heard herself say a prayer to send a stillness to drown out the sounds of the sizzling, crackling, and dancing and bring instead a softness with the fading sunset.

I need help.

And there, in the distance, past the matsuri moving in blurry masses, sat a small figure sitting still in a pool of light—just as she had wished:

It was the fox.

"*Maru,*" she heard.

She gasped and started to move slowly, as if going upstream, fighting the crowds and waves.

"Where are you going?" she heard a voice ask.

"Nowhere," she heard herself reply.

And then her eyes bored into the fox's bright yellow eyes, their connection holding them together as she moved with the parade and made her way down the street overflowing with flying sleeves and smoke that stung her eyes.

"*Ma . . . ru . . .,*" she heard again.

She was a few feet away from the fox.

The taiko beat steadily with each of her steps She counted her advances as fireworks began to burst when she passed under the torii.

"*Fight,* she heard the fox say."

The fox's tail flicked at her left side, and then it was gone.

She spun out of the parade and went down a road away from the main street that beat to the matsuri's rhythms.

As she stumbled along on the unfamiliar path, her mind was full of images of her father when she last saw him shouldering his rucksack and tossing his bags into the back of a wagon, his sedge hat askew as it caught the morning wind. He gave her a small smile and repeated his promise to return soon.

The image of that day, and echo of her protest, blurred into frightening thoughts. Maybe he hadn't left in a wagon. Perhaps he had taken his rucksack and thrown it over his shoulder, sheathing a sword into his robes as he mounted a black horse, smashing his heel into its side and vanishing into the night in a thundering of hooves as the samurai disappeared into the horizon.

And what if instead of begging him to trade in nearby ports, she had convinced him to stay, persuading him that he no longer needed to fight, and now that they were together in Kyoto where there was no war on their doorstep, their house was tall, and they were safe.

But he had insisted she would be protected inside the ochaya where nobody would suspect a shikomi was a samurai's daughter because it was sacrilegious. Memories she had long buried now surged like storm waves, wrestling with falsehoods she had comforted herself with through summer.

Her gaze adjusted to the encroaching dusk. She could see figures nearly hidden in the shadows. The pastel purple and blue hues of the fading sunset illuminated the edges of the buildings' stone foundations along the road. She saw the vines that climb into the iron chimneys and the wooden walls with rippling tiled rooftops. Eyes stared out at her from every nook.

And once again the fox was sitting at the side of the road, its golden fur alight, seemingly from within, and could be mistaken for someone's lost statue.

They stared at one another. Both were apprehensive about making the first move. She had pleaded the fox to bring news of her father, and finally the fox had come to see her. But there was no joy in their reunion. She could tell from its eyes that there was nothing to celebrate. The fox was pensive and still.

Boom

Boom

Maru

Maru

The loud noises of the matsuri fireworks woke Maru from her reverie. Suddenly the street was red and orange. Homes and shops were silent as their dwellers danced and sang at the festival, which had risen so quickly in the early dusk. Even the lamps were not yet lit.

The fox remained motionless. Faceless shadows were watching her. She approached the shadows and said, "Kitsune." Her tongue felt thick and hard to move.

The fox stood up, flicked its tail, and continued down the road.

"Kitsune, where are you going?" she hissed in desperation, grabbing onto a tall plant next someone's door to remain upright.

But the fox had turned around a corner. She had to push on.

They meandered south through the purple-painted paths and orange walls, keeping Fushimi Mountain in their sight.

Where were they going?

Maru's only choice was to follow the fox as he guided her on her their pilgrimage.

Boom

Boom

Maru

A war.

The war couldn't have been declared for the reasons the emperor told them.

His words echoed in her ears with each step beckoning her onward, closer to a truth that was finally within her grasp.

She knew the fox might have another plan in mind for the day. But in her inebriated state, she had staggered on, determined to follow the fox as closely as she could. She was desperate for what their conversation might reveal to her, even if she was oblivious to the tricks it might play on her.

A soft golden mist hung in the air on the shopping road, all the way up to the mountain. Cedars sparkled on the slope near the black poles with the wires for conducting electricity that jutted violently into the air. The poles and the silver wires obscured the soft colors of nature in the beautiful ancient city that had been scarred by the swift changes to fill the desires of the greedy emperor.

She hated him for this.

"*Ma . . . ru,*" she heard again.

The kitsune turned to lead her down another path. This one was familiar. Her intuition told her this was right, and the strange shadows behind her heels disappeared.

At the bottom of the path was a large pond covered with lilies. She knew she had been here before.

"Here, here! Stop, stop!" she cried out, and the fox came to a halt. A tightness gripped her chest. She sucked in the air deeply. It stung her.

The air smelled like it was filled with blood.

"There's something dangerous near us that we must find," she said breathlessly.

The fox nodded.

"You're sensing it too."

She heard whispering over her shoulder, and a black figure disappeared behind a tree.

It was Sakyou.

The fox was taking her to Sakyou.

"*Ma . . .ru,*" she heard.

There were yellow eyes in the forest, and the cicadas were silent. Even the sounds of the matsuri had died away.

Then she heard a whistle that sounded like a scream racing down from a windy mountainside.

She ran down the road, dashing past shanties until she came to a riverbank, nearly tripping over the sudden appearance of the silver rails of the train tracks.

"South—no, I must go north." She followed the tracks until a bend came in sight.

This was what she saw in her dream. It was the answer that had alluded her—the answer nobody was willing to confront.

"Here! The answer is here!"

She bent over the tracks, clawing her way, sleeper by sleeper, looking for traces of Sakyou. Perhaps she had left something behind. She picked up jagged rocks frantically searching for clues, tossing them aside when she found nothing belonging to her friend.

She was in the place in her dream where Sakyou's body was mangled, exactly where her robes lay on the rails, her leg bent beneath her unnaturally.

But there was nothing here. She had just seen her right here in her dream. How could she be wrong? She crouched to get a closer look, feeling the earth for a pulse as if it were a body.

Where was Sakyou's body? She stood up and looked up and down the tracks. She spied a dark pooling of liquid around the nearest poles with the hanging wires.

She lunged toward the first pole, stopping before she stepped into the thick black liquid that surrounded it. The thickness of the pole and the way it rose above the buildings leaking such vile poison was terrifying.

A buzzing in her head, a hum that roared louder, drew her closer. She felt the heat it was emitting as the buzz grew louder and louder. She clamped her hands over her ears to block it out, listened the voices calling her.

"Ma . . . ru!" The maroon shine on the black bubbles was calling her. She had to do something. She let her instincts guide her body forward until she found it.

She thrust her hands into the bubbles. A soft surface gave away easily as she plunged into the sticky sap. It felt like soft feathers and was hot. When she took her hands out, she found them stained with bright red liquid. In her palm she held a dripping kushi that once adorned hair.

It was not Satoshi's rust. It was Sakyou's blood.

"MARU!" she heard."

Voices were shouting over each other, as if the kami she called out to had just awakened with a start.

She held her hands against her chest and closed her eyes and bent to pray. The blood dripped down her chest and cheeks as she remembered Sakyou's beautiful face, and a wind swept up her words to take them higher.

Once she gave her final words of prayer from lightly parted lips, she collapsed. She was heaving as if she had released a rope in a tug-of-war in a final surrender to the other side.

Catching her breath, she pressed her face against her palms and realized two small children nearby were watching her, staying a safe distance away. When she waved to them, they turned and ran, shrieking.

"Oh, no," she said sadly and looked at her hands. They were still covered with blood, with drying chunks packed beneath her fingernails.

A new fear came over her: Would they think she was guilty of the crime?

She tried wiping her hands on the grass nearby, but the stickiness remained, pulling pieces of grass and dirt with it. Her hands and arms were layered with muck that made her look worse.

She started to walk along the tracks, trying to keep steady. Her head was spinning.

She had to find Sakyou.

And where had the fox gone?

"Kitsune," she called.

Maru paused, hearing a stillness come over the tracks and the land. She held her breath, watching the ground, realizing she was unsteady on her feet.

She thought it was drunk dizziness, but when her swaying became more erratic, she halted to regain balance, but found her feet shook even though she stood still.

This was an earthquake.

A blackened hand shot into the air, bursting through rocks between the rails. The figure pulled itself up, like a ghost resurrecting itself as it reached for the sky, growing taller and taller. An empty face looked down at her.

A ghost. Maru gasped and fell backward, stumbling away, trying desperately to scuttle away, but the earth shaking and the rail ties kept tripping her.

Behind the ghost she saw a young girl and two more creatures emerge from the woods. They were prying themselves from shallow graves, their entrails and blood flowing from where their bodies had been strewn across the tracks. They were now appearing before her eyes: They had been there all along.

And walking down the middle of the tracks, was Mitsu. She looked whole and alive.

"Mitsu!" Maru cried out. But she didn't budge. Mitsu's fox robes were faded; her face looked defeated. Maru tried to stand to warn her of the danger, but the shaking crumpled her knees.

"KITSUNE!" she screamed, willing the fox to appear. Her knees wobbled in an uncontrollable motion. When she was forced to bend over, she saw an elaborate hair ornament under some daisies. When she tried to pick up the ornament, there was a bigger jolt. She reached out to grasp the silver rails and saw the land was about to split open. But the silver was too hot to touch, and she couldn't steady herself.

Mitsu stood on the tracks staring at Maru. She was motionless.

"MITSU! You must leave!" Maru shouted.

Bodies of the remains from the fierce battle were rising from the tracks. Body after body of the charred soldiers who had fallen—all the agony she had witnessed over the summer—were now rising.

Up the mountain the land rumbled. Surely it was about to slide, taking the pagoda with it and knocking down the emperor's poles and wires and sweeping her away with the bodies no one had searched for.

Again, she saw the fox. It appeared behind Mitsu.

The broken bodies were creeping closer to her—and Mitsu was oblivious of the danger.

Maru tried to call out to her, but her voice faltered.

Some distance ahead, a shape that looked like a pair of shoulders lifted up out of the train tracks. Its hands reached up for the rails and the softly glowing, silvery figure pulled itself up.

Her heart stopped. The world quieted, as if she had sunk into the ocean, and she heard nothing but the sound of water rushing into her ears. The shape was familiar. She had seen it in her dream.

"Move!" she cried as she stumbled toward Mitsu, reaching out desperately to pull her back.

Mitsu didn't move.

"It will hurt you!"

But Maru could not reach Mitsu in time.

The shape grew bigger and bigger. Standing on its legs, the creature lifted its head. A lopsided bun was hanging from its shoulder. It's face as large as a platter above its pink blood-stained robes.

It was reaching for her. Its black eyes were boring into her as it glided over the rail ties with frothing black bubbles dripping from its pale lips. Mitsu was going to be taken. She was going to die.

"Kitsune!" Maru cried to the fox. "Make the creature stop! Protect yourself and Mitsu!"

"I cannot. I'm too weak."

"Hosokawa! We cannot take on the emperor! He will return fire on us tenfold!"

Maru wanted to shout and hurl a rock at the demon but her head was heavy and she was unable to hold on to the rail ties.

"Please fight!" she told the fox.

"I can't."

Go to the temples with me. Call upon all the kami; summon the demons.

And Sakyou opened her mouth, wider than was human, and an ear-splitting scream pierced her in the heart, knocking her back and rolling over her. A rumbling shook the land harder than before, and dark shadow appeared on the horizon.

It was a train.

We cannot! It's too dangerous, Hosokawa, no!

Maru saw it was barreling toward Mitsu, its black cloud of bubbles pouring its poison into the air, its front yellow eye blinding her as the blackness came closer and closer. She tried to lift herself up, but it was too late. Mitsu would be crushed.

We will bring the emperor a fight he cannot control.

"Fight!" Maru cried.

The fox began to double over.

She bellowed at the fox: "I can do it for you!"

"Are you strong enough?" she heard the fox ask.

"I will fight for you!" Maru shouted again. She had failed to get its pearl. It had no power. "I will share myself with you!" she shouted.

The fox bent its nose downward and stood, shining its eyes into her. A heat was filling her chest. She felt iron-hot, and her joints ached as an icy sting pierced her head.

The two eyes of the fox merged into one, and a bright yellow light filled her. She drew her tanto from her obi, knowing just where it rested. In a flurry, she ran to Mitsu, who was standing in front of the train, and brandished her tanto.

She bellowed and plunged her tanto deep into the eye of the train.

Then everything was black until she found herself opening her eyes.

Another scream coursed through her, and she saw the black ooze bubbling all around her, rushing down the silvery railroad. Wisps of spirits were floating out through the train's melting windows, their screams turning into faded whistles.

Her arms and legs stiffened and adhered to the tracks. Her skin was hardened and blackened as the tracks burned her skin up and down her body; the bubbling blackness taking over her.

Her neck stretched higher and higher. She thought she heard a snap as a fire shot up her spine.

She opened her mouth to scream and saw steam billowing from her mouth as she released the hatred and anger, and the pain and grief she had welled up inside her—all the things that had roiled around her guts all summer, the longings she had carried in her life and her secrets—were all spilling onto the tracks.

She dropped her head back and her legs buckled. She fell on the tracks in a heap of limbs, landing on her back beneath the shade of the water rush bamboo where the train should have been passing by.

The bodies disintegrated as the floating spirits settled into the bones that scattered across the tracks. The smoke consumed them just before they vanished into their graves.

Sakyou was gone. Mitsu was gone. The shadows were gone. The train was nowhere in sight.

"Get up," a voice commanded.

She hoisted herself up, and stars burst in front of her eyes; she rubbed them until they were sore. Older women sitting outside a shanty beneath one of the sleek black poles paid no attention to her. Rising from the brush, Maru saw the glittering hair ornament and tucked it into her robes. Had the women not seen the train? Or the yuurei? Or her?

"Here I am," said a voice.

"Kitsune!" she dove to where the fox lay as children stood over it, prodding its fur. She shooed them away. Its eyes were shut. It was struggling to breath. There were sores all over its body. She shook it gently, but there was no reaction.

The sound of the women laughing and whistling startled her, reminding she was in danger. She picked up the fox and held it close to her, taking it to the street away from the blackened pools, train tracks, and ghosts.

Maru went quickly past the onlookers, breaking into a run to escape their shouts and curious glances. The street her stage, the setting sun the stage light, brighter than the biggest kabuki theater.

The memories of her nightmares merged and fused as she clutched the fox she had never understood and ran through a ward that must despise and fear her. In her state of madness, she expected to see the train in pursuit of her.

Gasps and fingers pointing at her flew by as if they were arrows and bullets until she stopped to rest at Keage Slope's cherry trees, in a yard of vacant villa that once belonged to the shogun. She remembered her father's stories of the authorities pushing them out of their sprawling homes with stone gardens now filled with moss and coiled ivy.

She gently lay the fox down on an engawa that overlooked a pond and stroked its fur. It wasn't her fox at all. Should she leave its lifeless body here and go back for Mitsu? Or had she already turned into a yuurei?

Soon the ribs of the fox rose and fell with stronger breaths. Maru went to the pond and slashed water on her arms and face. The coolness awakened her senses and brought her some calm. There was nothing left inside her to make her ill. There was only peace. She had emptied herself from the poison of withholding the truth she couldn't explain, but her instincts told her was her reality.

"I'm not really mad," she told herself, cupping water in her hands to pour on the fur of the fox and coax some into its mouth.

It worked. The fox shook its head at the touch of the cool water and lapped up what she offered.

It was her fox. She swung her legs over the edge of the raised engawa, staring out into the forest while she gave it time to recover.

They sat in silence, letting the garden return to its twilight routine that was disrupted by their commotion.

"It was you all along," she dared to whisper, though still a little afraid of the truth.

"You tone is not accusatory."

A dragonfly dipped by them, awakening the first firefly of the season that had nestled beneath the lily pads.

"When I was in the tracks, my body felt different. I saw you stare at me and then—"

"We made a pact, did we not?"

The hum of the pond and the creatures hiding beneath large lily leaves stirred.

"I do not remember what I said to you. I know I didn't want to lose you."

"And you were frightened. When we are afraid, becoming what we fear is a way to overcome it."

"So, *you* were the ghost train!" She was breathless. Her fox was a trickster.

"I was, in the beginning. When man brought their train into our land, it hunted us. It went through our lands and distressed the spirits and kami. But we are not permitted to retaliate unless we are summoned to do so by a mortal. I had made a promise to be creative and devise a way to fight man, as we had a millennia ago."

All of the fairytales Maru had read of ancient battles between mythical creatures and man had been beyond her reach. Here in her lap was a creature of those legends.

"And one day, we had permission. Someone requested our aid. The kami were allowed to strike back at your emperor. At first, it was meant to be a warning. I assumed that formidable shape because I thought becoming the train's shape was the only foe that would scare the train."

Maru held her breath.

"Initially it was easy to use my shapeshifting to fight the train. But man's train kept taking lives of innocent spirits that wandered in error on the wrong path. The kami wanted revenge. They fueled the strength of my own train-shape. They were feeding it to get even with man."

She thought about the bodies of the children, the young girls spliced and torn and scattered across the tracks.

"Rogue warriors were taken. I thought there was enough chaos to satisfy the wish that had conjured the ghost train. But then one girl got in the way and became collateral, and the train took on a life of its own as a hungry yuurei."

The girl at the matsuri.

"I surrendered my shapeshifting. I thought we were even. But it was too late. The ghost train was a runaway with enough consumed spirit life to carry on its own. More wishes came in, such as demands to harm the emperor and destroy his machines. They fueled its strength. But it did more destruction than they intended. I tried to fight and dismantle it myself to keep it from causing more havoc and destroying the balance. After my orb was lost I became weak and unable to discern who an enemy was. Mistakes made today cannot spare pain in the future. Let this be a warning."

"You seem stronger," Maru said.

"For that, I have you to thank. By accepting me, you have become a shell I share. My energy had been depleted by trying to protect those who become weak from being in harm's way."

Evening bats clicked their tongues, chasing away the swallows in the treetops.

Maru said, "Those who were weak? The girls? They have had hard lives. It's unfair to call them weak."

"This is the balance of the world. Nothing more. You can blame your emperor for weakening them and making them vulnerable. Their bodies were consumed by another foe discarded as a sacrifice for the beast. Your changing laws empowered enemies since you often deliberate your decisions." The fox's eyes flickered. "The ghost train preyed upon hearts softened by tears."

The girls. Sakyou. Trapped in lives they couldn't escape.

"They became the rage of the ghost train," whispered Maru. "They sought revenge."

The fox said, "It went out of control when I stepped out. But without my orb, I couldn't prevent more people from being lured or harmed by man. I needed an ally. I was drawn to your spirit. In a way, your spirit called to me when you made a wish for your father."

"I don't feel as if I was suitable to be an ally."

"You passed all the tests of the yokai. Even when you were at your lowest strength, you resisted the temptation to follow them right into their trap and surrender your spirit. You fought death each time. It revealed what are willing to fight for."

Maru pulled herself in tighter, shivering at the thought of having been close to becoming a ghost.

Dusk's last gasp settling on the leaves across the pond painted the greenery in dark oranges and pinks, but all Maru saw was red. The emperor and his unjust laws and the way he leered and took the goodness from anyone who had helped him drove the samurai and the women to their deaths.

She asked, "Why would they use a way like this to find me? Were they using fear to encourage me to fight?"

"You needed to be convinced of the danger and comprehend the pain our world felt before I knew you were ready to take it on yourself."

Take it on myself.

"But what about Mitsu. She was standing there, helpless. I wanted her to be safe. When I came to, she was gone."

The fox told her, "Her life has been spared. Yokai use illusions as demons often do. But you protected her spirit. It seems it was the final motivation you needed to find where your heart truly lies."

"All I felt was the need to escape from them to protect you and her but also to—"

"You wanted to also set them free," the fox said. "You vanquished their cage. Now, you carry its key. You will tell the truth of your kind—the story of the black beast that is a ghost train."

"Yes, I understand that the ghost train is the beast."

"You must warn man of the dangers they play with when they grow too fast for their shell. I can hold back the yokai only so long. Kami are uneasy. They want the fight. As does your emperor. Once it is put into the air, a wish is impossible to return to where it was born."

To Maru, it felt a like a burden too heavy to deliver to the world. Who would listen? And how could she make them believe her if she told the emperor to remember the world of yokai? And what are the consequences of upheaval? And how could she explain that his decisions hurt both the kami and his own society?

And how can I tell him he has killed women who were trapped in life and trapped in death? And how men have used them as pawns, as a bait to gain power? She thought of the girls discarded so callously. They were killed to fulfill the emperor's desire for power.

The fox said, "I am sorry if I have burdened you; it was never my intention to give you anything you weren't strong enough to bear. I was too weak to carry this alone."

The fireflies glowed, their yellow bodies illuminating the lilies closing for the night.

She asked, "Do you remember your name?"

Did the fox smile, or was it a trick of the light?

The fox replied, "Our pact gifted me some idle strength, and yet it evades me. In time, it will come to me. Perhaps I do not remember because it is not so important to remember this."

She accepted the explanation. Having one more unknown between them wouldn't harm what they are. She had been alone, pushed aside, craving for someone to understand her. And here he is—her fox, she now shares a part of herself with, even if it is unexplainable or unholy to everyone else. When she was abandoned, the fox came to her and she responded to it. Her sadness now is the loss of Sakyou.

The fox asked, "Was she someone very important to you?"

Sakyou. Maru wasn't ready for that question. She focused on the flowers tangled in the pines and cedars in the garden before them. Sakyou's bloody kushi was still tucked in her obi.

She couldn't convey to the fox what she felt. Her guilt gnawed at her. She and Sakyou could have so easily traded places. Maru narrowly escaped a darker fate by something beyond her control. Sakyou was a girl no one cared about enough to protect, a girl with promise when she was younger, but had her chance of a good life ripped away from her unfairly. She could have been more than an oiran; she deserved a better fate. She died without answers to these questions she must have mulled over before she went to sleep at night. She had no one to soothe her worries. She had no friend to gossip with as they shopped at the market. Her last days were filled with pain.

The fox told her, "Spare yourself the distress about her death."

Maru dropped her head. She saw her mother die in bed and saw elderly people die in the fires. She'd seen those who were robbed by daimyo cut down and their bodies scattered as warnings in street corners. She knew a child had drowned in the river facedown without anyone knowing the reason.

But except for her mother, they were nameless to her. Maru was unable to stop being glad when a person who died was not someone she knew. But she knew Sakyou. She was her friend. It brought up the pain she felt when her mother passed.

She asked the fox, "But who harms them? You said when the woman and girls are killed, they are sacrificed for a purpose."

"There is always violence among humans. Some of this is random—perhaps from an unrequited infatuation or from greed or a hunger to possess something. Your emperor, however, has frenzied many people. He has riled them up and agitated them. They are often unfortunate people who want control over their lives, and a loss of security can be manifested as violence. With each decree there is an increase of unbridled energy that reaches its bursting point when there is nothing to do except lash out."

She thought of Satoshi's train under pressure until the boilers exploded; she thought of the screaming into the night. She thought of the boys who had encircled her, and Sakyou stepping in.

"Sakyou deserved better," she said. "There was no purpose she served that called for this fate."

"Spirits can be without expectation. It is torturous to force a spirit to adopt a purpose it does not want. You so fiercely defend her, but I do not detect any information that you were close. Yet, she has affected you so."

Maru stared at the fox. That can't be true. If Sakyou hadn't been special to her, why did she feel so terrible?

They had been classmates who spent days reading aloud poetry and lines of Confucius together. The stood in the grass watching boys wrestle each other for their attention while they plucked crepe flowers. They'd admired each other on Girls Day, dressed up as elegantly as their parents could manage. She'd given her a dried apricot when Sakyou dropped her apple in the dirt.

In these small pockets of memories, Sakyou had been special, and once had infinite possibilities in how her life was meant to go. If only the stars had revealed a better path for her. Her disappearance occurred when she was right under Maru's thumb: she felt responsible and that her passing was personal. Her loss was monumental to Maru in ways only now weighing her down.

She had many more unanswered questions. Yet a peace flowed through her, a comforting safety in which she didn't seek to know anything further. She was satisfied, as if she already had the answers inside that would unfold in time.

A group of rabbits munched on clover. She smiled, watching their innocent playing, not knowing how near she and fox were to them.

Maru heard the rattles of the matsuri; a jubilance she was not privy to, one that she'd never be permitted to experience again

She asked the fox, "The ghost train—is it gone?"

"It has become you. You can choose to destroy it or use it."

"How did I know how to become the train? Did you pass me that power?"

"You were leading yourself to it all along. The threats were all around you, disguised as beauty."

"Me? I've been wanting to know about my father. I have never seen the train before today."

Revenge had been planted in her heart long ago. It began when the train smoke first appeared on the horizon. It took shape in Kira's smirks and in Fujiwara's snide jests. She felt the anger when Adakichi struck her and when her father turned her back on her. Sakyou's shadow, and the laughter of the boys stirred her rage.

Revenge boiled in her now, just as it had for the women. And now their spirits were free of the burden, the injustice they'd suffered in life.

She had taken the fox's pain away, and the world had responded and bent to her will.

A thumping on the roof startled her. *Was it another ghost?*

"Adakichi told me that ghosts are inside us and are manifestations of mistakes and bad memories. She said that we need to set them free in order to truly vanquish them."

"She is right, in a way."

"Then what is the truth? Were they real?"

"You saw them, did you not? The grief you spoke of. The pain you carry."

"I don't carry pain. My life is—"

"Have you not been put down by your madam? You have wished many times for things to be different."

"Adakichi has been good to me. She took me in when it was a risk." She felt sympathetic toward her while she was here in the darkness thinking of the summer's drama and her flaws.

She asked the fox, "You will not become a train or a beast anymore?"

"No. It has been a long while since I took a new shape. I have no strength to do it again, nor would I want to. The consequences nearly wrecked our worlds. We will have no need to be a beast, and if you pass on the message, no others need to die. You will have that power in you to transform yourself when you desire to change. That capability transferred to you when you saved me.

"Take your grief and your rage, and unleash its power into a light of your own."

For those who no longer can, thought Maru.

"I have the answer you wished for."

Her father.

Everything else evaporated. The fox was fulfilling its promise.

"I heard his voice when the ghost train was coming."

"Release what holds you back—lies that cloud your truth and the pain others inflict. It's time for you to become what you are capable of and what they have prevented you from being. In a way, you can see this as the beginning of your own ghost story. Ghosts are all we become in the end."

The fox led her out of the garden and down a tall bamboo path, zigzagging at the right moments to ward off demons and confuse the ghosts.

Lethargic, she followed the flicker of the fox's golden light beneath a bridge, her guide as night now began to streak across the sky, swallowing the world in blue and purple. They passed stone cats who were waving, as crickets chirped in her wake. Discarded vases and pots were nestled in corners. They went higher and higher up a hill until they reached a wide street. It was not lined with statues or buildings with bamboo walls but with tall trees with the thickest trunks she had ever seen and the highest branches. A carpet of moss covered the curves of their huge roots. Under them she saw small, pale forest kami peering at her.

A large, dark stone entrance appeared through the thick branches, its columns blending in with the blackened trees. Beneath the entrance was a wooden gate carved with faces of demonic beings warding off intruders. Their claws clutched giant leaves as they braced themselves over the curving steps beneath them. She recognized symbols of Buddhism.

And there the fox stopped.

"Don't go in there!" Maru whispered, afraid to waken the forest.

But the fox flicked its tail and slipped through the opening.

Boom

Boom

Fireworks were muffled by the density of the forest and the thumping in her chest. The lights couldn't find their way through the branches, leaving her in a cavern tangled in cotton brush and the temple before her, only a bit of emerging moonlight pouring over the forest bed. It seemed empty. The mud at the edge of the doorframe and the dust settled on the first stone steps suggested it had remained undisturbed for many years.

She leapt over the step so as not to leave any marks and flung herself through the open door.

Inside, a path of white steppingstones in the mossy garden led to a natural path through the old forest. The loudness of silence almost took her breath away. It dawned on her that the cicadas, crickets, and critters had quieted themselves to show their respect.

She crept across the stones of the darkened temple. Its roof disappeared into the thick pines. A porch hugging its sides, created a bridge to another building, and she saw this was repeated from building to building, connecting them all as if they floated above the overgrown, grassy path. Nearby, there were moss-covered tombstones with faded carved names. Somewhere she heard a wind chime.

The fox's bright tail guided her beneath an open grove and along a sand garden that had been tilled and traced and then left behind. They reached the hall in the center where the garden opened, letting starlight dapple on a ceiling adorned with what looked like unusual carvings. Enormous columns held up the wall-less hall.

The fox was inside his destination. Even in the shadows, she could see its silhouette in the soft night haze.

And all at once, the hall erupted into daylight. Dragons painted high above in the ceiling glowed in a deep ocean blue, their teeth shining like diamonds, their tails swaying and their claws pushing through carvings of curly clouds. Their glistening scales shimmered.

The mystifying etchings cast a white glow on the floor and dozens of tall, thick columns were illuminated by a silvery light. Long shadows encircled her.

She watched in fascination as the dragons flew back and forth across the ceiling, diving through clouds of blowing smoke through their long snouts, their eyes scanning the temple, silently snorting fire every so often.

She didn't realize it was completely silent until she finally pulled her eyes away from the dragons to where the fox waited for her beneath a statue of Buddha, sitting high on top of his seat of gold. Mummified offerings from years past lay at his feet, the dried flowers and half-full sake bottles forgotten about as if one day the priest left and never returned.

How long had this temple been hidden behind a shut door?

She stepped closer to the fox and statue, fixated on his eyes that were emanating white light from the dragons above daring not to breathe, as if it was watching her come closer.

The fox flicked its tail. She flinched, breaking her gaze.

It nodded, bowing its head.

Maru remembered her manners and raised her hands with an intention to clap, her eyes catching Buddha's.

She put her hands down and, instead, closed her eyes. The beating in her chest was replaced by the sounds of horses' hooves galloping over distant hills and shouts of an army fading into the horizon.

She saw her father standing on a summit. He looked tired. His robes were stained, his skin darker, his wrinkles deeper. He was clutching a long rifle in one hand and leaning against a flag pole with his other. A long gun and sword hung at his side as a stream of mounted samurai and archers flew over the green hill, racing to a line of black-cloaked figures at the shore bearing canons. There were white sails behind them as they were poised to shoot.

"Now!"

A canon erupted into fire, hurtling toward the hill beneath the sun. It was dotted with the emperor's emblem.

Boom

Boom

There was a triumphant roar; she felt the earth under her feet rumble with hooves.

A flag with her family's crest pierced the sky to meet the fire that blocked out the sun, and something inside her soared, carrying a thousand words she wanted to send on the wind to reach him, to look in his eyes and tell him it was fine, that she knew his truth, and she was at peace. She accepted it, and accepted him.

She peered into the Buddha's illuminated eyes, which were soft brown, and whispered:

"Thank you."

• • •

She wasn't sure how long she and fox sat beneath the dragons who now rested comfortably in corners of the ceiling, their claws tucked beneath chins. Their eyes were closed as they snored peacefully. She remained mesmerized. Her head was spinning, lost in the twirling clouds. The blood that stained her hands had dried.

"Did you see him?"

Maru nodded, staring out at the statues in the sand garden, mindlessly trying to discern shapes in the darkness. A single, flickering lantern cast shadows and created new faces with each movement.

"And it feels right?"

She sifted through her thoughts. Finally, she nodded. *Who would be better to fight an emperor than his own victims.*

The fox told her, "It's your heart that has the answers. Use less of your mind. It's vulnerable to the demons."

Maru was quiet. "How was I able to see him? Did you show me what you saw?"

The fox looked over at her, it's eyes like the hills in her vision.

"You followed your intuition. You opened your heart and believed in yourself."

She thought of the reasons she could have lost faith in her father. The guards around Kira. The whispered rumors of the city. The other geiko at the bathhouse. The doubt in her friends' eyes. Adakichi's bowed face when he was mentioned. They asked her, but she never budged, certain he was away doing his business of trading. She protected him, almost by accident. Her memories were now lighting up the darkness she had suppressed in her mind for so long.

The fox had a tone of forgiveness as he continued his thoughts. "Lies become a comfort when the truth seems too difficult. But now, being rational is important to make decisions to help you to find peace. It is your instincts and feelings that lead you to discover the truth that seem to be buried in the deepest, darkest parts of a forest. And now you the power to enact change."

A warmth filled her. Could she really help her father?

She closed her eyes, basking in the image of her father galloping alongside the ocean past the spitting volcano. He was swinging his sword at the emperor's men as they raced out of his way, one by one blown back by his force.

She saw herself running alongside him, shouting at him to move away from his enemies, leap over ditches, and double back to aid the other samurai their hair whipping wildly in the wind; she heard the loud sounds of their clanking armor. They seemed almost feral, but were inherently true to themselves as warriors.

"My instinct of what is right seems a part of everything we do," she said, looking at the fox. "I never followed mine until you came into my life. You brought this to me. You showed me how to reach him. There was never a need for an astrology almanac."

She rubbed her eyes with the palms of her hands, and said, "I know you had a hand in it. You were also there, weren't you? You were running with him."

The fox seemed sad, almost despondent.

He said, "You know I am weak. I'm incapable of this unless my powers are restored to me. You must understand that you did this all on your own."

"I don't really know what I did."

"You will in time."

"I don't know if I have any time. He's there at the battle-field, and it's too late to repair my friendships, and my relation-ships at the ochaya."

"Time is the only gift this life gives you. Stop letting others take away this gift. It's all yours to spend."

The fox moved a little away from her to sit at the edge of the temple and gaze at the sand garden. Its body was illuminated by starlight and fireflies.

Boom

Boom

Distance drums rippled the floorboards. A soft whistle came from somewhere deep in the forest. The train barged through her mind, blowing away Sakyou's ghost that lingered in her thoughts. She pulled out the hair ornament to examine it. It was bloodied, with a jewel missing.

"What do I do about Sakyou? How do I tell them what happened? I thought Kira did this. I suspected people: Fujiwara and my okiya imouto, Mitsu. I'm ashamed."

"What do you want to do?"

"They need to know. As you said, they must know what this emperor is capable of—that his train and his society and rules are a danger to us. That he is the reason girls were driven to die! My father must have had some doubts. In fact, he must know something! Maybe he suspects the emperor is destroying the land, not the yokai and you, but—" She got to her feet. "The emperor will hurt all of us. He will drive us all mad. It's why my father would fight against him. The emperor knows his plans were a ruse, an ugly invention to cover an ugly truth. He wanted to do away with all we know and replace us and our knowledge with the ways of the West. My father wouldn't stand for this. I wish everyone knew that the emperor's plans are backfiring and killing innocents."

"You used the word 'wish.' There is one more thing you should know."

The fox nodded his head at a koro, emitting whiffs of sandalwood. The incense embers were smoldering as if someone had recently lit them.

She approached the koro, afraid to look inside. She found two pieces of curled paper and recognized her handwriting one:

I wish for my father's return and getting my life back. Her wish she made at Tanabata.

She dropped it gently and picked up the other one:

To summon chaos and destroy the emperor. Her father's handwriting.

She asked the fox, "How did you get these? Did he know how his wish would be fulfilled?"

The fox looked at her. and she saw disappointment and sadness in his expression. "The ghost train was created in response to a wish. Your father's wish was granted."

The burned paper slipped from her hand and floated to the temple's floor.

"So he *is* the reason the girls were used and the people who blamed him are right? And other samurai agree? But he would never hurt a girl. It can't have been my father who did this."

"You have already forgotten that once his wish was granted, the yuurei took on an uncontrollable life of its own. And by then, his desire to undermine and wound the emperor had come true. The women you speak of joined forces to fulfill his wish. They have sought their own vengeance after their lives were taken from them that certainly not their choice."

Maru knew well of folklore of women who had been wronged in life, and turned into demons upon death.

"And what about my wishes? Did my wish for a normal life counter his? Is that why I was found? Am I connected to his wish?" The edges of her wish's paper burned slowly until it was consumed in a deep red.

The fox nodded his head and said, "Only a daughter could undo the wish of her father."

There was a crescendo of humming from the cicadas that vibrated in her heart. Her instinct was to defend her father, knowing in her heart that he meant to heal, not to harm girls or anyone else. He was only seeking to right the wrongs inflicted on them; it was others who escalated the chaos.

"I've never known any anyone—or any being who considered me strong," she whispered, her voice suspended in the thick summer haze. "They usually say women are not as strong as men."

"All summer long you've been the strongest creature in Kyoto," the fox told her. "You evaded every ghost or human who tried to tempt you. You were able to overcome every strike and every pain inflicted on you when you thought your wishes went unheard. You stood up for yourself and your father."

The floor of the temple rose beneath her feet, carrying her upward toward the stars. A pale haze enveloped her tightly, lifting the burdens from her shoulders, letting her rise. Her family's flag broke through the clouds, and the chimes swelled in tune with the murmur of the forest with her heart drumming with their beat.

She now had peace. And it was time for her father to find peace. He had been unfairly betrayed in the wake of all he had sacrificed for the new world, and it was costing them the fulfillment of their dreams. And for the first time, she believed she was capable of taking it on. This emperor was changing their world. He gave his people opportunities but also a danger that if left unchecked could transform them into a beast that could swallow them all in madness. They needed the equality he promised. They needed the peace the country craved.

"You wish to join him?"

It would not make sense to go to Satsuma. There had to be other ways to help him. A fiery determination burned her belly.

"I am no warrior though. I am the girl they look at with mistrust. Even my friends think I am strange."

She heard another whistle.

She shook her fist, thinking of the train, the way it had barreled toward her, the way her tanto pierced it, and how it had vanished into the air with a fading scream.

"I am not the type who searches for revenge."

"That's why I found you. Your act will not be one of retaliation to others. I see the pain you feel when people turn away and frown on you. There is hope in your vulnerability, and you are resilient. You will make a choice just like your father did. He saw things that nobody else understood. And look at the decision he made. You may not be a warrior, but you are a samurai's daughter."

Her father knew he faced almost certain death: a horizon of ships and cannons, fortresses and formidable, impenetrable walls, Imperial men pointing guns at him in unison. Yet he took the risk of leaving home and turning his back on the emperor who betrayed him to stand up for a truth he held in his heart—even if it meant being alone.

If he could do this, so could she. Her father wasn't the only fighter in the family.

"What will you do?"

She stood. "I need to go. I want to finish what he started." *The right way.*

Outside, the sky was dark, and a wind coaxed her thoughts. She bowed her head and thought about that bright autumn morning at school. She remembered Sakyou's large eyes and gentle face she passed her the book in her small hands. There was an earnestness in all she did. She was a spirit extinguished from this life, leaving an impression that would last in many people's minds for the rest of their lives.

Maru reached over the burning embers in the koro. She dropped the hair ornament into the fire, watching the flame ignite and rise in a burst that lived much like Sakyou had—an elegant being whose fire breathed fast, ferociously, and for too short a time.

She took the stone path that wound through the trees, leaving behind the yuurei and yokai that wanted to tug on her ankles. But she couldn't be stopped. With each step, she saw hundreds of fireflies were launched into the air with the bursts of fireworks overhead, and the cicadas hummed louder.

Before she knew it, she was at the end of Gion watching the twirling robes, painted faces and parasols, drunken singing and chanting that shook the river kami.

Boom

Boom

The colors of the matsuri blended in streaks of yellow against blue. She stood on the precipice of a street suspended in joy that was never meant to be hers. They danced, unaware of the horrors she had seen. She lingered, a dark figure against a changing world that would always be unequal.

She heard someone say, "She's so pale. Maru, have you seen a ghost?"

It was Kiku and Tane with Ai lingering before twirling dancers.

Then Satoshi stumbled forth and cried happily, "Ah, there you are, Shikomi of Adakichi!" His cheeks were full of food and his lips were wine-red. This was a man who didn't believe in yokai, a result of men who fiercely and selfishly believe it is they who rule the world. She burned with a desire to show him the truth.

Nearby, Adakichi was scolding Mitsu. Mitsu spied Maru and motioned a "thank you" with her sculpted lips. The scars on her skin burned with the memory of Adakichi's lashes.

Maru stared at their faces, willing them to understand all she possessed inside, as a glow grew inside her stomach— something hot, something wicked, fiery and feisty— clawing its way up, brewed by steel-cold anger, stewed by the wild determination that she had to make this right, her pressure was building and building, her body demanding to give justice to Sakyou, her father, and the kitsune, and those whose lives were cut short by selfish men like the unmoving emperor. None of them had ever listened to her or cared, but now they would.

Her back bent backward, and

Cr
A
cK
e D,

until her neck was hanging backward, and her jaw unhinged. Black steam poured out from behind her bared teeth, her eyes turning bright yellow.

And she pushed out her scream: a bellowing, deep scream that echoed through the matsuri, shook the treetops on the hills, extinguished all the streetlamps—and released her ghosts.

Glossary

Aburagami: oil-cast paint across an umbrella to strengthen it in rain.

Akebono: a once acclaimed teahouse that was a favorite for samurai to converge; was one of the locations where samurai plotted to restore the emperor and overthrow the shogun. An assassination planned by the shogun destroyed the teahouse in a fire in the mid-1800s.

Amabie: a yokai that takes shape similar to a mermaid.

Atatori: an heiress to an okiya; typically the biological daughter of a geiko or geisha who is following in the footsteps of her mother.

Blackened Teeth: teeth exposed bone was sacrilegious according to Japanese Buddhism and Shinto practices, and unbecoming to show publicly in pre-modern Japan. Women in particular were careful to paint and blacken their teeth, often using charcoal for concealment.

Boshi: pickled plum.

Boshin War: The civil war in the mid-1860s when Imperial forces joined samurai against the feudal Tokugawa clans and power-controlling shogun and daimyo, ending their reign.

Bushi: meaning "nobility," of the warrior class, to which samurai belonged.

Chochinobake: a demon that possesses lamps and lanterns, making them flicker.

Danna: a high-level patron who exclusively sees one geisha, paying her a salary for entertainment on an on-call basis.

Darari no Obi (Darari Obi): a distinct style of long obi worn past the knees by a maiko.

Dashi: a large float in a parade, depicting a creature or blessings; people often ride on top.

Emperor Go-Yozei ruled from 1586–1611, and abdicated his position to his son at a time when the Tokugawa shogun were rebalancing the government to grant power in their favor.

Emperor Meiji ruled from 1868–1912, and is largely heralded for leading Japan through a Restoration Era, marked by industrial revolutions, social and diplomatic progress, and peace.

Enenra: a demon that covers land in smoke and darkness to disorient and swallow people.

Engawa: a porch or veranda-like architectural structure that wraps around a temple or home, especially prominent in the Meiji era. They are often raised above the ground, and open the building or dwelling to a garden.

Fukumimi: "lucky ears" said to bring money; the bigger they are, the bigger the wealth.

Fundoshi: a wrapped, thong-like undergarment worn predominantly by men and children, sometimes as their outfit in the heat of summer or at certain matsuri.

Furisode: long sleeves on a kimono, worn by maiko.

Gashadokuro: a giant skeleton formed by the bones of those who died in famine.

Geiko: geisha, Kyoto dialect. Singular and plural.

Geimaiko: a term combining "geiko" and "maiko," for when they are gathered together.

Geta: traditional footwear: elevated wooden sandals with a fabric thong between the first two toes that holds the foot.

Gion: entertainment district of Kyoto, considered unofficial capitol of geisha districts.

Gosho: formal, shorter name for the Kyoto Imperial Palace.

Guji: chief priest of a Shinto shrine.

Hanamachi: literally, "Flower District." Name for the entertainment districts.

Hanameishi: literally "flower card" that has a name or business listing on it; given as a souvenir by ochaya to patrons or potential clients.

He-gassen: literally, "fart competition."

Hiki Iwai: a formal goodbye event held for a geiko who is retiring.

Hikizurki: long hem that trails the back of a kimono, worn formally by geimaiko.

Hitoe: a kimono with only a single layer, traditionally worn in summer as to keep cool.

Hone-Onna: a demonic skeleton woman, referred to as a succubus, who lurks in the Hanamachi district and leeches off of vulnerable men she lures.

Honmono: a real thing; a genuine article.

Hotaru: fireflies.

Ichihime: evening bell, usually tolling 5 p.m., or end of the work day.

Iki: earthy-colored.

Imouto: term for "younger sister," both literally and figuratively.

Irori: a traditional, stone-lined, square Japanese hearth sunk into the floor.

Jinmenju: human-faced fruit from southern Japan, said to have a sweet taste, but are now extinct.

Kamado: a traditional ceramic barbeque and grill.

Kami: term for spirits and gods, but perceived differently from Western religion. In Japan, any item living or tangible are said to have a *kami* inside of it.

Kampai: a phrase meaning "cheers."

Kamon: a family or business crest.

Kanmuri: a formal hat of Shinto priests from the 8th century, consisting of a low cap with a tall knob on top and a long strip of lacquered clothing attached to the back.

Kanzashi: decorative hair pieces, typically made of flowers, gold pieces, or elaborate ties.

Katsuyama: a hairstyle worn by senior maiko to signify their ranking.

Kazurasei: a Meiji-era cosmetic and hair accessory shop exclusively for geisha and maiko until the twentieth century; still in operation today.

Kerakera onna: a yokai in the shape of a giant, middle-aged woman who haunts red lights districts, and can be identified by her cackle.

Kitsune: a fox spirit, often seen with nine tails, that is known for its mischievousness.

Kobuse: a style of steel.

Koji: name of the street the Kyoto Imperial Palace sits on, along with other aristocrats.

Kokki-fukurei: the act of putting one's own desires aside for the sake of society at large.

Koro: altar where incense is burned at a shrine, sometimes an ornate iron vase.

Kotana: a low table usually covered with a blanket in winter to keep feet and legs warm.

Kushi: an ornate comb, used for hair decoration. In Edo and Meiji eras, they were usually made of tortoise shell or sea shells. Today, they can be wooden and wrapped in fabric.

Machiya: meaning "wooden neighborhood."

Maiko: geiko-in-training, often for years, if not a decade. Singular and plural.

Matsuri: festival, singular and plural.

Mikka-korori: believed to be cholera, based on counts of symptoms, spread, and circumstances of arrival with Western visitors.

Mikoshi: a portable shrine, carried on shoulders in a parade.

Mochi: an unbaked dough made of pounded rice, usually used to make sweets.

Morijio: a small pile of salt placed outside a business, usually a restaurant, to block spirits and yokai from invading their space, and keeping it cleansed of evil.

Nanboku-cho: the end of the 14th century period of Japan when the Imperial court split and divided the culture and clans.

Nekomota: a famous fork-tailed cat-shaped yokai with supernatural talents.

Noderabo: a demon that hovers near temple bells, calling attention.

Noren: split tapestry, usually bearing family names, clan crest, or business name, in a door.

Nuppeppo: yokai that hangs around dilapidated areas or destroyed buildings, stinking of rot.

Oba-san: term for grandmother.

Obi: belt/wrap that ties a kimono together, usually with a bow on the back.

Obijime: a thin, twisted rope that ties outside the obi in a delicate bow.

Obon: annual late-summer matsuri honoring ancestors and the dead.

Ochaya: a teahouse used for entertainment of patrons, usually by geisha.

Ofuda: a decoration believed to invoke a kami to put in front of a door for different fortunes: ward away evil, illness, bring in good luck, protect household, or make a general wish.

Oiran: prostitute, typically high-class, sometimes considered an escort or a mistress.

Okaasan: "Mother" of an ochaya or okiya. Often a veteran geiko who has long practiced, and serves as the head to several other geiko and maiko as their senior; she will manage money, rent, and their overall business. Also translates to "maternal/biological mother."

Okiya: a dormitory where geisha and maiko reside, sometimes attached to an ochaya.

Omamori: a holy charm, typically obtained at a shrine or temple, to bring in luck.

Omedetou: expression for "congratulations."

Oni: types of demons and monsters specific to Japanese folklore, art and literature.

Otoko: man/male.

Otoroshi: a hairy creature that perches on high places, usually torii or temple gates, at night.

Ponto-cho: place for nightlife in Kyoto.

Raijin: god of thunder.

Ren: humaneness.

Sakoku: isolation period during the Tokogawa rule of Japan, from 1633–1868 when the Emperor's reign was restored and reopened Japan's borders legally to the world.

Sasamochi: bamboo-leaf-wrapped mochi.

Shamisen: a three-stringed traditional Japanese musical instrument with a long neck and a round body, similar to a banjo.

Shi-gakko Academy: established in Kagoshima (Satsuma) by Saigo Takamori, former council to Emperor Meiji, before becoming a general of an opposing army in the late 19th Century. There he trained other samurai rebels to fight the Emperor, ending in 1877.

Shikomi: assistant in a geiko house or teahouse. Singular and plural.

Shimabara: red light district of Kyoto; famous for both prostitution and geiko tea-houses up until the 1970s.

Shinise: multi-generational family business—the oldest in Japan still in operation is over a thousand years old.

Shinto: religious beliefs native to Japan. Comparable to Buddhism, with unique differences.

Shoji: traditional Japanese doors and windows made of latticework wooden frames, typically covered in translucent, weather-resistant rice paper.

Sugegasa: a sedge hat commonly worn by farmers harvesting fields and rice paddies; a triangular shape typically made of straw that protects faces from sun and rain.

Tabi: socks that separate the first toe from the rest.

Taian: "lucky days" optimal for business deals or making important decisions.

Taiko: large drums, typically brought out during a matsuri.

Takamura: literally, "tall pillow," a firm cradle placed at the base of the neck to help build strong neck muscles, particularly for geisha, and preserve a unique hair style. Some are encased in a cloth representing their ochaya; others are made of porcelain.

Tanabata: annual summer matsuri celebrating the joining of two stars Vega and Altair, representations of Orihime and Hikoboshi deities and lovers in the night sky. The story goes a strict father banished them from seeing each other after their blossoming romance distracted them from chores. They are allowed one night together a year.

Tanto: a short sword or knife.

Taruki: a particularly straight-type of timber, grown in Japan specifically for teahouses in a horticultural technique known as "daisugi"—the art of growing trees atop trimmed branches.

Temizuya: purifying stations of "holy water" near the front of a Shinto Shrine; in early Meiji era, they were large communal baths. Today, they are usually large fountains with small bamboo cups to wash one's hands and face before entering the sacred grounds.

Tengu: the most famous temple-guarding demon; often depicted as a long-nosed, bright-red giant with ogre-like features and a weapon brandished.

Tenugui: a thin towel that can be used to hold up hair.

The Oath was written in 1868 by Yuri Kimimasa, council to the Emperor, outlining five basic rules upon which the new government would abide to assuage public worry.

Tokugawa are a powerful clan that oversaw over two hundred years of rule in Japan, subverting the imperial family, and enacting laws and policies of their own.

Torii: a Shinto shrine gate of two columns and beams across the top, typically painted red.

Toyotomi Hideyoshi "The Great Unifier" was a samurai who led others through sieges to bring prefectures together as one. He was leading campaigns against Korea and China for years, working with the Tokugawa and keeping their ambitions in check, when he died.

Tsuyu: the rainy season, typically early-to-mid-summer.

Ubagabi: a fiery ghost of an old woman that can be found near the Hozu river in Kyoto.

Uchiwa: hand fan, usually with a bamboo handle

Ukiyo-e: woodblock print, specific to Japan.

Wakonyousai: "Japanese spirit of Western learning."

Waraime: also known as the kerakera-onna, or "the giant cackling, middle-aged woman" who haunts brothel districts, mocking the younger men who lurk, following and taunting them (if they can hear the laughter, it means they have a weakness).

The World Fair of 1868 spurred "Japonism" in art (Monet and Van Gogh), fashion (turning kimono prints into western pieces), and beginning of Japanese influence on the West.

Yamamba: a yokai that comes out when it snows to dance and play until its prey fall victim to its games.

Yanari: a yokai that lives in the walls and under the floors of a home, causing creaks, especially heard in the night, seemingly prompted by nothing at all.

Yatai: stalls or carts brought out for matsuri, selling cooked food, snacks, and other goods.

Yokai: a class of supernatural beings from Japan; can take the physical form of demons, spirits, and monsters for differing stories from across several eras.

Yukatabira: shorter, thinner robes, usually worn for sleeping or in summer.

Yuurei: a class of ghosts from Japanese folklore. Yuurei are unbound spirits, unlike yokai which are bound to a physical form.

About the Author

Natalie Jacobsen began writing fiction in high school, opening doors to hone her craft in creative writing programs locally and overseas. In college she turned her interest in storytelling into journalistic endeavors. After graduating, she wrote and photographed articles for magazines and worked for television and music studios in Japan, fostering her love of mythology, history, and untold stories. In Virginia, she reported on civil rights and defended the rights of journalists in court.

The award-winning journalist, writer, and marketer now devotes her time and talent to the public and nonprofit sectors, inspiring others to take action and change the world. In her spare time, she can be found at music festivals, boarding planes to faraway places, volunteering at local charities, or tucked away in a greenhouse. Hailing from the Pacific Northwest, Jacobsen lives in Washington, D.C. with her husband, a lawyer, and fellow Oregon "Duck," and their hundreds of plants and books.

Art Credits

Cover, main image:
View of Takanawa Ushimachi, Under a Shrouded Moon (circa 1879)
by Kobayashi Kiyochika (1847–1915), public domain.

Other imagery © istockphoto/

Red silk fabric: acprints

Dry brush strokes: Asya_mix

Japanese classic dance "YAGURA NO OSHICHI": banabana-sa

Origami paper—Japanese Pattern Asanoha: koko

Kitsune (fox): Natalia Vetrova